WOMAN OF CAIRO

Hart Muldoon had been a "no_____
against the Nazis, but now he_____
leave Europe and head back l_____
one more job working with a dubious agent named
Jeremiah Grant. A British bomber has disappeared
near Cairo, and Grant seems to know something about
it. And with Egypt ready to explode under the rule of
King Farouk, Muldoon's British contact doesn't have
time to operate under normal channels. A quick and
dirty espionage mission is called for. Muldoon needs to
get close to Gina Ferelli, the beautiful wife of Hans von
Bruckner, and penetrate the mysterious cult known as
the Sons of Mecca. But first he must deal with Siegfried
McCarthy, Grant's ice queen contact, and Marianne
Courbert, a French singer on a mission of her own. It
may be a dirty mission, but it has its benefits…

DEAR, DEADLY BELOVED

At the tail end of a long binge, Hart Muldoon finds
himself on the beautiful vacation isle of Venzola…in a
hotel room with a murdered man. Knowing he's been set
up, he only has a limited time to investigate. Suspects
abound. There's the French woman in Room 26,
Yvonne—she knew the murdered man. And the Bennol
women—Mamma, Gigi and Elsa. Gigi is married to the
victim, and Elsa was seen arguing with him earlier that
day. There's Elsa's husband, Pepe Planquet, the great
director, and his latest ingénue, the torrid Loretta Kelly.
Plus the mysterious Count Cassi; the corrupt cop,
Ferechini; the idealistic industrialist, Phillip Adams;
and the fabulously rich Babs Wentworth. They all have
something to hide, including a knife in the back of a
dead man. But can Muldoon find the killer before he
becomes the next victim?

Woman of Cairo

Dear, Deadly Beloved

By John Flagg

STARK
HOUSE

Stark House Press • Eureka California

WOMAN OF CAIRO / DEAR, DEADLY BELOVED

Published by Stark House Press
1315 H Street
Eureka, CA 95501
griffinskye3@sbcglobal.net
www.starkhousepress.com

ISBN-13: 978-1-951473-17-4

Book design by Mark Shepard, shepgraphics.com
Cover design by Jeff Vorzimmer, ¡caliente!design, Austin, Texas
Cover art from the original edition of *Woman of Cairo*

First Stark House Edition: December 2020

Intrepid Agent Hart Muldoon's Treacherous Paradise
by Nicholas Litchfield

Better known by his pseudonym, John Flagg, American writer John Rex Gearon (1911-1993) was an author of distinction whose early fiction was considered by some as standing alongside the likes of Graham Greene and Dorothy Hughes. His debut novel, *The Velvet Well,* published by Duell, Sloan & Pearce in 1946, was an immediate hit, proving popular among critics and launching Gearon's career as a novelist. *The New Yorker* said of the tale: "Things get tense indeed, so much so that the hardiest reader may find himself breathing heavily at the end." Even Dorothy Hughes commended it as an absorbing story "told with gripping tension, with ever-mounting suspense leading to a corrosive climax."

According to the 1949 Penguin Books reprint, a film version was also in preparation, with *The Los Angeles Times* indicating, in 1952, that it would be scripted by notable British novelist Philip MacDonald and released as *Strangers in Munich.* Eventually, in 1978, a movie adaptation hit the theaters, filmed by renowned French director Jacques Deray as *Un Papillon Sur L'épaule* (*A Butterfly on the Shoulder*) and penned by legendary Italian screenwriter Antonio "Tonino" Guerra and Jean-Claude Carrière, one of France's foremost screenwriters.

The success of his first novel no doubt convinced Gearon to continue in the mystery and crime genre. While it's debatable whether he truly stepped into the ranks of the masters of suspense with *The Velvet Well,* as some sources suggest, his canon of work, which comprises eight subsequent novels of foreign intrigue with landmark publisher Gold Medal Books, earned him positive reviews in leading periodicals like *The New York Times*.

Interestingly, Gearon's career might have been markedly different, if a decade earlier, the stage play he worked on with Pulitzer Prize-winning author Louis Bromfield hadn't received such disastrous press. The play, *De Luxe*, about rich American expatriates living in Paris at the end of the Coolidge era, opened with much fanfare at Broadway's famous Booth Theater in 1935, sporting a notable cast that included Melvyn Douglas (who, years later, would win two Academy Awards), Violet Hemming, Cora Witherspoon, and eminent gossip columnist Elsa Maxwell. There was an unusually large horde of distinguished luminaries in attendance for the premiere, including theatrical and motion picture magnates, but, alas, the play closed within two weeks amid a flood of criticism. The New York daily newspaper *Times Union* declared, after the opening night: "Louis Bromfield and his collaborator, John Gearon, have invented the most unpleasant set of characters ever set upon a single stage." Other newspapers were equally scathing. *The Brooklyn Daily Eagle* lambasted the writers, declaring them mediocre playwrights of a drama that is "a de luxe bore," and *The Brooklyn Citizen* called it "a long, incoherent, talky bore," offering this summation: "The trouble with 'De Luxe' was that too many of the characters were either dead or dying on their feet from boredom and moral decay, with the result that a funeral aroma was communicated to the play itself."

It doesn't appear that the torrent of negative press dampened Gearon's desire to continue in the theater. Articles in the *Daily News* that same year reveal he was collaborating with Edward Crandall on new plays titled "Without Guile" and "The Doctor's Confession," and selling "With the Wind" to producer Albert Bannister.

When not striving for success as a playwright, Gearon took employment as a salesman and in a department store and a refrigerator factory. He also worked as an associate in a literary agency and, before WW2, as a journalist, writing for newspapers like the *Detroit Free Press*. Earlier in his career, he was a dramatic radio scriptwriter for the Office of the Coordinator for Inter-American Affairs (OCIAA), which sought to boost political and economic relations between the U.S. and Latin American nations. Though a versatile writer, his ambitions to be a novelist came about almost by accident. According to Clip Boutell of the *Daily Press*, Gearon was playing around at his typewriter one day and produced four pages. Apparently, Gearon was deeply fond of what he had written and confessed, "Then I was caught and I had to find out what was going to happen."

Although rumored to be at work on a novel of suspense with a New England setting titled *Violence in October*, his subsequent book, published in 1950, *The Persian Cat*, was a postwar espionage novel that *The Cincinnati Enquirer* described as a mystery tale of "barbaric excitement" featuring "boudoir politics, murder, spying, oriental puzzles and strange perfumes used by stranger characters." Opening in Paris, the brisk action shifts to Tehran, with special agent Gil Denby recruited to bring a Nazi sympathizer to justice.

The novel holds special historical significance in that it was the first title released by Gold Medal Books. Sadly, the motion picture of *The Persian Cat*, said to be forthcoming from Warner Bros., never materialized.

Two further standalone tales of murder and international intrigue followed in rapid succession in 1951 before the author established a series character: freelance American agent Hart Muldoon. A former O.S.S. agent, the tough but refined Muldoon works as an undercover investigator for various individuals, organizations, and governments. His confidential work takes him to luxury hotels, whorehouses, politicians' offices, and gangsters' hideaways in Greece, Pakistan, Indonesia, and elsewhere, living (in his words), "a kind of paperback existence in which intrigue companions sex, and fact has become more unbelievable than the headlines." When not verbally sparring with volatile young females and multimillionaire playboys, he fends off the advances of lusty gals and attacks by mercenaries, narrowly escaping bullets and flying daggers. As author James Reasoner shrewdly notes in his introduction to the 2017 Stark House collection *Death and the Naked Lady / The Lady and the Cheetah*: "I suspect that Muldoon is cut from the cloth as Mac McLean and Rafferty Valois: smart, funny, and inclined to land in trouble up to his neck, often involving beautiful women, and set against exotic backgrounds."

Probably, Gearon's work with OCIAA and his experiences traveling Europe and the Near East as a youth greatly impacted his writing. His opulent settings and vivid descriptions of striking, strong-minded foreign women, shady government officials, and sharp assessments on unstable political situations in faraway climes are a staple part of his prose. Droll, pithy sketches of places like Marseilles go like this: "The weather was unseasonable and metallic; sky and sound were hot and hard, the palms stood like rusted iron in corrugated parks and at night the harbor waters seemed to hiss and steam against the piers and promontories of a city of brass. In the cafés, the waiters shook their heads and muttered while the tarts watched the trams rattle up the Canebiere toward the railroad depot with eyes as uneasy as those of the emaciated cats underneath the iron tables."

In *Woman of Cairo*, originally published in January of 1953, one might be forgiven for considering the character Muldoon an extension of Gil Denby. Throughout his ensuing four adventures, set in various parts of Italy and France, Egypt and the West Indies, violent incidences of civil unrest, dangerous alliances, and nefarious women crop up again and again. Fortunately, merrymaker Muldoon has an aptitude for ferreting out the truth, best seen in the series opener, where Muldoon is tasked by Max Kneber, an old colleague, now a big cog in British Intelligence, with discovering if black market trader Jeremiah Grant has information about a British bomber who disappeared on a flight from the Sudan to Suez. He must also find out if rich businessman Hans von Bruckner is connected with a revolutionist organization called the Sons of Mecca. To achieve this, the caddish hero needs to win the affections of von Bruckner's mistress, an aristocratic beauty with a face Botticelli might have liked to immortalize on canvas.

Though surrounded by the attractive high society types that appeal to him, Muldoon's mission is missing some of the "fun" Max insinuated there would be. Frustrating exchanges with Gina, frosty banter with the ice-cold Sigried McCarthy (Muldoon's inside contact), and guilt concerning his boorish treatment of Marianne Courbert, a pitiful French nightclub singer, wither his mood. And when not able to ply his wit and intelligence to seducing women, he needs all his wits about him in order to cheat death and avoid duplicitous spies, violent revolutionaries, and paid assassins.

Gearon excels at high drama, and the story is enriched by thrilling scenes and well-imagined locations and characters. Although criticized by eminent book critics like Anthony Boucher for his overly sexualized writing, you can forgive Gearon's inclination toward lurid elements and sensationalism. Throughout *Woman of Cairo* there are intimations to prostitution, homosexuality, rape, and incest, but, thankfully, his writing doesn't get too graphic and, certainly, it is never boring.

Interestingly, in the second book, *Dear, Deadly Beloved*, from April 1954, the protagonist's conduct has distinctly improved. The licentious Muldoon refrains from ungentlemanly, lascivious behavior and, instead, appears subdued and guarded. It's no wonder, really, considering the predicament he finds himself in at the start: discovering a murdered stranger in his room at the Villa Rosa, a moldering *pensione* run by insolent owner Mamma Peroni and her nephew, Pietro.

Having imprudently attended a party on a yacht in Cannes, a few days earlier, and having failed to board the ocean liner that would return him to the States after a three-year absence, he winds up on the fashionable (fictitious) island of Venzola in Italy's Bay of Naples. It's a lesser-known resort area to rival the chic neighboring island of Capri and, naturally, the "international set" that Muldoon favors surrounds him in numbers. He resumes his habitual frivolous lifestyle, rubbing shoulders with the charming, though peculiar, Count Armando Cassi; the mad old Duchessa di Cabrieni; the exhibitionist French film director, Pepe Planquet, and his promiscuous actress wife, Elsa; film financier Babs Wentworth; fading movie star Lorna Parks, and famed American industrialist Phillip Adams. Snapping at his heels is Signor Ferechini, *comandante* of the local *carabinieri,* an odious official who has ordered Muldoon to leave the island because of disorderly conduct the night before.

Muldoon, intent on learning who the dead man was and who framed him for murder and why, is up against the clock, striving to get answers before either the corpse is discovered or Ferechini puts him on the last boat off the island. Conveniently, Phillip Adams, at the suggestion of Max Kneber (their mutual acquaintance), then offers Muldoon ten thousand dollars to discover if his employee, a brilliant young Romanian electronic engineer named Georges Hertzy, is a secret member of a resistance group called the Balkan Eagles and is attempting to sell company secrets. Given that Hertzy is stretched out on Muldoon's bedroom floor, butchered with an Italian stiletto knife, Adams' timing couldn't be better.

Thus, Muldoon has thirteen hours to investigate Hertzy and unravel the mystery. Was he an industrial spy? Was he murdered for political reasons? Or was his murder a mistake and the knife actually meant for Muldoon?

The tense and twisty *Dear, Deadly Beloved* is an alluring, rapid-paced whodunit with a glorious technicolor panorama and a vibrant cast of oddball elite members of society. Unexpected revelations surface in practically every chapter, and the threat of death waits in the shadows of arches and moldering doorways all about the forbidding Villa Rosa.

One can't help but admire the author's capacity to thrill and intrigue, and you appreciate his masterful depictions of the colorful, eccentric, ritzy citizens who inhabit his rich, fascinating worlds. "She rose like some exotic flower from a pink cloud of a gown, and though she had assumed the attitude of cool hauteur there was a look in the depths of her eyes that might have meant she had been standing there in the center of this vulgar room waiting for me all of her life," his protagonist writes, with pulsating sensuality, of the highly desirable yet unobtainable Elsa Planquet.

In the author's dreamy, energetic mysteries, tycoons, aristocrats, royalty, and high-ranking officials mingle with Hollywood actors, directors, and producers, popular singers, and exotic dancers aboard luxury liners and steamships, at extravagant Masquerade balls, galas at casinos, cocktail parties in mansions and palaces, and roomy dining cars on railroad journeys along the Nile. But it's a treacherous paradise populated, too, by hustlers and harlots, revolutionists and agitators, and small-time crooks and big-time gangsters, where murder stalks the intrepid Hart Muldoon, and everyone is suspect. Watching this charmer goad and torment the hotbed of lunatics around him makes for great entertainment, and the reader's only disappointment will be that the series didn't span more than five witty, spine-tingling, sumptuous novels.

—August 2020
Rochester, NY

Nicholas Litchfield is the founding editor of the literary magazine *Lowestoft Chronicle*, author of the suspense novel *Swampjack Virus*, and editor of nine literary anthologies. He has worked in various countries as a journalist, librarian, and media researcher and resides in western New York. Formerly, a book reviewer for the *Lancashire Evening Post* and syndicated to twenty-five newspapers across the U.K., he now writes for *Publishers Weekly* and regularly contributes to Colorado State University's literary journal *Colorado Review*. You can find him online at nicholaslitchfield.com.

Woman of Cairo

By John Flagg

Chapter One

Max was smart as hell. He caught me at exactly the right moment. I walked out of the Baccarat rooms of the Casino de Mediterranienne in Nice to find him sitting at a table in the lounge café, grinning at me like a Cheshire cat.

"You old son of Satan," I said with a laugh. "You've jinxed me!"

"Cleaned out, old boy? Too bad. Sit down. Buy you a drink. Funny thing. Just thinking to myself; wonder what ever happened to Hart Muldoon."

"The answer is simple. Croupiers and women. Bad combination. Might have been president otherwise. I know your being here is no accident Max, but it's good to see you."

I was glad to sit down and have a drink with Max. He was part of the old days, one of the good guys. I hadn't seen him since the spring of '43 when we had planned some cute headaches for the Nazis in a farmhouse outside Dijon. In those dreamlike faraway days I had been a noble O.S.S. boy while Max was British liaison with the French *maquis*. Times had changed! Someone out in Pakistan had told me Max was a big wheel in British Intelligence heading up some kind of hush-hush unit. It was always the hush-hush units you heard about first, even in Pakistan.

Max exuded a cherubic kind of innocence. But I knew he didn't expect me to swallow the "casual encounter" routine. There was nothing casual about Max. We talked about the possible evolution of the Bikini bathing suit and other weighty matters over a couple of drinks, moved on to the subject of Nice by night and finished in the aching glow of shared experience in those other days. This last took us on to dinner. It wasn't until we had left the restaurant and were walking along the Promenade des Anglais, ostensibly in search of the obvious, that Max came to the point.

"So you were wiped out tonight at the Casino, Hart, old boy," he said with a cheerful smile.

"What's so damned funny about that?"

"Maybe not funny. But convenient to me."

"You knew I was here in Nice?"

"The minute I heard you were heading for a couple of Riviera weeks I felt better. I knew you had put away a few dollars from that job out in Pakistan and were planning finally to make it back to the

States. But when I heard you were approaching the Casinos I knew you wouldn't get home so quick."

"You kept a file on me, Max?"

"Naturally. I hate to see good talent go to waste. You could—and can—come to us any time you choose."

"Not me. I've given up long-term contracts. With any government!"

"Too bad. You see, Hart, the danger of being a free lance in this uncertain century is that you can never be free enough. No more islands and all that sort of thing. Takes cash and cash means dollars these days."

"I'm immune to orientation lectures! Now if you want to discuss that blonde across the street on that café terrace ..."

"Later."

He stopped and looked down the boulevard. The pavement was deserted. He moved in to the sea wall and lit a cigarette.

"We have dollar reserves for just such emergencies," he said ironically. "You might as well take ours. They're as clean as any these days."

"Max," I said, "I'm fed up with the whole stinking mess! I've peeked under too many beds in the last few years. I just want out. A farm in Maine maybe. A *hausfrau*. A dog. And maybe an atom proof cellar. I say, a plague on both your houses!"

"You don't mean that, Hart. Come home. All is forgiven."

"Home is where I make it! I get along fine. I've got a little United Nations all my own. Name of Hart Muldoon!"

"All right. All right, old boy." He hesitated a moment, then said, "I have a job for you, Hart. It might pay enough to get you back to the States and that mythical farm. But beyond that ... I need you."

"God!" I said. "I never thought I'd live to hear a Britisher say that to me."

"I can trust you. I can't use one of my own men on this. Situation is too delicate. I need a good operator like you and an American. I've come all the way down from Paris to get you."

"You've wasted a trip, Max."

"Maybe." He was staring out across the beach and moonlit sea. "There's a chap been shopping around Paris and Berlin and Vienna for a smart operator. We're very interested in his activities but we can't locate his paymaster. His name is Jeremiah Grant."

"That creep!"

"You know him, then?"

"Ran into him once or twice. Rather forget it."

"I know. His dossier reads like a case history. But up to now he's never been involved in actual espionage. When we heard he was looking for someone to do his dirty work we thought of you."

"Me? Grant knows better than to try me."

"That was before," he said calmly.

"Before what?"

He turned and looked innocently up at the moon.

"My men have been dirtying up your name, Hart. All over the map of Western Europe. You've been highly recommended for the job."

"Why you lousy son!"

"Easy, old boy." Suddenly Max's voice wasn't so mild. "This creep Grant ... he's peculiarly interested in certain characters who reside in Cairo. This is important to us, Hart. No holds barred. You've got to come our way."

Still simmering from Max's highhanded methods I started to turn away but he grasped my arm.

"Listen, Hart. One of our bombers has disappeared on a flight from the Sudan to Suez. Into thin air. None of my men can get even a whiff. This is desperately important."

"Maybe to the Empire. Not to me. Anyway it sounds like something for Downing Street."

"Not at this time. Not with the lid about to blow off around the canal. There have been no notes, no publicity. As far as we know Farouk knows nothing. But oddly enough we have reason to believe that maybe Grant knows something."

I cooled off a little. There was something in Max's voice that recalled the old days. But I thought, it's only the money that interests me. Nothing more. Maybe this could be my last job.

And Max, seizing on that moment of hesitation, said quickly, "You'd be on your own. We'd have to disown you loudly and publicly if things got too hot. But you'd be on your own, Hart."

And I heard myself say, "I could listen."

Max laughed. "Now that you mention it that blonde has certain interesting points but it's the redhead that catches my fancy. We'll talk business later."

I grinned. "You still look like a delinquent boy scout when you drool, Max. Let's go."

And it began that way.

Max had been certain that things would begin to boil before the end of the month; we had set it up that way. But I was still waiting around Marseilles in the last week of November and I was getting worried. The weather was unseasonable and metallic; sky and sound were hot and hard, the palms stood like rusted iron in corrugated parks and at night the harbor waters seemed to hiss and steam against the piers and promontories of a city of brass. In the cafés, the waiters shook their heads and muttered while the tarts watched the trams rattle up the Canebière toward the railroad depot with eyes as uneasy as those of the emaciated cats underneath the iron tables. The atmosphere of the city was getting me down. Time to think was the last thing I needed. I resorted to the local talent and Courvoisier.

But on December second at two in the morning I stopped worrying. At least for a time. They rose to the bait a little late maybe but just as we had figured it, rose to the bait in the person of Jeremiah Grant. I walked into my hotel room after detaching myself from a winning blonde at the Mirimar to find him sprawled in the sagging arm chair, pipe in mouth, tweedy, deceptively affable. I hadn't seen him since 1950 in Tangier. At that time he had been conducting a lucrative trade with the black markets of France. For once I was glad to see him.

"What are you doing here, you bum?" I said, playing it cute.

"With the permission of madame, your landlady. I promised to sleep with her."

"Still got delusions of grandeur, eh, Grant?"

"I see," he said with satisfaction and a look at the peeling wallpaper, "that you have lost yours. Too bad."

"Temporary," I said. "Waiting for a deal."

"Maybe I got it."

It was coming quicker than we could have hoped for in our most optimistic dreams. Play it down, I thought. "How did you know I was here?"

"The grapevine. You know how bad news travels."

I knew all right. Good old Max Grant would have a shock if he suspected how well that grapevine had been rehearsed.

"The low-down on Hart Muldoon! Caught with his two paymasters showing. Can't pick up a job this side of the Iron Curtain!"

"The boys exaggerate." I acted appropriately depressed.

"Tsh, tsh," he said mockingly. "One of my few illusions shattered. Superman crashed to earth. Right down to the level of us fallible humans. Enough to make a cynic of me. Or drive me to drink. By the way, you got a drink?"

Without enthusiasm I dragged a half empty bottle of cognac out of the dirty linen and passed it to him. He took a long pull, wiped some of the drops from the pinkish beard he had worn ever since some dim-brained woman had told him he resembled Hemingway. He went back to his pose of thinker-with-pipe.

"Get to the point, sweetheart," I said. "I need sleep."

"Why? You've got nothing to get up for. Not unless you listen to me. I'm a humanitarian. Come to help an old friend in his hour of need."

The hell you have, I thought. I knew he hated my guts almost as much as I hated his.

"You always were a little too much of a do-gooder for my blood, Muldoon. But you're a helluva slick operator. I can use you."

"Never mind the editorial comment. How much?"

"Five grand."

"For what? The murder of Stalin? A piece of the moon?"

He swung one leg over the arm of the chair and sucked thoughtfully at the pipe. He was enjoying himself.

"I got facts."

"What else? The eternal file keeper. In what capital? For what government?"

"I need more facts. Your specialty."

"I'll listen."

"About time, too! It may surprise you to know that this job is legit."

It *would* have surprised me—if it were true.

"Where I am, that's irrelevant."

"Ever heard of the Marsden Foundation?"

I smothered the grin. The Marsden Foundation was a highly respectable philanthropy endowed by an American millionaire. Among its objectives was better understanding with the Arab world. The idea of Grant being involved with anything to do with the brotherhood of man had its comical aspects. I gave him A for imaginative effort. I nodded.

"I'm heading up an undercover investigation for them into certain conditions in the near East," he said.

I took a drink myself on that.

"So?"

"It's a delicate job and dangerous. I need an expert like you."

"The five G's has a nice sound. You interest me."

"Ever heard of Hans von Bruckner?"

"Vaguely. Cairo big shot, isn't he? Made a fortune in diamonds or something."

"Or something."

"I see. You want to get to that 'something'?"

"Not me, baby. The Marsden Foundation. This comes under the heading of cultural research."

"Like what?"

He hesitated, looked toward the hall door and lowered his voice. "The boys along the grapevine tell me you're an expert on the Sons of Mecca."

"That crackpot outfit?"

"You're not that dumb, Muldoon. Things are steaming out in Egypt. Farouk is getting it from all sides; the Commies, the British, the Wafdists ... the same old show ... and the Sons of Mecca."

"I had a few dealings with some of their prize members out in Pakistan. They make a lot of noise but draw no blood."

He leaned forward. "What's Von Bruckner got to do with them?"

"Never heard him mentioned in connection with them."

He sat back disappointed. "I heard different," he said. "That's your job. I've got to know how deep in he is."

I went carefully now. This was the tightrope walk.

"That's a little out of my line. I don't know ... I've got no ins in that crowd."

"Listen, Muldoon—if that's all you're worried about—I've got the in. This ought to be a cinch for you."

My pulse began to beat faster. "Five grand isn't enough for my old age."

"That's clear. You get your expenses at Shepheard's in Cairo. Steamship fare out."

"And return?"

He grinned. "What kind of a schnook you take me for?" I walked to the window, a picture of indecision. I could hear him beginning to breathe hard in the room behind me. Outside across the rooftops came the peacock cry of the P.L.M. night express from Paris. It sounded like a harsh warning. One-way passage, I thought grimly.

"There's more to it, Muldoon. Fun while you work. We want you to get next to Von Bruckner's mistress."

"Who is she?" I asked as though I didn't know.

"An atomic cocktail by name of Gina Ferelli. Widow of an Italian diplomat. Stranded in Cairo during the war, without funds. Von Bruckner liked what she had fine ... as who wouldn't. Now she queens it over Cairo's smart set from a palace on the banks of the Nile."

"What do I do, walk in and introduce myself?"

"No. She's been in Paris. Returning to Egypt from Marseilles on Friday on board the Chambord. You sail on that boat. Woman named Sigried McCarthy will contact you and arrange the introductions. You should be able to handle it from there on in?"

I turned and yawned. "I'm going to get some sleep."

He stood, losing a little of his cool poise.

"You're not turning this down?"

"I'll sleep on it. Where are you staying?"

"The Noaillies. I'll give you till ten in the morning."

"Fair enough."

"If you have any sense left you'll be in my room then. You can't get another job on the continent. I know!"

At the door he turned. He looked uncertain. "You wouldn't be playing coy, Muldoon?"

"Not with you, sweetheart."

"Wise boy. There's only one paymaster in this job. That's me. You'll have to stay away from your old pals on this trip. I've been known to play rough."

"So I've heard."

"Boy scouts are my specialty. You remember that and we get along fine."

"I'll remember."

After he closed the door I took a good swig of Courvoisier. The old feeling of excitement when I was beginning something new was back. But something bothered me. Something just slightly out of focus we hadn't figured on. I waited an hour and then put in a call to Lyon. Max's bright voice, never sleepy, answered.

"Yes?"

"Got the job with Aunt Yvonne."

"Good."

"Friday with the help of the Good Shepherd."

"Yes."

"Aunt Yvonne's health uncertain though."

"Oh?"

"Her doctor is unknown."

Max started to say something but suddenly I wasn't listening to his voice. There was another sound much more interesting and much closer than Lyon. It was the bare whisper of a sound, the faint squeak of a hinge in movement. I didn't wait to investigate but threw myself down beside the bed. Something whistled through the air and finished in a sickening plop. Footsteps receded, fast, over the worn carpet of the hall. I heard the dreamlike sound of the self-service elevator gate clang to. But by the time I got out into the hall the car was rattling downward in its ancient cage. I dropped that one quick. By the time I could have got down four flights of stairs whoever was in the elevator would be lost in the endless narrow streets. I went back to my room and closed the door. The knife still trembled in the peeling wallpaper. I pulled it out and recognized the craftsmanship of Damascus. Knife throwers yet, I thought.

I picked up the receiver.

"Still there?" Max's voice was reassuring.

"Luckily. This is going to come the hard way."

"Take it easy. I'll expect to hear from you after you consult the doctor. Don't expect word from home until then."

He hung up. I sat there with the receiver in my hand and I couldn't think of anything funny. Out of the receiver came a sinister, sputtering sound. I smashed it down into its cradle.

Chapter Two

The Chambord, pride of the Marseilles-Saigon run, was built just before World War II, built for the superior white man—preferably French—on his tour of native populations or just plain monkey business in the Colonies. Not too large, but in the luxury class, her former arrogance seemed, in a changed world, somewhat pathetic and even courageous. Fifteen minutes after her white hull slid past Chateau Dif, outward bound from Marseilles, Mrs. McCarthy presented herself in my stateroom. She was a surprise that seemed, at first glance, pleasant. Blonde hair in old-fashioned Bavarian braids about a well-shaped head, blue eyes with the outdoor look of ski runs and mountain lakes in them, a body lithe, compact, put together like a swimmer's, covered casually in a simple white linen dress that was exactly right. She looked young, not more than twenty-two or three.

Unembarrassed, she closed the door behind her. "Mr. Hart Muldoon?"

"Yes."

"Sigried McCarthy."

She didn't offer her hand.

"Things are looking up," I said.

She gave me a cool once-over. "I'm relieved. I rather expected a prize fighter. Jeremiah is wiser than I would have expected."

She rattled this off in a somewhat British accent in which there were traces of middle Europe. She smiled. It was a pictorially effective smile completely devoid of warmth. A wind seemed to whistle down the fjord.

"This surreptitious nonsense goes against my grain," she said. "Let us not waste time."

"I'm not putting a stop watch on you."

"I've told Gina that a young American I knew in London is aboard. You're going to Egypt to get material for a book. She has a weakness for what she imagines are artists."

It was a simple statement without apparent malice. But she might have been talking about a washing machine or a typewriter for all the humanity in her voice.

"What kind of a book?"

"Oh, archeological, of course. Nothing contemporary or dangerous like 'the world situation.' She never discusses politics."

"You don't seem to think much of her mental capacities."

"Gina doesn't need a brain. But as a matter of fact she has one. A good one." And then mechanically she added, "She's a dear."

The single stateroom was tiny. It was impossible not to stand close to one another yet she made me feel a frozen distance between us.

"If I'm supposed to be an old friend of yours, I'd better know something about you."

"A little is all that's necessary. The little all Cairo knows. I'm a couturière. My own shop in Cairo. I've been to Paris for the spring showings. I spent a few weekends in England. We met at the country house of Lady Barton. In Sussex. Gina doesn't know her so you can avoid any awkward questions on that score."

"You've had this Cairo shop a long while?"

"Two years. It's no secret that Gina set me up. She is very kind." The last was added as a sort of conventional afterthought.

"And Mister McCarthy?"

"Dead. Three years ago in Tangier. He was British. Not that it matters. No one will speak of him."

Her voice was completely indifferent.

"And before?"

"In Cairo we never talk about before."

I indicated the only place in the room on which to sit. She looked at the berth and then into my eyes.

"This is just business to me, Mr. Muldoon."

"What did you think I was suggesting?"

"I know what you will eventually suggest. I've met Americans of your type before. It is perhaps just as well that you understand now and at the beginning that I have no interest in fornication with you or any other man on board this ship."

Miffed, I said. "Who asked you, baby?"

"These things are better understood immediately."

"You think every man who invites you to sit down is planning an affair with you?"

"I have found the ratio high enough to establish a theory. Yes."

"Very well!" I was annoyed enough to say it. "Better understand everything from the beginning then. This woman Gina Ferelli set you up in the dress shop. She is a friend."

"Yes." And then in answer to my ironic look she said: "You're being melodramatic. My understanding is that in no way will Gina be affected by whatever it is you're up to."

"How naïve can you get?"

"I'm a business woman," she said coldly.

"With a heart?"

"The heart," she said, "has the perfectly obvious function of distributing blood through the body."

The soft voice, the cool classic beauty of her face, the lovely body held so very well, the youth and detached sophistication all resolved into something cold and repellent; the Zombie woman of today's Europe, streamlined and avaricious and empty as last night's bottle of Scotch. I had met her in many parts of the world in the past few years and out of charity would try to remember the bombs wailing down through the night and the shattered childhood that had gone into her creation. But at the moment it seemed to me that this one took first prize in the international broom riding contest.

"We'll dispense with the soft music," I said. "How do we proceed, Little Eva?"

She hesitated, perhaps sensing what had gone through my mind, started to say something, stopped and said instead, "Gina will be in the café in fifteen minutes. We will be there when she arrives. My part in this ... this business, whatever it may be, ends after the introduction."

"That's fine with me."

If it hurt, no scars appeared. "One thing more. Gina's young brother Guido. I've been having difficulties with him. If he seems over curious about you, you can put it down to adolescent jealousy—no more."

"Nice to have your hand in on both sides of the family."

"Yes, isn't it?" And then a little flame of anger came and went out of the clear blue eyes. "But I just don't happen to—I think you would say—work that way."

One hand on the door, she turned. "Oh. I almost forgot. You'd be expected to know. The people I know best call me Kitty."

She looked impassively into my eyes as I laughed. "I thought you'd better know."

"I'll try not to gag when I say it!"

I followed her through the main lounge to the gaily decorated little café overlooking the bow. Here the Frenchman had been able to find a bit of Paris off the coast of Malaya or in the sun-drenched loneliness of the Indian Ocean. Done in a pseudo provincial manner, there were red checked tablecloths, wooden beams, brash abstractions over the tiny bar and iron lanterns, lit now against the last lurid light of the sunset. Ordinarily, at this time of year, the ship would have been crowded with wealthy tourists heading for the winter season in Egypt. But the trouble along the canal looked for real this time. It was inconvenient but wiser for the escapists to miss tea dancing in the shadow of the pyramids until things quieted down again. As they always had before, old boy. And yet a few well-dressed people sat over cocktails talking softly and now and again a woman's laughter would rise above the murmur in a carefree manner that would have warmed the heart of any Sahib. Sigried McCarthy, known for reasons beyond my comprehension by the nauseatingly coy and lovable nickname of "Kitty," waved to several expensive-looking people with the gay and professional manner of an actress making an entrance, and led me to a large table by the plate-glass window at the far end of the room. I ordered a Martini for her and a double Gibson for myself.

Out of the tight silence I said, "Where did you stumble across Grant?"

"In Tangier. Four years ago. I hadn't seen him since then, until this trip to Paris."

"Does he impress you as a master mind?"

Her hand darted out for one of the flowers on the center of the table. She tore the petals from the stem. I don't believe she was aware of this action; her eyes were fixed on some point above the bar. She said nothing.

"Sorry," I said. "We'll skip that. Let's get on the weather. Or Cairo. How do you like Cairo?"

"I like any place where I can survive on a subsistence level."

"You seem to be doing much better than that."

"I've earned it!"

"Like, for instance, like the way you're now earning a little extra pin money from Papa Grant?"

She looked down, noticed the destroyed flower, swept it from the table.

"This undertone of high morality is a bit ironic."

"That's funny. The sermon usually doesn't come until after the fourth drink. I'll get it out of my voice."

She laughed. "You American boys! Mouthing the bromides of sweetness and light while you trample us all to death."

"I've stopped screaming for the eagle long ago. Still ... it seems to me the trampling's being done by someone else."

"Granted. But the someone else at least you know about. You see the scowl from miles away. With you Americans it's different. You dazzle us with your smiles before the boot falls."

Despite the bitter words some of the hardness seemed for the moment to have been thrust aside.

"I refuse to be trapped into being patronizing," I said.

"Let me tell you about yourself," she said. "It's a game I'm good at."

"It's a good subject. Shoot."

"Middle West of the United States?"

"Yes."

"Small town?"

"Fairly small."

"Loved F.D.R."

"Right."

"State University?"

"Two and a half years."

"Ah, yes. The world had to be saved for Democracy again. Out of the classroom and onto the battlefield to show the beast of Germany a lesson...."

"You make it sound trivial."

"Married?"

"Slightly ... and for a time."

"Ah. And now?"

"She's sleeping legally with the guy who had an in while I was sweating it out over—why the hell am I telling you this?"

She continued in her detached fashion: "And then the waking up and the end of that war and home with the medals and the war profiteers and the cynical politicians and all the others who didn't know or care to know and the feeling of alienation from the fairly small town and everything else. And waking up one morning thinking, the devil with them all—from now on it's me and the rest can—an impolite word. Packed a bag and turned home-sweet-home to the wall. Back to dying Europe where the rats scurry about the ruins with 'deals' in their teeth. Became, shall we say, an international bum who asked the price first and the questions after."

"Some of the facts are right."

"But—?" There was a look of intensity in her eyes that baffled me.

"As a biographer you have slanted your material."

"Ah?"

The waiter interrupted whatever she might have said. After he left she stared down into her glass. Suddenly her voice was tired.

"And yet ... you and your kind ... you could have had our hearts had you known. Now it's too late."

The note of despair seemed highly out of character. I looked at her suspiciously. She avoided my eyes. I was uncomfortable. There was something disturbing beneath the travesty of all that had been so important to me once. It came over me that maybe Grant was right, that my sense of detachment was a myth. I was on the same rotten sleigh ride with Grant and the woman at my side. The years had done a helluva lot to the intense young man who had left college to join the air force in 1940.

And then it occurred to me to wonder about Sigried McCarthy. Had there been a time when she too, believed? If so, believed in what?

"I, at least, have learned to accept facts," she said. "I learned this many years ago."

"In Germany?"

She put down the Martini and looked through the plate-glass window where the white wake rolled back into the approaching night.

"I told you," she said. "In Cairo, there is no before time."

I turned from her to find a woman standing in the café's entrance, looking toward our table. I knew immediately that she must be Gina Ferelli and felt a shock of surprise. By any standards she was a raving beauty. She appeared to be in her late twenties or early thirties but it was difficult to be certain. Tall and aristocratic yet suggesting warmth and sunlit skies, black hair pulled back into a chignon from a Botticelli face dominated by enormous dark eyes, magnificent breasts almost scandalously exposed in a very low-cut cocktail gown, she made a picture that sent a tingle of excitement up my spine. The cool chic of Sigried McCarthy, which despite its steely quality, had offered, up to this moment, at least a challenge, floated off into an Icelandic mirage. Since Marta in Bombay three years before, no woman had, on first sight, such an explosive effect on me. And, in the next moment came misgiving. This woman could have any man she wanted. This was no pushover. It looked like a tough campaign.

Chapter Three

She caught my eye and, to add fuel to the heat that was quickly rising to the top of the thermostat, smiled. It was a damned disconcerting smile, intimate and apparently only for me. Maybe Santa will be generous after all, I thought.

Sigried brought me back to earth. In an undertone she said, "You're supposed to be the fisherman, not the fish!"

I got hold of myself and stood as the apparition floated across the room to our table.

"You are, of course, Kitty's Mr. Muldoon."

"Mine until this moment," Sigried said with a laugh.

"Nonsense, Kitty darling. Do sit down Mr. Muldoon. I accept your silence as a tribute to my age. Would you be very sweet and order me a vermouth. Forgive me, please, if I chatter on a bit. Writers unnerve me. They see so much."

They certainly do, I thought, and if they were permitted to see much more madame would be thrown in the brig for indecent exposure. The edge of the green silk dress seemed perilously suspended.

"It will be such a pleasant two days. Quiet and friendly, no? Kitty and Guido and Mademoiselle Courbert and you, Mr. Muldoon. Just our own little family. I make a point never to encourage intimacies on shipboard. People usually turn out to be something altogether different than represented. You play bridge, of course?"

"Indifferently."

"Good. You and I must defend ourselves against the sharks. Guido and Sigried play as though they had been plying the French Line for years. I'm a rank amateur."

Her speech was very Mayfair with only now and again the slurred softness of Italy. But despite the fashionable clipped words and their meaningless context I sensed something questioning, alert, even wary in her attitude. The atmosphere of camaraderie which she so quickly established was, in its way, a clever armor, impregnable to the threat of any genuine intimacy.

"My brother is furious that we didn't fly back. He looks down on anything that moves less than three kilometers an hour!"

"He flies himself?"

"I'm sorry to say, yes. He is the private pilot of Mr. Hans von

Bruckner."

She spoke casually of the man who, according to Grant, was keeping her. But again I sensed the question beneath the surface.

"Where is Guido?" Sigried asked quickly.

"I sent him to fetch Marianne from her stateroom."

"He must have loved that!" Sigried laughed.

"Ah, yes." There was a subtle change in Gina Ferelli's voice, a suggestion, a bare suggestion, of something that might not yield. "Now that you mention it, Kitty, there is something that I wish understood."

"Now, Gina—no lectures, please."

"But I have asked you and Guido to be kind to the poor girl. You both have behaved like bad, naughty children."

"Poor girl! Really, Gina, you can be naïve. And you can't blame Guido for being somewhat fed up with playing nursemaid to your pet charities."

"I do not consider Marianne Courbert an object of charity. She's an artist!"

"My dear, you heard her sing at some party in Paris after too much champagne. The girl wheedled herself into your graces; you thought she was Yvette Guilbert or something. Why has she never sung in Paris?"

"I'm sure I don't know."

"And why was it so important for her to go to Egypt?"

"It's not an unnatural desire."

"But Gina, you know nothing about her. Yet you went ahead and arranged a booking through Signor Gazioni of the Club Lido. The most fashionable nightclub in Cairo. When Gazioni sees what you have to deliver he will tear his hair out by the roots."

"I cannot understand why you dislike her so."

Sigried hesitated. I was aware of the moon rising slowly out of the sea.

"Guido and I both feel she has imposed on your kindness. As so many others have done. She is ungracious and sullen and, I believe, unpleasantly neurotic."

Gina turned to me.

"Forgive me ... you don't know the young lady. She is really quite sweet and pathetic. I'm certain there is some dreadful unhappiness in her past. She is not used to ... well, frivolous people, like Kitty and myself. I hope very much for her success in Cairo."

"I see."

I was thinking that it was somewhat brazen of Sigried to object to

Mrs. Ferelli's generosity.

"Perhaps you will be kinder than Guido and Kitty—they are too young to know."

Was I mistaken or did I detect a slight inflection of irony? Surely she could not think that Sigried was just fresh from a convent.

The woman under discussion came into the café followed by a dark, handsome young man who was obviously Gina's younger brother. Marianne Courbert was a thin young woman, pale and rather ill looking, wearing a cheap and unbecoming black dress. There were two little lines of strain between her eyes, eyes which never quite met a direct gaze. She seemed uncomfortable and almost painfully ill at ease. It was almost impossible to believe that she could command an audience in a smart nightclub, or for that matter, a Greenwich Village dive.

There was a flurry of introductions. Mademoiselle Courbert acknowledged them in a listless manner. Guido grunted a resentful and barely polite greeting before he turned, the competitive male, young and too intense, to Sigried.

"My dear," Gina said to Mademoiselle Courbert, "where in the world have you been? I asked you to meet me in the lounge at seven. I was worried. I had to send Guido to fetch you."

"I am so sorry, madame. I was feeling that perhaps ... You are all so very gay. I do not seem to be gay. I thought ..."

"Nonsense! You're part of our family now."

"You are too kind, madame."

"Do stop calling me 'madame.' I am your friend, child. To my friends I am Gina. Now then, a little wine will cheer you up."

I noticed that the girl clutched a handkerchief in her right hand. Her fingers were wrapped tight about it.

Guido said, "Why don't you tell Gina the truth, Mademoiselle? Or at least what you told me."

"Ah, no! Please!"

"I insist!" His voice was far from sympathetic. "It is not every day that we can hear such an exciting story of escape."

"Escape?" Gina said. "Escape from what?"

Guido sighed and said, "A murderer."

In the sudden silence a woman at the far end of the room laughed. The sound was harsh and completely devoid of humor. We all looked at the French girl. Her hands were clasped tight on the table, the handkerchief crushed between them. She seemed embarrassed to be the center of attention. A hint of color dyed the pale cheeks. She looked down at the clasped hands, then suddenly jerked her head up towards Guido.

"You are making it a joke! I was upset. I never should have told you."

Guido said, "Oh, come now."

He and Sigried exchanged a quick look of amusement. Gina was not amused. In fact it was her expression that convinced me this was far from a joke.

"Pay no attention to Guido, Marianne. What is this all about?"

"You see! *Voila!* I appear—immediately the joy, it is gone from everything!"

"Stop apologizing!" Gina said impatiently. "What did you tell Guido?"

The girl hesitated. She darted a swift look at me. Despite her nervousness there was something speculative and appraising in that look.

"It sounds incredible," she said. "But I will tell you. It was soon after the ship left the harbor at Marseilles. My cabin it was very warm. I go up to the boat deck for air. The deck was deserted. Or at least, so it would seem. I stay there for a very few minutes because I remember I have told madame that I would meet her in the lounge at seven. Instead of using the inside stairs I go to the little iron stairs that lead down so steep to the promenade deck."

She stopped. She looked from face to face as though pleading for belief. She gave an apologetic and mirthless little laugh. "So unreal. So unreal."

"Go on Marianne."

"I went to the top of the steps. It is no more than an iron ladder in reality. I put one foot down to the first step. And then ..." She spoke quickly now; "And then someone pushed me from in back. Very hard. Strong hands."

"My God!"

"My head ... it snap back ... so! I fall forward. My feet are in air. My right hand go out ... see ... like this. I grasp—grasp on nothing and then, *mon dieux*, suddenly beneath my fingers is the guard rail. I manage to hang on to this rail, sliding, sliding all the way down to the promenade deck. I was hurt very little, all but this ... *Voila*, my hand."

She held out her hand and opened it palm up. It was almost raw. Guido looked at the hand. The color rose to his face.

For a moment no one spoke. Then Gina gasped, "But this is monstrous! What sort of beast would do this thing?"

"I don't know," Marianne said. "When I looked up no one was

there. I was afraid to go back. There was nothing, nothing except this."

She opened the handkerchief and placed on the table a small object. It appeared to be a crudely made wooden crescent painted in garish red and yellow.

My first instinct was to ask what in hell it was. To my surprise no one else at the table shared it. They stared at the curious object as though hypnotized.

"Of course," Marianne said, "there may be no connection. It was at the foot of the iron steps when I got up."

After a long moment Gina said, "Have you reported this to anyone?"

"Ah no! I have a morbid fear of publicity. What good would it do? There is no way of knowing ..."

"Guido!"

Gina's voice was a command.

"Yes Gina?" The young man's manner had changed completely. The cynicism had dissolved into abject misery.

"How could you have been so callous when you found poor Marianne frightened nearly to death? You will take her to the ship's doctor immediately. The hand must be attended to."

"It is nothing, I assure you, madame."

"Nonsense! Do as I say, Guido!"

"Of course. Mademoiselle, can you forgive me?"

Guido's remorse had not spread to Sigried. She sat there stony faced, staring at the tiny wooden object on the checked tablecloth. Protesting, Marianne Courbert was led from the room by Guido Ferelli.

Gina said, "It's like a bad dream."

The wooden crescent lay where Marianne had left it. I picked it up and turned it over. It looked handmade and extremely primitive and wholly without meaning.

"Have you any idea what it is?"

The two women exchanged a quick, frightened glance. Then Gina said, "Not the faintest." Sigried decided to investigate the sunset. I slipped the crescent into my pocket.

"Kitty," Gina said almost imploringly, "what do you make of all this?"

Sigried turned from the window. "Something that would be no mystery to a good psychiatrist."

"And what does that mean?"

"She craves attention."

"How can you say that? Her hand ..."

"I don't know how she managed that messy business. But that sort of mutilation is fairly common among psychopaths."

"Kitty! How can you be so unkind?"

"It's quite easy, I assure you."

"But the Mecca Crescent. It ..." Gina stopped. She gave me a quick frightened look. "Or whatever it is. How do you explain that?"

"Don't be a fool, Gina," Sigried said icily. "If you ask me that creature was born with a lie on her lips!"

"The Mecca Crescent?" I said.

Gina stood, almost spilling her drink in the process.

"I don't know why I said that. It looks similar to certain objects I have seen from Mecca. If you'll give it to me ..."

"I'll keep it for the time being."

She put her hand out, checked its movement, let it drop to her side, turned on Sigried. "I don't understand cruelty Kitty. I know you don't really mean it, but sometimes ..."

Sigried was looking at her unmoved. There was something she said with her eyes. A warning? A threat? Whatever it was throttled Gina's sentence. Instead she said distractedly, "You really must excuse me!"

For a moment she looked down into my eyes. What I saw in hers startled me. She was very near to hysteria. He pupils were dilated and I believe that at that moment she was completely unaware of us. The arrival of the waiter with the wine that had been ordered for Marianne brought her back. She managed a shaky laugh and summoned up her armor. "Later," she said with supreme irrelevance, "we will have our bridge, Mr. Muldoon. We will forget this nightmare."

I watched her leave the café, walking like a princess through her court. Sigried said coolly, "If I were you I would drop that obscene little wooden object overboard and forget you ever saw it."

"So you really don't think the girl was lying."

She shrugged. "For her sake, I hope so. Order me another Martini please. I can't bear scenes."

Chapter Four

For two days and nights Gina Ferelli avoided being alone with me. She kept her group tight about her like a protective battalion, marshaling us to the bridge table, the café, the dining salon or the promenade deck. She had gone to the ship's officers with the story of the attempted murder (had she mentioned the wooden crescent?) and with some indignation and open skepticism they had conducted a discreet and fruitless investigation and reluctantly posted a guard at the French girl's stateroom door. Once in a while I would look up quickly to find Gina regarding me with a sort of intensity that added fuel to my desire but in the end left me up against the blank wall of her gay social manner. However, on the morning we were due to land at Alexandria, I had a few moments alone with her in the lounge. Quickly she tried to block all personal contact by a long monologue ending with an invitation to luncheon in Alexandria before she would motor to Cairo. But suddenly her words died and we were left suspended in silence filled with pleasant tension. Uneasily she lit a cigarette and looked toward the door as though for the help of one of the members of the group.

Quietly I said, "Why are you afraid of me?"

She laughed sharply. "Afraid? How absurd!"

"When may I see you?"

"I'm sure we will see one another in Cairo."

"That's not very satisfactory."

She looked directly into my eyes. "It is not up to me to find easy solutions," she said candidly. "I have always understood that was the male prerogative."

The implicit promise in those words took me by surprise. I had expected a polite brush-off. But, once said, the words seemed to alarm her.

The ship was nosing through the busy harbor toward the pier. Gina stood. "I must see that my maid has everything packed. We will meet later at the Majestic Hotel for lunch, then."

"Yes. But Gina ..."

It was the first time I had used her first name. She turned.

"Well?"

"My methods may be somewhat crude, but—"

"Crudity would be fatal," she said calmly. "You must have guessed that I cannot, nor would if I could, be indiscreet. There is a circle. If you remain on its outer limits all will be gay and amusing. If you choose to step beyond its limits ..." She shrugged. "You step into a world of danger."

Her hand brushed mine for just an instant and later I was not certain whether or not it was by accident or intention. Then she went off toward her stateroom.

With mixed emotions I finished my packing and went ashore. Away from the piers and warehouses of the water front the great sprawling city seemed curiously still and empty. Lonely figures sat quietly in deserted parks and the wide boulevards of the modern city gleamed white and silent under a noonday sun. I checked my bags at the Majestic Hotel and joined "the group" for lunch. There I discovered that Gina, Sigried and Guido were proceeding to Cairo in Gina's limousine and that I was expected to accompany Marianne Courbert to Cairo by train.

When we came out of the Hotel Majestic the square was empty and still. The inevitable shadow of the street Arab bearing obscene postcards approached and, rebuffed, slid down the façade of the hotel and out of sight. The Rolls Royce limousine with its liveried chauffeur standing at the curb looked disturbingly like a shiny fortress.

"All of Alexandria is behind doors," I said.

"It's not the first time. These things always pass."

There was a certain amount of bravado in Gina's voice. I didn't share her optimism. Ever since we had left the ship that morning the signs of serious trouble had been everywhere. I was too familiar with the expression I saw on the faces in the streets. I had seen it in other parts of the world, usually just before the lid blew off.

Gina had detained me in the shadow of the hotel entrance. Sigried had already disappeared into the limousine. Guido waited impatiently by the side of the white-robed Nubian doorman who held the car's rear door. The luncheon in the hotel dining room had been saturated in labored gaiety.

"Wouldn't it be wiser for you to change your mind and take the train?" I asked.

"Nonsense. I only wish there were room enough for you and Marianne. However you will probably be relieved to escape us for a bit."

"An honest answer would be indiscreet!"

She smiled. "I will accept it as a compliment. Hart, it is so very kind of you to watch out for Marianne."

"I may regret it."

"I know that frightful episode aboard the Chambord must have been perpetrated by some half mad person, perhaps a member of the crew or ... still, I am very worried for her."

"Don't worry," I said with more conviction than I felt.

"I must go to Luxor for a few days but will be back in Cairo by Friday in time for Marianne's opening at the Lido. I expect you to be in my party there. In the meantime don't hesitate to call on Sigried at her shop. She's not really as cold-blooded as she would have you believe."

I kept my silence on that one.

She lowered her voice. "It is odd, you know."

"What?"

"I've known you only two days. Your interests and your life are quite remote from mine. Yet I feel that in some curious way ... what I mean to say is ... I feel I can trust you."

Fortunately I had, many years before, forgotten how to blush.

"Thanks."

"There is one thing you must promise me."

"Yes?"

"Later I will explain this to you. You must not mention to anyone that ugly little wooden crescent."

"So!" And then impulsively I said, "Gina, you're in some sort of a jam."

"Not now. In Cairo."

"Gina!" Her brother called from the curb. "We will never reach Cairo before dark if you waste more time with Mr. Muldoon."

Her fingers tightened for an instant on my sleeve.

"*Au revoir*, Hart."

Her voice was soft and tinged with sadness. I stood in the entrance and watched her cross to the limousine. Guido gave me one last resentful look and followed his sister into the car. The chauffeur touched the gears and it slid across the nearly empty square and was lost in a narrow street to the south. On the far side of the square, above the roofs of the modern apartment buildings, a minaret stood bold and phallic against the white afternoon.

I went back to the dank lobby with its carpets and wicker furniture and potted palms strewn across a great tile floor. My uneasiness increased. The lobby was as quiet as a bank vault. I thought of the arrogant Rolls Royce purring through the clusters of mud huts and barefoot women and children and dark eyes full of pent-up hatred on the road to Cairo. A man in a shiny dark business suit cleared his throat, sent a rustling sound through the dim room as he shifted in his wicker chair. I crossed to the concierge desk.

"Your tickets, sir. The train is the Luxor Express. It leaves in forty minutes. The taxi will be at our door in fifteen minutes. The luggage is checked through."

"Good. Thank you very much."

"Yes." He left off the "sir" this time. His voice was barely polite, his face carefully devoid of expression. "I have telephoned Shepheard's in Cairo as you asked. They have confirmed the reservation of Madame Courbert, and a room will be awaiting you. On the same floor."

I paid for the railroad tickets, bought a copy of the Cairo Times and found a chair near the entrance where I had promised to meet Marianne, who had excused herself immediately after luncheon on the plea of some necessary shopping in a nearby store. The clock over the clerk's desk sounded loud in the antiseptic silence.

The headlines were not reassuring. The English language paper was filled with carefully sinister understatements. Britain stands on the letter of treaty. Wafdists throw parliament into uproar with demands for evacuation of British troops from Suez and return of Sudan. Trouble on the canal. Students stage peaceful demonstration. Position of the King. Farouk cautions against violence.

Violence. All about us the city crouched, tense with waiting. In the cotton fields and all across the delta the Fellah was nearing the end of a century of patience.

A shadow fell across the newspaper. I looked up into the face of a young man in well-tailored tweeds and a fez. His eyes were bright and hep. He had the smart look of a New York advertising executive. He carried a portfolio. Right away I knew it didn't contain slogans for soap or cigarettes. The guy had "official" shining from every pore.

"Mr. Hart Muldoon?"

"Yes."

"Fares Gebel. In the service of his majesty King Farouk."

"Ah. Sit down. Please."

"Thank you. A matter of routine. I knew you lunched here and thought it better to dispose of this business immediately."

"Routine, eh? I've heard that phrase before."

"I have no doubt of that."

The irony was gentle. He pulled up a wicker chair, sat down and opened the portfolio.

"It will take only a moment."

"Good. I'm taking the Luxor Express in half an hour."

"Yes. I know."

"His Majesty's service is pretty damned well informed."

"Yes. You intended to stop at Shepheard's."

"Right."

"A delightful hotel. Full of memories and nostalgia. A monument to times—shall we say—more privileged?"

"If you like." He purred too much for my blood.

"Now then, it is not customary to ask these questions, especially of a citizen of your great country, but as you well know, this is a time of crisis."

"Shoot."

"Why are you in Egypt?"

"The Pyramids. The Sphinx. Fun. Sun."

"Your reputation is not that of a frivolous tourist."

"My reputation?"

He looked at the portfolio. I lit a cigarette.

"Need we waste time on details? I assure you we have it in black and white. Employed during the autumn of 1950 by Anglo-Iranian Oil. UNRRA, Greece, January and February 1951 on confidential investigation. Pakistan, June to July of the same year on mission for an official of the government of India. Just last month you were in Indonesia where your employer was unfortunately unable to take advantage of certain facts produced by you. And that is not all. You have been for the past five years an undercover agent for many individuals, organizations and governments."

"Your English is excellent."

"And my facts?"

"Admirable."

I meant that. They were surprisingly accurate.

"Is there any reason, therefore, why we should assume you have deserted your, er, profession in favor of a Kodak and a Baedeker? Come now, Mr. Muldoon."

"No logical reason."

"Well then?"

"My business is of a private nature. There are no politics involved."

He showed his dazzling white teeth in an unbelieving smile, sat back and sighed.

"My country has become almost immune to agents, Mr. Muldoon. The streets and hotels of Cairo are jammed with mercenaries and spies. In some cases we have been able to learn more from them than they learn from us. We have become cynical watching the G. P. U. man dancing with the girl from British intelligence or the Falange representative drinking with the clean-cut young man from your state department. They wait with lighted matches around the gasoline tank. It is possible that they will be the first to go in the explosion."

I looked toward the hotel entrance. What the hell was keeping the Courbert girl?

"This is all very interesting, Mr. Gebel, but—"

"I could prevent you from continuing to Cairo. It is even within my power to see that you leave the country within twenty-four hours. Or less. I don't intend to exercise this power."

"Why not?"

"Put it down to curiosity."

"So." I managed a laugh. "Don't waste your men on me, Mr. Gebel. What they would turn up is embarrassingly trivial."

"In that case, you could have no objection to satisfying my curiosity now."

"My first loyalty is to my client."

"I see." He snapped shut the portfolio and leaned forward. He lowered his voice. "His Majesty's government will not countenance interference in the internal affairs of Egypt. Any infraction at this time would mean your immediate arrest."

"Fair enough."

"Furthermore, if in the course of your private business you should stumble across anything that might be of importance to the government, any concealment on your part will be viewed with extreme gravity."

"So that's it!" I laughed. "Let's get down to cases. If and when—how much?"

An expression very near to hatred came and went from his young face. But he hid it quickly. He thought for a moment, not having planned to face this decision so soon. He hesitated, then said, "I doubt that you will be able to produce anything not already known to his Majesty's government. However ..." He took a deep breath and said, "We are prepared to be generous."

"Good enough."

He took a small pad and a silver pencil from an inner pocket and quickly wrote something, tore the page off and handed it to me. "When and if, as you say, you can reach me at this Cairo number. In the meantime, I have warned you."

He stood, very efficient once again, alert and flashing his Madison Avenue executive smile. We shook hands.

"As you well know," he said, "anything to do with the matter of the

Mecca Crescent would be received with interest. Ah, I see your young lady has arrived."

He left me, crossed the lobby, stepped aside to let Marianne pass as she came up the steps from the street, and then went out into the deserted square. Marianne turned to watch him go. My left hand closed about the wooden crescent in my pocket. It was too late to question Gebel now. At last my reputation had not only caught up but whistled past me. Gebel thought I knew.

Chapter Five

The Luxor Express, Egypt's crack de luxe train, slid through the suburbs of Alexandria out toward the green expanse of the Delta. Because of the wide-gauge rails the cars were more spacious than those of Europe and no train in the world matched it for ornate luxury. Designed to speed multimillionaires up the Nile from Alexandria, she was all gilt and pink paneling and soft carpets and silk-shaded wall lamps. Only an ominously few passengers had got aboard at the Alexandria station. Apparently most of the traffic was heading in the opposite direction.

I was not too pleased to find that Marianne Courbert and I would share a first class compartment in exclusive grandeur for the trip to Cairo. It was the first time I had been alone with her. After the melodramatic scene in the ship's bar she had flitted like a shadow around the edges of "the group." Always there when Gina beckoned her into the light but avoiding any intimacies. Although I discounted Sigried's initial theory about the psychopathic lie, the girl's odd behavior, a mixture of self-abasement and listless indifference, certainly seemed to indicate some neurotic difficulty. Under repeated questions from Gina she had firmly denied knowledge of anyone who might wish to take her life. Now I resented having to play big brother to a girl I suspected, despite her air of helplessness, was more than capable of taking care of herself.

She got into my thoughts with disconcerting speed.

"I'm sorry, Monsieur Muldoon."

"For what?"

"You must not feel you have to stay here with me and be bored. There is a restaurant car on the train and ..."

"Doesn't it ever occur to you that people might enjoy your company?"

"Oh, yes," she surprised me by saying.

"Well then ..."

"But people like Madame Ferelli and her brother and Mrs. McCarthy—I have had little experience with such. I suppose I am like a Cinderella who feels only uncomfortable at the ball."

I had not expected nor wished such a quick plunge into the personal. But now that we were there I decided to dig deeper.

"You mean the rich make you uneasy?"

"Yes. Not because of envy. Or disapproval even. I think it's wonderful to be gay and brilliant and beautiful and to make of life a party. It is only that I don't belong there."

"It's hard to know just where you do belong."

"Am I so strange?"

"It's as though you belonged only in some world of your own. That there was some sort of—well, obsession, to which you are constantly turned."

"Obsession?" She looked at me gravely. After a moment she said, "You think I am ill?"

From far up ahead the locomotive screeched a warning. I felt an unaccountable chill.

"No. I didn't mean—"

"Perhaps you're right. One becomes ill out of one's time and experience. Perhaps you're right."

As I looked at her I got a shock. The gown seemed purposely designed to make her appear thin and gauche. For the first time I saw beneath its straight lines a beautiful body. And for the first time I became aware that Marianne Courbert was not only young but attractive. And immediately I had the feeling that she had revealed this to me at the first opportunity after we had left the others. Why?

Her breasts rose and fell in an agitated manner. What emotion or sensation was robbing her of her breath? Ego patterns began to take over. Well, well, I thought, it's worth investigating.

"Where did you meet Gina Ferelli?"

"At a party in the studio of Herjes, the painter. Someone I had known in Rio took me there. I was persuaded to sing. Madame Ferelli was extremely kind and flattering. When I told her that I had always wanted to go to Egypt nothing would do but that she telephone the manager of the Lido in Cairo. It was arranged in twenty minutes. Patrons like Madame Ferelli can make or break a place like the Lido, you know."

"Why did you wish to come to Egypt?"

"Let us say ... my obsession."

"Money? A rich marriage perhaps?"

"No!" The answer was unnecessarily vehement. Then she smiled. "There! I will depress you with seriousness."

"Not necessarily. You look too young to be knocking around nightclubs."

"Too young? For what?" She mocked me now. Was there also the suggestion of an invitation?

"You don't look like a professional entertainer."

"I am a professional all right. Since I was fifteen. Seven years. A lifetime really."

"But is it not better for your career to sing in France?"

"I have never sung in France. I sang all over Central and South America. And I can assure you in nothing so elegant as the Lido."

"Why not France?"

She shrugged and looked out of the window. The train was flying across the flat country. A white sail seemed to be moving down the middle of a cotton field. A dromedary stood rigid near an ancient water wheel. Somewhere over there was the Nile.

"You do not feel uncomfortable with me?"

"No," she said without turning from the window. "There is something about you I understand. I have known men like you."

And then into my silence she turned quickly. "As friends."

"That spoils my idea about your obsession," I said. Right away I knew I was going too fast. She stared at me coldly.

"In that case I am glad!"

"It was a bum joke."

"Yes, of course."

But she breathed even faster. Her hands were clenched tight in her lap. She looked toward the closed door and then almost guiltily back at me.

"I'm afraid ..." She stopped.

"Of what?"

"It is impossible to explain. I want you to like me. That is more than I can say about most men. I want you to ..." Again she stopped. The color rose to her cheeks. I began to get really interested. Two days of Gina Ferelli's veiled but frustrating play had keyed me up to this moment.

"Surely," I said, more crudely than I had intended, "in your profession a young and attractive girl has—"

"No," she said flatly. "No."

I tried mental cold water. "About the wooden crescent...."

"What about it?"

"Surely you have some idea."

"I wish I did."

"You have no idea who gave you that shove?"

"No."

She reached for her big, ugly leather handbag, unsnapped it, fished for a lipstick and mirror. I don't think she thought out the gesture. In the midst of touching her lips she stopped suddenly and the color came back to her face. Awkwardly she pushed them back into the bag and snapped it shut.

Despite myself I laughed. "You're like a schoolgirl. Quite charming, really. I'm sorry I missed it before."

"A schoolgirl?"

"Why so solemn?"

The heat was on again and this time I went along with it. Her agitation was all too apparent. I got up and put the latch on the door and pulled down the shades that opened to the corridor.

When I turned back she was hunched into the corner by the window watching me with wide terrified eyes.

"You don't have to put on the reluctant virgin act with me, baby."

"Please," she whispered.

So certain was I that her fear was simulated, I bungled it as badly as any callous farm hand. She fought like a tiger but I assumed it was part of a professional game. I had managed to loosen the offending gown until it hung about her waist and the brassiere was dangling off one lovely shoulder before I realized she was fighting for her life. Her fingers dug into the back of my neck and she opened her mouth to scream before I came to. I pushed her away and got hold of myself as best I could. I turned my back while she made the necessary rearrangements to the accompaniment of hysterical sobs. When the sobs had subsided to a whimper I said,

"I made a mistake."

"It's not your fault. You didn't understand."

"I don't want to hear," I said harshly. "Let's go to the restaurant car and get drunk."

"You don't want me to ..."

"Damn it, come on!"

I heard the snap of the handbag and the rustle of silk as she repaired her face. Then she was beside me, one hand on my arm.

"You are kind," she said simply.

"And you're nuts!"

I followed her down the swaying corridor fighting down my anger and bewilderment. This was one I couldn't figure. Nothing in my repertoire fitted the picture. I stopped to light a cigarette. When I looked up I saw her standing very still and tense at the entrance to the ornate restaurant car. I came up behind her.

"Well, let's go," I said. I gave her elbow a push but she didn't move. I looked over her shoulder. Save for the white-robed waiters and two men who sat at separate tables the car was deserted. Both men were facing us. One was absorbed with the menu. The other stared out the window. The one with the menu who was nearest to us was a tall distinguished-looking guy of about fifty. He held himself very straight and was examining the menu as though it were a state proclamation. I didn't like the rigidity of the face or the thin lips or the steely glint of the pale blue eyes. The other man sat further back on the opposite side of the car. I recognized him immediately as a chap named Pete Larson whom I had known in India as a British agent. His hawklike face looked tired and ill. I had remembered him as cynical and even gay; now, unaware that he was watched, he seemed sunk in some overwhelming depression.

I had been so surprised and pleased to see Larson that I was hardly aware at first of Marianne's arms moving swiftly, until I heard the snap of the handbag. It wasn't until I saw the sudden shaft of light reflected off metal that I got it. I moved as quickly as I ever moved in my life. I swept one arm down in front of her, hard. The gun fell to the thick carpet. She kicked at me and stooped to pick it up, but I was ahead of her. I snatched the automatic up and shoved it into my pocket with one hand as I got a half nelson on her with the other and dragged her back into the corridor of the next car. She stopped fighting almost immediately and sagged against the window. Fortunately no one was in sight. I was fairly certain that no one inside the restaurant car had been aware of what was taking place outside the glass door.

"So that's it!" I said. "Which one?"

"Seven years," she said in a dead voice. "And now I've found him."

"Are you looking to get yourself pinned on a murder rap?"

"Nothing can stop me, Hart."

"Except maybe me. Come on. Get back to the compartment before someone sees you looking like Dracula's daughter out for blood."

She went along docilely enough. I got her inside the compartment and locked the door again.

"And now will you kindly tell me what in the name of God you are up to?"

To my amazement she laughed. For the first time since I had met her she was giving a damned good imitation of happiness. It made my blood run cold.

"I knew I was right. I knew I would find him!"

"So this is the obsession!"

"Nothing will stop me, Hart! Nothing. Maybe not today or tomorrow, but soon. At last!"

Caught in some macabre gaiety she threw her arms about my neck and pressed her body tight against mine.

"Hart," she said passionately. "Hart..."

Chapter Six

On the following morning I was troubled with an uneasy dream. I was drowning in an angry surf and then I realized I wasn't drowning and that it wasn't the sound of surf I heard but people shouting in unison. Shut up, I thought, shut up, and then slowly, reluctantly, awakened. I was in a large bed with mosquito netting and canopy and a woman asleep beside me.

That's just fine, I thought, fine. Where and whom and why? And what was all the shouting about? I managed to prop myself up on one elbow. For a moment I thought my head would refuse to come up with me. It was throbbing like a faulty gasoline engine. Fine. I examined the woman beside me with some interest. She looked familiar. The face, childlike in sleep, evoked some disturbing association but the body, relaxed now yet suggesting inner tension, the breasts turned upward with bold unawareness, the slim thighs, the hand flung outward toward me, brought back something that had been more than merely pleasurable.

But I was still only half awake and it seemed part of sleep, a vague and fantastic dream. Struggling for reality, I pushed aside the mosquito netting and managed to get out of the bed. My toes bumped against an empty champagne bottle. Yeah, fine, fine, I thought uneasily. I went across the sunlit room toward the window and the sound of shouting. It sounded vaguely like a boy-scout rally. I pushed aside the draperies. Down below, two stories down, was a vast terrace on which some well-dressed people sat in wicker chairs at iron tables. Steps led down from the terrace to a wide boulevard. Lined up at the curb were carriages with gay red tassels and some expensive-looking limousines. In the middle of the street a crowd of young men and women were marching carrying placards reading "Down With England" and similar immoderate slogans. The moment I saw the terrace I thought, why this is Shepheard's Hotel in Cairo, and in that instant everything came back.

Yet it all seemed part of the dream, the chattering people who ignored the placards of the marchers, the chauffeurs leaning against their limousines watching the young people with amused detachment, the orderly politeness of the demonstrators, the yellow tram waiting for the parade to pass, the Nubian waiters hurrying about the terrace with trays of drinks, the room behind me with the sleeping girl.

A kind of panic took possession of me. Time had passed, too much time. I found my watch on the bureau. It was almost noon. I should have been out of this room and back to my own before dawn. Damn the management anyway for not being able to arrange adjoining rooms when we had arrived the night before. I looked back toward the bed, remembering. Marianne. Marianne Courbert. How innocent and childlike she appeared in sleep, all the knowledge that had made the previous night possible eradicated from her face. Better go, I thought, with heroic self-discipline, or you'll never leave this room today.

Still somewhat stupefied I began to dress. I hadn't planned it this way. I'd had no intention of getting involved with the French girl. But after the episode in the Luxor Express, nature had taken its course. And with a vengeance! For sheer physical passion Marianne Courbert was extraordinary. Yet despite her almost frightening detachment from sentimentality I remembered an expression in her eyes that had disturbed me. It reminded me of a devoted hound I'd owned as a kid. If I let this affair continue I might end up with one of those "my man" characters on my hands.

I buttoned my shirt after a fashion, threw the tie about my neck, and reached for my coat. But I stood there a moment still watching the sleeping girl. After the gunplay in the corridor of the restaurant car she had gaily but firmly refused to discuss it with me. And my mood on the previous night had been far from businesslike. I'd put off the questions in what I suppose was a perfectly normal manner. But now they came crowding back. Was she some sort of a mental case as Sigried had implied? And if not, which of the two men in the restaurant car had she planned to murder? And for what reason? I knew one of those men fairly well, and remembering Pete Larson as a quiet, rather prissy Englishman who took his job very seriously, it seemed improbable that he could have done anything to goad a woman into attempted murder.

Who was the other man? Had Marianne rushed into an act of

passion with the specific purpose of preventing me from making inquiries?

I tried to shake the cobwebs out of my head. Had the girl planned it this way? Was it her intention, her job perhaps, to divert me? My hand closed around the wooden crescent in my pocket. Time to get to work.

Quietly, I opened the door and walked through what seemed to be miles of corridors to my own room which was on the same floor but on the opposite end of the long rambling building. I bathed, shaved, had some eggs and coffee in my room, dressed in fresh clothes, got out the telephone directory and made a call.

When the voice at the other end said "Yes," I said, "Phidias?"

"Who is?"

"Ah! Good. Muldoon. Remember? Colonel Wells' delight. Together we cleared the road to Tunis."

"Son of a bitch! I thought you were dead, sweetheart!"

"Not yet. Maybe this time. When can I see you?"

"Now. Any time. I'll come to your hotel."

"No. Stay at your office. Clear it out. I'll be there in about a half hour!"

"Sure, Hart, sure."

I hung up and went down to the vast lobby where phony Moorish architecture fought a losing battle with all too authentic Victorian. One look around at the cosmopolitan crowd told me that nothing had changed at Shepheard's. Here within the walls of one of the world's most famous hotels, you would have thought the good queen still reigned over the Empire and that all was well with the world. No hint of the political tension in the city was permitted past the terrace. Millionaire playboys, well-heeled tourists, international ladies de luxe, members of Cairo's legation crowd rubbed elbows with confidence men, paid assassins, spies and black market profiteers. But it seemed to me that the conversation in the lobby was a bit too shrill, too synthetically gay. I bought an English language newspaper and moved into the renowned bar. There in mahogany grandeur wealthy Egyptians were breaking the rules of their faith with a pre-luncheon Martini among newsmen and rubberneckers and the inevitable contingent of British Colonials who evidently had not heard of recent history and who stayed aloof in their own icy group.

I ordered a drink and cased the newspaper. The news from the canal was damned serious. There had been riots in Suez and Port Said and the British had no intention of giving up the canal. But the stories were restrained and optimistic, even though King Farouk warned against violence, and Britishers and Americans were advised to leave the country. A great deal of newspaper space was devoted to legation dances, houseboat parties, the races at Heliopolis, the attractions at the supper clubs and chitchat about the international set. There was a note to the effect that Signora Ferelli had returned from a visit to Europe and planned to give a party at the premiere of the new singer at the Lido. I looked in vain for mention of Hans von Bruckner.

I folded my paper and was about to pay for my drink and leave when I saw Pete Larson. He was standing at the far end of the long bar, several feet separating him from his closest neighbor, staring down into his drink. Once again I was struck by the extraordinary change that had come over him since last I had seen him in Pakistan. His face was drawn into a tired and indifferent mask.

I walked down the length of the long bar and took the empty place beside him. He looked up from his drink. For an instant his eyes lighted up, then the light died and an expression of cynical indifference took its place.

"Muldoon of the red, white and blue, I presume. Honored."

"Hello, Pete. What's eating you?" I ordered another round of drinks.

"Ulcers," he said shortly. "I might as well warn you if you're here on business you'd better not be seen drinking with me. I'm outside, you know. Way outside. No decent Sahib would touch me with a ten-foot pole."

"I'm not a decent Sahib. Anyway stop acting like a character out of Maugham."

"Funny thing about those characters. They're true. Serious what I said. I'm taboo, old man. Man without a country and all that."

I managed to hide any shock I felt. Larson had been one of those plodding, good-natured, efficient types, as British as roast beef. I remembered some vague talk about a girl waiting back in Manchester and the appalling life of respectability they planned some day in one of those suburban houses with a garden.

"Want to talk?"

"Why not," he said in a tired voice. "Might as well hear it from me as the others. They gave me a choice. Damned generous. Stay away from England from now on out or face a trial for treason."

His voice broke slightly on the last word.

"You're joking."

"No. Wish to hell I were. Sweet little bitch with gold earrings up in Karachi. She got me drunk and talking. It seems she turned everything over to the NKVD. It wasn't much but it was enough to finish me. No appeal of course. Well ..."

"Cripes! Surely they knew you better ... gave you another chance."

He laughed sharply. "You know as well as I do that you only make that kind of a mistake once. I suppose they're right. I never visualized life away from England. I—I think maybe I'll have just one more, old man."

I ordered another drink quick.

He lit a cigarette with shaking fingers. "Must be a masochist to come here. Somehow can't keep away. Looking for an island. Some chaps who have bitched out like me do well. It's different for me. I was never much good at this cloak and dagger stuff. I was a career man. Glorified office boy. What government wants an office boy to-day? You hear of one and tell me. I'm not choosy."

"The hell you're not!"

"Don't give me that hearty optimism, Muldoon. My stomach's not too steady as it is."

"How long you been in Egypt?"

"Two months. Moving on when I can afford—I mean soon."

"I see. Ever run into a French girl named Marianne Courbert? Not here in Egypt. Anywhere."

He looked at me blankly and shook his head. I decided immediately he had not been intended for Marianne's target practice.

"Forget it." I looked down the length of the bar. I turned very quickly in time to catch the intent gaze of an extremely handsome young man standing about midway down the room. He suddenly discovered his glass very interesting. I pointed him out discreetly to Larson.

"Know him?"

"That little frog," Larson said contemptuously. "Young playboy. Name of Armand Trouvier. Has the ladies of the legation set panting in public. Bachelor with a penthouse on top of the Alexander Apartments. Dashes around the country in a silver racing plane and owns a string of polo ponies. French and too damned good looking to be anything but a cad."

For a moment Larson had reverted to type. I didn't smile.

"What do you think will happen here in Cairo, Larson?"

He took a long swig of his drink. After a moment he said, "Not that it's any of my business but there are plenty of trouble makers around. The Commies and the local fanatics—they'll exploit this situation for all it's worth. I think it's very possible that all hell will break out. All it needs is a spark."

I took a deep breath, counted three and said, "Hear anything about missing aeroplanes?"

He jerked his head up, looked me in the eyes.

"So you're in that. Everyone in Cairo knows about a missing British bomber. Everyone in Cairo doesn't know what I know. And no one will know unless they pay a price, goddamn it."

"Even for the Union Jack?"

He looked away. "That's not my business anymore."

"The hell it isn't. But anyway, when and where can I see you?"

He hesitated. Then without looking up he said, "This evening. If you can afford it. Pension by the name of Capri. A rat hole over beyond the Hotel Victoria." His mouth curled into a cynical bitter grin. "Ask for Madame Gebhardt."

I put a bill on the bar.

"I'll be there."

As I walked across the room I was aware once again of the young Frenchman following me with his eyes. I went out through the lobby and the great Moorish arch onto the terrace and then down to the street. The demonstrators had disappeared. Traffic had returned to its usual madhouse proportions. Modern Cairo glittered all about me like an overdressed whore. But up on the hill the great ancient citadel looked down on the miles and miles of narrow alleys and tenements which the tourists called "quaint" and in the dark passive faces I sensed a tension of waiting nearing the breaking point. I tried not to think of Larson and his shattered life. This was no time to be soft. There was a job to be done.

Chapter Seven

At the Luna, I turned away from the Boulevard Fouad I and cut out across the park to a narrow street that hugged close to the rear of the Opera House. Very little of the bright sunny day filtered down into this rancid-smelling alley. Windowless walls, pierced by single doorways, here and there an "office building" erected early in the century and long ago abandoned by most Europeans, now and again a stall-like shop presided over by an indifferent and lethargic Arab. The sounds of city traffic faded into the background like sounds in a dream. I found number seventy-six and entered an arched door into a small musty lobby. On the wall several places of business were listed in Arabic but there was one in French. I went up a narrow stairway between hot stone walls, lighted only by a single dim bulb on each landing. It was difficult to believe that any business was being conducted in this building or for that matter any life at all; it was as quiet as a condemned tenement. On the third floor I went down a uselessly wide corridor, found the door marked "Amour de Nile, Parfumeur" and pushed it open.

Phidias Imperator sat in almost exactly the same spot where last I had seen him, during the third year of the Second World War. Behind a paper-strewn desk, he leaned back in a swivel chair, cigar clutched fiercely in his mouth, staring blankly at an equally blank stone wall on the other side of the narrow street. He was short, thin, dark and completely bald and for some reason he made me think of an olive. He turned and grinned as though I had just been out for a few days instead of several years. He hadn't changed.

"Son of a bitch!"

"How's the perfume business, you old swindler? Still taking the tourists with that colored water you call amber?"

He shrugged. "I should not complain for the past. But tourists scare easy. I may have no clients tomorrow."

Phidias spoke a curious English compounded of accents from many sources. I think the most predominant influence had been a British consul for whom he had once worked as a valet many years ago in his native Athens, and the Americans during the war to whom he had given valuable information before Montgomery's advance toward Tunis. I had been helpful in clearing red tape so that his son could get into the States to be with his Yankee wife. The son now ran a successful Greek restaurant in lower Manhattan. Phidias was not one to ever forget a good turn.

"I have an illumination," he said. "I will close the office. I will take you back to my house in Heliopolis. You will meet my new wife. Daughter of a sheik. I have made a heathen out of her. She is a regular baby factory. Gave me three children since we were married. A fourth on the production line. Very—"

"Not today, Phidias. Maybe tomorrow or the next day. I've got a helluva lot to clear up in a short time."

I sat down, avoided an offered cigar, and for a few minutes we talked about old times. Phidias had lived in Cairo for the past thirty years and in some ways knew it better than the native born. Especially on the level of fast deals and under-the-counter politics. After a bit I said, "You know where all the bodies lie in this town, Phidias. Maybe you can give me some information."

He laughed. "These days I have found that by merely giving directions to the Pyramids at Giza I can be paid. More useless 'information' I have sold for hard cash this past month to clever, clever agents."

"I've been to the Pyramids and I have no expense account this time."

"With you it's different," he said simply. "Fire ahead."

The room was very still and hot. No sign of life came from anywhere else in the building.

"Guy by name of Von Bruckner."

He frowned. "Hans von Bruckner. You ask about one of whom I have little knowledge. Who knows. Cotton speculation, diamonds in the South, black markets in Europe ... who knows. If he works for any government it has not come to my ears. Perhaps he is not as rich as he would have people believe."

"You think it may be a front?"

He turned his hands out expressively. "Very possible."

"What's his racket?"

"He is clever. Plays the social role. Has a woman named Ferelli whom he has set up in a luxury villa out on the river. All Cairo goes to her parties. He stays in the background. As far as I know he has no legitimate place of business in Cairo."

"Any ideas?"

"Plenty. But only hunches."

"Like?"

"He has been intimate with the ex-Mufti. It is possible that he tries to establish better relations for the Mufti with certain power groups. I have no proof. Only a hunch."

"What about her? The Ferelli woman."

He grinned. "Ah ... what a woman. Every man in Cairo would like to change places with Von Bruckner. She was the wife of a minor official in the Italian Legation, came here as a young girl just before the war. He died and she disappeared from sight. When she turned up again it was as Von Bruckner's mistress. It is said she has no other lovers. She has been very successful as a hostess. Maybe she gets the people Von Bruckner wants into her house."

"He's German of course?"

"Decidedly. The story is that he got out in '38 because he couldn't stand Mr. Hitler."

"You don't believe it?"

"He is Prussian to his fingertips. Boots, spurs, riding crop—besides, you know how friendly the ex-Mufti was with Hitler. It figures."

"Is he connected with the Sons of Mecca?"

Phidias put down his cigar. The flippancy went from his face.

"So ... that is your business. I am sorry to hear it."

"Why?"

"It's unhealthy."

"How unhealthy?"

"It's been known to be fatal."

"As I hear it—it's a sort of fanatical lunatic fringe group pledged to carry out some of the ex-Mufti's policies. Sort of on the order of the Ku Klux Klan in the States. And just about as ineffective."

"Ineffective? In these days anything could happen."

"They would need some dramatic *cause célèbre* to get the masses of the Arab world behind them."

He looked at me sharply. "I had never thought of Von Bruckner in that connection. Now that you mention it, I am told that since the trouble with the British up on the canal they have recruited many new members. Perhaps ..." He stopped. He looked uneasily over my shoulder toward the hall door.

"Since it is common knowledge that I sided with the Americans during the war, I am not too popular with certain groups in this city. I have made a point of not meddling. After all, I must go on living here long after you are gone."

"I don't want to put you on a spot, Phidias."

I got up, went to the door, looked out into the hall. It was empty. I stood there a moment listening. Somewhere a door closed softly. I shut the door tight and went back to the desk and leaned over close to Phidias.

"Have you heard any aeroplane stories?"

He looked away. After a moment he said in a low voice, "It is common knowledge in Cairo that a British bomber is missing in a flight from the Sudan, if you mean that."

"It could be what I mean."

"I see." He hesitated a moment. "In times like this there are many wild rumors. Personally I believe the plane went down in the Red Sea. Still the tales multiply."

"For instance?"

He laughed nervously. "Just stupid wild tales ..."

"Tell me."

He sighed. "Yesterday I spoke to the dragoman of a caravan just in from Saudi Arabia. He told of sighting a great plane flying low about a hundred kilometers southeast of Cairo. A British plane. If it was the bomber it would have been many miles off its course. I think the story is not trustworthy. The dragoman wanted to be an important fellow."

I thought, Phidias is probably right. Yet it was a straw. "Where can I see this camel driver?"

Phidias leaned back in the swivel chair and for the first time his eyes were unfriendly. "I will not be involved in this, Hart! I cannot afford it."

"I'll keep you out of it."

"I am old now and cynical and indifferent to everything but the security of my wife and children. It is a mistake to have moral convictions in this town. I don't intend to acquire any. It is none of my goddamned business and I intend to keep it that way."

"I seem to have heard this all before."

"The war—it was different. Besides I had sense enough to get on the winning side. This time I don't know."

"You're not kidding me, Phidias. You know you hate the guts of the Mufti and his kind."

He looked worried. "I have never said such a thing!" he said in a loud voice.

I straightened up, puzzled. Phidias was not the type who scares easy. Eight years before he would have laughed at a group like the Sons of Mecca.

I reached into my pocket, drew out the wooden crescent and held it out toward him. The effect was immediate and disturbing. I might have been offering him a rattlesnake.

"Where did you get that?" he whispered.

"Does it matter?"

"It is a death symbol."

"The Sons of Mecca?"

Instead of answering he said, "You shouldn't have come here. If I had known—you would be wise to leave Cairo on the first train out."

I laughed. "You ought to know me better than that. Where can I see this dragoman?"

He stood. His face was cold. He bent down and wrote something on a pad. Then in a loud voice he said, "I can't give you any information at all. I know nothing."

He took the paper from the pad and handed it to me.

On it he had written, "Café Noir. Ban-en-Nazr Gate. Ten o'clock tonight."

I stuffed the paper in beside the wooden crescent. I felt suddenly warm and happy about the human race. Phidias was standing there a picture of cool dignity, unsmiling, remote. I grinned. "It's good to see you again, Phidias."

"Son of a bitch," he said in a low voice.

I went out into the hall. A dapper little fellow with a wax moustache was entering an office down at the other end. He didn't turn in my direction but I had the feeling that he had managed to get down that hall damned quick. His fez slipped forward as he bent down over the knob. Then he went inside. I thought, don't begin imagining things. I hurried down the narrow stairs out into the tunnel-like street. Somewhere out in the city another mob was shouting. My hand closed around the wooden crescent as I walked quickly toward the sunlit park.

Chapter Eight

During the afternoon I tried several other contacts, less reliable than Phidias, and, as it turned out, even less informative. The very mention of the Sons of Mecca was enough to produce a sphinx-like silence. This, combined with the effects of my long night with Marianne, didn't do much to make me a sunshine kid. By four o'clock my mood was, if not black, certainly a very dark gray. I couldn't seem to get my mind clicking properly. And what went on in it didn't make much sense. What possible reason would the Sons of Mecca have for attempting the murder of an obscure little French nightclub singer? Was that gun she toted intended for a political victim? And, if Hans von Bruckner were connected with the Sons of Mecca, was it more than mere coincidence that Gina Ferelli had sponsored the girl's trip to Cairo? Gina's brother Guido was Von Bruckner's private pilot. Did that mean the boy was involved also with the Arab group? And was Gina innocent of Von Bruckner's activities, provided that my hunch about him was correct?

At four o'clock, hot and in ill humor, I found myself walking back toward Shepheard's along the Boulevard Fouad I. The afternoon papers carried black and ominous headlines. Were the threats and counterthreats merely political juggling this time? Not far from the hotel I noticed a smart little shop with the name "Mme. Sigried" in scroll gilt letters on its show window. I'd almost forgotten about the German girl. Where did she fit in? I pushed open a plate glass door and entered a small but elegantly appointed little room.

In the perfumed silence a middle-aged woman came forward with a mechanical smile of greeting. There were no other customers in the place.

"Monsieur?"

"Is Mrs. McCarthy in?"

"Madame Sigried? She is in her office." She indicated a door at the rear of the shop. I started for it. "Oh, monsieur, madame is engaged at the moment. If you will give me the name ..."

I paid no attention. I opened the office door and stepped over the threshold. A man was bent over the desk engaged in a low-voiced and apparently urgent conversation with Sigried McCarthy. She caught my eye and said in a warning voice, "Oh—Mr. Muldoon!"

The man straightened up quickly and turned. He was the handsome young Frenchman Larson had pointed out to me in the bar at Shepheard's. He was obviously startled.

"Sorry to barge in." I said.

"That's quite all right," Sigried said coolly. "Monsieur Trouvier was just going."

"Ah ... yes. Yes, of course."

She introduced us formally. The young man seemed nervous. He managed a smile. "Without Sigried I would be lost.... My lady friends admire my taste in gifts but, I assure you, it is a reputation founded on Sigried's advice."

"Yeah," I said in no mood for social chitchat, "haven't we met before?"

Trouvier stopped smiling. "It is possible, of course, monsieur. If you have been to Cairo ... I meet many people."

"I mean before Cairo."

He frowned, his face a picture of charming candor. "Paris perhaps ... I am sorry. I have no recollection."

"Everyone knows Armand," Sigried said.

I was sure I had seen the guy somewhere but nothing clicked.

"Well, I must go," the young man said into the uncomfortable silence. "You are joining Guido and me for a cocktail, Sigried?"

"That would be lovely."

"Say six?" Then he looked at me and added dutifully, "Mora insists on the red gown, Sigried. I'm counting on you to dissuade her. The girl is sweet but if let alone would appear at the Polo Club looking like an American fire engine."

"I'll do my best," she said.

Trouvier nodded pleasantly to me and left the office. Sigried lit a cigarette. "Are you always so insufferably rude?" she asked.

"I was just curious."

"You sounded like a house detective with delusions of grandeur. You acted as though you had seen poor Armand's face on a 'criminals wanted' poster."

"Poor Armand."

"Well, rich Armand, then. Most women find him charming. It is considered a mark of attainment to be taken for a trip in his racing plane or to sit in his box at the International Club while he is dazzling Cairo on the playing field."

"What's he doing in Cairo? And with whose money?"

"Don't be dull. Sit down and stop looking so sullen. Am I to consider this a business call?"

"If you like. How long have you been working for Von Bruckner?"

Her face didn't change expression. She tilted her head back and blew a stream of smoke upward. Then she looked me in the eye. "You must be drunk," she said.

"I wish I were. I haven't time for subtlety."

"That's obvious. You're behaving like an oaf!"

"That's no answer."

"You can see for yourself. I run a very successful dress shop. Gina helped me start it. Von Bruckner has nothing whatsoever to do with it. In fact, I have never been told what his business is."

"You've never been curious enough to ask Gina?"

"Why should I? I don't give a damn!"

"Even for her sake?"

She looked down at her cigarette and then smashed it out. Then she said quietly, "Perhaps I should have. I'm worried about Gina. I think she's frightened to death."

"Of what?"

She shrugged. "Perhaps Von Bruckner. She is too proud to confide in me." She looked up, eyes candid now, too candid. "I don't quite know why I'm telling you this. Perhaps it's even more dangerous. I don't know what Jeremiah Grant is up to. I assume it has nothing directly to do with Gina that could mean harm to her. If I'm wrong ..."

"Well?"

She clasped her hands tight on the desk before her. "I probably appear hard and efficient to you. In some ways I am. But ... but I'm frightened, too. I mean for her."

"Conscience?"

"You can call it that. I'm going to tell you something. Gina is an odd person. Her name has never been linked to any man but Von Bruckner. She has never even shown the slightest interest in anyone else before—"

"Before?"

"Before you."

I was dumfounded. This was the best news I'd had that day or that week or that month or, for that matter, that year.

"It's not easy for me to admit that," she said coldly. "Your ego is the last thing that needs inflating. I'm only telling you because I want you to know that I realize you are in a position either to hurt or help Gina."

"Help?"

"She might tell you what frightens her."

"And?"

"And you could do one of two things; either turn over what you find out to that devil Grant, or ... or ..." She hesitated and then blurted out, "Be the sort of decent man I believe you to be at heart."

"I don't figure you."

"Don't try. It's not important that you do. The important thing is what you do to Gina. If you make the wrong choice I'll tell her that you are employed by Grant."

"You're forgetting that you're in this too, baby. After all it was you who played contact for Grant."

"Nevertheless." She said coldly. And then quite suddenly her voice changed. "Hart!" she cried. "I'm taking a terrible risk. But—but I feel certain that you're not really working for Grant at all!"

A warning bell rang in my mind.

"The heat is getting you sweetie," I said.

"You don't trust me!"

I laughed.

She sank back in the chair. "I can't blame you."

"Grant should give you an L for loyalty!"

She flipped her hands out in the classic gesture of defeat. "I thought you would understand. I thought—"

Instead of thinking, I said curtly, "How about telling me a little about Von Bruckner's connections with the Sons of Mecca?"

Her face tilted up in shocked surprise, or at least a good imitation of it.

"You're joking."

"It's just an idea," I said easily.

"You're trying to frighten me!"

"The only thing that could frighten you, my sweet ice cube, is a heat wave."

"Get out," she said.

"Get your report to Grant straight. Don't doctor it."

"Get out."

I went to the door and turned. She was sitting there looking suddenly limp. I laughed. "Not even a good try. Too damned obvious. I expected better of you."

"Hart."

"Oh, for God's sake!"

I turned on my heel, left the office and slammed the door behind me. I couldn't understand my unreasonable anger. After all, I had no illusions about Sigried McCarty. I'd pigeonholed her after our first meeting. I intended to keep her there.

Still simmering I left the shop cursing myself for being such a schnook. My gaff about Von Bruckner's connection with the Sons of Mecca had resulted only in putting her on guard. I could only hope that her loyalty, if any, was more to Grant at the moment than Von Bruckner. I counted on that.

When I got back to the hotel the terrace was filling up with the fashionable tea crowd. I called Marianne's room. There was no answer but at the desk I found a message from her saying that she was at rehearsal and would meet me on the terrace at five. It was almost that now. I managed to get a table for two at the far end and ordered a cool drink. I needed something cool. And time, too, to remind myself that after all this was just another job to me; like Phidias the fate of empires was only incidental to the cash involved. Thinking back on the last few days I felt again a twinge of repulsion. I was sick to hell of the lying and the cheating and the schizoid course of my days. The cabin in Maine and the book-lined room and the roaring fire in the dead of winter were more attractive than ever. But who to share it with? The main object of my desires at this moment was a sophisticated woman of the world, and I could not picture her in my wildest dreams settling for the rustic life. The phantasy of Gina Ferelli giving up a life of luxury in exchange for heating a can of beans over a two burner was laughable.

I watched Marianne come up the steps of the terrace from the street. She looked childlike and plain in this smart crowd. The eagerness in her face as she looked around sent my spirits lower. Fun was fun and in a way I felt sorry for her but I had no intention of allowing an unwelcome attachment to interfere with my plans about Gina. The fact that the girl was Gina's protégée only complicated matters.

She saw me and smiled shyly. She came across the terrace as though no else there existed for her.

"*Mon ami* ... Hart."

"For God's sake, sit down," I said more gruffly than I had intended. "All Cairo will know we are sleeping together."

"*Ce n'est rien*," she said gaily, sat down, removed her beret and placed it on the table beside her place. "The management is very disappointed in my rehearsal. He thinks I will have a dismal failure."

"Nonsense," I said without much conviction.

She smiled. "I have failed before. It will be nothing new."

"You act as though you don't care."

She shrugged. "Other things are more important to me."

"Like the Frankie and Johnny act you started to pull in the train?"

"*Comment?*"

"An American song about a girl who went gunning for a guy who done her wrong."

She stopped smiling. "Cannot we talk of other things just for today? I feel that time is so precious."

"Doesn't the management feel they may have to cancel the opening because of the political situation?"

"On the contrary." She laughed "You could not guess who has a reservation for the opening tomorrow night. I should be frightened out of my wits."

"Who?"

"The king."

"I'll be damned."

"It is fantastic, Hart. A month ago I could not get work in the lowest *boîte*. Now ..." She stopped very suddenly. An expression that I can only describe as dumfounded came over her face. I turned and followed the direction of her gaze. Sigried and Guido and the young Frenchman Armand Trouvier had just come up the steps and were waiting for the maître d'hôtel. Guido and Sigried were chattering with some people at the table nearest the top of the steps. But Armand stood apart staring at our table and for once his careful suave mask had deserted him.

He stared at Marianne as though hypnotized by an unpleasant apparition. Then Sigried turned, caught the expression, gave us a curious glance, said something in a low voice. Trouvier got hold of himself and followed Guido and Sigried to the opposite end of the terrace.

I looked at Marianne. She had gone very pale.

"What now?" I asked exasperated.

"Hart." She said in a low voice, "I beg of you not to question me. I am not feeling well.... perhaps the rehearsal. You will forgive me."

And before I could stop her she rose, and hurried towards the lobby.

I gulped down my drink. I thought, God Almighty! What now?

Chapter Nine

They were dancing in the patio restaurant at Shepheard's when I left the hotel at nine o'clock that evening. From the side streets came the shrill sound of records screeching out Arabic songs in the native all-night cafés.

There was a long line of limousines in front of the Opera House where a special gala performance of *Aïda* was being given. But the streets were uncommonly deserted and dark faces moved aside impassively, usually not quick enough to hide the anger smoldering in the eyes. A quiet tension seemed to be spreading over the city; the calm before the storm.

The Pension Capri was as Larson had described it; a depressing sort of a place, one step above a flophouse. In the small, evil-smelling lobby an ancient redheaded woman sat under a pink light behind the desk. I asked for Madame Gebhardt and was then directed to Room 23. I walked up a flight of ill-lighted stairs into a long narrow hall where one red light burned eerily over the exit door at the far end. With some difficulty I found 23 and knocked. After a moment's hesitation the door was opened an inch to reveal part of a woman's face. After a moment she spoke. "Well?"

"Pete Larson?"

Behind her, Larson's voice, thick and unsteady, called, "Let the poor fool in!"

I stepped into a small room dominated by the inevitable bed draped with torn mosquito netting. There was just about room for two uncertain looking chairs and a large bureau. Through the open bathroom door I could see women's lingerie hanging to dry.

Larson, dressed to receive visitors in nothing but shorts, reclined on the bed, glass in hand. He grinned and waved his glass unsteadily at the woman and said, "Hilde Gebhardt. War casualty. Viennese. She keeps me."

"Pete," the woman said sharply.

I looked closely at the woman. She was tall and blonde and probably in her early thirties. If it had not been for the shadow of strain and perhaps illness she might have been pretty. But now only the hair had received proper attention, coiled lovingly in ropes about her head like the symbol of something remaining that could not be defiled.

"Chap I told you about, Hilde. Democratic. Talks to the lower orders and lepers. Pour him a drink."

I didn't refuse though I knew how precious the half empty bottle must be to him. The woman indicated a chair and I sat gingerly, half expecting it to collapse. "Treat him well, Hilde. At the moment he's my client but if that falls through ..."

"Pete!" She turned quickly to me. "Don't mind him. He hasn't been well today."

"She means I've been potted since noon. Great girl Hilde. Couldn't do without her. Took her off the streets when I was still in the chips. She stuck when the going was no longer de luxe. Now it looks as though she'll have to go back to the streets to keep me in whisky."

"Stop being a bastard," I said.

"It's the truth. Tell him, Hilde. Tell him."

She stared at him a moment then looked quickly at her hands. I had not been prepared for this melodramatic masochism in Larson. He was behaving like a man that he himself would have described in the past as "a cad."

"Her husband was a big-shot department store owner in Vienna. Had the misfortune of being a Jew. When Hitler moved in they murdered him and confiscated everything. Hilde managed to get out. She landed out here without a tuppence to her name. She never learned to be anything but a lady. The training was useful in her work."

"He doesn't mean to be cruel," she whispered.

"I know."

"What's she saying? What's she telling you about me?" He pushed himself up on one elbow. In doing so he spilled part of the drink on his chest. The liquid trickled down across his stomach unheeded.

"Perhaps you will excuse me," Hilde said. "I was washing some things."

"Of course."

She went quickly into the bathroom and shut the door. I heard the sound of running water. I wondered whether she was weeping.

Larson's bravado vanished. "She hasn't sense enough to walk out on me, the poor little fool."

"For God's sake stop being sorry for yourself."

"Forgive, old chap. The heat you know ..."

And then with an almost pompous dignity he rose from the bed, dragged a dressing gown from a closet, wrapped it around himself with great care and sat once more on the edge of the bed.

He grinned. "We Britishers never let down as you can see—chin up—make a good example for the inferior natives—dress for dinner every night in the tropics. You will find us the best-dressed receiving end of every revolution. When our heads go the white bow tie goes with them, by God."

"Is the decision in London so final, Larson?"

"It's not only London." He looked down into his glass. "It's me. I always despised the sort of chap who was weak and—well, now look."

"Oh, come now, it isn't the first time there has been an accidental leak. You're taking it too big. Things will change. You're still a valuable man."

He looked me directly in the eyes. "Not anymore. Not ever again. I know where I am."

"You're making it worse for yourself."

"I'll tell you something, Muldoon. I'm finished with the whole show. Trouble with me I was too conscientious. Everyone else was skimming the cream from the bottle but me. You can have it—family, country, friends, respectability—to hell with it all. It belonged to another man." He jerked his hand toward the bathroom. "She's the only damned thing I care about. She has the misfortune to love me. I love her."

There was nothing much to say. Embarrassed and annoyed I resorted to drink.

"I've got something to sell. You'll like it. But I only talk for cash."

I thought quickly. Neither Max nor Grant had provided for such a contingency. It would have to come out of my own funds. I didn't think too long about it.

"How much?"

"A hundred pounds."

"It's a deal."

He leaned forward. "In the bar at Shepheard's you asked about a missing plane. I was saving what I have for a little blackmail. But it's too dangerous. Too much for me to handle. You can have it."

"Well?"

"If that's the job you're on you might tell your superiors they might have looked up the files on some of the members of the bomber's crew."

I pricked up my ears. "Maybe they have."

"The hell they have. I know how they work. After all I was part of it once."

"Well ... assuming they haven't."

"I did a little research once out in Pakistan to do with the Sons of Mecca."

"Ah?"

"It led to some interesting places. They have contacts in the British armed services, believe it or not. And one of them is a captain in the air force. A little bastard named Havervard. Ian Havervard. Was once mixed up with Mosley's Black Shirts in England."

"Well, you sent in your report."

"That's just it. I was canned before I had the chance. I've been saving it for a rainy day. Luck is with me."

"In what way?"

"The commanding officer on that missing bomber was Ian Havervard."

I watched Larson carefully as he spoke. He seemed overwrought, too anxious to please. And yet I believed him.

"So?"

"Don't you get it? The blighter, the lousy little blighter has probably turned over the plane to the Sons of Mecca."

I laughed. "An air force of one outmoded bomber? What good would it do?"

"Damned if I know. But that's what happened."

"Have you any proof?"

"Hell no. What do you want for a measly hundred pounds?"

"But it doesn't make sense. Where the devil would they conceal a bomber with the whole British Empire searching for it? Not to mention Farouk's men."

"That's your job, not mine."

"You said you did research on the Sons of Mecca. What else did you come up with?"

"Not much that isn't pretty well known. They're a crazy bunch. Never been able to get a very large following in the Arab world. But now with the fuse about to go off here in Egypt, they might manufacture some sort of incident. It would swing things their way."

"Who is the big shot here in Cairo?"

"I can't say for certain. There are a lot of ex-Nazis, army officers, mixed up in it along with some feudal Arab leaders. But they've played it real cute here in Cairo. I don't know who gives the orders."

"Anything else?"

"What do you want? Blood?"

I stood up. "It's a pretty wild tale, Larson. Capturing one British bomber and its crew isn't going to get them very far. They can't be that rocky."

"Muldoon. I gave it to you straight. You're not welshing?"

I looked toward the bathroom door. "No. Come to my room at Shepheard's tomorrow morning about noon. I'll have the hundred pounds for you."

"You think I dreamed this up because I'm desperate?"

"No," I said wearily. And then out of embarrassment I added, "If anything comes of it I'll see you get credit in London."

For a moment hope lighted up his eyes. "Maybe your word. Maybe ..." He stopped. "The hell with credit, I'll settle for cash. It's just luck that I didn't sell this to the other side."

"I know better than that," I said quickly. "Say good-by to Hilde. Maybe next week we can all get together."

"The hundred pounds will get us up the Nile to the Sudan. There's a Dutchman offered me a job—not much but still ..."

He got to his feet.

"What I've told you is on the level, Muldoon."

"Sure," I said, turned quickly and left the room. I went through the dingy hall down the stairs to the lobby. The redheaded woman was talking into the phone in a low urgent voice. When she saw me she hung up quickly and gave me a glassy stare. I went out into the street, walked to the Boulevard Fouad I and found a carriage. I directed the driver to the Café Noir near the Ban-en-Nazr Gate, and leaned back trying to shake off the depression resulting from my interview with Larson. The chances of his story being true were one in a hundred. The idea of the Sons of Mecca stealing a British bomber was fantastic, idiotic. It didn't make sense. Still it was at least worth checking up on the lead about the commanding officer.

The carriage left the lighted boulevards and streets of the European quarter. We bumped down narrow cobblestone alleys between darkened windows. Once we drew aside to let a camel caravan pass. The dark faces in from weeks on the desert were like an apparition from the Arabian nights. The hooves of the camels clattered off into the distance. When we got closer to the Ban-en-Nazr gate we skirted the Souks garishly lighted and full of life and noise even at this hour. But the Café Noir was on a small square away from the bustling life of the markets, in the shadow of a mosque. It was a small place with a dirty plate-glass window where a torn velvet portiere hung on a wooden rod. Inside, the room was stifling. Cigarette smoke hung thick under the low ceiling. A few blank-faced Arabs in from the desert sat sipping lemonade while the less orthodox city Arabs were indulging in wine or cheap whisky.

On a small platform at the end of the room, a fat woman was lethargically performing the inevitable stomach dance. Phidias sat in a corner table, well chosen for its lack of light. The clients eyed me in an unfriendly manner but there was no open hostility. I sat down opposite Phidias.

"Well?"

"He promised to be here at nine-thirty. He's twenty minutes late already."

"The dragoman?"

"Yes. He doesn't know what it's about. I've led him to believe it's a caravan leaving Cairo on Friday." He lowered his voice. "I was followed here. There are a couple of bruisers hanging around the entrance to the mosque."

"I appreciate this, Phidias."

"You should. I wouldn't have done it for anyone else. Not even for money."

"Does he speak English?"

"No. A little French."

The waiter brought my whisky and placed it before me contemptuously. I had intended to tell Phidias about Larson's screwy theory but when I saw the curtained doorway too close to the table, behind the vacant chair, I changed my mind. Anyway, at that moment the dragoman arrived.

He was a short, bearded, shifty-eyed character who slid into his place with a sort of sneering defiance of the cold stares he got from the rest of the room.

Phidias introduced me as a radio salesman from the United States who wanted to get a shipment of portable radios through to Saudi Arabia on a caravan leaving Cairo on Friday.

Phidias in the role of agent haggled about price for a good ten minutes. Then having apparently arrived at a price and the commitment to come to Phidias' office on the following day, Phidias laughed and inveigled the driver into talking about his adventures in the desert. There were some interminable talks of sandstorms, recalcitrant camels, thieving drivers and gunrunning. Finally Phidias asked him to tell again the story of the plane he had seen flying low in the desert near Cairo.

Unsuspecting, he began shrilly to assert that the story was true.

"Come now," Phidias said in French, "what would a British bomber be doing near Cairo?"

"Effendi, on the word of Allah, I speak the truth. It came low over the sand hills ..."

"Where?"

He shrugged. "It is not easy to say in kilometers. A day and a half journey as the camel travels. Near the oasis of El Sha-en-Reb."

I had been watching him very closely as he spoke. I was convinced that he was telling the truth. And as a result I began to wonder whether there might not be something in Larson's story after all.

With rising excitement I leaned forward and said, "This oasis—it is a village?"

"No, effendi, it ..." And then a look of mild surprise came over his face. He reached back as though to slap at an insect but his hand never completed the gesture. He came falling across the table, face down among the glasses, arms flopping like cloth. In his back protruded a long-handled knife.

It all happened in an instant. Before the rest of the room was aware of what had taken place I was up and through the swaying red curtains of the doorway in back of the chair the Arab had occupied. I found myself in a narrow hallway. At the far end a white-robed figure was climbing through an arched window. I sprinted down the hall with the sounds of an uproar beginning in the café behind me. The white-robed figure dropped from sight beyond the window. I vaulted up onto the wide ledge and leaped through, falling further than I had expected, into a small enclosed court. I stumbled for a moment, caught myself up, saw the white robe vanishing through an open gateway. Without thought I followed.

On the opposite side of the gateway was a narrow alley running along the rear of the Great Mosque. For a moment I saw no one. I took a step forward. Something moved out of the shadow. I ducked to one side as a metallic object hit the cobblestones. Blindly I struck out. My fist crunched into something soft and I heard a sharp curse of pain. I swung around to the right. My assailant turned also so that the moonlight fell on his face. Despite the Arabic costume I saw that he was blond and blue-eyed. The expression was startling in its fear and hatred. His fist caught me on the chest and then before I could recoil his other hand came down, palm open, and sharp fingernails slashed across my cheek. I felt the warm blood trickle down my chin.

I put the full weight of my body behind a right that only grazed his chin. And then his knee came up between my legs and I went sprawling to the cobblestones. I saw the shoe raised above my face in time and rolled out of the way as he brought it down viciously. I reached out, almost blind with pain, and clutched at his leg. But he snatched it away before I could get a decent grip. I rolled over again up against the stone wall, doubled back, managed somehow to struggle to my feet. He could have taken me then; the pain had made me almost helpless. But, perhaps because he hadn't realized the effectiveness of that kick, he didn't follow up. When I straightened up the white robe was disappearing around the corner of the mosque. I was in no condition to follow. From behind me I heard shouts and the sound of a police whistle. I drew back into the shadow of the wall and leaned up against it until my breath began to return.

The blue-eyed son of a bitch! I thought.

I moved away from the café, around the corner of the mosque into a large dimly lighted square. A carriage was just emerging empty from the direction of the Souks. I intercepted it, hopped in and told the driver to get the hell to Shepheard's as quick as his nag would take him. There was no use going back to see how Phidias was faring. Phidias could take care of himself.

Chapter Ten

Despite the growing tensions of the day, a goodly portion of Cairo's international set had turned out for Marianne's opening at the Lido. I suspected that Gina had had a great deal to do with persuading her friends to appear here tonight in the face of the scare headlines in the evening papers. The stunning room with its revolving glass dance floor, modern decor and enormous picture window adjoining a moonlit terrace that looked out over the Nile, was a perfect setting for the lovely Paris gowns and the breathtaking display of jewels. An American dance orchestra specializing in tunes from current musical comedies alternated with a rhumba band. Originally Marianne's appearance had been scheduled for eleven-thirty, but because of a last minute midnight curfew ordered on all night clubs and cafés, her performance had been moved up to ten. At our table on the floor were Sigried, Guido, Armand Trouvier and Gina Ferelli who was, of course, the hostess. An empty chair awaited Hans von Bruckner. I looked forward to this first meeting with Gina's mysterious "protector" with mingled feelings.

My initial sight of Gina that evening had revived the flame of desire that had been with me ever since she had walked into the bar of the Chambord. She wore a daring purple satin gown that set off perfectly the olive skin and the dark eyes. It seemed to be only a temporary and decorative restraint to the breasts that all but burst forth from the tight cloth.

No one mentioned the dangerous situation. The talk was of polo and scandal and Farouk's latest indiscretion. But underneath the studied gaiety I sensed a personal tension at the table. Gina was unusually curt in her remarks to her brother and in turn I caught him glowering at her several times with open hostility. I wondered whether the friction between them was based on Gina's disapproval of his flying activities for Von Bruckner.

Armand Trouvier, however, exuded charm and laughter and at times I thought that his eyes mocked me. On the other hand Sigried, trim and chic in a white gown, seemed uncommonly silent and depressed. For once her brassy indifference had deserted her. She lighted one cigarette after another, glancing now and again nervously toward the empty chair. The minutes ticked away toward ten, and my own uneasiness increased. I was certain that whatever Marianne's talents, they were not appropriate to this worldly and jaded audience.

I asked Gina to dance and we moved about the glass floor to the rhythm of the rhumba. Pressed close to me I was aware of every contour of her body. She didn't resist when I drew her closer. I began to think of other things but dancing and felt the perspiration rising on my forehead. Perhaps sensing the situation she said, "Come. You must see the view from the terrace."

We went out through French doors onto the moonlit terrace. For the moment we had it to ourselves. Side by side we went to the rail. Below us was the Nile, black ink flowing to the sea. The bridges to the island were diamonds on velvet and the glow of the city's lights rose up into the soft night. Out there, beyond the edge of the desert, the Sphinx squatted in the sands holding the riddle of the centuries between her outstretched paws.

For a moment neither of us said anything. I reached for her hand. Her fingers closed about mine. I felt a thrill of hope. Maybe Sigried hadn't been kidding after all. I decided not to risk breaking the silence. But when I moved closer she suddenly withdrew her hand and said, "The room behind us is buzzing. I have caused a minor scandal by coming out here with you."

"Does it matter?"

"No. I have always had a great contempt for gossip. Still ..." She laughed. "I should not like to be executed for a crime I have not committed."

"Perhaps you will be kind enough to give them some justification."

She turned and looked up into my eyes. "Hart ... you may not realize it. I would not have walked out onto this terrace with any other man in Cairo. There is something I must say."

"Why say it, Gina," I whispered. I tried to draw her close but she pulled away.

"I am not a schoolgirl," she said. "I have been aware from the beginning that you and I—that there was something inevitable. But I have brought you here to tell you that it must go no farther."

"You can't stop the inevitable!"

"Hart!" I was startled at the seriousness in her eyes. "I feel as though my world were slipping through my fingers. As though everything I'd ever known was useless really. I am dreadfully concerned. I don't know where to turn for advice."

"Concerned? About what? About whom?"

"My brother Guido."

"What's wrong?"

"I don't know exactly. That's what worries me. He used to confide in me—we were terribly close. I have always thought first of Guido. But during this last year he has become terribly secretive, ever since Hans made him his pilot. I know nothing of these things. I'm dreadfully stupid about politics, but ..."

"Ah! You think Guido is involved in something dangerous— something to do with Hans?"

Her hands closed over the rail. In the moonlight the emeralds were green fire at her throat. She said nothing.

"Gina! You're frightened to death!"

She reached out and clutched my arm. She spoke quickly in a low voice. "When my husband died I was frantic. Hans came along. Everything has been for Guido—I wanted so much for him—and now he and Armand Trouvier are both engaged in some nasty business with Hans. Hans just laughs at me when I question him. Guido refuses to answer. I feel as though he were sinking into some dreadful whirlpool. He's so young and foolish, and spoiled I guess, and I am unable to do anything. I need help!"

"Gina!"

I tried to draw her to me but she resisted. Urgently I whispered, "You've come to me for help. You're right, Gina, anything you ask. But you turned to me—why, Gina?"

"No!" she said and pushed away.

"What is it? Why do you turn hot and cold?"

"I don't mean to," she said almost angrily. "I do not have any respect for the type of woman who leads a man on and then says no."

"Well then?"

"You must try to understand. Hans has been kind not only to me but to Guido and—"

"Kind enough to get him mixed up in some lousy political mess.

Maybe kind enough in the end to have him up before a firing squad!"

"No!" she said sharply. "You must not talk such nightmares!"

"You'd better face reality. It's all around you, Gina. This is no party where the guests play it polite. The ball is almost over."

"I owe a great deal to Hans," she said in a dead voice. "Since it began, I have had no lover. No one."

"Then why did you bring me out here?"

"To ask for your help. I knew the very first time I met you that ... that ..."

"That what?"

"Oh, Hart!"

But as I tried once more she stiffened.

"Very well!" she said with sudden emotion. "I will tell you. I might have been fool enough—I mean with you, Hart, but I'm not the sort, whatever you might think, who can be casual ..."

"Who says it will be casual!"

"No," she said. "I understand you. And now that you are involved—"

"Involved?"

"Don't deny it. I have seen it in the poor girl's eyes. I can't hurt her, Hart. I won't have you hurt her. Marianne has had enough unhappiness in her life and ..."

"Oh," I said suddenly deflated, "so that's it."

"Now perhaps you understand."

"For God's sake, Gina. I like the girl and all that, but at the risk of sounding like a heel—it's just one of those accidental things."

"Not to her! I know."

"Gina. You can't let that stand between us."

"Oh, but I can!"

I thought, Easy now. Too many words could spoil the coming attractions. She seemed disappointed that I didn't say more. After a moment she said, "I have been honest with you. Perhaps it is expecting too much to ask your advice."

"No. I meant what I said. Anything."

Her hand touched mine gratefully. "I have many powerful friends in Cairo. Farouk has been very kind to me. He's dear, really, but in a way he's like a boy—very gullible. And even if I dared ask for his help I can do nothing to hurt Hans, you see. What should I do?"

"For the moment nothing. But when the time comes I want you to answer every question I put to you honestly. Then maybe I can help—and above all don't allow Von Bruckner to think that you're worried about anything. Things will turn out all right, Gina."

"You reassure me. You sound so confident."

The sound certainly didn't reflect my inner thoughts at all.

"Perhaps I exaggerate. Perhaps it's only the dreadful tension in the city...."

"About Marianne. Don't be too concerned for her."

"It is not altruism I assure you. It is self-protection. With you I might have lost my head. I might ..."

And then for a moment she was suddenly close to me. But the moment was so brief our lips never met. Then she pushed me away and said almost gaily, "Now we must go inside before the gossips have a juicy tale for Hans."

There was nothing more to say at the moment and obviously nothing more to do. I followed her back into the main room of the nightclub trying not to reveal my bitter disappointment. For a moment I resented the French girl for inadvertently having put a spoke in my wheel. I was a long way from giving up as far as Gina was concerned but it was going to be tough. Why did Marianne's emotional state have to show for all the world to see?

The house lights began to dim just as we sat down at the table. Sigried gave me an ironic smile. Guido glared. Armand Trouville seemed too obviously interested in a party at the next table. There was a roll of drums and a pale master of ceremonies appeared in the spotlight to announce with marked indifference that we were to have the pleasure of hearing a few songs from Mademoiselle Marianne, "direct from triumphs in South America." Gina applauded enthusiastically but the other patrons were barely polite. I forgot my frustrating scene with Gina long enough to feel uneasy for Marianne.

The master of ceremonies disappeared into the smoky haze that hung about the edges of the dance floor. The orchestra struck up a simple little French provincial song. The house lights were extinguished altogether.

The chatter of the crowd which had abated somewhat for the announcement started up again. Gina cast annoyed glances toward the neighboring tables. Into the midst of this unreceptive audience walked Marianne wearing a plain, rather badly cut black dress, her arms and throat innocent of jewelry. She looked more like a department store clerk than a nightclub performer. Someone laughed. I began to suffer for her.

But she stood very still and calm, directly in the center of the glass floor as the spotlight narrowed down to a pinpoint that picked out only her face, an eerie disembodied face floating in the smoky darkness. The elegant patrons, probably having expected an expensively gowned Parisian beauty with the all important attribute of "chic" went on chattering in an openly rude manner and underneath the babble of sound was the derisive note of those who feel cheated. But that face floating above the glass dance floor remained impassive. Marianne made no move to begin her first number. Behind her the orchestra was silent waiting for her signal. In an angry undertone Gina said, "They will not give her a chance!"

Guido laughed, "You can't blame them. At these prices they certainly did not expect a midinette."

Bored, Armand said, "I must make an important phone call. You will excuse me." And before Gina could remonstrate he left the table and made his way toward the foyer.

Disaster was in the air. The house lights slowly began to come up. And then just when it seemed Marianne would be forced to leave the floor a miracle happened. A miracle in the guise of a stout, mustached character who had apparently entered the club while the house lights were down and was sitting now with his party at a table on the edge of the floor. He half rose from his seat and gave a loud "shush." The effect was astonishing. In an instant the room was silent. Marianne had found a momentary ally in no less a personage than King Farouk of Egypt!

In the dramatic stillness Marianne bowed graciously toward the king's party, a bow that subtly recognized the gallantry without in any manner destroying the fiction of the monarch's incognito. So relieved was I for Marianne that for a moment I could almost forget the stupidity of this adolescent, fat libertine who squandered millions in nightclubs, European resorts and the gaming table while his country hurtled toward the abyss of revolution and chaos. It was almost incredible that in the midst of the dangerous tension existing in his country the king would appear publicly in a fashionable nightclub.

Yet wars or revolution or international crisis notwithstanding, his desire to hear Marianne had saved her from complete failure and in fact, before she even opened her mouth to sing, assured her success.

Guido hissed, "The fat fool!"

Sigried said, "Be careful, Guido!"

"Let him drink his champagne while he can!" Guido went on angrily, "he hasn't much longer!"

Someone at the next table shushed him. The music began and Marianne started her first song, a wry little love song of the working class French girls. After that there were simple peasant songs,

songs of the *maquis* and one dramatic, almost violently cynical ballad of a Parisian street walker. By the time she had finished her fourth number they were cheering. Aside from royal endorsement and the almost absurd remoteness of her material from this rich crowd, the girl had the simplicity and command of an artist. Although she was somewhat similar to Edith Piaf, the great French *chanteuse*, she had her own individual style, drier, softer, yet at the same time as incisive as a hot needle. At the end of her last encore it was obvious that she had made a tremendous personal success.

"I told you so!" Gina cried victoriously. "It is marvelous. Even Farouk applauded. Tomorrow all Cairo will be talking about her!"

I thought to myself that "all Cairo" had more important things to talk about at the moment than nightclub performers but I felt an almost paternal pride in Marianne's success. I looked at the others. Sigried was staring at me, very pale and obviously moved. She said nothing. Guido refused to admit circumstantial evidence. "It is funny," he said. "What appears first-rate in Cairo might be laughed off the boards in Europe. Still ..."

Gina put her hand on my arm and whispered, "You must go to her dressing room and fetch her. It is only fitting that you be the first to congratulate her."

After inquiring directions from the maître d'hôtel I made my way between the tables to a door behind the orchestra into a long cement hall leading away from the main room. The place was about as gay as a bomb shelter, curiously deserted and sepulchral. Behind me the beat of a rhumba seemed to be coming from underwater. Instinctively I walked softly. And a moment later I knew my instinct was right. Almost at the door of Marianne's dressing room I stopped, arrested by the sound of a man's voice inside, raised in sudden anger. The door was only slightly ajar but I heard him say distinctly, "I will not have it. You will leave Cairo tomorrow."

Marianne said, "Do not be absurd!"

"I am warning you. If you do not go—"

"Quiet!" Marianne said. "Someone is out there."

Almost before I had a chance to get a nonchalant expression on my face the man came striding out into the hall. It was Armand Trouvier. He was not pleased to find me but summoned up a polite smile. "I have beaten you to it, monsieur. I have been the first to congratulate mademoiselle on her success. I take pride in such things." There was a thin note of irony in his voice. He bowed and walked swiftly past me down the hall toward the main room. He never looked hack. I remembered he had risen from the table on the excuse of making a phone call just after Marianne had come out on the floor. Had he waited in her dressing room all during her performance?

I went into the dressing room to find Marianne, pale and tense, back to the mirror, hands folded tight before her.

I dived right in. "How long have you known Trouvier?"

She seemed barely aware of my words or my presence. After a moment she said listlessly, "This young man? I never before saw him. He arrived to offer congratulations."

"You're lying. He's the guy who sent you into a tailspin on the terrace of Shepheard's this afternoon."

She shrugged and looked down at her clenched hands. "You have not the right to question me in this manner."

"Not knowing to whom to apply for that right, I'm on my own! Is he someone you slept with once?"

That brought her out of it with a vengeance. For a minute I thought she was going to strike me. Then she turned, sat down at the table and furiously began to apply cold cream to her face. I tried to catch her eye in the mirror without success. I decided to put off the inquisition until later. The rich young French playboy was beginning to gain the proportions of a very large question mark. Gina had implied that her brother and the Frenchman were involved in Von Bruckner's machinations. Why should he be so interested in getting Marianne out of Cairo? Later, I thought, and I figured about when. Now that Gina had given me the ice treatment I recalled the previous night with Marianne with some pleasure. I was getting in the mood for a repeat performance. Why not combine business with pleasure? Why not, indeed!

"I'm unnaturally curious," I said. "Forgive me. Straight off I should have told you that you have just wowed the rich effendis!"

"Wowed them? This wow is something good, yes? If so I thank you." She didn't smile.

"Doesn't it mean anything to you?"

She shrugged. "The management he offered me four extra weeks and a raise in salary as I come from the floor. I am not naïve. This king—this absurd King Farouk—it is he I should thank. But you Americans have the expression ... 'stoge' ..."

"Stooge?"

"Oui ... stooge. Farouk is the stooge of the people who are here tonight. They depend on him to keep the gold flowing. But if Farouk goes tomorrow, where will my audience be?"

"That's pessimistic. From all I hear Farouk isn't due for an exit visa yet. Not until the army makes up their mind who top man on the totem pole is going to be."

"The people have a way of not waiting for the army. They have so much patience and then pff!—no more!"

"That sounds vaguely radical."

"Does it? I have no politics. Certainly I have only observed."

She wiped off the cold cream with tissue and applied her street make-up. Then she got up, calmly slipped off the rough dressing gown and stood before me in nothing more than sheer silk panties, stockings and shoes. Completely unconcerned over my agitation she asked me to help her adjust her brassiere. I took my time about it.

"Hart!" She gave a sharp little laugh.

"Tonight?"

"You're incorrigible. I'm flattered. Yes, of course—but not now...." She broke away and slipped into one of those unbelievably unbecoming black gowns which seemed to be the mainstay of her wardrobe.

Her head came out of the neck of the dress and she pulled it down tight around her body. She gave me a quizzical look and said with disconcerting insight. "So she turned you down, eh?"

"She—who?" I blustered like a guilty husband.

"It is obvious. Well, perhaps her foolishness is my gain. She is not for you anyway."

And before I thought I said, "Why not?"

She laughed for the first time. "You see! You give yourself away so completely. Luckily I am not a jealous woman. I am used to being second choice. I am—how you say—adjusted to the role. But you are too much of the little boy to play with such a sophisticated and ... subtle woman."

"You make the words sound derogatory. I detect a meow."

"Never mind *mon cher* ... you are not rich enough anyway. You have come to me and I am perhaps a philanthropist, *n'est pas?*"

"Some philanthropist. But I like your charity sweetie—the currency is solid!"

"Ah, well ..." The smile died. She turned and regarded herself in the mirror, as though looking at a stranger.

"Baby."

"*Oui?*"

"What is it?"

She passed her hand before her eyes. "Everything it is so unreal to me. So terribly unreal. Sometimes I am walking in a dream. I dread going out to Gina's table and all the gay laughing people. I long to be locked in my bedroom with you, Hart. I think to me that is all—the only thing that is real."

Her eyes met mine in the mirror and I saw the reflection of despair. And then with incredible swiftness the dark shadow evaporated into a gay smile. "I am too serious. You will be bored. Come. I am ready. But let us leave soon!"

She snatched up her wrap and bag and we went back to the main room. Our progress to Gina's table was a slow one, impeded by the loud congratulations of Marianne's new public. A maître d'hôtel approached and whispered in Marianne's ear. She signaled for me to go ahead to the table and she followed the head waiter to where King Farouk waited. I hoped for her sake his attentions would be confined to polite congratulations. I'd heard of the royal touch in the dark. The king apparently distributed his somewhat doubtful favors in a manner that might be described as exceedingly democratic.

But I forgot to watch her interview with royalty when I saw the newcomer seated next to Gina. He was stocky, almost rigid from the waist up, like an over-fed pigeon; narrow lips, pomaded hair, eyebrows that looked plucked, fat small hands, expensive and well-fitting dinner clothes. Even with his face half averted I recognized the man who had been seated in the restaurant car of the Luxor Express; the guy, apparently, for whom Marianne had come to Egypt on a hunting expedition. Guido and Sigried were dancing. Armand Trouvier had not returned to the table. I stood there unobserved for a moment, watching the newcomer talking in a low, urgent undertone to Gina. Her face was set in a mask of resignation. She saw me first, put her hand on the stranger's arm and smiled up at me. "Hart. I have been telling Hans about you. Hans, this is the young American writer, Mr. Muldoon. Herr von Bruckner."

The man stood, precisely, very straight and turned to face me. I saw then that what appeared to be strength from a distance was an illusion created perhaps by cosmetics. The studied expression, the almost military mask, seemed about to disintegrate at any moment into a twitching ruin. The powdered skin under the eyes jumped to the rhythm of a tick and the corners of his mouth trembled slightly. The eyes were cold and impersonal and yet there was beneath the light blue surface a suggestion of some sort of unnatural intensity; the hint of paranoia, of some fanaticism; sexual or religious or political or perhaps all three. He looked me up and down as though I were a prize bull. For a moment an ironic smile lighted up those strange eyes as though we shared, or should share, some secret.

"I am most interested to meet you, Mr. Hart. You have made far too much of an impression on Gina. I must discover your formula—aside, of course, from vulgar good health and obvious youth."

His gaze held mine with the puzzling question in them. I began to feel uncomfortable. I didn't like the thought of Gina going to bed with this character. I tried to put it out of my mind. Gina had a polite social smile on her face but there was the flicker of a warning in her eyes.

"I'm afraid you're wrong," I said. "As a matter of fact Madame Ferelli has underestimated my age. A blow I can assure you."

He raised an ironic eyebrow. He looked over my shoulder. "I am relieved to see that your friend the young French girl has escaped the royal patronage for the moment. For her sake I can only hope that the condition remains—" And then he stopped. For just an instant his mask slipped into something like consternation. I turned. Marianne was coming across the room. Her eyes were on Von Bruckner. She saw nobody else. She came on, chin held high, eyes as cold as death. She came right past me and stopped before Von Bruckner. She waited. Von Bruckner had recovered. He smiled mechanically as Gina introduced Marianne.

"I have been told that you have a great success, Mademoiselle. I am sorry business kept me from seeing your performance. Perhaps another time."

Marianne said nothing. Gina gave her a quick, puzzled look.

"Do sit down," she said quickly. "I did want you to meet young Armand Trouvier but it seems he is having difficulties with some dull girl. Armand is constantly placating some idiotic female."

Marianne sat like a marionette being lowered into place. Her face was deadly pale.

Quickly I said, "Mademoiselle is not feeling well. She has a headache. The strain of the debut, you know. I think I should take her back to the hotel."

Marianne said, "Yes."

"Not even one glass of champagne, Mademoiselle?" Von Bruckner's voice seemed to suggest a significance beyond the words. Marianne shuddered.

"My dear!" Gina said. "You do look ill. Poor child. Hart—you must take her immediately."

Marianne got to her feet. She was clutching the ungainly handbag. She didn't look at Von Bruckner again. He stood with mock solicitude. "My car is at the door. I insist that my chauffeur take you to your hotel."

"No," Marianne said.

Gina frowned and looked to me for help.

"We'll take a carriage," I said. "A little air should do her good."

Vaguely I was aware of Guido and Sigried on the edge of the dance floor watching us curiously. I managed the good nights and got Marianne out into the foyer.

I found a carriage at the end of the long line of limousines and town cars and told the driver to take us to Shepheard's. We sank into the back and Marianne moved close to me. She was trembling.

"Baby."

"It's too late." she sobbed. "The moment is gone. Why did you stop me yesterday in the train? So many years, and now ... I can't ... I can't."

I breathed a sigh of relief.

"It's nice to know that I'm going to bed with a lady who, after all, is not a potential murderess!"

Chapter Eleven

Here, so close to the endless silence of the desert, even in the hour of sunrise, there was the echo of camels' hooves in distant streets and now and again the purr of a motor outside on the Boulevard Fouad I. But the dawn seeping through the window of Marianne's room and the mosquito netting of the bed had an oddly sinister quality, as though this day would lighten on horror and madness.

"So, Hart ..." Marianne said. "So...."

Every few moments her face was dimly illuminated on the pillow as I drew on my cigarette. The last hours had been, to say the least, tumultuous. Marianne had been possessed of a passion that went beyond pleasure into some secret despair. Now, exhausted, she lay very still, talking in a manner that was quiet and yet almost compulsive.

"You are shocked, *mon cher?*"

"Hell, no!"

"Most men are afterwards. I am the sort they fight to get but revile in the morning!"

"Nonsense!"

"Oh no. They think of their mothers or their sisters or their wives. It has been always my opinion that the man, he is a big hypocrite in these matters. Far more so than any woman."

"No apologies necessary, or explanations, sweetie."

She laughed shortly. "You are more gallant than most. *Voilà*—you are still here. It is not polite to eat and run, no?"

"My mother taught me good manners!"

"I thank her." And then after a moment, "You know it is strange. Always I am told a woman must love a man before it is—what can I say—right for her. This for me is not a fact. I have not loved. I have never loved."

"Never is a helluva long time."

She laughed that oddly touching, bitter little laugh. "You are relieved, no? Yet perhaps the male ego it is somewhat hurt?"

"Now that you mention it—a little."

"Ah, yes, you are accustomed to the woman who tells you how insanely in love with you she is? Ah, well, they have spoiled you. I believe that some of them even have meant it."

"Thanks. Is the lecture over, Professor Freud?"

"No."

I was beginning to feel uncomfortable. I drew in on the cigarette and saw her face turned toward me on the pillow, eyes wide and serious.

"It is odd. You are infatuated with Gina Ferelli, you are drawn to a fire that can only burn. Like all Americans you feel anything is possible."

"Never mind that."

"You are annoyed. I tell you something. If I were to pick a woman right for you, right in the years to come, you would never guess...."

"I'll do my own picking, thank you. I'm doing pretty well at the moment."

"Nevertheless. I believe as a good friend I would choose for you Sigried McCarthy."

"What!" I was genuinely startled. "That icicle?"

"You do not understand her at all. I know her as only one woman can understand another. She has been hurt. But she is warm and full of life and she would love one man—only one."

"At a time! I'm losing respect for your feminine insight. Well, as the Senator said, it's time for me to dress and go home!"

"Hart."

"Yes?"

"Not yet."

"My God!" I said.

"No. Not that.... But you have waited and I have not spoken. I will tell you now."

I leaned back and blew smoke up into the darkness. Her hand came along my body to my face. Very gently her fingers touched my nose, my lips, my brow—then my shoulder and down my arm to my hand.

She said, "Like a blind person I know you so well. So very well. In the dark, even in some lonely faraway place I will remember."

There was nothing to say on that one. Nothing was better than the near commitment.

Very quietly she went on. "Perhaps even I could have loved you. Before anything happened to me. In another life."

"You're a strange child, Marianne."

"No. I am not a child. My body is young perhaps. But inside I am old and tired and empty. Milestones have crushed me. No longer will I strike back. I knew that tonight."

Her hand on mine tensed, then was still.

"I wish to tell you this. I have never spoken it to anyone. I want you to understand. It was during the war, the Nazi occupation. The Wehrmacht officer in charge of the occupation forces in my village was a pig by the name of Shmidt. Captain Shmidt. He had been a waiter in a Munich café before he joined up with Hitler. He rose quickly for his services to the Vaterland. He was good at the most unsavory jobs, *n'est pas?* A real patriot!"

"You lived in this village with your family?"

"I lived with an aunt on a farm outside. My mother she died, thank God, before the Germans came. My two brothers—they were in the army—were both captured in the first weeks of fighting in the North. My father was away. He was a doctor. Very respected in the district. He—he was a very great man!"

Her voice broke but she got hold of herself and went on talking in the same remote, almost indifferent manner.

"He was the chief liaison for the underground in our province. He was betrayed. The Nazis arrested him. They gave him the sentence of death!"

The fingers touching the palm of my hand twitched slightly.

"It was a Thursday in May. I remember so well. A breathtaking day with the trees bursting into bloom and so difficult to think of death and war. I went to Shmidt's headquarters in the Hotel de Ville. I went there to plead for my father's life. Like a bad cinema, no? I went there against the orders of my aunt and the wishes of my father. He would have been humiliated—his daughter begging mercy from the Nazi pigs. But I loved him. I loved my father. I wanted him to live. I went to this Shmidt."

"And?"

"Yes. Yes. I didn't have much hope. But I was admitted. And then— the dream—it began. He asked the other officer to leave the room. He tell me that if I would spend a week end with him in a hotel in Lyon that he would commute the death sentence. I didn't hesitate. I agreed."

Darkness was fading into deep gray. In the distance I heard a plane droning low over the city.

"Oh everything it was arranged with great dispatch. Prussian efficiency! I told my aunt that I was spending the week end at the home of a girl I knew in the next village. I had done this before, you understand, and nothing was thought strange. Shmidt's staff car picked me up at the appointed crossroads two miles out of the village and took me to the hotel in Lyon. I was brought upstairs immediately. A suite on the third floor. Shmidt was there with two young officers. I never left that room for three days. The two officers and Shmidt—it was a nightmare. I cannot tell what happened. I couldn't tell anyone. I was ... out of my mind."

"But surely you must have guessed?"

"No. Not that. You see, Hart, I was a virgin. And I was only fourteen."

"Fourteen!"

"Well, I was fourteen when I entered that room. I was forty—oh, a hundred and forty when I left it. Such things I could not have dreamed of. Shmidt's young men and—"

"The bastards!"

"It was late Sunday night when I got back to my aunt's. She would not allow me to enter the house. Already news had spread through the village that I had given myself to Shmidt. They thought I did it to better my position like other girls had. I was ill, and I believe half insane when the miller and his wife took me in. They spared me the news for three days."

"The news ...?"

"On that Saturday night, at the very time I was in that hotel room, my father had been executed."

I clenched her hand tight as though the act might shut out the terrible memory of that moment. I wanted to smash out the intervening years and the days of that nightmarish week end— smash out the past so that there would be another chance, a chance for a young girl to find happiness.

She went on in the same monotone as though it were the story of someone she knew but slightly, distant, clinical, remote and unreal. "In the village I was an outcast. I no longer cared. I planned to kill

Shmidt. But he was transferred back to Germany that week. The months went on. When the Allies landed they—they shaved off my hair as a collaborator. It didn't matter—my brothers were still interned in Germany. I went to Paris and I worked in a cheap revue as a nude, then I went to Rio with the manager of a nightclub. All the time I tried to find out where Shmidt was."

And then at last I got it.

"Shmidt! Von Bruckner is Shmidt!"

"Yes."

"But his story is that he left Germany before the war—that he didn't approve of Hitler."

"Is it? Like everything else about him it is a lie. The Munich waiter is now a rich gentleman! He is a monster, Hart."

"But where did the money come from?"

"This I do not know. You are ahead of my story."

"Go on."

"Soon my Argentine manager he grew tired of me. I found another man. I worked in second rate cabarets. I had many men. Oh too many, Hart ... it was always as though the next time I could wipe out the memory of those nights and days in the hotel in Lyon. And then one night in a water-front dive in Rio I met an ex-Nazi. I got him drunk and after a while the fool began to talk. He knew Shmidt. He told me he was living in Egypt under the name of Von Bruckner. He thought it was a great joke. It was all I needed. I had enough money to get back to Paris. I heard that Von Bruckner's mistress was in Paris. I managed an introduction ...: the rest you know."

We were both quiet for a moment. Then I said, "I'm sorry I stopped you from using that gun on the train. If I had known I would have helped."

She sighed. "It was the end of waiting ... but the moment went. Tonight when I saw him I knew that it mattered no longer. I am too tired, beyond caring."

I was more moved by her story than I cared to let her know. But I was after Von Bruckner for another reason and time had a habit of ticking on too goddamned fast. Max would be getting impatient.

"Do you have any idea of what Von Bruckner ... Shmidt ... is up to?"

"None. Except it can't be pretty."

"Where does young Armand Trouvier fit into your picture? Where did you know him?"

She didn't answer. She withdrew her hand. Finally she said, "I knew him a long time ago. It was unfortunate that he recognized me this afternoon."

When she didn't reply I suddenly realized she was weeping. Gently I touched her face. "Poor kid—that bastard is going to pay!"

"You must go now, Hart. Perhaps I should not have told you. You must go."

"I don't like leaving you like this."

She managed a brave but strangled laugh. "Little boy ... such nice manners. Tomorrow everything will be different, *n'est pas?* I promise not to play tragedy always. We will laugh."

After a bit I left the bed and dressed. From behind the mosquito netting Marianne said, "Whatever comes to us, Hart, I am grateful to you."

"Grateful?"

"For being ... decent."

But when I had one hand on the doorknob she suddenly cried out, "Go away from here, Hart! Go back to your own country. Go back to your own kind before it's too late for you!"

"Don't worry about me, honey."

I waited and after a moment she said, "Good-by *mon cher* ... my very good friend."

It wasn't until I was in the hall that that "good-by" made me uneasy. There had been something so damned final in the sound of her voice. I hesitated, half tempted to return to her room. But the sudden appearance of a Nubian waiter at the far end of the long hall brought me back to reality. I had to get some sleep. If I didn't I wouldn't be much help to Marianne or Max or anyone. There were things to be done this day. A helluva lot of things. And I knew now that most of them would lead to one center; a center dominated by a sonofabitch named Shmidt!

Chapter Twelve

The jangling of the phone by my bed woke me out of a heavy dreamless sleep. I looked at my watch. It was only eight-thirty A.M. What kind of a sadist was resorting to this means of early morning torture? Half drugged I decided to find out. I lifted the shrilly offensive instrument and grunted, "Well?"

"Fares Gebel."

"Who?" My night with Marianne weighed heavily. I pushed through some of the cobwebs and remembered. Gebel, Farouk's agent who had interviewed me in the lobby of the Alexandria hotel.

"Tell the king I can't come to the palace until after lunch. He'll have to wait."

"I have no time for jokes. I must see you this afternoon. It is most urgent."

"So why wake me at eight? You practicing up to be an alarm clock?"

"There may not be time later. The situation is most tense. I cannot discuss it further on the phone. You will come to the Golden Horn Hotel at four o'clock sharp. Give your name to the desk clerk. You will do this."

"Will I?"

"Decidedly. If not you will be picked up for questioning."

"On what grounds?"

"Certain events leading to the murder of a dragoman two nights ago in the Café Noir."

"You're dreaming. Or maybe I am. I need sleep." But I didn't feel so casual anymore.

"This is serious, Muldoon. You will take my advice."

"I'm curious," I said. "I'll be there."

"Good!"

The phone clicked and Gebel was gone. Before I had a chance to hang up the hotel operator came on and said with sickening brightness, "Good morning, monsieur, I have for you another call waiting."

"What is this—an invasion of Zombies?"

There was some sputtering, then a woman's voice, cool and matter-of-fact said, "Sigried McCarthy."

I came up out of sleep an inch more. "I'm not in the mood honey, try me later."

"A wisecrack for every occasion," she said acidly. "These are normal hours for me. I'm a working girl. However maybe you won't have a wisecrack for the news I have."

"Try me."

"Jeremiah Grant."

"What about him?" I asked sharply.

"It appears that, quite correctly, he does not trust us. I have just been informed that he was on the night plane from Paris that landed at the Cairo airport two hours ago. I thought you had better know."

"Is this a bum joke?"

"I wish it were."

I tried to figure some sense into this one. My head wasn't up to it.

If she were lying her motive was beyond comprehension. And there was something beneath the studied coolness of her voice that might have been panic.

"You're taking a chance baby—after all I work for the guy."

"So do I, theoretically. Maybe I'm warm-hearted. I don't like to see dogs run down in the street."

"You should see me sit up on my hind legs and beg. Let me come to your place tonight to prove my bite is worse than my bark."

"You're barking now," she said coolly, "and boasting. I imagine that even you need a few hours respite. Besides I'm choosy about my dogs. Anyway you might not be around by that time and I have no use for a dead dog."

"You're morbid."

"I'm a realist. And I have no more time for chitchat. I don't feel funny. Not at all funny. And there's something else ..."

"Bad too. I can tell."

"It might be. I've been trying to get Marianne's room but they tell me she cannot be disturbed. If you are in a position to disturb her please give her a message."

"Well?"

"Tell her not to leave her room until I have a chance to speak with her."

And with that she hung up. I lay there a moment knowing I should get into the bathroom and take a shower and begin moving. But the thickness of my head said no. Just an hour or so more, I thought; an hour at the outside. I'll be better able to handle this with sleep. And then I made one of the really bad mistakes of my life. I did the ostrich act, buried my head in the pillow and in one minute flat was dead to the world.

How long I actually slept I would not know until many hours later. It seemed to me only a few minutes when I was awakened once more by the phone. Mechanically I reached for it. No one answered. I put the thing down wondering whether the loud roaring sound was in my head. The ringing resumed in a strident hysterical manner. I picked it up again only to get a frantic buzzing on the other end. Then I became gradually aware that the roaring was not in my head. It came from outside the hotel. It was the concentrated roar of many voices, angry fanatical voices, and I didn't need to hear the sickening sound of wood splintering to realize that this was no routine "student demonstration."

I jumped from the bed and went to the window. Three floors below, the terrace, usually occupied by well-dressed Beys and Shahs and wealthy foreigners, was swarming with red fezzes. Tables were being thrown out to a seething mob that filled the Boulevard Fouad I. The fezzes swarmed like angry ants, converging on the entrance to the hotel lobby. I stood there transfixed, not quite certain that I was not still dreaming. Certainly the screaming mob behaved like characters in a sinister nightmare. All down the wide fashionable boulevard bricks were being hurled into shop windows and even as I stood there, too stupid for action, smoke began to curl out of the windows of the exclusive Carlton Club down the street, just beyond Thomas Cook and Sons.

Smoke.

And then I knew it was the nightmare come true, the nightmare of every good Sahib.

Smoke. Not Shepheard's. And like the sahibs I thought, they wouldn't dare. Not Shepheard's. After all the famous hotel was one of the king's favorite playgrounds. But the acrid odor grew stronger.

Out in the hall someone screamed and it was that scream that hurtled me into full wakefulness. I grabbed for my trousers and shirt, stuffed my wallet into my hip pocket, and still struggling into this scanty wardrobe got out into the hall. Halfway down the hall, in the central rotunda by the elevators, a thin line of blue smoke was floating gently upwards. A dowager-like woman emerged from the opposite room, dressed immaculately in a tweed suit and ancient black hat, clutching a small bag that probably contained jewelry. Behind her came another tweedy character, a male counterpart, carrying an old-fashioned alligator skin bag. They were as cool as figures in a nightmare and just as unreal.

"I'm afraid, my dear," the male said, "that it is inadvisable to use the lift. The fire stairs are at this end of the hall."

"It's an outrage," his mate (for she could have been nothing less) announced. "They simply can't do this sort of thing!"

"I'm very much afraid they have."

Unconsciously she had been watching me adjust my trousers, and suddenly aware of the object of her gaze, stuck her chin up disapprovingly. "I must say," she said and marched majestically off to the end of the hall opposite to the elevators where more guests, less nonchalant, were flocking into the entrance of the fire stairs. All this happened in the few seconds it took me to adjust my trousers and belt. Still barefooted I went quickly towards the center rotunda towards the long reach of hall that led off beyond it toward Marianne's room.

More guests, pale and frightened now, fled past me away from the rotunda towards the fire stairs behind me. In only a minute the wisp of smoke by the elevators had developed into an ominous black column billowing up swiftly from below. There was a dangerous updraft here in the center of the hotel and the open bedroom doors all along the corridor were not helping matters. I ducked through the wall of smoke, bumped into someone, straightened up and faced Sigried McCarthy. She was deathly pale, no longer the cool ice number, but trembling with fear and something more. She clutched at my arm.

"Go back, Hart—the other way. The forestairs—there isn't time."

"What the hell are you doing here?"

"Not now ..." She tried to drag me back.

"I've got to get Marianne."

"It's too ..." She stopped, looked wildly beyond me. "Oh Hart please, please come with me."

"Get the hell out!" I said harshly. "I'll see you later at your place."

She gave one last despairing look, then turned and fled through the smoke back down the hall toward the fire stairs. Down below in the bowels of the ancient hotel there was a dreamlike rhythm of shouting. And then for the first time I heard the ugly sickening sound of crackling flames eating their way up through the dry wood. The damned place would go up like a paper box.

The halls were suddenly, ominously empty. I stumbled down to Marianne's door. It was ajar. For one moment of hope I thought she had already gone. But I had to make certain. I stepped across the threshold. I saw the shadow huddled on the bed beneath the mosquito netting. Evenly, very evenly I walked across the room and drew back the netting. Marianne lay where I had left her, arms flung back on the pillow in a gesture of supplication. Her eyes were open. There was a knife in her throat.

There wasn't much blood on the bed. She couldn't have been dead a long time. On the pillow beside her was a wooden crescent.

I thought, No.

And then I felt my knees beginning to buckle and reached for the bedpost. Only a few hours before I had held this girl in my arms. She had said not "*au revoir*" but "good-by" almost as if ... For the first time I noticed how small and delicate were her hands.

Dully I thought, it's getting damned hot. I stood there unable to move. Her hands are like those of a child, I thought. They are the same—the same hands that had stiffened with terror back in that hotel room in Lyon.

Something glittered on the rug. Mechanically I stooped down and picked it up and stuffed it into my pocket.

"I'll do it, *ma chérie*," I whispered idiotically.

The carved Damascus handle of the knife seemed to tremble, reflecting some new light. Flames were reaching up outside the window. I turned and walked very slowly from the room and closed the door behind me. Closed it very gently.

The crackling had developed into a dissonant roar. Smoke and flames were rushing up through the center of the hotel. There was no chance of crashing that wall of death to reach the fire stairs. Feeling strangely remote and calm I went into the room opposite Marianne's, shut the door behind me and crossed to the window. This room faced the inner court and down below in the garden where only the night before an orchestra had played for dancing and a smart supper crowd had drunk champagne, guests and servants of the hotel were huddled into frightened groups, still too shocked for further action. On the window ledge of a fourth-floor room a woman in sheer lingerie tottered precariously, shrieking for help. The room behind me was like a furnace. I watched the screaming woman with a kind of terrible fascination. I wanted to shout to her to hang on. But I was too far away and others were attempting the same warning from below. But she was beyond thought or hearing. A great cloud of smoke billowed out of the room behind her. With one last unearthly scream she leaped out. She fell like a rag doll, turning headfirst in mid-air. A deathly silence had fallen over the garden. She struck the marble dance floor with a sickening crunch. I turned away and was sick. Down below a woman began to laugh hysterically and then suddenly the sound was throttled. When I looked back someone had thrown a coat over the body.

With a kind of awful precision I climbed out onto the window ledge. Between my window and the next was a copper pipe which ran to the ground from the roof. I thought, I won't miss. I threw myself sideways and grasped the pipe. My feet swung under me straight down. My hands, moist from sweat, slipped down the copper. The pipe was blistering hot. I began to fall faster but managed to hang on. I hit the ground fast and hard but got to my feet unhurt, except for raw palms. I looked about. No one paid any attention to me. I felt as though I were an extra who had wandered into the wrong movie set. I wondered why the infuriated mobs had not invaded the inner court of the hotel. I thought, they're lucky. So far. A girl was leaning against a young man in a neat white suit, weeping quietly on his shoulder. They looked like Americans. I suspected they were on their honeymoon. No one looked toward the inert figure on the marble floor. I saw blood trickling out over the shiny stone.

Then for the first time I saw the police. Four or five of them began herding the guests toward an arched gate that opened into a narrow street behind the hotel. Lethargically I followed.

And then someone touched my arm. I looked down into the face of Phidias Imperator.

"Son of a bitch," he said urgently. "You look like you are sleepwalking."

"Do I?"

"Come with me."

I permitted him to lead me across the garden to a small door near the entrance to the kitchens. We went through a corridor oddly free of smoke. We came out into a narrow street. Up near the middle of the street I saw hotel guests being herded into busses and limousines. Both ends of the street were guarded by armed men. The king's troops. Humpty Dumpty, I thought. We walked a few yards and then he tugged at my shirt and practically pulled me into a doorway. He opened the door and we went into a long, cool hall. He shut the door behind him. I followed behind him through the hall and out into an enclosed garden. Three veiled women, impervious to the horror taking place outside the dreamlike garden, sat near a well. They turned their faces away as we crossed it to another door. I turned back to look for the last time at Shepheard's. She was roaring into the bright sky, burning the years behind her. I saw it not so much as a symbol of the end of an epoch but as the funeral pyre of a lonely French girl whose hands were like those of an innocent child's.

Chapter Thirteen

The time between my escape from the burning hotel and the moment when I left the house of Phidias Imperator's Arab friend (the uncle of his wife I discovered later) is somewhat blurred in my mind. I had, since the discovery of Marianne's body, become a fanatic with but one purpose and everything not related to this purpose was vague and dreamlike. I have a dim recollection of Phidias hovering over me in his friend's house, imploring me to stay out of sight until the riots died down, yet at the same time supplying me with the burnoose and sandals that I had requested; of servants coming and going as though this room were a thousand miles from Cairo; of a passive Nubian sent off with a message to Gina and of the waiting while Phidias droned on, predicting sudden death if I didn't listen to reason. At three-thirty the Nubian returned with a note from Gina. I tore it open and read:

"Thank God you are safe. The king has sent a military detachment to guard my villa. In answer to your question about Hans. I have not seen him today and have no idea where he can be reached. I have received instructions from him to proceed at seven P.M. to his houseboat which is anchored above Abureash. If Marianne is with you go to Sigried's apartment, the Palais Royale Apartments in the Rue Napoleon. My car will fetch her out to my villa in time for the trip to Abureash. I insist that you and Marianne accompany her; that you both will be my guests until this dreadful uprising has been put down. I will not rest until I see you, Hart."

At another time the suggestion of promise in that note would have been exciting. Now I found only frustration in the fact that Gina had been unable to tell me where I could find Von Bruckner. Despite obvious disapproval Phidias had been at work on some of his contacts but with no success. Even his pipeline into the royal palace had proved fruitless. But there were two or three people who might lead me to him and one of them was the man I had promised to meet in the Golden Horn Hotel at four P.M., Farouk's agent, Fares Gebel. The chance that he would still keep the appointment, considering the upheaval in the city, was remote but I decided to play it that way.

At three-thirty the radio was demanding that the crowds cease violence immediately at the King's orders. A curfew was declared beginning at ten P.M. Rumors seeped in to us that the National troops, suspiciously absent from the scene until now were beginning to appear with some effectiveness along the main boulevards. The hatred of the mobs had been confined for the most part to British property and person, yet it seemed improbable that even Farouk could have been so stupid as to use this crude weapon for negotiations. This flame had been well tended, well planned. But by whom? Phidias was of the opinion that the instigators had been not one group but many, the Communists, the more fanatical Wafdist, the army elements who wished to embarrass the king and the lunatic fringe elements in the Arab League. He suspected that some sort of a deal had been made at the palace before the army

agreed to appear in the streets. He was more optimistic than I
about the riots not spreading into a nationwide conflagration. He
was of the opinion that only some fantastically stupid act on the part
of the British could make matters worse.

But when I was more or less disguised as an Arab, feeling like a
character at the Beaux Arts Ball in the flowing burnoose, he said,
"The dragoman who was murdered in the Café Noir died because of
what he knew. It must have had something to do with the missing
British bomber. So we can deduce that he was telling the truth. Yet
I am unable to find any oasis on the map known as El Sha-en-Reb.
It is very puzzling."

"I'm not interested," I said.

He frowned. "But I thought—this is your job."

"It was. I have a bigger job now. A personal one."

"I do not like the way you talk, my friend. Or the way you look. This
new job—it is no good?"

"It's good enough. Someone has to do it. It might as well be me."

"Ah? And what is this?"

"The job? Simple enough. To kill a snake."

That stopped him. He shrugged.

"I do not hear you," he said, "if anyone asks later. I do not hear."

"Good."

"On this job, count me out!"

I followed the Nubian servant to the door.

Phidias called after me, "On second thought ..."

I turned and managed a smile. "Thanks, Phidias. But this one is
strictly on me. If I make it I'll buy you a drink next week at the Mena
House—if it's still standing."

I followed the poker-faced Nubian through back alleys away from
the main streets of the European section. In the distance a pall of
smoke hung over the center of the city but back here life went on as
usual. Come death or high water or revolution the life of the fellahin
went on as usual. Although my disguise could not have been very
convincing no one molested us in our zigzag course towards the
western sector. There in a quiet native quarter we came to the
entrance of the Golden Horn, a small hotel whose façade was hung
with iron balconies and peeling gingerbread. I told the Nubian to
wait outside and entered the dim lobby which had an unpleasant
dampness in it like that of an earthen cave. The only daylight
entered through the main doorway. The rear of the small room was
lighted by a gilt chandelier which looked like something lifted from
a mosque. A little Turk, resembling a nervous monkey in his fez,

watched my approach from behind the desk. There was no one else in the room. In the fraction of a minute it took me to cross from the street door I had the feeling that his bright little eyes missed nothing.

"I expect to meet someone here," I said. "The name is Muldoon."

He nodded immediately. "Yes. O.K."

He banged on a hand bell. An old servant came out of the darkness. The Turk said, "Follow him."

He jabbered something in Arabic to the servant. I was led down a long evil-smelling hall, up three steps and into a bedroom that was not unlike that of a medium priced mid-western hotel. There was nothing of the glamorous East here. The servant went out and closed the door behind him. It was very still here at the back of the building. I made a quick examination of possible points of exit. The one window opened on a dark areaway. Opposite was the blank wall of the neighboring building. It looked like a cul-de-sac. The only other way out was through the door I had come through. I lit one of the cigarettes that Phidias had given me and sat down in an oak armchair. There was a desk, a double bed direct from Grand Rapids neatly made up for the night and on the bedside table a metal lamp. The place was surprisingly clean. I almost expected to see a Gideon Bible on the table. But there was not a book or a scrap of paper or any other sign of an occupant. The open closet door revealed unused hangers and a wall shining with varnish.

The silence became oppressive. I wondered whether I would be waiting here for Gebel the rest of the day and whether it had been worth coming in the first place. I felt inside the robe for the Luger Phidias had given me in such an offhand manner. I had smoked half the cigarette when I heard a sound in the hall. I got up out of the chair quick and crossed the room, placing myself flat against the wall beside the door. The knob turned gently, then the door swung in. Gebel stepped nonchalantly into the room and without even turning to look at me, closed the door behind him and said, "You're more nervous than I would have thought."

"Just careful," I said.

He walked to the window, pulled it down tight and turned to me. He grinned. "You look like one of the tourists dressed for a trip to the pyramids by Thomas Cook."

"From what I've seen today, Thomas Cook won't be dressing many tourists for a long time to come."

"Unfortunate. Very. Sit down."

"I'm all right where I am."

He shrugged. He lit a cigarette. I noticed that his hands weren't too steady.

"You must think I can give you something important," I said, "to keep this appointment at a time like this. Your boss must be pretty damned worried."

"My boss?"

"The King."

"Oh," he said, "of course."

He surprised me on that one. I waited. He enjoyed his little bombshell.

"In government work," he finally said, "it is never advisable to tie oneself irrefutably to one boss."

"Does that mean the king is through?"

"Certainly not. However ... there is always tomorrow." He grinned. "I can say this here. These walls have no ears. It is a relief to speak it."

I looked at him, suddenly regretting my decision to keep the appointment. "Who the hell are you really working for?"

"My country," he said with a grin.

"If I knew the national anthem I'd sing it. You touch me."

His eyes narrowed. He spat out some smoke. He choked a little, then got hold of himself.

"Neither of us have time for the philosophical aspects of politics, Mr. Muldoon. I have a job to do. My interests may coincide with yours. If they do not, that is unfortunate for you. To come to the point. A subject of his Majesty the King of Saudi Arabia was murdered two nights ago in the Café Noir. I have irrefutable proof that you were sitting with him at a table in this café at the very moment he was murdered."

I waited on that one.

"Now then ... I am a man of some liberalism. I believe very much in what you Americans call 'give and take.' I am prepared to be liberal in return for candor."

"And if I refuse to play?"

"I will then have the unpleasant duty of arresting you on a technical charge of murder, along of course, with your accomplice, Mr. Phidias Imperator."

"You're bluffing. There were plenty of witnesses. He was stabbed in the back by a knife thrown through the curtains of the adjoining hall."

"On the contrary," he said calmly. "I am in a position to produce at least four witnesses who will swear that they saw Mr. Imperator hold the poor devil while you knifed him. Very crude and ruthless."

I lit another cigarette. I watched him closely. His eyes were cold as marble. He meant it. At that moment I was more concerned with Phidias than myself. After all I had got him into this mess.

"You must want something bad," I said.

"Something quite simple. We have discovered that the dragoman who died so abruptly at the Café Noir had been telling a fantastic story around the bazaars. A story involving a foreign plane. It is my duty to track down all rumors no matter how absurd. You will give me the location in which the dragoman claims to have seen this— this—mirage."

I hesitated. There seemed no particular harm in telling the little I knew. After all even Phidias who was an expert in these things had been unable to find any such oasis as the dragoman had mentioned. But if it were the only bargaining point I had, I decided to hang on a bit longer. I'd come here for a little information of my own.

"What guarantee do I have that I get safely out of Egypt and that Imperator is not pinned on a phony murder rap?"

"My word, sir."

I laughed. His face darkened. He dropped the cigarette to the rug and stamped it out.

"You force me to be more explicit, Mr. Muldoon. I am being more generous than you deserve. I am possessed of certain incriminating facts."

"Like what?"

"You are here in Egypt as an employee of a notorious character of the Paris underworld by name of Jeremiah Grant. You have busied yourself with investigating the activities of one of the most distinguished ladies in Cairo. You have questioned the reputation and motives of Herr von Bruckner who has had the confidence of the king. You cannot expect much consideration as the right hand man of an international blackmailer."

"Is that all?"

"Not quite." His voice was ominous now. "Last night you spent in the bedroom of the French *chanteuse* who made her debut at the Club Lido. It may interest you to know that the fire was not entirely successful as far as her murderer was concerned. My men found her body one hour ago. And the knife in her throat."

"You're not accusing me?"

"I have not time to waste," he snapped. "Either you co-operate or you will find out what the inside of a Cairo jail is like. Make up your mind."

And then suddenly it came over me that the whole setup was a phony. Gebel knew as well as I that I had not murdered the Arab or Marianne. I would have been picked up long ago. Yet his implication that if I supplied the information he wanted I would be free didn't ring true. For the first time I considered the possibility that he was one of Von Bruckner's men trying to find out how much the Arab had really spilled.

But I had come here for one purpose. I had to play the long shot.

"Listen, Gebel. I'll give you what you want. But first—I want something."

"Well?" His eyes glittered with anticipation.

"Where can I find Von Bruckner?"

The light died from his eyes. After a moment he said quietly, "I speak now for my government. Your interest in Von Bruckner is at an end. We will not countenance any more meddling. If you give me the information I am seeking I will see to it you are on a plane for Paris in the morning. Otherwise you will be under arrest. That is the beginning and the end of my bargaining."

"Where is Von Bruckner?"

I took a step toward him. He stood his ground, face dark with vexation. He snapped out a phrase in Arabic. The door behind me opened. I wheeled about. Armand Trouvier stepped across the threshold. His face was deathly pale. All the playboy insouciance was gone. He looked like business. So did the gun in his hand.

"Well?" he said sharply to Gebel. It was the voice of employer to employee. Gebel said, "He won't talk."

Armand slammed the door to behind him.

"Fool!" he snapped out. "I should have known better than to depend on you. You're not worth the money you draw."

"His fee is too high. Besides, I cannot pay it," Gebel protested.

"What is it?"

"He wished to know where he can find Von Bruckner."

Trouvier's eyes darted back to me. I didn't like what I saw in them. It occurred to me that there was some sort of madness in this young man.

Very deliberately he said, "You are scum to me. Grant's tool. I do not play soft like our friend Gebel. If you do not speak—if you do not divulge the nature of your conversation with the Arab at the Café Noir I will have no compunction in killing you."

And he meant it.

He stood between me and the closed door to the hall. Behind me, barring the dubious escape possibilities of the window was Gebel. I thought, I will be only telling him what he already knows as one of Von Bruckner's men. Yet if I tell him their suspicions will be confirmed. I will never leave this room to repeat it. Heads or tails I was on the losing side. And then I decided to use desperate means, a sort of shock treatment that would either get me a bullet in the guts or the unguarded moment I needed.

"One minute!" he said coldly.

"O.K. I'll talk." The hand on the gun relaxed just a bit. "But first I must tell you something funny."

"Funny?"

"The girl I slept with last night told me you were lousy in bed. Her name was Marianne Courbert."

The effect was even more astounding than I could have hoped for. Trouvier's face twisted into a grimace of shock and hate. The very intensity of his emotion immobilized him for the moment I needed. Before the gun could come up again I threw myself into him, knocking him backward against the wall. I wheeled about just as Gebel fell on me, twisted him about, got his body between mine and the infuriated Frenchman's, and pushed him forward into Trouvier's outstretched hand. I tore open the door, stumbled out into the hall just as I heard the crack of Trouvier's gun. Something went "plop" in the wall to my right. I got down the hall to the lobby in one minute flat. I heard them coming behind me down the narrow hall. The crack came again. The Turk ducked down behind the desk. Something ricocheted across the tiles. I plunged into the sunlight. The Nubian jumped to his feet startled. Two men down at the corner of the hotel started running toward me. I had time to see one of them pulling a gun. I ducked down an alley, vaulted a low wall, found myself in another alley almost identical. A woman began screaming from a doorway opposite. Down at the end of the alley I saw the sunlight of a small square. I ran as fast as the burnoose permitted. I thought I'd never make it. I could hear footsteps on cobblestones coming from behind, coming very fast. I ducked out into the square almost directly into the path of a careening trolley. The side of the car hissed across my back as I got beyond it. A curse of alarm echoed back from the car and I heard the crackle of electricity and saw blue sparks spattering from the overhead wire. A crowd of Arabs suddenly erupted from a street to the right pursued by uni-formed police on horseback. I dived into their midst, risking the plunging horses to lose my pursuers. I fought my way across the angry panic-stricken crowd to the opposite side. I left then as a swimmer leaves a swift current in midstream and found myself in

another deserted street. I kept running. I knew now that my
pursuers would be everywhere. From now on it would be me or Von
Bruckner. But only a well-placed shot would keep me from stalking
my prey to the kill. I ran blindly on until there was nothing but
silence behind me.

Chapter Fourteen

It was five-twenty when I entered the chic little foyer of the Palais
Royale Apartments near the French Legation. The tricolors were
prominently displayed before the entrance of the ultra-modern
building. The mobs had done no damage here but I could hear them
still howling not more than three blocks away. Two soldiers blocked
my path but when I pulled aside the hood of my burnoose they
shrugged in a bored manner and let me pass. Apparently they had
become adjusted to some odd disguises since the riots had begun. A
jittery woman at the reception desk was so nervous that she
dispensed with the usual formality of announcing me and gave me
the apartment number in a distracted manner. I entered the self-
service elevator, pressed the button and rose silently through the
building.

The pink walls of the second floor hall were discreetly lit. Pale green
doors stood down its length at wide intervals. The carpet was soft
and thick. I found Apartment 28 at the end of the hall and pressed
the pearl button at the side of the door.

After a moment the door was flung open by Sigried McCarthy. The
look of tension on her face changed to pleased surprise. Or at least
a good imitation. I stepped past her over the threshold into a lovely
sitting room, pastel and sunlit with a large picture window
overlooking the square. She closed the door behind her.

"Hart! I can't tell you how relieved I am. After seeing you in the
hall—that terrible nightmare!"

Without turning to her I said, "You had just come from her room!"

When she didn't answer I turned. She looked very cool and smart
in a well-cut linen sports dress. She had one hand on the back of the
sofa, holding on to it tightly. "Well?"

"I went there to warn her," she said in a dead voice.

"Very kind of you, I'm sure. And what was the nature of the
warning?"

"Don't be cruel, Hart. I can't stand much more."

"Oh, hell, stop acting."

Her head came up sharply. She closed her eyes. "I don't expect you to believe me. Last night at the Lido, after you left, I went into the foyer on my way to the ladies' lounge. The foyer as you remember is an ell shaped room. At the corner of the ell I heard Armand Trouvier talking to Guido. I—I listened. They couldn't see me of course. They were close to the wall around the corner of the ell. I heard Armand say, 'I'll take care of the French girl. It's my job. Leave it to me.' And Guido said, 'You'd better do something quick—and drastic—before she messes things up.'"

"And?"

"That's all. They went away then."

She didn't look me in the eyes. Yet for some reason I wanted to believe her.

"Why didn't you tell me this when you phoned this morning?"

"I was a fool. I've got so I don't know who to trust. I decided to go there myself when I couldn't get Marianne on the phone. The operator kept saying she could not be disturbed. The riot began when I was on my way up to her room. I—I walked in. The door was ajar. I found—oh my God, it must have just happened. I don't know how long I stood there. I was in shock. I came out into the hall and there was smoke. Then I saw you."

"Why didn't you tell me what you had seen?"

"I tried to keep you from going to her room. But I couldn't tell you that way. I knew how much she meant to you ..."

"I think you're lying in your teeth," I said.

"Hart!"

I got to her quick and threw her to the sofa. Her back hit the arm and she recoiled in pain. But she lay there looking up at me with a sort of hopeless resignation.

"This is what happens when you touch mud. You sink into it and it won't come off!" Her voice was remote.

I bent over and hit her hard across the face with the palm of my hand. She began to weep.

"How long have you been working for Von Bruckner?"

She shook her head wordlessly. I hit her again, this time harder. An ugly red mark cut across her cheek. She didn't even try to protect herself. She lay there looking up at me, her mouth trembling, tears slipping down across the welt.

"You're only hitting back at yourself, Hart. You know it. You—"

"Answer me."

"What's the use? You won't believe me. That unspeakable business with Jeremiah Grant. That's all, and I only did that because ... because ..."

"Why?"

Suddenly fear came into her eyes. "Never mind!"

And automatically I raised my hand and brought it down across her mouth. A little trickle of blood appeared in one corner of her lower lip. She didn't cry out. She closed her eyes.

"How long have you known Armand Trouvier?"

"Six months—perhaps a bit more. What does it matter...." She made no effort to wipe away the blood. I began to feel slightly ill. I fought off the weakness. If she had only fought back it might not have been so difficult. Yet the blow this time was even more brutal. Her head snapped to one side.

"You know Trouvier works for Von Bruckner!"

"No. I know that Hans is fond of him. But then that's only to be expected."

"What does that mean?"

She put the back of her hand to her mouth, drew away, regarded the spot of blood, let the hand fall listlessly to her side. "Surely you know. Hans likes young men."

"What!" She really had stopped me cold.

"It's common knowledge. Handsome and young."

"But ..." I said flabbergasted, "Gina. I thought—"

"Who knows? Perhaps she represents prestige to him. I don't know. I don't know."

"You mean to say he doesn't sleep with her?"

"Anything is possible, of course...."

Suddenly I remembered Marianne's story of the weekend in the Lyon Hotel. The presence of the "two young officers" in that room took on a new and sinister meaning. Somewhere in the back of my mind was a glimmer of relief. Perhaps Gina had never really been his mistress. If so ...

"You know more about Armand Trouvier than you will admit. What was he doing in your office when I barged in on you both? And don't tell me he was buying clothes for a girl friend."

"He was questioning me."

"About what?"

"If you must know, about you."

It was possible. Considering the scene I had just been through at the Golden Horn it was more than possible.

"All right," I said, "I'm going to give you a break. I'm going to assume for the moment that you're not working for Von Bruckner.

That still doesn't mean you haven't any idea of his racket."

She opened her eyes and looked directly into mine. Deliberately she said, "I would have answered that had you asked. I believe Hans von Bruckner is the brains behind the organization called the Sons of Mecca."

"Why didn't you tell me this before?"

"It's not a thing you talk about in Cairo. Besides there is Gina to consider. I think she suspects. But one cannot make accusations without proof. I tried to imply it to you in my office when I told you that Gina was afraid of something. I hoped she might confide in you."

I stood there a moment looking down at her. Then harshly I said, "Do you know where he is now?"

"No. I got a message from her an hour ago. She insists I go to her villa at six and accompany her to Hans' houseboat. What should I do?"

"If you can get out to her villa, go."

"Is that all?"

"Get up and put some cold water on your face."

She rose with dignity, looked through me, walked past me toward the bedroom. I heard the sound of running water. I felt like a heel but she had me puzzled. I began to feel again time pressing on me, time running out. Gebel's men might be closing about me at this very moment. I had to escape that net until I got my hands on Von Bruckner.

The house phone began to ring. My nerves began to jump. Sigried came out of the bedroom, avoided my eyes, picked up the instrument and said "Yes?"

Her face went tense. She put her hand over the mouthpiece and whispered, "Jeremiah Grant is in the lobby. What should I do?"

"Ask him up."

Into the phone she said, "Tell Mr. Grant to come up."

She hung up and stood there, one hand still on the phone, staring at me. "Now what?"

I took out the Luger. "I'll be in the bedroom. If you're on the level play it cute. If you're not ..." I brought the gun up significantly.

She sighed and looked away. "Yes," she said almost indifferently, "all right."

I went into the bedroom leaving the door slightly ajar. From behind the door I got a good view of at least half the room.

She walked out of sight to answer the door. There was a nervous moment of silent greeting. Had she betrayed me by a look? Then she walked back to the sofa with Jeremiah panting behind her like a drooling terrier. He looked pleased with himself. I didn't like it. He sat on the sofa with a sigh.

"I could use a little shuteye. I haven't slept for twenty-six hours. And the way things are going I probably won't get any for at least fifteen."

"Why fifteen?"

He shook his finger at her roguishly. "I'll tell you all about it, honey. Someday when we are safely tucked away in a twenty-room villa outside Cannes. Or do you prefer Spain?"

"It's sweet of you to offer me countries," she said coolly. "What are you doing here?"

"Surprised?"

"I knew you were in Cairo. I knew you landed this morning. In Cairo it's wise to have friends everywhere. Even at the airport."

"You sure have smartened up, baby, since I first knew you. You've gone a long way."

"That is a matter of opinion. Why did you come here?"

"How about a drink first. Got any cognac?"

Sigried hesitated. Her gaze slid across the door behind which I was concealed. Then she got up and poured him a drink.

"How about yourself?" I remembered that tone of voice. Jeremiah Grant the lady-killer. Jeremiah in the role of Don Juan. I wouldn't think it was going to work any better than it usually had worked for him. Not unless my impressions of Sigried were dead wrong.

"Do I need one?" she asked.

"Maybe. I came to warn you to steer clear of Hart Muldoon."

"Why?"

"Yesterday, about noon, I got a tip. He's working for the British. I got the first plane I could."

"How very interesting," she said. I thought I detected a note of elation in her voice. Maybe Grant did too. He said sharply, "He won't get far. Don't worry, honey. He hasn't got anything on you. I'm the only one who has."

"I thought you expected to get some valuable information from Muldoon." She was playing it very cute indeed. I'd have to do a lot of making up for those blows to her lovely face.

"I got that. I got all I need for both of us, baby."

"Both of us?"

"Enough to make us rich."

"You keep using the plural."

"That's the way it's going to be. You and me. I've looked around. I haven't found anything I want more. Two or three more days and we'll clear out of Egypt with enough loot to make the pharaohs turn over in their tombs."

"Are you making a proposition? If so be specific. I'm a business woman now, you know."

He hesitated and for the first time looked around the room suspiciously. Sigried managed to keep the business interest on her face. He frowned slightly, started to get up, looked at her, then shrugged, obviously dismissing the passing doubt. Ego saved me. The damned fool thought she was all for him, from now on in.

"I've finally got the goods on Von Bruckner."

"Oh?"

He leaned forward. "It's bigger than I ever suspected. He'll pay through the nose. And keep paying."

My pulse began to quicken. Sigried played it cool, very, very cool. She said, "Knowing men, I've also known many promises. I don't take promissory notes these days. It's cash on the line."

He leaned forward, throwing caution to the winds.

"Listen baby," he said, "I'm going to tell you this because I know it's safe with you. You can't go anywhere else. And besides, you've got a head on your shoulders."

"Yes," she said, "that I have."

"Von Bruckner is one of the big shots in the Sons of Mecca. He's been working for the rich Beys and Shahs who back the organization."

"That's not news," she said.

"No? Well maybe this is." He stood and grasped her shoulders in an excited manner. "This morning I fell right into it. Manna from heaven. A German mechanic I once knew in Tangier—smart little rat named Kurt Benz. Been through some tight little deals. But even he finds this one a little too tight. He wants out but out with plenty of cash. Needs someone to negotiate. Someone like me. He spilled the beans on the condition that I cut him in. We can see about the cut later. It's fantastic."

"Well?"

"Von Bruckner. The crazy bastard somehow got hold of a British bomber."

A chill went up my back. My hand tightened on the Luger. Sigried managed to keep the shock out of her face. She laughed.

"That's not cash. That's a fairy tale."

He shook her. "It's the God's honest truth. I know this Benz baby well."

She looked skeptical. "It's absurd. How could he get hold of a

British bomber and anyway what good would it do him?"

"I don't know what his screwy plan is. All I know is that he has it. Ready to go, bombs and all."

"A one plane war—against whom?"

"Listen, you little dope, this is on the level. And that information is going to keep us in mink and liquor for years to come. Von Bruckner is going to pay through the nose!"

She backed away.

"You're not going to try to blackmail Hans von Bruckner? You must be mad."

"Oh, no I'm not! I've figured it close and neat. He's going to know that I've left a letter with the British Consul to be opened if anything happens to me. Nothing will happen except a draft on the Paris bank. Tomorrow this time you and I will be on a French airliner."

When she said nothing, he said, "I don't blame you for being struck dumb. A quarter of a million anyway."

"Tell me," she said very carefully, "where is this bomber?"

"Where?" Something in her tone warned him. He stepped back and looked quickly toward the door of the bedroom. Looked right into the muzzle of my Luger. He had too much sense to try to move.

"You heard the lady," I said quietly.

In the silence the ticking of a little gilt clock on the mantel seemed abnormally loud. The color drained from Grant's face.

Without looking at Sigried he said, "You double crossing little bitch!"

"Yes," she said, "and delighted."

"Where is the bomber? Quick, Grant. My finger is itching."

"I don't know," he said in a hopeless monotone. "Somewhere out in the desert. An oasis."

"Go on."

"Eighty some miles southeast of Cairo. Listen Muldoon—be reasonable. This is big stuff and there's enough for all of us."

"Where is Von Bruckner?"

"I don't know."

I took a step forward. "Don't give me that. How did you expect to put the bite on him?"

"I ..." He gave a frightened look toward the gun and spoke quick. "Kurt is arranging an appointment with him. On some houseboat up the Nile. Near Abureash. Ten tonight."

I saw that for once panic had forced him into telling the truth. I waited.

"That's all I know, I swear it. Now that you see—you're no fool,

Muldoon. There's enough for us all—I'll handle it."

"The hell you will. Sit down."

He sat with the jerking movements of a puppet. He was scared almost to hell.

"You can't prove anything against me," he said.

I looked at Sigried. She hadn't moved. She was looking down at Grant with an odd almost disinterested expression.

"What's he got on you?" I asked.

He looked up at her, imploring her to silence. Her expression didn't change. "Jeff, my husband Jeff ... we were in Tangier. He was very ill. Tuberculosis. We were broke. I was desperate. Someone introduced me to this—this creature. He offered me a job. It was running black market things into France. I took it. I would have done anything for Jeff. When I came back from my third trip Jeff was dead. I left Tangier and went to Cairo. I tried to forget Grant ... and then when I was in Paris this trip he found me. He threatened to expose me if I didn't co-operate by introducing you to Gina. That's all. Except for one thing."

"Well?"

"Jeff didn't die of tuberculosis, He was shot in the street. No one saw it happen. No one knew who did it. I do now."

Her expression had not changed. Grant sank back on the sofa and gave me a wild look. "She's nuts."

I turned to Sigried. "Well?"

She nodded. I said, "On a day like this one shot more won't be noticed."

She sighed and closed her eyes. Grant put his hands up before his face. "No," he shrieked, "she's lying! It's a frame-up—you can't."

I let him have it. He snapped forward like a jackknife, his hands pressed tight to his stomach. I let him have it again. There was a gurgling sound and he went sprawling to the carpet. Once more I let him have it ... this time in the back of his head. That was a mistake. It made an unpleasant mess on the pink rug.

The phone began to ring. Sigried came out of her unearthly calm. She stepped over Grant's body and picked up the instrument.

"Yes?" And then after a moment, "I'll be right down."

She put the phone back in the cradle.

"Gina's car is at the door. Come with me, Hart."

I stuck the Luger down inside my burnoose. "You go on out to Gina's villa. I'll be at the houseboat before ten. Don't say a word about anything. If I don't get there—"

"Well?"

I shrugged.

"Hart," she whispered. And then her hands fell to her sides. "Something inside has atrophied," she said. "I feel nothing. Absolutely nothing."

"Keep your head. Later there will be questions."

I went to the window and looked down toward the hotel entrance. Gina's Rolls was standing there. In the front seat, beside the chauffeur, was a soldier carrying a Tommy gun. He wore the uniform of the King's Guard. Maybe it still paid to know Farouk.

I turned back to the room. "You go down now. I'll follow in a few minutes. When they ask questions you don't know a thing. This happened after you left the room. Leave the rest to me."

"I think," she said quietly, "that I love you."

"Get out."

She took one last look at the remains of Jeremiah Grant.

"I'm free now," she said. "Maybe someday ..."

She left the rest unfinished, took the bag that she had apparently packed before my arrival and went to the door. She didn't look back. She left me in the silent room where the only sound was the relentless ticking of the little gilt clock.

Chapter Fifteen

The woman behind the reception desk gave me a puzzled look. "The other gentleman?" she asked.

"He won't be coming down. Take a look at my face. Remember it well."

"I don't understand, monsieur."

"You will. I had trouble with the other gentleman after madame left!"

She frowned. She looked about the empty lobby as though for help. I went quickly out into the amber light of late afternoon. My figuring was cold and relentless. Grant had said that Von Bruckner would be at the houseboat at ten. He would keep on ice until then if I did! There were a few things I had to settle first.

I left the vicinity of the smart apartments and zigzagged back through the seething city through back alleys until I reached the house of Phidias' Arab friend. Luckily Phidias was still there. I suspected he had remained put where I could find him. Quickly I told him what I needed. He looked doubtful but, mercifully, did not lecture me this time. He knew I was beyond listening. What I asked wasn't easy but he finally shrugged and said, "You're crazy. I will try. If I am successful you will find me at the pier of the Tutankhamen Cigarette Company. Above the bridge at Giah. Red brick warehouse. You can't miss it. Give me one hour."

That was enough for me.

I left the house and took a roundabout course for the Luna Square. This time I had more trouble. A couple of shots sang by, pretty damned close. I had the feeling that if I had been in European clothes instead of the burnoose the soldiers might have proved better marksmen. I used the roof of the Opera House as a point of orientation and in fifteen minutes I was at the Pension Capri. The mobs had ignored the tawdry hostelry—apparently poverty was the most protective of international passports these days.

Larson and his woman had just finished packing. For a change he was dead sober. After one look at my face she left us alone on the excuse of going to talk to the manager.

"We're clearing out at eight," Larson said. "An Arab friend is taking us up the Nile to meet my Hollander at Luxor."

"Maybe you'll change your mind."

"No. I have no alternative. It's a good way out."

He went to the window, turning his back. He spoke with some difficulty. "I'm damned glad you showed up, Hart. I didn't think you would welsh on your bargain. I—I need the cash badly."

When I said nothing he went on nervously, "You did bring it, didn't you? Naturally, I couldn't keep my appointment to come to your room at Shepheard's but I knew you'd come here. You did bring it? My Arab friend is counting on passage up the Nile."

Instead of answering I said, "What do you think of all this business?"

"The damned fools!" he said angrily. "They'll never be treated so well again as they have been by the British. The stupid, blundering idiots!"

"Hail Britannia!"

"I keep forgetting," he said, "it's not my fight anymore."

"Maybe it is," I said.

"To hell with that!" And then, doing a double take, he turned. "What are you driving at, Muldoon?"

"Easy does it. What do you hear about the mess in the city?"

"Rumors, all of them contradictory. Farouk will abdicate. Farouk will not abdicate. The Beys and Shahs solidly behind him, the Beys and Shahs selling out to the fanatics. The Wafdists and the Commies and the Brotherhood of Islam all doing battle to get on top. Farouk about to can his Prime Minister in favor of a more moderate man who will listen to reason. If you noticed, the troops didn't appear on the streets for a helluva long time. My guess is that they refused to show until someone got his terms."

"Any idea who?"

"My bet would be on General Naguib. In that case the Beys and Shahs and even Farouk himself had better get their cash out while there is still time."

"Where does the wooden crescent fit into the picture?"

"It fits in like all the other crackpot groups, but it doesn't figure big. They haven't got the large popular backing of the Wafdist or the Brotherhood of Islam. Still, they represent the most fanatical elements in the country and if the British make some kind of a stupid blunder at this time anything could happen."

"I see." I lit a cigarette. "A guy like you would be pretty damned valuable to Downing Street at this moment."

"What the hell are you doing? Rubbing it in?"

"I didn't bring the cash," I said quietly.

His mouth fell open. Then it shut in a tight line. "Why, you rotten son of a bitch!"

"I didn't bring the cash," I said, "because I'm going to give you something much better."

He took a threatening step towards me. "It better be, damn it!"

"What I'm going to give you is all wrapped up and ready to deliver."

"Like where?"

"The British Legation."

He stopped. I saw the beginning of hope begin to flicker back in his eyes. It was good to see. I was glad that I had been first to see it.

"You're joking, Hart."

"No. You deliver what I give you and all will be forgiven."

"You don't know the brass!"

"On the contrary, I knew one important piece of brass very well. He's a good guy. From this minute you're working for him."

"I don't get it. I ..." He stopped. "You've been working out of London!"

"This is it. The missing British bomber is at an oasis about eighty miles southeast of Cairo. It is now in the custody of Hans von Bruckner."

The color drained from his face.

"My God! Von Bruckner ... that little louse, Havervard is working for him. But what in God's name does Von Bruckner want with one of our bombers?"

"That's for your superior officers to figure. Your little bombshell should be enough to satisfy them for one day."

"But it's incredible! Insane! The audacity of the man. Eighty miles from the capital? What the hell do you suppose it means?"

"I wish I knew. Mine is not to figure where or why. Now, this is the dope. I was given the name of an oasis called El Sha-en-Reb. Unfortunately there is no such place on any map. However, there can't be too many oases in a radius of eighty miles. Especially southeast of here."

"They'll laugh at me. They'll think I'm off my rocker."

"Insist on putting a call through to Lyon. This is the number and the name. Ask for Max. Tell him you've been working for me. They'll snap to then."

I wrote the number in Lyon on a piece of hotel stationery and handed it to Larson. He took it like a sleepwalker.

"Why are you handing this over to me, Hart?"

"Because I'm no longer working for any government. I have a job to do on my own. But I had an obligation. It will be fulfilled if you take this to the Legation."

"You're taking a chance. How can you be sure of me?"

"I'm sure Larson. I'm damned sure!"

His lip began to tremble and he turned from me. "It's a chance," he said in a muffled voice. "A straw ..."

"It will work. But now comes the gimmick. I want something from you."

"Anything."

"It has to do with Von Bruckner. The way I remember British legations the machinery won't get under way for hours. Check and double check. But I don't want Von Bruckner touched until after ten tonight. He's my baby. My own personal baby."

"But how?"

"I'll leave that to you. I know you can manage it."

"Yes," he said after a moment and it was good to hear the first sign of authority in his voice. Then he frowned. "I don't like the way you're talking, old boy. Like a chap who is making his last will and testament. Where can I reach you?"

I grinned. "Don't call me, I'll call you!"

"Muldoon ... I don't know how to thank—I don't know."

"Give my best to the lady. And to the White Cliffs—you'll be seeing them soon."

He followed me down the hall and from the top of the stairs began

calling his woman in an excited tone of voice. I passed her on the
landing and it gave me a kick to know that for once she was rushing
to hear good news. I hoped Larson wouldn't leave her behind if he
ever made his way back to tea at the Polo Club and lunch with the
vicar.

Out in the city the riots were beginning to simmer down. Across
Luna Square I saw several overturned cars still burning and a black
smudge hung low against an orange sky over the European section.
All that remained of the once glittering Shepheard's Hotel were
blackened walls. The military were much more in evidence, armored
trucks roared in and out of the streets opening off the square, foot
soldiers were dispersing demonstrators and now and again a shot
rang out in the dying afternoon. But beyond these activities an eerie
silence seemed to be descending on the city. Would the night,
marching in so swiftly from the desert, bring with it horrors even
more terrible than those of this bloody day?

In the midst of this desolate sunset scene it was startling to see a
battered old tram lazily coming down the Boulevard Fouad I from
the railroad station. Nearby, from an open doorway, a radio was
making shrill pronouncements in Arabic. A soldier turned from a
shattered shop front, saw me, raised his rifle threateningly. I ducked
quickly down a side street. Windows had been boarded up and
there was not a living soul down the whole length of the street. It
was like a thoroughfare in a nightmare. I got to the end of the street
and turned west toward the river. The orange sky was turning to
deep red. I hurried faster. Soon I was stumbling through a district
of incredible squalor and filth. Open sewers ran through the deserted
twisting alleys between crumbling yellow walls. Veiled women
clutching children whose eyes ran with disease watched my passing
with indifference. A mosque reared out of this garbage heap of
poverty and from its delicate minaret a white-robed figure was
wailing toward Mecca and the setting sun. For a few minutes I lost
my sense of direction completely. I was possessed of the near panic
of a child caught in some hopeless maze. An old man dumped a
bucket of slops from a second-story window, missing me by inches.
His laughter followed me, its cackle reverberating against stone until
I was out of his sight. Then, just as I thought I might have to
retrace my footsteps and make a new start I saw a glimpse of the
Nile, a tiny picture bright with the colors of sunset, far down at the
end of a long dark alley. In a few moments I had emerged from the
miserable ghetto to a street lined with wharves and warehouses.
Several blocks upstream was the Napoleon Bridge and beyond it,

looming dark against the lurid sky, the warehouse of the Tutankhamen Cigarette Company. This street, usually bustling with trucks and camels and draymen, was deserted. Where a main boulevard crossed it to the bridge a soldier stood guard. His back was to me. I moved in close to the warehouses, moved quickly, a mere shadow in the gathering dusk. The street lamps had not yet been turned on. When I was several yards from the soldier I ducked low and started across the boulevard. It wasn't until I was almost across that I heard the muffled shout. I didn't stop to listen. I kept right on, and fast, into the great shadow cast by the cigarette warehouse. There were no shots and after a moment the shouting died. It was very still now, ominously still.

I crept around the corner of the warehouse, slid down its width, came out on the water side. Down in the protective darkness under the pier I could make out the bulky silhouette of some kind of craft. I reached the end of the pier. Someone grabbed me from behind. I wheeled about. A rifle was level with my face. The guy behind it said something in Arabic. Knowledge of the language was unnecessary to know that I was being told to get the hell out. I tried to move back so that the last rays of the sun would not catch my face. He leaned forward and peered at me suspiciously.

He got a nasty expression on his face. I didn't feel too good. And then suddenly behind me someone whispered a few words in Arabic. The guy with the rifle hesitated, shrugged, lowered the gun and turned away. I was damned glad to see Phidias.

Silently I followed him out onto the wooden jetty. He went first down a slimy rope ladder. I followed him and dropped into an ancient, fat launch. It was grunting down there under the pier like an aged dog complaining at the order to rise. At the wheel was a villainous looking Arab. Phidias sank back on the wooden seat, said something fast and to the point, calmly lit a cigarette. The old Arab pulled a lever and there was a frightening sputter and then dead silence. Up above I heard footsteps running down the wooden jetty. The Arab pulled again and this time the old launch coughed once, twice, sputtered, caught again and then began to chug lethargically. I didn't think we would make it out of there in time. But the launch began to move, dragging behind it a little black skiff; moved in a majestic circle beneath the pier just as a leg came into sight, right above Phidias' head, on the rope ladder. With great deliberation Phidias reached up and tugged hard. The leg came spilling down with its body, arms askew, rifle flying off into the dusk. The guy didn't have time to shout before he hit the water.

Disdainfully the launch moved out from under the pier and began to grunt upstream. I moved my feet out of the bilge water and sat beside Phidias.

"It might be advisable to duck," he said.

It was. The shot splintered wood off the gunwhale. The old Arab didn't budge. The second shot went wild, zipping into the water several yards to the port side. By the time the third shot came dusk had moved between us and the pier. The little skiff, following at the end of a long rope, was like a duckling who never could quite catch up with its fat old mother duck. I sank back, took one of Phidias' cigarettes and lit up. Night was coming with swift smothering wings. Somewhere out across North Africa a red ball of fire was sinking down beyond the rim of the desert. Out here in the river it was suddenly very quiet.

"Thanks," I said. "Thanks, Phidias."

"Don't always be so certain," he said. "I have no magic lamp. Only my head. And my connections."

"It wasn't necessary for you to come."

"It's been a trying day. A nice cool sail on the river is just what I need."

I grinned. "How far up is Abureash?"

"About twenty miles. With luck we will be there by nine-thirty. This is the only way we'd get there. You can't go through the road blocks without a pass."

"Won't they be patrolling the river?"

"Yes. But the Nile is a wide road and dark. They have their hands full. River traffic must go on as usual. They won't stop everything with a hull. Especially if it's moving away from the city."

"This may be a one-way trip if things don't go right."

"I've always come home before," Phidias said. "My wife she will never forgive you if I am not in her bed before midnight. That woman! My God!"

I pointed to the Arab. "Who's the cutthroat?"

"My wife's cousin. Prides himself on being one of the best pimps in Cairo. Fine old family. Tonight won't be too good for his trade. He gave the girls a night off. He likes Americans. I told him you were the son of President Truman."

The lights of the city trailed off behind. Out in midstream we saw the occasional flash of red and green as a government launch prowled the main channel. But the Arab kept the launch close to the shore, so close that the bulrushes scraped against its decaying hull. My nerves began to unravel a little. Phidias gave me the latest bulletins. According to the grapevine Farouk was furious over the wanton destruction of his favorite hotel. For once even the army seemed somewhat impressed by his anger. Orders had gone out to shoot to kill. There seemed no immediate danger of a *coup d'état*. The handwriting was on the wall but apparently the king refused to read it correctly. Naguib was going to give the monarch another try. In the meantime, however, one false step from the British would start a conflagration that would be beyond the control even of the army. It was a time for breath-holding.

Soon Phidias stopped talking. The waters of the Nile whispered against the fat prow. Somewhere off to the left the pyramids of Giza rose from the cooling sands and not far away the Sphinx crouched, gazing off into the vast desert darkness toward the East. Out across the endless miles of rolling sand, robed figures moved with their camels as they had moved since the beginnings of recorded time, their lanterns bobbing like fireflies in the blessed cool of night. And out there, still further, were walled cities where the minds of men were sunk still in the Middle Ages. What had happened that day in Cairo was only a spark compared to the terrible fires that might be awakened in the hearts of millions of fanatical men.

And yet, at this moment, as we moved up the ancient river among the monuments to a long forgotten grandeur, as we moved, driven not by the fate of nations but my determination to avenge the heartless murder of a lonely French girl, I found myself thinking, not of the man I intended to kill, but of the woman with whom I was desperately infatuated. Gina, who fascinated me as no other woman before her. Gina, who was like some exotic bird caught in a silken trap, fluttering hopelessly toward the sunlight. Despite her surface sophistication there was something terribly lost about her, something tense and waiting. Something of the child, surrounded by a world of evil which she had never made. Nor understood.

Why had she become Von Bruckner's mistress, if indeed technically that was her role? Caught in Cairo without money, a profession or hope, she had seen in Von Bruckner a chance to ensure the future of the young brother she adored. I was fairly certain of this. Yet, even if this were not entirely true, even if her motives had been more selfish and mercenary, I was still helpless to resist the flame of a desire she had created in me. In a way I knew that my desire had no future beyond tomorrow. Should I live to escape the consequences of the act I contemplated, it was impossible to visualize Gina sharing my life. I could never hope to give her the surroundings and mode of existence she had come to accept with Von Bruckner. Yet logic didn't help. The thought of her smoldered hot beneath every other thought and action. Phidias brought me back to the urgent present.

"It is perhaps callous of me, but I must ask a vulgar question. What is it you are planning to do at the end of this delightful evening voyage?"

"You know Hans von Bruckner's houseboat?"

"Of course. The Golden Cloud. Everyone in Cairo knows it. It is the most luxurious private houseboat on the river except, of course, Farouk's."

"This is our destination."

"I am surprised. Usually it is anchored at the Royal Yachting Club just above the city."

"Tonight it is at Abureash. Somehow I must get aboard without being seen."

"His woman is aboard?"

"If you mean Madame Ferelli, yes."

"Then it won't be easy. At a time like this Von Bruckner will have his woman well guarded. Besides, she is a friend of the king's— between these two men she will have an iron guard."

"She expects me. Perhaps she'll manage."

"What! Surely you are not such a fool as to have warned her of your coming."

"I know what I'm doing!" I said angrily.

Phidias sighed. "I risk my life and reputation so you can try to climb into the bed of a—"

"Shut up! This isn't a pleasure trip. I have another job. Now listen. If the houseboat is anchored in midstream it may be difficult to get aboard. If it's tied up at some pier I'll manage. If I'm not back in a half hour, get the hell back to Cairo and forget you ever saw me."

"I forget easy."

"What is Abureash?"

"A heap of mud huts on the West bank. An odd place for a fashionable houseboat. Very odd ..."

We lapsed into silence once more. The launch seemed to be the only moving object on the vast expanse of the river. Occasionally the lights of a village huddled between the river and the rim of the desert slid past. The gigantic dome of the star-strewn night seemed to be expanding into infinity. Our craft seemed terribly small and impotent in the midst of the hush of darkness. The soft chug of the engine became hypnotic. I dozed off. I dreamed of a small cottage high over the coast of Maine. There was a woman in the house but I couldn't make out her face. Yet her movements were cool and sure and reassuring and vaguely, only very vaguely, familiar. Even in my dream I tried to obliterate her image. What was she doing there? It wasn't Gina.

A poke in the ribs awakened me. The engine had died to a gentle sputter. Phidias pointed out across the river to where a row of soft lights were reflected in the water.

"That's The Golden Cloud all right. But what the devil is she doing, anchored on the East bank?"

"Why shouldn't she be?"

"There's no village over there. Nothing."

"That's wise of Von Bruckner. Only a fool would keep that million-dollar affair near a village of poor natives in times like these."

We had gone upstream and now, with engine cut, were drifting down across the river current toward the gaily lighted houseboat. It was eerie, hearing suddenly the sounds of the Rosenkavalier waltzes drifting across the swift black river. When we were a couple of hundred yards upriver from the craft, the Arab slipped the anchor quietly overboard, close up to a high mud bank covered with bulrushes. It was extraordinary how noiseless were his operations. In the silence there was no sound but the distant music. Not even the suggestion of a breeze stirred through the reeds.

I looked at the illuminated dial of my watch. It was nine-twenty-five. Was Von Bruckner already aboard? One look at the dense undergrowth on the muddy bank convinced me that it was not feasible to approach the houseboat from the land. Anyway, that approach would probably be well guarded. I held a whispered confab with Phidias and he passed on the instructions to the phlegmatic Arab. The casual pimp pulled in the small skiff. Phidias whispered, "Where do you want the body sent?"

I said, "The Smithsonian Institute. Get back to your wife."

"I'll stick a while. Lovely view."

I lowered myself into the skiff and felt around for the small wooden paddle. The thing was as fragile as an eggshell but far more practical. I moved gingerly to the stern and squatted down. The river waters seemed about to pour over the gunwales. "Now," I whispered and Phidias let go his end of the rope. For a moment the skiff swung crazily about in the current, then I dug the paddle in deep, used it as a rudder, felt the boat lurch in the right direction, and started to bear down on The Golden Cloud more swiftly than I had counted on. Perhaps I imagined it but I thought I heard a soft whisper coming to me from the launch, "... luck ..."

Chapter Sixteen

The Golden Cloud would have done justice to Cleopatra. Bargelike, intended only for the Nile, she rested against the bank, white and gold, a wide hull built low in the water surmounted by a high superstructure, broken by glass doors and picture windows set in wide decks which were covered by scarlet awnings. In the low hull was a line of square windows, silk draped, emitting pink light just above the water. Across the stern on a wide deck which jutted out over the hull, several people were seated in comfortable chairs sipping drinks as a white-robed servant passed among them with a tray. The music of *Der Rosenkavalier* came apparently from a recording machine placed in one of the softly lit rooms which opened off the rear deck. The scene was fantastically dreamlike, a pauper's vision of ultimate luxury, divorced completely from the seething city twenty miles downstream or the ancient village huddled on the opposite bank.

All of this was absorbed in the brief minute while the skiff swept down from the launch toward the glittering houseboat. I saw also, with some satisfaction, that the port deck facing the river was deserted. I managed to bring the prow around in the powerful current in time to prevent a collision and grasped wildly for the stern anchor cable. I knew that if I missed, my chances of getting back upstream against the relentless river were slim. But for once my timing was perfect. The skiff tried for a moment to get out from under me as I hung on to the cable, then suddenly decided to cooperate and swung like a well-trained pet, close into the hull under the projecting stern. I got the slimy rope around the cable and held fast, listening for any sign of alarm. Up above there was only the music and the unintelligible murmur of polite conversation. Apparently no one had noticed the little skiff bearing down out of the darkness. Here under the projecting stern deck it was like a black cave but the houseboat was built so low in the water I had to keep my head low. I crouched there, thinking ahead to the next move.

The Golden Cloud was anchored firmly against the high mud bank. On top of the bank I could see an Arab standing, a few yards from the boat, leaning on a rifle. Fortunately his back was to me; apparently trouble was expected only from the land side. Beyond him, in a clump of river palms, was a jeep. The Arab looked relaxed.

I strained my ears trying to identify the voices above me. There had been time only for a glimpse of the stern deck; I had been unable to make out any of the faces. Now I heard merely a low babble of lethargic conversation. It was impossible to marry the sounds to any known face. I examined the rope that I held about the cable. It was not long enough to allow me to play it out very far. Using this method, I could at best reach only the middle of the barge. I figured, however, that that was about right. There, amidship the port deck, had been deserted. Further down near the prow must be the crews' quarters and I didn't fancy mixing up with any of Von Bruckner's guerrillas.

Carefully I began to play out the rope. The skiff behaved like a thoroughbred, swinging back into the current without a sound, whispering down across the stateroom windows where pink draperies were discreetly drawn. Then suddenly, almost directly amidship, there was no more rope. I took a deep breath and jumped up, grasping the mahogany rail. I felt the skiff slide swiftly out from under me. In a moment it would be swirling madly downstream toward Cairo. I pulled myself up, got one leg over the rail, and in the next moment made the deck. The people in the stern were out of sight, around the corner of the deckhouse. The port deck was deserted for the moment. I ducked in under the scarlet awning close to the wall and edged toward one of the glass doors. Inside was an exquisite sitting room, as extravagantly decorated as a luxurious town house, all pink and blue and gold. A servant came into the room from the rear deck, carrying an empty tray. I ducked back while he crossed to a door on the opposite side and disappeared. Once again the room was empty. I moved fast, got through the glass door into the room, crouched on all fours and made my way to one of the rear windows. The music was louder in here and I realized that it emanated from an expensive cabinet in the far corner. When I was directly under one of the silk-draped windows I got the Luger out and released the safety catch. Then carefully I inched up along the draperies, drew back a silken corner and peered out. There were four people on the rear deck; three men and a woman. The woman was Sigried McCarthy. Beside her sat Guido, looking more sullen than ever. The other two men had their backs to me but I saw at a glance that neither of them was Von Bruckner.

For a moment I had the eerie impression that Sigried was staring directly into my eyes. But, if so, she gave no sign. She turned and looked off toward the river and then with a nervous movement took a long swig of her drink. Here on the night of blood and death in Cairo, she wore a smart white dinner gown. She looked down into her glass. I could see that her hands were clenched tight about it. Guido lit a cigarette and looked impatiently at his watch.

Through the open window his voice was distinct. "Hans said he would be here by ten. It's almost that now."

One of the men whose back was to me got up and walked to the stern rail. "I heard the sound of a motor several minutes ago. I assumed it would be Herr von Bruckner's launch coming from Abureash. But now there is nothing. It is odd, no?"

His accent was German. I wondered if he was the mechanic with whom Jeremiah Grant had planned the split. If so I would have given a great deal to see his face when he heard that Jeremiah lay very cold and very dead in a position where he would never again cut in anyone on any deal. The fourth man reached for a cigarette on a glass table and as he did so his face came into profile for the first time. I recognized him immediately. I'd had that pink face, that round chin, the blond hair carefully combed into two unlikely waves, the pudgy hands, in my mind ever since the night the dragoman from Saudi Arabia had been murdered in the Café Noir. This was the guy I had tangled with in the alley back of the café.

He spoke now in a nasal voice that had in it more than a trace of Cockney. "He'll be here all right! I'm not worried. I think he had an appointment at the palace. If Farouk doesn't listen to reason he'll be one unhappy king come tomorrow."

The German at the rail said quickly, "Shut up!" He gestured toward Sigried.

The pink and blond Cockney got a cigarette between his lips. I noticed that his hands were shaking. "It doesn't matter...." he said with a thin bravado.

Sigried took another drink. "This party is damned dull!" She looked at the blond young man. "I don't think I like you. The fact that no one has even bothered to introduce you bothers me not at all. I prefer it that way."

"Call me Eric," the blond said.

Sigried said, "Not if I can avoid it."

"Sigried!" Guido's voice carried a petulant warning. The blond said, "Water off my back, dearie ... you're just another woman to me."

The German said, "Eric. Stop with the liquor. Hans will not approve. You have a job ahead of you."

"I'm best drunk. In and out of bed!"

Guido said, "Gina insists we wait dinner until Hans arrives. I'm starved. Sigried, how about a turn around the deck?"

I ducked back from the window, bent low, crossed the room to the door through which the waiter had disappeared. I found myself in a small foyer. On the opposite side, an arched door led into a mirror-lined dining room where a long table sparkled with linen and silver. In the center of the foyer was a gilt railing and steps leading downward. I descended quickly, holding the Luger ready. Below deck was a wide carpeted hall. Six white and gold paneled doors opened off the hall. I stood there trying to figure which door. I heard someone move in the foyer above me and then a smothered footstep on the stairs. That made the decision simple. I reached for the knob of the nearest door, pushed inward, stepped across the threshold and shut it softly behind me.

I was in a small but elegantly appointed sitting room. Light streamed through a door to the left. I stood very still, listening. The footsteps receded down the hall and were cut off by the click of a closing door. From somewhere came the sound of splashing water.

The scent of a delicate perfume—excitingly familiar—hung in the air. My pulse began to do double time. Luck had brought me through the right door. I took a deep breath and crossed to the threshold of the lighted room. I was certainly not prepared for the sight that faced me.

Before me was a fantastic bedroom, the walls of which were hung with green silk covered with boldly painted figures that might have stepped from one of the tombs of the Pharaohs at Thebes except that they were engaged in erotic activities more in keeping with some of the frescoes of Pompeii. The room was dominated by an astonishing bed, shaped like a boat, encrusted in gold leaf coming forward to a pointed prow that was surmounted by a serpent, rigid and erect, ready to strike. To the left of the bed, through a half-opened door, I saw a woman seated in a black marble bathtub. Even though her back was to me I knew it was Gina.

I stood there in the doorway, too stunned to move. The implications of this room were unmistakable. These were not the surroundings of a subtle woman whose favors were bestowed with discrimination. This was the bedroom of a slut, brazen and vulgar, underscoring the tastes and activities of its occupant with all the modesty of a Broadway neon sign. And the woman who chose to live in such blatant surroundings had played demure and hard to get with me for ten days. What a laugh she must have had!

But the anger that began to simmer to a boil was fused and finally obliterated by a stronger sensation, caused by the sight of Gina rising from the tub. The satin sheen of her back was still turned to me. She reached for a towel and lazily began to dry herself. Then she removed the plastic protector from her head and allowed the shining black hair to spill down her back. She turned now in profile, leaned back and vigorously shook her head. The line of her body was breathtaking. She turned and came out into the bedroom, discarding the towel on the pink rug.

The onrush of unreasoning desire made me dizzy. The discovery of Gina's true nature, revealed in that blinding moment when I first stood on the threshold of this erotic room, aroused in me an almost sadistic passion; a necessity to possess, to hurt, to violate. My real reason for being on this houseboat went swirling off into limbo.

Unaware of my presence in the doorway she stood before a mirror, reached for a perfume bottle, took out the glass stopper and touched it to the tips of her breasts. She smiled and drew the stopper down across her stomach as though it were alive. She half closed her eyes and brought her hips back in an unconscious and completely sensual movement.

I moved on her in a kind of hectic urgency. She wheeled about, eyes wide with fear. But almost instantly the fear died and even before I reached her it was replaced by an expression so primitive in its meaning that whatever sense I had left deserted me. Blindly she pushed aside the Luger in my hand. I'd forgotten that I held it. The gun went thumping to the rug unheeded. She laughed breathily and moved to the bed. She stood there for an instant, one hand resting on the golden serpent, eyes reflecting a smoldering challenge.

Neither of us said a word. Somehow I got out of the burnoose and then what happened was too dreamlike to recollect with any accuracy. I know that the gold seemed to reach out and envelop us and I remember the light dancing crazily on the rigid serpent. In this half world of contempt and desire the serpent seemed, by some trick of the light, to rise higher and higher until it was poised trembling for a white moment before it struck again and again into the depths of the room. And then I was aware of the arrival of a cold silence which carried in it the reek of perfume and the echo of her last whispered obscenity.

I pushed her away and sighed deeply.

She laughed. My head was throbbing and I became aware of another throbbing, very real and urgent; the throbbing of a powerful motor approaching very fast from the river. She left the bed and for a moment I felt as though I never would move again, as in a nightmare when one's feet refuse to budge before the sinister pursuer. Somehow I got out of the bed and struggled into my clothes. Yet, even caught as I was in a sort of fumbling panic, something caught and held my gaze, something very simple, really, that should not have had such a chilling effect. It was a bracelet flung among Gina's jewelry on the glass dressing table. A gold bracelet hung with tiny green pendants that must have been jade. It was the sparkle of the green stone in the electric light that brought back another picture, clear and sharp. Stone sparkling in sunlight. One of the green pendants was missing.

Mechanically I dug deep into my trouser pocket and brought forth the tiny object that had been there since early morning, forgotten in the stress of the day's events. I held it before me in my open palm. It caught and reflected the light and sparkled green.

And then, too late, I realized that Gina had come forth from the bathroom clutching about her a flimsy negligee. She was standing just inside the door, staring at my outstretched hand. Then she looked up directly into my eyes and what I saw there told me everything.

Told me too late. She swooped down and snatched up the Luger which was almost directly at her feet. I heard the safety catch snap.

Very quietly she said, "You will be good enough to return that bit of jade. It's worried me."

Chapter Seventeen

She meant business.

I flipped the pendant at her feet. She didn't bother to pick it up.

"I lost it last night in that boring nightclub."

The sound of the motor was now a roar. I felt nothing except an extreme weariness. I thought, everything I ever knew doesn't count. Neither of us had moved. She held the gun steady. After a moment I said, "Did you stick the knife in her throat yourself ... or was it one of your paid assassins?"

"I haven't the faintest idea of what you're talking about," she said coldly. "Not the faintest."

Outside the motor sputtered and died. I heard footsteps on the upper deck.

"That will be Hans," she said.

I indicated the rumpled bed. "Good. You may have trouble explaining that away."

She smiled derisively.

"How naïve! Hans has no interest whatsoever in my

divertissements as long as I don't poach on his territory."

"Just business, eh? Just cold, slimy, rotten business!"

"Yes. We understand one another. And one another's tastes."

"Convenient."

"Yes, isn't it!"

We eyed one another. I took a tentative step. The gun came up. I stopped.

"Why did you do it?" I asked. My voice sounded oddly disinterested, merely vague and curious. "What did Marianne ever do to you?"

"You're talking nonsense!"

"Was it because she might have revealed the fact that Von Bruckner is really Shmidt, a former waiter in a Munich café and one of Hitler's hatchet men? Was it because your social position was at stake? After all it's rather smart to be the mistress of a known sex criminal and worse, but a common waiter—never! Or was it merely business?"

Her chin went up. "I could use this gun, you know. No one would ever doubt it was anything but self protection."

"Why don't you?"

She hesitated. Then she said in a low voice, swift and urgent. "Hart! Stop being a stupid sentimental American. We can use you. I can use you in particular. Life can be exciting, Hart—with the blinkers off, I mean. The survival of the fittest on a de luxe scale. Power; I can give you anything if only—come—you're not a complete fool. What do you say?"

What I had to say was said in a few well-chosen words, pungent words, short words and to the point.

The hand tightened on the gun. I think if the door had not burst open at that moment she would have used it. As it was she looked beyond me and forced a smile to her lips.

Behind me Van Bruckner spoke. "Well! How very amusing!"

She shrugged. "It was, for a time, in a primitive, gauche, American manner. If you've ever had an American you'll know what I mean darling."

He laughed a staccato, explosive laugh.

"Is there anyone like you, my dear Gina? Cool like the cucumber. Good! You are better than cheese ... you have led the rat to the trap. Good!"

"Hans. I'm tired of holding this damned thing!"

Von Bruckner came into sight and took the gun from her, holding it on me almost indolently. He eyed the rumpled bed and leered at me.

"You have had more than you deserve, young man!"

"I've had better."

Gina went to the bed, sat on its edge, lit a cigarette and watched me with eyes as cold as marble. Von Bruckner ordered me to sit on the chair by the glass dressing table.

"What kept you so long Hans? I was worried!"

"I had a few uncomfortable moments. I was called to the palace and put through a few hours of annoying questions."

"What!" She snatched the cigarette away from her face and held it straight out.

"No need for alarm," he said coolly. "It seems a minor official named Fares Gebel had spread an absurd rumor about the palace to the effect that I had in my possession a British bomber! Ludicrous, is it not?"

"Well?"

"He could produce no proof. My friends near the King scotched it as pure fantasy. I was permitted to leave. When I left Gebel was still trying to reach General Naguib. He was accompanied by a man with whom he worked. A French government agent."

"A French agent?"

"Yes. I must say I was a little annoyed when I discovered the identity of this agent. For once I have been completely wrong. I think it will come as an unpleasant surprise to you also."

"Who?"

"None other than the charming, the deceptively irreverent Monsieur Armand Trouvier."

Gina dropped the cigarette to the rug. She ground it out with the heel of her slipper and leaned forward. "Hans! You're joking."

"I wish I were. Thank God I was never fool enough to take him into my confidence. I never did fancy Guido's friendship with him."

"Guido? Hans, you don't think Guido ...?"

"*Nein!* You must not even think such a thing, Gina. Guido is absolutely loyal to me. This I know. But perhaps he has been impulsive and weak and assumed that Armand was one of us. Fortunately the dear boy knows very little."

"I wonder.... Hans—" She stopped and looked at me. "Armand and this Gebel. Suppose they convince Naguib that it is not fantasy."

"It will be too late. In fact in five minutes it will be too late. Except for Eric and the mechanic there is no one on this boat who knows where the plane is or why—" He stopped.

"How stupid we were not to suspect Armand!"

I listened to all this with growing excitement. So this was the explanation of that interview in the Golden Horn Hotel. Gebel had been working with Trouvier. Probably doubling in brass. It seemed incredible that they had not been able to convince anyone connected with the government that Von Bruckner had a British bomber somewhere in the desert. If only I could discover where it was and what Von Bruckner intended to do with it before it was too late.

"The jeep is ready," Hans said. "I came only to say good-by. Tomorrow at this time we may be celebrating with champagne, perhaps even at the royal palace!"

"Hans! I don't like it. Suppose someone listens to them. Suppose they come up the river."

"I can depend on you to handle them. You simply know nothing. Time is all we need. After tomorrow it doesn't matter what they think or say."

He turned to me.

"And now ... this problem."

Gina stood. "Get rid of him. He will only cause trouble."

"Yes. I'll have Eric do the job."

He called out an order to someone in the hall.

As calmly as possible I said, "I will cause you more trouble dead."

Von Bruckner's eyebrows went up. "Impossible."

"You'd be surprised."

"What are you driving at?"

"Jeremiah Grant," I said.

"Grant!" The eyebrows came down like Samson's pillars. He looked out of the corner of his eye to Gina. "Has Grant been here this evening? I had an appointment with him here on the boat."

"Grant? Why no. I don't understand."

"He's not that much of a fool," I said quietly. "He sent me to negotiate."

Von Bruckner laughed. "Negotiate! That's good! The most he would get from me is a bullet where he needs it. He is a ludicrous amateur. You don't imagine I would fall for such a cheap blackmailing trick!"

"If I am not back in Cairo by seven A.M. Grant will go to the British Embassy with what he knows."

"What he knows is nothing!"

"I wouldn't be too certain. You see he had a very interesting chat with that Kraut. Your compatriot and mechanic, the guy who waits for you upstairs."

I'd guessed right. Von Bruckner took a step back. He blinked uncertainly.

"Benz!"

"Benz is right."

"Benz and Grant?" He thought about it a moment. What he thought he didn't like. "It is true. I know for a fact Benz once knew this Grant ... but I cannot believe he would be such an idiot. So! Benz!"

Gina came forward. "Hans! He's bluffing."

Von Bruckner looked uncertain. "It is possible. Still ... Gina, we have not time. Nothing they can do will stop us now. I have dreamt of this for two years, planned every move. Neither Armand nor Grant nor Benz nor this man ... no one will stop me!"

"No, Hans. Not now!"

"But if this blundering American is telling the truth he must be kept alive. Grant will not go to the British—not yet. But he will try to bleed us dry after. This man will lead us to Grant."

Gina didn't like this. "Hans, listen to me! You must get rid of him. Here is Eric. Let him do the job."

The blond guy with the round chin walked into the room. "You sent for me, sir?"

"Hello, Havervard, you son of a bitch!" I said coldly. "How much does a traitor get these days? As much as Hitler used to pay?"

He took a step forward. Von Bruckner intervened.

"The last time I saw you, Havervard," I went on, "was the other night back of the Café Noir. You weren't very convincing in that Arab outfit. Still ... you managed that knife trick almost as well as the lady does it."

"Pay no attention," Von Bruckner said. "Get back on deck. Have the jeep made ready immediately. We have a two hour desert trip ahead of us. Keep your eye on Benz until I come up."

"But I thought ..."

"Do as I say!"

"Yes, sir!"

Havervard clicked his heels and left the room.

"Now, Gina," Von Bruckner said in a businesslike voice, "I will leave two armed guards on the boat. Guido will be in charge."

"Guido! Hans, I—"

"You heard me, Gina. You are too harsh with the boy. I trust him absolutely. I will send him down here. The McCarthy woman will be locked in her stateroom. She has seen too much tonight and I doubt that she can be bought off. Eric will take care of her when we return."

"But Hans—the government—if they send a boat—"

"You will have warning. In that case Guido will see to it that Mr.

Muldoon and Mrs. McCarthy are, shall we say, liquidated? The river will take them out of sight before the government boat comes alongside. You and Guido can handle the rest!"

"As you say." She clasped her hands nervously. "Hans, are you certain everything will go as planned?"

"To the second. Tomorrow night Egypt will be in the hands of the Sons of Mecca. My job here will be finished. After that there is no limit!"

Was the guy really off his rocker? What in God's name could he do with a lone British bomber to bring about a situation where the Sons of Mecca would seize power? But there was something in his face and in Gina's that chilled me to the bone.

Muffled through the hull of the houseboat came the sound of the jeep warming up. From somewhere came a shrill whistle. Von Bruckner thrust the Luger into Gina's hands.

"You will keep this just to remind Guido. The dear boy is so impulsive."

She took the gun and pressed her lips tight.

"You and I will talk business tomorrow, Mr. Muldoon, that is if you're lucky."

"You're the one who needs the luck."

His parchment face tightened. "With me it is never luck. It is always the plan. You will understand tomorrow!"

He left the room. Gina cocked the gun in my direction. We waited. I heard the jeep open up. We listened to the sound of its motor dying in the distance. I looked up at her and said, "It's either me or you."

I started to rise.

"Abdullah!" she said sharply.

I whirled about a second too late. I saw only the white robe descending on me from the sitting room and the upraised arm. After that I saw nothing but infinite blackness.

Chapter Eighteen

The darkness had movement like billowing velvet. Then there was a pinprick of light. I opened my eyes. The first thing I saw was Gina sitting on the edge of the gold bed, a half-smoked cigarette in one hand, my Luger in the other. I managed to turn my head slightly. Bending over me was Guido.

"He's coming to."

Gina yawned and said, "That's too bad."

An Arab in a white robe forced some water down my throat. He was the guy who had hit me. I pushed myself up into a sitting position, my elbows dug into the pink rug. The effort sent my head spinning.

"A drink might help him," Guido said.

"By all means," Gina said. "Make it arsenic."

"Bring whisky," Guido ordered the Arab. The man left the room. I touched the back of my head and felt an egg there. If the Arab had hit any harder he would have cracked open my skull.

"Get the hell away from me," I said to Guido. "I'm all right." Guido's back was to his sister. He frowned. Was it meant to be some kind of warning?

"Concussion is an odd malady," Gina said. "You feel all right for an hour or so and then suddenly you keel over, quite dead."

I said, "I'm arranging this so it won't happen that way."

"You bore me," she said. "Get up and sit in the chair by the dressing table. That is if you can get up."

I managed it without groaning. I just managed though. The chair rose up to meet me.

"For God's sake, Gina!" Guido said angrily. "Pull that negligee around you. You're sitting there like a—"

She laughed. "My, how modest! Remember, my dear, when you were thirteen? You used to be co-operative in those days. Remember how shocked my husband was when he walked in that afternoon?"

"Shut up!" he said harshly.

"Lorenzo shocked so easily. Ah well ..."

I felt my flesh crawl. I didn't want to hear. The expression on Guido's face was open hatred. I didn't want to see it or think of what it meant. Guido reached for a champagne glass he had apparently brought with him from the upper deck. I looked at my watch. It was ten after eleven. Guido threw me a cigarette. I lit it with shaking fingers. Time was running out.

The Arab brought me the whisky and left the room, shutting the door behind him. I downed it in one gulp. I began to come to life. Had I misinterpreted the expression on Guido's face? I looked at him. He was deeply interested in his champagne glass.

"The American is shocked," Gina said.

Sullenly Guido said, "Everyone isn't born a Vencelli. Everybody isn't born poisoned!"

Gina laughed. "How melodramatic, my dear Guido. I'm afraid your association with French spies has instilled in you an unbecoming morality."

"French spies?" But the surprise on his face was obviously simulated. I began to hope.

"Your great hero, Armand Trouvier. The one who was going to make a man out of you. Or some such rot!"

"Armand a spy? What the devil are you talking about, Gina?"

Gina regarded him with malevolent disdain.

"I don't happen to share Hans' weakness for you, my pretty one," she said scathingly, "I know you too well! You've been playing a dangerous game. It's lucky for you Hans is so blind. As usual I will cover up. You see, it's too late for your hero to play superman. Much too late."

"I don't know what you're talking about."

"Wouldn't you like to know where Hans has gone and what he will be doing in a few hours? Wouldn't it be charming to rush down river with the news for Armand? Well, forget it! Come to your senses and listen to me."

Guido tilted back his glass, said nothing.

"What a damned little fool you are! Almost throwing everything away! You don't deserve all that I've done for you!"

Guido laughed unpleasantly. "Ah, yes. I'm apt to forget all you have done for me, Gina! Are you referring to the night just after Lorenzo died, when Hans came to dinner for the first time? Are you referring to the discreet manner in which you left me alone with him after dinner? Surely I couldn't be so ungrateful as to forget that night. After all it was my fourteenth birthday!"

"Fourteen!" I said. "That seems to be his favorite age."

"It is!" Guido said and spat.

"Oh come, come," Gina said mockingly. "At fourteen you were already very wise. Very wise. After all we are the same family. That you can't escape. You had four hundred years of wisdom behind you."

"And fourteen years of excellent tutelage. You were a thorough teacher, Gina."

"I don't know what's got into you! You bore me!"

She stomped out her cigarette, reached for another on the small table at the head of the bed. In that unguarded moment Guido was up and across the room. He took the gun from her almost before she realized what had happened. He backed away. She snapped her head up, trying to keep the panic from her eyes.

"Guido! What are you doing?"

"Hans left me in charge," he said quietly. He went back and sat down, reaching for the champagne glass with one hand, holding the Luger ready with the other.

Gina sat very stiff now on the edge of the bed. She drew the negligee about her as though for warmth. She forced a smile to her lips.

"You're drunk," she said.

"Yes. I wanted to tell you. I've been working with Armand. I've supplied him with everything I know about the Sons of Mecca!"

The smile stayed fixed. "My God! You sit there and calmly admit this to me!"

"Why not? I have the gun."

Slowly the smile died. She narrowed her eyes, looked from Guido to me, swiftly, then toward the door beyond.

"It's no use, Gina," he said almost sadly. "I told Abdullah to stay close to the stateroom in which poor Sigried is locked."

There was a tense silence.

Slowly I got to my feet.

"Tell him to sit down!" Gina cried sharply.

Guido said nothing. I took a step toward her.

"Guido! Without me you're nothing—nothing at all. These Armands and their like, they will do nothing for you!"

I took another step. Slowly Guido lowered his gun.

"We're sick, Gina," he said in a dead voice. "You were born sick and you made me sick too. Armand taught me what it might be like to be well."

"You're mad! You've been hypnotized. You can't change, Guido, you never will. I know—I—"

She threw herself backward across the bed. My whole weight came down on her hard. She twisted from beneath me, half fell to the rug, scrambled to her feet. I reached out, got hold of the negligee and jerked back. There was a ripping sound as the garment tore loose. She lost her balance, my hands clutched her thighs and I pulled with all my strength. She came toppling back onto the bed. She fought now like an animal, her breath hissing from her in terror. Her fingernails slashed down across my cheek, dug in, held, ripped the flesh away. I managed to get her arms in a tight grip, rolled over on top of her, pushed myself up on my knees, straddled her, shifted my hands purposefully to her throat. Her legs and arms flailed out wildly. And then, quite suddenly, she stopped fighting. She lay there very still, eyes wide with resignation, looking up at me. I relaxed my grip.

"Yes, I will tell ... anything ... anything. Only you will not harm me ... and you will tell the authorities I have nothing to do with Hans' business."

Looking into her eyes I lied. "Yes," I said.

"Oh, Hart...."

"Go on. Talk. Fast."

She rolled her eyes towards Guido, then closed them.

"Hans ... he ... he has the British bomber."

"Where?"

"Somewhere in the desert.... I do not know."

"You're lying." My fingers found her throat again. Her head came around. I relaxed the hold.

"All right—I will tell. Only please ..."

"Well?"

"It is at the Oasis of Neifer."

"Then there's no such place as El-Sha-en-Reb?"

"That was the ancient name. It hasn't been in use since the Turks left. The Arab from Saudi Arabia knew only the old name."

"So that's why we couldn't find it on the map! All right, what's he going to do with this bomber?"

"Hart, you promised. You will not let them harm me?"

I lied again. "I promise!"

She looked at me intently. Then an odd expression came into her eyes. A sort of hopeless realization and with it relief.

"He has a crew—the Englishman, Haververd, and the German and four others. They take off at dawn on a mission."

"What is the mission?"

She closed her eyes and whispered, "They will drop their bombs on the holy city. On Mecca."

I was so astounded I loosened my grip. She made no effort to wriggle free. She lay there waiting.

I managed to say, "Mecca! But my God, why?"

In a dead voice she said, "Surely you must see? It is a British bomber. It will go into the city flying low. Thousands will see the markings of the plane. All that will be known is that a British bomber dropped its bombs on the holy city. Any explanations the British will make after, will sound incredible. The whole Arab world will rise; the moderates will be thrown from power; the Sons of Mecca will take over in Egypt and elsewhere!"

"It's the dream of a madman!"

"Perhaps. Hans planned it all. Even his Arab confreres know nothing. It will work."

And suddenly I knew she was right. This incredible deception would set off one of the bloodiest holy wars in history. A red sea of fanatical revenge would sweep throughout the Middle East. The diabolical scheme engendered in the mind of a paranoiac might actually plunge the world into a global war.

I looked at Guido. He was staring fixedly at his champagne glass.

I believe at that moment, despite my determination to avenge the heartless murder of Marianne Courbert, Gina might have escaped the consequences of my blind rage. But her next words were like a death sentence, self-imposed. She looked at me and said something incredibly obscene. And laughed.

A kind of black insanity closed about me. My fingers dug into her throat. She didn't fight until almost the end. Then at the last minute she tried feebly to tear away my hands. Finally the last horror died in her eyes. They became fixed on space. Her mouth sagged open. There was a dreadful gurgling sound and then nothing.

My hands fell away. They ached. In death she was still beautiful but already there was about her something corrupt and reeking of the grave.

I got off the bed. I was sobbing. Guido hadn't moved. The gun lay inert on his knees. I took it from him. He looked up at me.

"When we were children," he said, "we used to play on the terrace of my aunt's villa at Rapello. Gina was twelve. I was six. I had a pet dog. I loved this dog, this little cocker spaniel named Nichi. She killed it. She wanted to have a funeral with a Black Mass. My aunt thought it amusing. I thought everyone in the world was like Gina. I'm tired...."

"Get up," I said harshly. "Open the window."

"I thought all the world was filled with people like my aunt and Gina and Hans von Bruckner. I didn't expect anything else until I met Sigried and Armand."

I pulled him to his feet. I got the wide window open. It was just above the water line. He held the window open as I went back to the bed. Gina's body was terribly light. I didn't look again at her face. I got her through the window. She slipped into the Nile without a sound. One stiff hand whirled for a moment in the black waters, then was gone. Guido let the window slam back into place. He leaned up against the wall.

"She worked for Hitler during the war. She wanted power. She never loved anything nor anyone in her life. Everything she touched turned to evil ... everything we touch ..." He stopped and passed his hand over his forehead.

Out in the river I heard a growing buzz, the sound of boats, not one but several, roaring towards us. Guido didn't seem to hear. He looked at the crumpled bed, kicked out at the empty champagne glass on the pink rug and without another backward glance, left the room.

Chapter Nineteen

There hadn't been much of a fight. The crew and Von Bruckner's guerillas were taken by surprise, turning to Guido for orders and realizing, too late, that the orders would never come. The gray government launches descended out of the darkness and from them erupted a cataract of olive drab. One of the Arab guards received a leg wound, and a French chef who maintained the artist's neutrality got an arm broken for his innocence. But by midnight The Golden Cloud was firmly in the hands of the small military contingent under the command of none other than Fares Gebel.

At one A.M., I lay sprawled on a sofa in the pink and gold lounge, weary almost to the point of indifference. Cool and chic, apparently immune to crime, treason, and gunplay, sat Sigried McCarthy, her chair drawn close to me. Guido stood with his back to the room, gazing out into the river, talking over his shoulder. Phidias and his disreputable relation by marriage, the Arab who had piloted us up the river, were on the far side of the room, retrieved by the law from the fat old launch and doing very well on Hans von Bruckner's Scotch.

Fares Gebel, flowering in his moment of recognized authority, stood stage center playing to an imaginary audience while a thin young Egyptian in an expensively cut uniform took notes at the white and gold desk. Outside on the deck I could see the backs of soldiers standing guard against the sinister desert darkness.

Guido had just finished his statement.

There was a moment's silence. Then Gebel said, "The facts seem to check with what we have already learned from Monsieur Trouvier."

"Where is Armand?" Guido asked.

"He was scheduled to be at the pier of the river patrol at ten-thirty. We could not wait longer. Apparently he was delayed by other business."

Wearily I asked, "What's holding up the show, Gebel? Time won't wait for official reports. Von Bruckner plans to take the bomber up at dawn."

Gebel looked anxiously at his watch. "The trucks are to be ferried across the river from Abureash. They should be here now."

"Why trucks? A couple of army planes are what you need."

Gebel looked away and lit a cigarette. "I will handle this, Mr. Muldoon. We are grateful to you for the bit of information you have supplied, but...."

"Bit of information! I've only given you the exact location of the plane! Without it you were helpless."

"I'm certain that His Majesty's government already has this information."

"The hell they have!"

Gebel's lips tightened. "You might have avoided a great deal of trouble this afternoon, Mr. Muldoon, if you had given me that information in our interview at the Golden Horn."

"I didn't have it then. Besides, how did I know that you were doubling in brass? How was I to know you were working for the French?"

The thin young man taking notes looked up at Gebel in surprise. Gebel flushed. "I work only for His Majesty's government, Mr. Muldoon. You have had enough fantastic notions for one day."

I laughed. "That means Farouk stays on for a while, eh? You're on the winning side as usual."

"You are impertinent!"

Sigried said softly, "For God's sake, shut up, Hart."

I was too beat up to care. "Come down to our level, Gebel. You couldn't get an air-force plane. You couldn't even get a detachment. All you could manage was a handful of green trainees. That's all they would spare you. They don't believe the story of the captured bomber. They think maybe you're sick. But they're willing to give you a chance. If you can prove your point you'll be hot with any new government His Majesty may form. Between the roulette tables, of course!"

"I have been very patient with you, Muldoon. It is within my power—"

"I've heard that record before. You better see what the hell is keeping your boy scouts. If they don't get their tender little fannies moving pretty damned quick you'll never reach the oasis in time. As it is—"

"I'm in charge here!" he shouted. Phidias took a swig of Von Bruckner's liquor and grinned. Gebel, suddenly a not too convincing military figure, strode toward me.

"Now then, there are some things that puzzle me. One thing in particular. Von Bruckner's men, whom we now hold below deck, claim that Madame Ferelli was aboard this houseboat and that she never left it. Yet we find no trace of her."

Before either Guido or I could say a word, Sigried spoke up very coldly. "I'm terribly worried about Gina, Mr. Gebel. I'm terrified that ..."

"That what?"

"Well you see ... Mr. Muldoon and Guido and myself were having a drink in the main lounge when Von Bruckner went down to see Gina, just before he left. He was very angry about something." She turned wide and innocent eyes to me. "You remember, Hart? You were disturbed about it."

I grunted something that Gebel took for assent.

Guido said, "Von Bruckner was jealous of Hart. He thought that Hart and Gina—"

"He probably thought right," Gebel said. "Then what happened?"

"He came up after a few minutes," Sigried said. "We all noticed that he was very pale and tense. Almost immediately after, he and his crew set off in the jeep. Gina didn't come up ... I assumed that she was dressing for dinner. And then before any of us had a chance to go down, you and your men appeared."

Gebel looked from one to the other of us. There was open skepticism on his face. After a moment he said, "The large window in her stateroom has been opened. I'm afraid Madame Ferelli has been murdered."

"How sad," Sigried said, without the slightest emotion.

"Three witnesses," I said. "You'll have to accept it, Gebel."

"We shall see about that!" he said. But there was no conviction in his words.

At last we heard the loud complaining chug of the tug approaching the east bank from Abureash. Gebel signaled Guido to follow him out on deck. The thin young secretary gathered up his notes and left the room.

Phidias stood and yawned. "I have been ordered to stay on the houseboat until morning. My wife will never forgive you, Hart. I will now get some sleep. Such comfortable beds downstairs."

He jerked his thumb at his wife's villainous-looking cousin and they walked toward the foyer. On the threshold he turned.

"You need a rest cure, Hart. No more politics for a while. No more hunting, no more women."

When he had gone Sigried lighted a cigarette and said coolly, "No more women? He's an optimist."

"At the moment he's dead right!"

"How unfortunate."

I gave her a sharp look. "Goddammit, don't start—"

She laughed. "I'm not starting anything, my dear Hart, not yet. I'm not that much of a fool."

"Thanks," I said, and stood. I stretched and yawned. "It looks like we will be kept here until they get back from the desert, if they do get back. I'm going to close my eyes for a couple of hours and forget."

The look she gave me made me feel uncomfortable. I started for the foyer.

"Hart."

Impatiently I turned. What I saw surprised me. She was standing, her arms at her sides, her mouth trembling, tears in her eyes.

"Well?"

"What kind of a dreadful world are we in that makes us into murderers?"

"Shut up!" I said harshly.

"I'm as guilty as you," she said. "It's something we will always share, that secret. We have our guilt, you and I—it's a sort of bond."

"I don't want to hear—" And then I stopped. It came over me that she was right. What bond could be stronger than that of the secret of murder? Grant and Gina, both dead by my hand. Could I ever calmly shut them out of my mind? Could I ever really justify having taken revenge into my own hands?

And when I thought of Marianne I suddenly thought, yes, yes. And then, perhaps.

We stood looking into one another's eyes, silent in our secret knowledge, and I suddenly saw her not as efficient and cold and heartless, but a woman alone and terrified, hiding her true nature in a protective shell.

Whatever road my speculations would have taken was suddenly blocked by Gebel appearing in the doorway.

"Come on," he said curtly.

"Where?"

"You will come with me to the oasis. I need every man I can get!"

"Listen. I've done a job tonight. I'm finished."

"Not yet! This is a command."

"Ah, I see. Afraid I'll get back to Cairo with a scoop. Afraid I'll steal some of your thunder."

"Mr. Muldoon! You will come immediately."

I shrugged and went with him from the room without another glance at Sigried. I didn't want to see what was in her eyes; not now.

Two small tractor trucks had been transported across the river on a flat barge towed by a river tug. They were now near the same clump of palms where Von Bruckner's jeep had stood. I got into the front seat of the leading truck beside the driver. Gebel squeezed in next to me. Four young soldiers were seated across the wooden seat behind us. In the second truck were three more soldiers. Except for a Tommy gun the only weapons visible were rifles. Three men had been left behind to guard The Golden Cloud and its prisoners locked now below decks. I grinned as I saw Phidias and his wife's cousin being dragged, protesting, into the second truck. Someone shoved a rifle at me. I pushed it away and drew forth the Luger I had retrieved from Gina's room. Guido, remote and very straight, came down the gangplank like a dream-walker and got in beside Phidias.

It was almost two A.M. when we finally nosed off to the east. Soon we were bumping along the hard gravel-like surface of the desert, no billowing soft sand like the Hollywood desert; here in the headlights there was even a semblance of sickly vegetation. Soon that disappeared and there was nothing but endless darkness and stony emptiness. I would have given a great deal to know how the hell the driver knew where he was going. I lit a cigarette. The drowsiness left me. I wondered how many men Von Bruckner had out at that oasis and whether our handful of untrained men could prevent his taking off. If we arrived in time.

We rattled along for what seemed hours. To the east was the first flush of dawn. My nerves began to jump. We hit a bump, bounced high, almost overturned. Gebel cursed. The headlights behind us leaped crazily, swerved to the left, froze on a steady beam to the north. Gebel gave a sharp command. We wheeled and circled back to the second truck. It listed to one side like a foundered ship. Guido and Phidias and the young soldiers were picking themselves up from all around the wrecked vehicle. It didn't need an expert mechanic to see that the front axle was busted.

Exasperated, Gebel shouted to Guido and Phidias to come with us. There wasn't room for more. The two men leaped aboard and we left the others staring helplessly at the disabled truck. It must have been a lonely feeling, watching our lights disappearing off to the east.

The terrain became more sandy, a great sea of long rolling hills. The dawn was coming up too damned fast. I began to think we wouldn't make it. Up ahead, as far as the eye could see, was a great gray-pink expanse of nothing.

And then we suddenly topped a small rise. Before us was a wide valley and in the center of the valley was an oasis. It was completely dark but we could see the shadows of low buildings clustered tight among the palms.

"This is it," Gebel whispered.

I thought he was nuts. There wasn't a sign of life. But almost as I opened my mouth to tell him so, I saw a great batlike shadow, moving slowly across the flat tableland on the opposite side of the oasis. It had to be the bomber. I knew that we would never make it in time. The oasis was a good four miles distant. Gebel shouted at the driver to put on more speed. We rocked down a sandy hillside hanging tightly to whatever we could find. I was filled with a sudden sense of helpless anger. We weren't going to make it.

And then suddenly someone clutched my shoulder from behind. I whirled about. Guido was bending close, his face turned upward, pointing with the other hand. I looked up. There, coming low across the desert, coming like a jeweled dart, was a plane, glittering silver in the first rays of the sun. But my first feeling of elation was dashed. This was no bomber, no fighting plane, it was a single-seater racing plane.

"Armand!" Guido cried. "It's Armand's plane." Fascinated, we watched it as it came on directly at us, swooped low in a kind of salutation, then rose almost straight up into the pink sky.

Puzzled, I looked toward the bomber. She had turned and was lumbering across a makeshift runway, gathering speed for the take-off. Gebel shouted something. We came to a sudden halt. The motor was cut. We sat there in the silence, watching the silver plane mount higher and higher into the sunrise. Then, when it seemed that she would continue into space, she suddenly turned and began to plunge toward the earth.

"She's out of control!" I cried. But something in Guido's set face silenced me. I watched, my stomach falling with the silver plane, falling, falling through the sunrise toward the desert. It wasn't until the very last minute that I realized the truth. She fell straight as an arrow toward a goal, fell deliberately and with plan. She struck the great bomber just as it was leaving the ground, struck it directly in the center.

First there was a great ball of fire and then seconds later the sound of the explosion. At that moment, another ball of fire edged up over the eastern horizon. Its red rays fell on the remains of the two planes, mere smoking rubble scattered over a quarter mile of desert. No one in either plane could have survived.

In the dreadful silence that had ended Von Bruckner's evil dream I was aware of Guido sobbing.

I heard my voice croak, "Why?"

"She was Armand's sister," he said brokenly.

"She ... who?"

"Marianne," he said.

In the vastness of the desert the tiny figures scattering like ants from the palms of the oasis ran aimlessly, without purpose, off into space.

Chapter Twenty

It was four days later when Max saw me off on an American Export Liner at Alexandria. He had flown in from Paris the day before, as laconic and soft-spoken as ever. He came aboard and we found the ship's bar for a farewell drink.

"Next time we expect you to bring our planes back intact!" he said with a grin.

"There will be no 'next time'!"

"I seem to have heard that before."

"This time I mean it, Max."

He toyed with his drink. "Maine? The cabin? The dog? Thinker with a pipe?"

"Damned right."

He looked innocently down into his glass. "Very touching."

"What's so damned funny, Max?"

"Funny?" He stopped grinning and looked me in the eyes. I was startled to find a shadow of bitterness there. "On second thought, it's not a bit funny old chap, I suppose it's rather sad."

"Sad? In what way?"

"Sad that at your age and with your experience you should still carry with you the delusion that you can return to decent society."

"I don't get it."

"Don't you, Hart? I'll try to explain. You and I—we belong outside. We belong to the hunters and the hunted. We belong to a world of violence and deception, a world that makes its own laws. We lie and we steal and we kill because it is our job to do it. And you can't go back, Hart, you simply can't go back."

Suddenly the vision of Jeremiah Grant sprawled on Sigried's pink rug and Gina Ferelli's body slipping through the window of the barge into the black Nile rose up before me. I tried to shake it off. I gulped down my drink.

"This is one baby that is going back," I said. "I've had enough!"

Max shrugged. "Time is on my side," he said cynically.

I ordered another drink and changed the subject as quickly as possible.

"What about Larson?"

"Touchable again. Next month he'll be back on a desk job where he belongs, in London."

"Good."

"He's marrying some woman he knows out here. A Viennese, I believe."

"Glad to hear it."

Max took a swig of his drink. "Tell me, Hart, old boy—Did Hans von Bruckner really throttle his lady love?"

I looked him in the eye. "I think I'll have another drink," I said.

"And the demise of our old friend Jeremiah Grant. Is it really true as the official report has it—death at the hands of person or persons unknown during the civilian riots?"

"Make it a double Scotch, waiter," I said, disregarding Max.

After the waiter had gone he shrugged. "Fares Gebel seems satisfied. Now that he has a position of some importance I suppose that's all that matters. Except, of course, for those bad dreams at night."

"Shut up, Max!"

"Sorry, old boy."

He downed the rest of his drink and stood just as the warning whistle came for visitors to go ashore. I finished off the double Scotch and walked with him to the head of the gangplank.

"I suppose you know," he said casually, "that this ship stops on the Riviera before heading out into the Atlantic toward New York."

"What of it?"

"Do you really think you will make it past the Casino at Cannes?"

"I'll stay locked in my stateroom while the ship is in port."

"I wonder," he said mockingly.

We shook hands. Something in his expression made me uneasy. He moved to the top of the gangplank. "Matter of fact I am flying up to Cannes day after tomorrow. If you do come ashore, look me up at the Carlton. I have a job that might interest you."

"The hell you have! You've seen the last of me right now, Max. Never again."

For answer he smiled, turned and walked sedately down the gangplank toward the pier. I watched him saunter off into the crowd. I felt suddenly depressed. There was something in the back of my mind—something or someone—that had been with me for the past two days. I needed another drink.

The bar looked cold and cheerless. After a couple of more Scotches I went down to my stateroom.

Sigried McCarthy was sitting on the edge of my berth. "What the hell are you doing here?"

She smiled. "It's a free world. At least this part of it. I'm going to the States."

"In my stateroom?"

"Don't be absurd. I have a perfectly good stateroom of my own on B deck. But I met you first in your stateroom if you remember. I thought ..."

"Who told you I was aboard?"

"Phidias. He came to my shop yesterday. My last day there. I've sold out to a courageous Italian. Phidias thought you might need me."

I slammed the door behind me.

"What kind of routine is this? What are you up to?"

"I think it's quite obvious what I'm up to," she said calmly. "When I make a decision I stick to it."

"Listen, Sigried—"

"Why fight it, Hart?"

And suddenly looking down at her, it came over me that her question was perfectly sensible. But she warded off my next move.

"No, Hart, not like that. I want you to understand something. I love you. You've brought me back to life. I've been dead, really, since ... since all that terrible business in Tangier. I love you but—"

"But what?"

"I could only continue loving you if you really mean to go back to the States and stay there where you belong. I couldn't face a life of uncertainty, of threat and violence and death. I've had too much of that."

"Who asked you!" I said angrily. "You're assuming a helluva lot."

She smiled. "I'm not conceited. I'm merely a woman. But I know."

"Well, you'd better know this then," I said. "I don't intend to play house. Even with you."

"Why not, Hart?"

The anger left me. The uneasiness returned. "Face it, honey. I'd give any woman a hell of a time."

"I could take my chances."

"Is this a proposal?"

"Yes," she said. "On the condition that you settle down in the States and give up your past life altogether."

I lifted her to her feet and began to unbutton the jacket of her suit.

"No, Hart. I mean it."

"Sure you do, honey...."

I got the jacket off. She stopped resisting. There was the soft sound of the zipper down the side of her silk blouse.

"Oh, Hart, if you could only be—"

"Sure," I said. "Sure."

She gasped and pressed close to me, her hands answering frantically to my touch. "Oh, darling," she whispered, "I'll see that you make it home this time."

Through the porthole I saw the last of Egypt, a thin line on the edge of the sea. I thought, maybe she's right. Maybe I will make it this time. Maybe it's the end of wondering, the end of nightmares. Even as the thought went through my mind, her lips pressed on mine, speaking not of death but of life and this moment. The past days went swirling off, a mirage in a sandstorm, and once again only the present had any reality. Yet the edges of this present were touched by a dim future where, as in a vision, I seemed to see the face of Max, smiling like a satyr, smiling skeptically, smiling and waiting. Waiting.

THE END

Dear, Deadly Beloved

By John Flagg

Chapter One

THE VILLA ROSA, 9:05 P.M.

The knife—one of those exquisite little stilettos manufactured with loving care in Sicily—lay at the edge of a red stain, slow-spreading on the worn carpet, and just beyond it was the body of a dead man. I stepped in across the threshold and automatically shut the door behind me. Someone had left on the electric light, a dusty, dim-burning bulb under a faded pink shade upheld by a sleazy cupid. Downstairs in Mamma Peroni's bar, almost directly under my room, Pietro was singing softly to his concertina. The tune was plaintive and only half resolved, a decadent echo of the Neapolitan streets and beyond that Greek antiquity, infinitely self-pitying, infinitely sad.

I leaned back against the door, closed my eyes, and tried to think. Now at the tail end of a long binge, it wasn't easy. Yet, even though many hours of the past three days were blacked out of my memory, I was fairly certain that this had nothing to do with me. When I kill a man I make it a point to be sober.

It was damned inconvenient.

The timing couldn't have been worse. Only twenty minutes before I had finished a heart-to-heart talk with *Signor* Ferechini, *Comandante* of the local *carabinieri* and symbol of what little law and order was permitted on the island. He had been patient but firm. It wasn't that he objected to my singing four choruses of the unex-purgated version of "Frankie and Johnnie" on the steps of the Mayor's home just before the last dawn; he had been quite willing to concede, without benefit of translation, that the song was a lyric hymn to better American-Italian relations. After all, the island was prepared to accept the eccentric behavior of crazy Americans and mad Britishers in the sacred name of Tourism. But now that Venzola was fast becoming a retreat for what is loosely termed "the international set" and even had made inroads into the lucrative trade of the neighboring island of Capri (visible on clear days far across the bay of Naples), my uninhibited performance could be condoned only if I had the bank account of a rich patron to justify it. Ferechini had made it a point to unearth the depressing fact about my financial status. It hadn't been too difficult for him. It was quite apparent that no well-heeled tourist would have an address such as the Villa Rosa in the somewhat disreputable Via Cellini. With exquisite Italian subtlety the good Ferechini had made it quite clear that my presence on the lovely island of Venzola was not desired and, in fact, any further transgressions would result in a fast one-way ride by government launch across the bay to Naples. I didn't want to leave Venzola just yet.

My reason was named Elsa Planquet, wife of a crazy French film director who lived in a pink villa up on the mountain. Elsa's talents as an actress were the least of her attributes. As far as I could remember, I had already established a more or less firm beachhead on the threshold of her bedroom, and with proper strategy in the next day or so should be able to take the capital. It didn't suit my battle plans to leave the island yet.

The unpleasant development on my bedroom carpet didn't help matters. Ferechini was in no mood to listen to reason. Tolerance of crazy Americans did not extend to murder. I had an idea that any explanations on my part would be after, not before, the handcuffs. At the moment I was a sitting duck for Ferechini. Someone had played me for a patsy.

I didn't think about it long. I opened my eyes. The guy was still there, of course, as decisively dead as ever, half turned on his side, facing me, one leg buckled up under him where he had fallen. The eyes were fixed in an expression of childish wonder. He had olive skin, dark eyes, black hair, but I knew he was not an Italian. He was stolid and square-built with something of the East European peasant about him. He wore a lightweight dinner jacket—cut much better than the one I had managed to get into before Ferechini's men had come for me—and mixed with the odor of death was the scent of expensive lotions. He appeared to be—or to have been—in his middle thirties.

I crossed, bent down, fished around in the inside pocket, and retrieved a thin gold cigarette case and a wallet. Inside the wallet were five thousand lire, membership cards to the Lake Michigan Yacht Club, the Midwest Engineers Club, and the Detroit Athletic Club, and a Social Security card. They all gave an address in Grosse Point, Michigan, and were made out in the name of Georges Hertzy. Of more immediate interest was a sheet of pink stationery from the swank Hotel Miramar up on the hill, on which was written one sentence: "Hart Muldoon is your man." The handwriting was small, neat, tight, and the "t" was crossed with a miserly horizontal line that was nearer to a dot than a bar. I stuffed the pink paper with my name on it into my own pocket, replaced the wallet and cigarette case, stood, lighted a cigarette, and thought about it some more. "Hart Muldoon is your man." Who had given me the cryptic reference? "Your man" for what?

The name of Georges Hertzy didn't ring any bells. In appearance the guy was vaguely familiar to me, but I figured that during the past hazy and alcoholic three days I had probably seen him at the beach club, the Casino, the Miramar, or one of the all-night bars, or perhaps at some party in one of the villas on the mountain. The island was not large—no more than eight square miles; social relations were, to say the least, casual, and everyone knew or purported to know everyone else. Yet, dredging the past brandied hours, I couldn't dig up anything that resembled the sound of his voice or words that he might have spoken to me.

I looked at my watch. It was twenty-six minutes after nine. I had made a date to meet Elsa at a little joint called the Caffè del Porto at nine-fifteen. Later she and her husband were giving a supper party at the Casino, and this was to be one of those between-trains things. At least, it seemed to me that was how we had arranged it. Elsa knew everyone on the island. She might be able to give me some dope on the dead man. My head seemed stuffed with cotton. There was something that bothered me about that date that had nothing to do with whether or not I would be able to keep it. Something elusive, 'way out on the edge of my mind. Better go down to the bar, I thought, and get a shot of brandy, then try to reach Elsa by phone at the Caffè del Porto. In the meantime there were Mamma Peroni and her nephew Pietro to question. Life at the Villa Rosa was, to say the least, free and easy; visitors to its bedrooms on the second floor came and went unquestioned and most often unseen. Still, there was just a chance that Hertzy had asked for my room, and, after him, the murderer. I couldn't seem to get rid of the cotton. Maybe three shots of brandy. I looked at the body. It was unlikely that anyone would enter my room before the maid came to clean, about eleven A.M. Unless someone had tipped off Ferechini, that gave me a little over thirteen hours.

Thirteen hours.

After a moment I went to the door, opened it a crack, and looked out into the narrow hall. A dim light flickered near the head of the stairs. There was no sound except for the dream music from the bar and the faint plop of mosquitoes against the spattered light bulb. At the moment, the hall was deserted, an unusual state of affairs at the Villa Rosa before midnight. The French girl over in Room 26 must have closed down early for the night. The transients, apparently, were snug behind locked doors, up to what you might expect of transients at Mamma Peroni's uninhibited premises. Quickly I stepped out into the hall and, for the first time since I had been in the place, locked the door behind me. Then I went down into the lower hall, where damp cracks cut across the peeling plaster. Ahead was the street door and, to the right, beaded curtains across an archway to the bar. It was all too simple to reach the second floor from the street without being seen by anyone in the bar. With a heroic effort of will I put off the brandy for a moment and went in to the ancient telephone protruding from the wall in a dank corner behind the stairs. I was grateful for the cover provided by Pietro and his concertina.

For a few moments I wrestled with the archaic telephone system, but finally, amid ominous explosions, I managed to make contact with a voice at the Caffè del Porto. With some little pride the voice finally identified itself as the manager.

"*Signore*," I said, "do you know by sight the *Signora* Planquet?"

"Planquet? Who calls? Why do you wish to know—"

"I had an engagement to meet her there. I have been detained. I thought—"

"Ah. The *signora* has left. They left some time ago."

"They?"

"The gentleman she was with."

I hung on for a moment, wondering. "Who was he?" The voice laughed. "I am sorry, *signore*."

"How long ago did they leave?"

"Oh, over an hour ago. Yes, certainly an hour ago."

My hand tightened on the receiver.

"Are you certain?"

"Yes, *signore*. Very certain. Now if you please ..." And the voice was gone.

A sputtering began in my ear. I put the receiver back into its hook and stood there feeling the dampness of the plaster hall. Had I been wrong? Had I actually made the date for eight-thirty and not nine-thirty? What was this thing—this little black cloud—off there on the far edge of my mind? A word spoken in a dream?

I stood there by the phone and thought, This place, this hall, is like a tomb. I reached for a fresh cigarette. Behind me I heard the soft rustle of the beaded curtains on the archway into the bar. I wheeled about. The beads still trembled in glassy agitation, but no one was there. Somewhere up on the second floor there was the soft click of a door being quietly shut.

Chapter Two

THE VILLA ROSA, 9:25 P.M.

I pushed aside the beaded curtains and went into the bar. A couple in slacks, striped cotton pull-overs, and sandals—the daytime uniform of the island—were sipping wine at one of the four zinc-topped tables. At first glance their sex was indeterminate and at second glance even more so. One seemed older than the other. They seemed caught in a state of trauma, produced perhaps by a Capote novel, while Pietro, who by day was one of the young fishermen who actually still engaged in fishing, sang dreamily to his concertina. Pietro gave me a humorous wink, swift and barely perceptible, disturbing only momentarily the outrageous mask of romantic dewy-eyed yearning. The only other person in the room was Mamma Peroni, owner, manager, and absolute monarch of the Villa Rosa, who sat behind the bar ferociously counting up the day's receipts. Lately some of the smart crowd had taken to dropping in at Mamma Peroni's for a pre-dinner drink, swooning over its "atmosphere" and ignoring the bad brandy and Mamma's studied insolence, but it was not considered a late-evening spot and rarely stayed open after midnight. The couple looked like a hangover from early evening. They eyed me balefully as I went to the bar and ordered a cognac. Mamma Peroni poured it disdainfully, set it before me, shrugged as though my case were hopeless, and returned to her eternal war with the ledger. She was massive and dark, encased in the black cloth she was reputed to have worn for fifteen years, since the death of her husband, possessor of angry eagle eyes and unlikely gleaming white teeth that were exposed in a smile only for enemies, who were, apparently, legion. For her beloved nephew Pietro and a few favorites she reserved a perpetual scowl. When she didn't smile at me, I considered it a good sign. Perhaps I had risen in her favor since two of Ferechini's men had interrupted me as I was dressing to go to the Casino and invited me to headquarters. Ferechini was definitely not one of her favorites. I watched her closely as she battled with the ledger. If she knew about what was up in my room, she was playing possum the convincing way.

"Ferechini let me off on trial," I said in Italian.

"Ferechini!" she muttered contemptuously. "He is a bad artichoke.

You peel off the leaves—the scraping, the bowing, the kissing of rich feet—and you have inside the heart that is nothing. All rotten. Like most of the Venzolanese—rotten!"

"His manners are excellent."

"*Sì!* The manners of the bootlicker! During the time of Mussolini he kissed the boots of the *fascisti*. When the Americans landed he denounced the *fascisti* and kissed the boots of the generals. Now, with the Communists gaining in Naples, he takes no chances. He kisses their boots and the boots of the visiting millionaires. He has kissed so many boots in his time he has turned to leather. Your shoes, are they wet with his spittle?"

"Hardly. I'm not important enough."

"*Sì!*" She nodded her head vigorously. "Still, you should know better than to sing on the steps of the Mayor. The old goat thought you were serenading his wife. By this time every potent male on the island has had a turn in her bed. Besides, if you must sing, it's wiser to choose Verdi. Ah, that son of a pig, Ferechini, he would like to put me out of business. I tell you, the honest Venzolanese—the few of us left—we have no chance these days. Mother of God, what garbage I have to contend with!" Her eyes turned expressively to the couple. Fortunately, I suspected that Mamma's express-train island patois was unintelligible to them. I grinned.

"You're a fraud, Mamma! Any messages for me?"

"Anyone would think I am a telephone bureau! The woman you had in here last night—the wife of that monster of a film director—she called just after you went away with Ferechini's minions."

"Ah?"

"I told her to try the jail. She laughed. Perhaps she was right."

"What else did she say?" There it was again, that shadow off on the edge of my mind. If Elsa had known I was being questioned by the *carabinieri*, why had she then gone on to the Caffè del Porto? Even granted I had made a mistake about the time of our date and it actually had been eight-thirty, she must have known after her call to Mamma Peroni that I could not possibly be there on time. Ferechini had dragged me out of my room at seven forty-five.

"She says if you return to remind you that you are expected to be at the Casino by midnight. Garbage!"

"Nice garbage."

"Bah!"

Her eagle eyes leveled. She hesitated, then dug into the fold between her enormous breasts and drew forth a slip of soiled paper.

"An hour ago this message by phone. The caller demanded I write exactly what is said. Anyone would think you were De Gasperi himself!"

I spread the crumpled paper on the bar and read in Italian, "It is urgent that you come to the suite of Mr. Phillip Adams at the Hotel Miramar no later than ten-thirty."

I stared at it in shocked surprise. From my murky three days I managed to retain the memory that the arrival on the island of Phillip Adams had created a stir in the local newspaper. He was one of America's top industrialists and the fact that he had come to Venzola rather than Capri had been hailed as another sign that the island was surpassing its more famous neighbor as a resort for the very rich. But what did a guy like Adams want with me? And why the urgency? I took a healthy swig of the burning raw brandy and considered. It was possible that there was some connection between this note and the riddle in my bedroom.

I crumpled up the note and turned in time to catch Mamma's eyes unguarded for a moment, narrowed and intense with something that might have been only curiosity. She looked quickly down at the ledger.

As casually as possible I asked, "Anyone call here for me in person?"

For a moment I thought she had not heard. Then quietly she said, "There was a man, dark, built like a boxer. Very elegant in evening dress such as you yourself choose to wear at the moment. He did not give his name."

"What did he want?"

She shrugged. "He did not choose to impart any information and I certainly did not demand it. He sat and waited for a few minutes. Then the French girl, Yvonne in Twenty-six, came in and joined him. They seemed to know one another. At any rate, he went upstairs with her. As far as I know, he's still there."

"He could have left," I said quickly. Too quickly.

She looked up, speculative again. "It's possible," she said carefully. Again I was aware of the curious intensity of her gaze, the power of the unspoken question in it.

But this was a new angle. I had no doubt that Mamma had described Hertzy. And he had gone upstairs with the French girl. There was work to do nearer home than I had expected.

"What do you know about her?"

Mamma shrugged. "No more than I know about you. Except she is in some kind of great trouble. That is enough for me. I give her enough time to catch her breath. That is the least one can do. All the same, she is a problem."

"In what way?"

Mamma sighed. "What people do behind the bedroom door is their own business, but I do not run a brothel." She regarded my glass distastefully, returned to the ledger.

"Mamma Peroni ..."

Without looking up she said, "I, too, have troubles. My business is my own. Yours belongs to you!"

I stood there indecisively and then decided on just one more brandy. Mamma poured it angrily and shoved it toward me. Behind me one of the characters at the table spoke, revealing its gender as feminine.

"Sometimes I believe there is only cruelty ... and filth. Filth! People like Pepe—" She broke off, and then after a moment, "Everything happens so gradually, Freddie, you hardly know, and then you wake up and ... Oh, God!"

I gave her a sidelong glance. The close-cropped boyish bob didn't suit her. The face, which had obviously once been beautiful and even now retained a shadow of that beauty, was beginning to sag in the wrong places, and there were tight little lines of desperation around the gray eyes.

Her companion, whom she addressed as Freddie, spoke soothingly in a voice that verged more or less on the opposite sex. "Pepe is a living bitch, darling. But I beg of you not to spoil things. We can't go anywhere but forward now, sweet, and it's for laughs. Please, beautiful, don't go cold on us. For Freddie's sake, go back and change into your maddest rags and appear at the Casino in a blaze of glory and dare them—just dare them! I wouldn't dream of letting a little bitch like—"

He broke off as she touched his arm in warning.

"You're so understanding, Freddie. I don't know what I would do without you."

The conversation didn't make much sense, but I had pricked up my ears at the mention of the name Pepe. Could they be referring to Elsa's husband, Pepe Planquet?

"We should ... I really think we should ..." Freddie's voice died out in a whimper.

"How long have they been here?" I whispered to Mamma.

She shrugged. "Two hours. Maybe more. Underneath they are competing for Pietro. They are wasting their time. I have seen to it that Pietro, at least, does not go the way of the other boys on this ruined island. Not yet, anyway. Garbage!"

She slapped down her pencil, raised her voice, and croaked in broken English, "*Signori*, we now close shut!"

"Just one more glass of wine, Mamma Peroni?"

"Impossible!" Mamma said firmly.

Already Pietro was packing away his concertina while his black eyes flirted shamelessly with the two customers. They seemed completely unaware of the cynical humor behind Pietro's charade. Mamma said something sharp to him. He shrugged and laughed.

I turned and cased the woman again, wondering why she seemed vaguely familiar, like an object seen through several fathoms of water, dim and unresolved. And then suddenly I recognized her. It was Lorna Parks, who, in the days of my youth, had been a top Hollywood film star. I had some recollection of an attempted but abortive comeback several years before and a disastrous assault on the Broadway theatre. She was taking to the forties the hard way and at the moment was type-cast; the sort of woman who is all too familiar in such places as Cannes, Porto Fino, St. Jean de Luz, Marjorca, and now Venzola. Her escort I knew to be one of the army of busy young men who appear from under the local rocks at the advent of celebrity, doubtful or otherwise, running interference like sassy pilot fish and pretending to write or paint or to do something obscure with papier-mâché and wire and who assume an arrogant matriarchy over the sort of "art" that is taken quite seriously by American women's clubs, advertising executives, and tired book reviewers. Mistaking sexual aberration for genius, they quote Freud and Gide for their own purposes and manage to bring a certain *fin-de-siècle* chic to such unlikely fields as right- and left-wing politics, Dadaist philosophies, and even religion. It has been said, perhaps with exaggeration, that they can be credited with having once again made God fashionable. Lorna Parks's companion, Freddie, raised plucked eyebrows disdainfully, and dismissed me into the limbo of the poor, the uncelebrated, the unbelievers.

But the expression in Lorna Parks's eyes startled me. The pupils were wide and too fixed, rigidly concentrating on innocence as though looking into a camera directed by D. W. Griffith, but behind the vacuous innocence was fear. And oddly enough I sensed that for some reason it was my presence that aroused this fear. For just an instant there was a flicker in those eyes, some sort of desperate attempt at silent communication. I wondered.

I finished the second brandy, went out into the hall and up to the second floor to the door of Room 26. I knocked and after a long wait the door was opened about a foot, just enough to frame the pale and childlike face of the French girl, Yvonne. There was no welcome in her eyes.

"*Oui?*"

"I'm Hart Muldoon," I said in French. "I'm in Room Twenty-four."

She switched to her own version of English. "Yes, I know."

"May I come in? I'd like to talk to you."

She hesitated, finally shrugged, pulled wide the door, stepped aside to let me pass, closed the door behind me when I had crossed the threshold. She wore a flannel robe that came to her knees and, I suspected, nothing else. There was something listless and ill about her that mitigated a sort of picture-postcard prettiness. The room was permeated with the faint sickly odor of disinfectant; her clothes were tossed carelessly in and about a sagging armchair, the iron bed was rumpled, and on a small table near its head was a small bottle of patent medicine and a glass of water.

"I'm sorry to bother you."

"What difference?" She shrugged. "I tried to sleep without success. In a few moments now I will be going out."

I noticed the cheap little black dinner gown thrown over the chair and on the floor the tarnished silver slippers.

"You know a man by the name of Georges Hertzy?"

She sighed, went to the small window overlooking the alley, asked over her shoulder, "Why?"

I took a chance now, gambling with the knowledge that these words might later be used against me.

"He was supposed to meet me here at the Villa Rosa. He hasn't shown up."

She turned placidly and looked into my eyes.

"It was my understanding that he would await you in your room."

"Ah?"

"He asked me which was your room. I told him."

"He came up here with you?"

She shrugged indifferently. I said, "You had an appointment to meet him in the bar?"

"Not precisely."

"What does that mean?"

She tossed her head back impatiently. "Why these questions? You are as bad as Ferechini!"

"You've had dealings with Ferechini?"

She laughed shortly. "I am to leave the island by the morning boat. It seems I have offered too much competition to the fine ladies in the de luxe hotels. Or maybe my prices are lower than theirs!"

I gave her a moment to cross to the table and extract a cigarette from a sodden pack. I lit it for her, but, as my hand touched hers, she flinched away.

"That bad?" I said.

"All of you!" She said tensely, "All of you!"

"Let me apologize for my sex."

She laughed harshly. Then the effort to remain on her feet seemed too much. She sat on the edge of the crumpled bed. The robe fell open, exposing one small firm breast. She caught my eye and drew the robe closed.

"How long has this been going on?" I asked.

"Comment?"

"When did you establish rates? When did you begin ..."

"Oh. If you mean did I sleep with pigs for money before I came to this island ..." Her voice died out and then after a moment went on: "Before ... before ..." She sucked in her breath sharply and said in sudden anger, "You're as bad as he was."

"He?"

"Monsieur Georges Hertzy!"

And slowly I said, "Was?"

She stared up into my eyes. I saw the pupils contract and the fingers tighten about the cigarette. After a moment she said, "Is. Was. What is a word? What difference? He was full of questions, too."

"About what?"

"Like you. Full of curiosity about how and why, but it didn't keep him from crawling in between the sheets!"

"Questions about what?"

Something in the tone of my voice made her look away. After a moment she said listlessly, "Oh, stupid questions. Mostly about a ... a man named Cassi. Count Cassi."

"A friend of yours?"

One corner of her mouth turned up in a half-smile.

"If you mean a customer, no. Women have no interest for him in that way. I have been of some use to him ... how I do not care to discuss."

"What did Hertzy want to know about Cassi?"

"He thought I might know about some of Cassi's friends. Something political, I believe. I did not know. I couldn't help him."

"Political?" I gave that a moment. She was staring at her cigarette. "You knew Georges Hertzy before?"

"Before? No. We met downstairs in the bar two days ago. We came to an understanding. You know.... I saw him again tonight at another bar. I came back here and he followed some time later. He was waiting for you. There was, apparently, spare time. So ..." She shrugged. "He wanted diversion."

"Do you know why he wanted to see me?"

"No."

"How long did he stay with you?"

"Fifteen minutes, more or less. Then he said he would await you in your room."

"You say you ran across him in another bar. What bar?"

"The Caffè del Porto," she said.

Something turned over in my stomach. "He was there alone?"

"Oh, no. He was there with a woman."

"Did you know who she was?"

She stood up. She crushed her cigarette in a saucer on the bedside table. Then she looked at me again in that oddly placid manner.

"Oh, yes. The woman is quite well known on the island. It was Elsa Planquet."

The room was very still. In the silence she reached for the water and took a sip, held the glass for a moment between her hands, then listlessly replaced it.

"And he left her there—Madame Planquet—left her at the Caffè del Porto?"

She sighed. "I don't know. They were still together when I left the café. He came here a half hour later. Perhaps he did leave her there. They were having some sort of a quarrel."

"What about?"

She wheeled about now. In a tense voice she said, "Something has happened. I am quite aware of that from what you say. All this is none of my business. I have other business and I have only a short time in which to get it done."

Her pale hands moved restlessly over the lapels of her wrapper. I took a step toward her. She held her ground.

"Who was—who is Hertzy?"

"A man," she said with cold contempt.

I waited a moment and then said, "Yvonne, why did you come here to Venzola?"

Her face remained set in the indifferent mask for almost a minute. When I didn't say more she suddenly collapsed. She put her hands to her face and began to sob.

"Go away."

I went to her side but didn't touch her, knowing that she would flinch away.

"Ferechini is sending you off the island tomorrow. You will go home?"

"Home!" She sobbed. "No. It doesn't matter. I wanted to. I ... But now ... What difference ..." With a convulsive angry movement she wiped away the tears and said with unexpected violence, "I will not leave this island until—"

"Until what?"

She stood. "The only decent persons on this island are Mamma Peroni and ... Never mind. Oh, go. Please go."

I went to the door and turned. "You won't tell me who Georges Hertzy is?" She said nothing. "Yvonne," I said gently, "someone has given you a raw deal. If you will tell me I might help."

"I need no help!" she said coldly.

"I've said that in my life and regretted it. Was it Georges Hertzy?" She turned her back.

"Maybe you'll change your mind. I'll be at the Casino after eleven if you do."

I opened the door and almost inaudibly she said, "I, too, will be at the Casino."

There was something in the way she said it that froze my blood. I hesitated. Her back was still to me. After a second I stepped out into the musty hall and closed the door behind me.

Chapter Three

THE VILLA ROSA, 9:40 P.M.

I left Room 26, went past the door of my quiet room with its rigid secret, and went down into the lower hall. Through the beaded curtains I could see Freddie paying up at the bar and Lorna Parks preparing to rise. I went back to the phone and finally got the Planquet villa. A maid answered and in a moment I heard Elsa's voice.

"It's good of you to call," she said coolly.

"How long will you be there?"

"I don't see that that's any of your—"

"Answer me, Elsa."

There was a moment's silence, then she said, "I must be at the Casino no later than eleven-fifteen."

"Is he there?"

Again the silence, then, "No."

"Good. There's something I must talk to you about. I've got to see someone else first but I should be no later than ten-thirty."

"Hart, what is it?"

"Not now," I said, and hung up.

I was aware that someone else was behind me in the hall. I lit a cigarette and turned. Lorna Parks was standing there waiting. She moved toward me urgently.

"You're Mr. Muldoon."

"How did you know?"

"Freddie ..." She stopped. "It doesn't matter. I must talk to you." She looked nervously over her shoulder to the bar, where Freddie was still talking to Mamma Peroni. Her hand on my arm was tense and I knew this was no reflex of latent nymphomania. The glandular imbalance had other causes; it was obvious that fear was pumping gallons of adrenalin into the fading movie star.

"I will be at the Casino by midnight," she whispered, "and later at Babs Wentworth's party."

A cool feminine voice said, "How nice of you to invite people to my party, Lorna."

We turned. The woman who had just come in from the street was, in her early forties, still handsome and very smartly dressed.

"Babs ..."

"Who is this man?" the woman said coldly.

"Babs, I ..."

"Oh, for God's sake, Lorna, am I to spend my life taking you out of dark halls with strange men?"

Freddie came through the beaded curtains bubbling. "Babs, darling! As usual you look divine. Divine!"

"That's more than I can say for you, Freddie. What ideas have you been putting into Lorna's head? What are you people up to?"

"We people?" Freddie gave me a haughty look, a queen's glance for the presumptuous peasant. "He's not one of us, darling. Although, I must say—"

"Shut up, Freddie!" the woman said angrily. "Come on. I have the car up on the Via Minerva. I'll drop you off at Armando's. He's seething. He thinks you're still panting after that Hertzy person. Stop giving a performance, Lorna. It's not a good one, I assure you. I don't intend to have you spoil things by a drunken scene. Too much is at stake." And then again, "Who is this man?"

"I came to fix the refrigerator," I said.

"A comic," she said. "I'm fed up with comics. Whoever you are, leave Lorna alone. Lorna, come along. I have enough on my mind tonight.

I'm in no mood for slumming."

Lorna Parks laughed shrilly, made some inane remark, and they all went out into the street. I could hear Mrs. Wentworth's steely voice cutting metallically through the night air, fading as they climbed up toward the Via Minerva. I went back to Mamma Peroni.

"I want to speak with Pietro."

"Impossible. He's gone."

"Gone?"

"He has some errands for me. Later he has been engaged to sing at some fancy party on the mountain. I warn him that if he does not confine his entertainment to the concertina, I will give him the beating of his life."

"What party?"

"The villa of that American woman who was just out in the hall. The rich one. Mrs. Wentworth."

"I see." I lowered my voice. "What's going on, Mamma?"

She looked at me inscrutably. "What goes on more or less every night. Animals! Sick animals!"

"I didn't mean that."

"So?"

"Who is Count Cassi?"

She moved her powerful hand on the bar, seemed to find it suddenly interesting. After a moment she said, "A beast."

"Is he mixed up in politics?"

"Who isn't? He is a friend of Ferechini's. Need I say more?"

"A Fascist?"

"Ask the one who was in here. The one they call Freddie."

"Mamma ..."

"Yes?"

I decided against it. "Never mind. Watch out for the French girl. She's in a bad state. What ails her?"

Mamma scowled. "I do not betray confidences. Now don't bother me. I am busy."

Before I reached the arch she called after me, "Do not shut your eyes for an instant!"

I turned. "What does that mean?"

"It means," she declared with all the melodrama of her countrymen, "that the gods of evil have come from slumber and death is everywhere." And calmly she went back to her ledger.

I went through the hall into the narrow Via Cellini. It was no more than a cobblestoned alley climbing steeply up the hill from the harbor between the sagging tiles of ancient houses. Down below, trim white yachts serenely rode the darkness before the Royal Marine Club, and up against the municipal mole, fat fishing craft were huddled together, complaining softly in the gentle swell. Far across the bay, Naples sent a luminous glow into the April sky, and to the northeast the edge of a lump of red moon was just appearing over the rim of Vesuvius. Except for a few water-front cafés, the lower town was dark and still. But from up above, where the wedding-cake Casino burned bright among the ornate resort hotels, came the faint, dreamlike sounds of dance music. Higher up the mountain and strung along the four-mile coastline like diamonds on a broken necklace were the lights of the luxurious villas belonging to wealthy foreigners and the flashier, more international elements of Roman society. The air was permeated with an odd rotting sweetness, a combination of dead fish, lemon trees, bougainvilleas, the open sewage of the lower town, the pungent aroma of native wine. Drunk the night before, I had even imagined the musky odor of incense burning before the altars of antique Roman gods, emanating perhaps from the ruined temple on the mountain top, built, it was said, by the Emperor Tiberius.

There was something strange and dark in the April night air of Venzola, something disturbing and intangible even after one had sorted out all the separate odors. And climbing the deserted alley toward the lights of the new Via Minerva, I had the odd sensation of climbing back in time and breathing in the exhaust of dead centuries. The island was rotten with history, but in the rot was a sweetness like some exotic aphrodisiac. It was old with beauty and old with evil and old with words unspoken hanging like a filmy mist over its palaces and gardens and decaying roofs.

Mamma Peroni's pronouncement about the gods of evil coming out of slumber whispered in my ear. Had they ever slept? I tried to shake off the morbid fancy. Somewhere up above I would find a logical, rational answer to the riddle of the dead man in my room. Behind me the old street was hollow and empty, time stoned in; but up ahead was the modern world and sanity.

I had almost reached the Via Minerva when a small shadow detached itself from a dark archway and intercepted me. It materialized into a boy, no more than ten years of age, with one of those perpetually upturned faces, old and knowing far beyond its years, so familiar to postwar Europe.

He tugged at my sleeve. In childish broken English he said, "Nice girl, *signore*? Nice virgin girl?"

I stopped and looked down into the unsmiling little face. I dug into my pocket and brought forth one of my last hundred-lira notes and thrust it at him. In Italian I said, "Go buy food for your sister, *bambino*."

He snatched the note but to my surprise stayed rooted before me. And then I saw an odd frightened tension in his eyes. He was trying to keep my attention but out of the corner of his great black eyes he was watching something else, something behind me. I leaped to one side just in time. The knife went whistling past my ear and clattered up against a stone wall. The boy turned and ran off down the hill, his bare feet making no sound on the cobblestones. I wheeled around. Another shadow, larger than the boy, was vanishing down the narrow alley. I knew it was useless to pursue it through the maze of narrow twisting streets.

I hurried more quickly now toward the lighted boulevard. And for the first time it occurred to me that perhaps the murder of Georges Hertzy had been a mistake. Perhaps that knife beside the dead body had been intended for me. Someone on this island wanted to kill me. But why?

Death is everywhere, Mamma Peroni had said.

Up above, among the glittering lights, music rose gaily in the soft April night of Venzola.

Chapter Four

HOTEL MIRAMAR, 10:00 P.M.

Green crystal glittered against saffron walls and out among the lemon trees in the garden a pianist was playing a Cole Porter tune for those few guests who were not at the Casino or at private parties or dancing to the Dixieland band down at Lady Negly's swank beach club. The clerk at the desk came away from the house phone and told me Phillip Adams was waiting for me in his suite. I waited for the lift to descend from above. The pink paneled doors finally slid open and I found myself face to face with Pepe Planquet, Elsa's husband. The French film director was stocky and powerful and he looked like a bull dressed for some comic circus act. White silk trousers, scarlet dinner jacket, a tie that looked as though it had been snatched from an old production of *La Bohème*. Standing next to him in the lift was a gorgeous redhead in a tight green sequined gown that did little or nothing to conceal her generous curves. The operator

of the lift stood to one side like a wooden doll and they came forth
from the perfumed box.

Planquet smiled at me, a set smile with some left-over irony I didn't
like. "Ah!" he said in his deep resounding voice. "Elsa's young
American!"

"Hello, Planquet."

The redhead eyed me with cold curiosity. Planquet made no move
to introduce her. She moved beyond us and waited for him in the
middle of the lobby.

Planquet laughed. "You have not the effrontery, young man, to—
how you say—stand up my charming wife."

"I don't know what you mean," I said. I'd got the seeking quality
in his voice, the device of candidly seeming to accept a situation that
in fact he had not accepted at all in order to get information.

He laughed and winked. "Elsa must have her amusement. As long
as it is harmless. *Nest-ce pas?*"

The elevator boy, a young Venzolanese with dark curious eyes, was
waiting. Suddenly Planquet dropped the smile, came close, and
said in a low voice, "You are to be our guest at supper in the Casino
tonight?"

"If I can make it."

"Be sure you do. I have something to discuss with you that might
prove of some interest. Of more interest, perhaps, than anything else
you might be offered this evening."

With that he moved past me across the lobby as though it were a
pasture and the laconic redhead a waiting heifer. I got into the
elevator. The doors slid silently shut. The machine rose, like a silk-
draped coffin, up among the rooms and corridors, and deposited me
in a pink-lit hall. I was still wondering about Planquet when I was
admitted to Adams' suite.

I found the industrialist in surroundings entirely appropriate to
contemporary royalty. The sitting room was vast and startling in its
decor, dominated by an enormous window that looked out over the
rooftops of the town and the fantastic panorama of the Bay of
Naples.

Phillip Adams was so different from what I had expected that I
spent the first few moments readjusting my preconceived picture of
him. Slim and tall, carrying his fifty-odd years and six feet with the
slightly arched dignity of the intellectual, he had a gentle and
scholarly manner, an impression heightened, perhaps consciously,
by old-fashioned rimless glasses. His dinner clothes were somewhat
askew.

Apparently his preconceived picture of me was, on one level, fairly accurate; Scotch and brandy, soda and ice were waiting on a teakwood commode. He fixed me a stiff one, poured a phony for himself as though the gesture were all too familiar—the moderate in a world of extremes—indicated a chair, and sat near me, looking at his watch.

"You're invited to have supper with the Planquets?"

"Yes," I said.

"Good. I'll be with them too. I left a cocktail party at the Count Cassi's in the hope you might show up. We have very little time. And I wish, at this point, to squelch rumors, rather than start them. I hope I didn't take you away from anything interesting."

His eyes were mildly curious. I wondered just what "interesting" connotated. Death? But after a moment he raised his eyebrows and gave the word its more obvious smoking-room meaning. I gave a noncommittal shrug.

"The morals of this island are, I suppose, deplorable," he continued. "Still, in a world that is fast conforming to uniform gray, I find it quite stimulating. My board of directors, my political advisers, and my Yankee conscience don't approve. But oddly enough, I find myself surrendering to the place's scandalous charm. Is it the sun? Why are the normal moral standards extra baggage here?"

"My interest in Venzola is not particularly anthropological."

"Ah, I daresay." I suspected that the small talk and the mildness were a cover while he gave himself time to size me up. Where I expected Rotary and a Midwest twang, I was getting Harvard.

"Who gave you my name?"

"Max Kneber."

That straightened me out for a moment. If Max had recommended me to the American industrialist, the deal must be a big one. Max was upper brass in British intelligence. I had done a couple of off-beat jobs for him in the past. I had first got to know him during the Second World War, when I had been a bright-eyed O.S.S. boy assigned to work with him in occupied France. Max had dragged me into deals I'd tried to avoid in the past, but he was, all in all, one of the good guys.

"Is Max on Venzola?"

"No. He's a personal friend and I took the liberty of calling him in London this afternoon. I couldn't go into details on the phone, but he understands I need someone trustworthy and discreet. He gave me your name and the address on the Via Cellini."

"How in God's name did Max know I was here?"

He shrugged. "You'll have to ask Max. Incidentally, Mr. Muldoon, how *do* you happen to be in Venzola?"

"An accident. I had no intention of coming here. I was at Cannes preparing to board a liner for the States when I made the mistake of one last farewell party. The next thing I knew, I was coming to, three days later, on somebody's yacht and entering Venzola harbor. I'd never seen my hostess—sober, I mean. What I saw when I stopped rocking disturbed me. I jumped ship four days ago. Since then I've been trying to make up my mind."

Adams smiled. "Max tells me that you've been trying to get back to the States for the past three years but at the last minute something always intervenes. Roulette or a woman, I understand."

"Damn Max, anyway! He should know. He's made good use of my failings a couple of times."

"Yes, I know. Very good use, I understand. I'm told that you are tops in your field."

"My field? Did he tell you I was the prostitute of the legations? The guy who isn't too particular about what government or individual supplies the cash?"

Adams smiled again. "He told me you would talk like this. But he also told me you have been pretty damned particular about your employment."

"Max is prejudiced."

"He told me that you have done very valuable work—in your own manner, of course—for the Allied cause."

I gave that the horse laugh. The direction of the conversation made me uncomfortable. The guy was treading on the edge of quicksands on which I had long since turned my back. Or had I?

"Max also told me that you were fed up with Europe and causes and wished only to get back to the States—away from it all in a cabin in the Maine woods, I understand."

"That's where I was headed at Cannes when people and liquor got in the way."

"Well, Mr. Muldoon, your dreams are your own business, of course. I am more interested in your worldly attributes, the talents that have made you unique. If you will direct those talents to my problem, I will make it possible for you to retreat into your log tower."

"How possible?"

He hesitated. "If you can manage to accomplish this assignment without any publicity, I will pay you ten thousand dollars."

I froze. For once I had no comeback. The body of Georges Hertzy had been uppermost in my mind, not cash. But I needed cash badly, not only to get back to the States, but for a bargaining point with Ferechini should matters get too hot to handle. Besides, a patron like Adams would do no harm; the bootlicking *Comandante* would think twice before railroading me if Adams stood somewhere in the background.

"Well?" Adams looked impatiently at his watch. "You must need help badly."

"I do." When I still hesitated he stood and said sharply, "Max led me to believe you were more decisive, Mr. Muldoon."

"I was giving it a moment to sink in. It's sunk. It's a deal."

Never before had I jumped into a deal so blindly. But a sixth or seventh sense, plus the mental picture of a cool ten thousand vanishing from my fingertips, acted more strongly than reason.

"Good."

The word was soft but oddly cold and final. I had a momentary attack of unaccountable misery. Here it was again; the word, the bond, the leap into the pattern I'd tried so hard to escape. For I had no doubt but that behind the word lay the all too familiar world of the pursuers and the pursued; the region of dark paranoia that has become the norm in our times. Yes, after all, this seal of agreement was merely anticlimactic; actually I had been plunged back into the murky labyrinth at the moment when I had crossed the threshold of my room to find before me the body of Georges Hertzy.

Adams was looking down at me, waiting for something. He had the look of a collector waiting to be told that his casual purchase is, beneath its false veneer, a Rembrandt.

He inserted a fresh cigarette into a stubby amber holder. I noticed that his fingers shook slightly and suspected that it was not from any chronic illness. There was great tension behind that carefully calm exterior.

"As you probably know, my plant in Detroit is engaged in turning out jet engines."

"I've heard."

"What you probably haven't heard—at least I hope not—is that we are well past the experimental stage in the development of an entirely revolutionary principle—something far in advance of anything of its kind."

"Good news."

"Naturally, the enterprise is top secret. And, until recently, we have had no reason to doubt that our security has not been absolutely airtight."

"Ah. That serious, eh?"

He hesitated, then said wearily, "I don't know. I don't know. I can't be certain. That's why I need you."

"You don't want me. This is for the security officers at your plant, the F.B.I."

Abruptly he turned his back and went to the window. Over his shoulder he said, "God knows I am as patriotic as any Fourth of July orator, despite my enemies' attacks on me as an 'internationalist.' But ..."

"But what?"

"This is a situation that may involve my political future."

"Political?"

"At the moment I'm in line for the nomination by my party for Senator at the convention in August. It's the culmination of many years of work."

I laughed. "Hell, you don't have to be a Senator. Your kind of guy could own a couple of private Senators of your own!"

Coldly he said, "Apparently you don't know much about me. I just don't happen to operate that way, Mr. Muldoon."

A certain anger flickered through his voice. Again I readjusted my sights. Behind that proper façade there burned, apparently, fires of idealism, even some sort of fanaticism. The culture of Eastern cities, Yankee singleness of purpose, Western skepticism, ambition, and dreams of the best of all possible worlds were all thrown together in one cocktail that might prove to be explosive.

When I made no comment, he went on: "The nomination means a great deal to me. For many reasons. I feel, perhaps egotistically, that I have a contribution to make to my party and my country. But I represent the new, more vigorous wing of my party, and I must buck the opposition of some powerful enemies."

"From the opposition party?"

"Of course that. But much more important at the moment, within my own party. What I have considered enlightened has been attacked as 'internationalist' by certain powerful leaders. So far they have kept a sullen silence as to my nomination. But they would not be displeased by some sort of scandal that would upset my political applecart. Do I make myself clear?"

"Why do they object to you?"

"They are skeptical of my somewhat modern point of view toward labor-management relations. But above all they are opposed to my warm espousal of the United Nations and my chairmanship of the E.R.I.A.I."

"Translation?"

"European Refugees in American Industry."

"Sounds formidable."

"Not really. It's quite simple. I have worked with a group of like-minded businessmen in sponsoring refugees and displaced persons and placing them in American industry. We believe that in treating the politically persecuted of Europe as friends, instead of with truculent suspicion, we are making a contribution to world peace and strengthening the morale of the Allied world."

"I can see that you might run into trouble."

"Actually the plan has been extraordinarily successful. For example, it has worked very well in my Detroit plant. Or at least I thought so."

Through my glass wall I saw the moon rise full and red above Vesuvius.

"Mind you, we have not been merely stupid idealists or dreamers. None of these persons have had contact with what we refer to as Project D until we were absolutely certain of their loyalty. There would have been no Project D to begin with if it had not been for one of these displaced persons. A brilliant young Rumanian electronic engineer who came to us eight years ago. It was his work that made the entire project possible. His background in Europe was irreproachable. No youthful political mistakes or temporary blindness. He became one of my most trusted associates and, I might add, a close friend. I have never had any reason to doubt his loyalty."

"His name?"

"Georges Hertzy."

Chapter Five

THE HOTEL MIRAMAR, 10:20 P.M

Somehow I wasn't too surprised. Almost from the beginning of this carefully planned conversation I had felt there was some connection between the American industrialist and the dead man. Yet things were falling into their expected pattern a bit too easily. The fact that Hertzy might have been murdered for political reasons was almost too pat. I took it slow and easy. There was something here ... something that had to do with that elusive cloud off on the edge of my mind.

"What made you suspicious?" I asked finally.

"Yesterday morning I received an anonymous note. I immediately called Max Kneber in London for advice. Strictly off the record, of course."

"An anonymous note is seldom firm evidence."

"Ordinarily I would agree." He avoided my eyes. Yes, I thought, there's something here. "But after reading it I began to remember certain odd things. Little incidents, a word here, a word there ... nothing I could put my finger on exactly, but ..."

"What did the note say?"

He hesitated, still not looking at me. "Ever heard of an organization called the Balkan Eagles?"

I managed not to laugh. "Vaguely."

"What do you know about them?"

"Suppose you tell me."

He snapped up his head and for just an instant color rose to his face. "I understand it's a hangover from the old Iron Cross gang of Rumania. Fascist in nature. They've been trying to get recognition from Washington and London as a genuine resistance movement. Both governments have so far stayed clear. It is suspected that they are actually encouraged by Moscow for the purpose of trapping members of authentic underground movements."

I looked him in the eye. "Pretty dangerous boys," I said with a certain inflection that wasn't lost on him.

"Well, I don't know," he said impatiently. "One can't afford not to take these things seriously."

"And the note?"

"It claimed that Georges Hertzy is ... has become a secret member of this organization, and that he has arranged a rendezvous with someone on this island for the purpose of passing on his knowledge of Project D."

"And you believe it?"

He came back to the sofa, bent quickly, snuffed out his cigarette. "I don't want to believe it. But I can't take a chance. You see, it was Georges who persuaded me to come here. I had had no intention of a European jaunt. I intended merely to take a short holiday at my plantation in South Carolina. But Georges and Gigi, they are like members of my family."

"They?"

"Georges and his wife." He looked quickly away. "I have made myself solely responsible for Georges. You can see that if there is anything at all behind this terrible accusation ... Well, publicity of any kind would boomerang against me politically."

I waited. Almost compulsively he added, "My wife is in Rome visiting friends. We—we have been separated for over a year. Georges suggested that we fly to Italy and spend a much needed rest on Venzola. Mrs. Hertzy's mother and sister are here and she had not seen them in some time. Mrs. Hertzy's sister is Mrs. Planquet, wife of the director." He stopped. "Something wrong, Muldoon?"

"No," I said rather faintly, "nothing at all."

So the dead man was Elsa's brother-in-law. And according to the French girl in Room 26, she had been with him at the Caffè del Porto only a short time before his death. Why had she met her brother-in-law there? Why had they quarreled? No doubt she would tell me. No doubt....

Almost angrily now Adams said, "I can't bring myself to believe ... and yet Georges has been acting peculiarly since we have been here."

"In what way?"

"He disappeared earlier this evening from a party at the Count Cassi's without a word of explanation to Gigi or me. He is not the sort who would engage in any cheap sexual intrigue. I mean ..." The color rose again to his cheeks. "I mean ... Well, damn it all, I want you to find out what I mean! It will be between you and me. I pray my fears may be proved wrong."

"I see."

"Georges is a friendly sort of person. He will be at Mrs. Planquet's supper party at the Casino. Pepe told—" He stopped, recovered, went on quickly: "I understand you are invited. It makes things convenient."

Almost too convenient, I thought.

"How you operate from then on in is, of course, your own business."

I watched him closely. Did he really believe that Georges Hertzy would be at the Casino? I looked toward the moon-drenched bay. If I told him the truth, the deal might be off. In fact, at the moment, the death of Georges Hertzy might prove to be singularly convenient to the millionaire. But if I played along with him—played it his way—I might win the deal yet. I decided, with some misgivings, to play it close to the chest. There was something in Adams' voice I didn't like.

"Let's see the note."

"Yes. Yes, of course. It's in my bedroom. One moment."

But as he turned toward the bedroom there was a knock on the hall door. For a moment he seemed suspended there, half turned, trying not to hear that knock. Then he gave me a quick worried look, crossed to the door, and opened it.

A blonde in a magnificent white and gold evening gown stepped over the threshold, mouth half open to speak. When she saw me, she checked her words and came slowly into the room. Adams had his back to me but I saw her eyes, curious, surprised, and then wary.

"I'm so sorry to bother you, Phillip. But I thought Georges might be with you."

"Georges?" Adams hesitated a moment, then shut the hall door.

"Then he is not here?" She stopped smiling for a moment. "That's odd. He said he was going to ... Ah, well. I should have phoned you. As it is, I've interrupted—"

"Gigi," Adams said quickly, "this is Mr. Hart Muldoon. He's a friend of Alec Bentley's from Cleveland. This is Mrs. Georges Hertzy."

"Ah, but I know Mr. Muldoon ... by sight." She smiled again. "He lunched yesterday with my sister at Lady Negly's club."

"Yes," I said, remembering for the first time.

"But I had no idea you were a friend of Mr. Adams." Her voice was unexpectedly childlike, with only the faintest trace of a husky Balkan accent. She was one of those shimmering blondes with hair floating in a luminous cloud over pale skin, blue eyes, and a wide sensual mouth. Plump breasts moved restlessly beneath the dangerously low neckline and she walked in a manner that suggested a strip-tease artist, and about her was a general atmosphere of melting softness, sweet perfume, and breathlessly parted lips. She was a girl-girl, the kind no man would ever refer to as "pal." Her femininity was so pronounced that it approached parody. As an extra dividend she seemed to be well down in her twenties. Her sister, Elsa Planquet, was an orchid type, delicate, subtle, and shy beneath a veneer of sophistication, with something of mystery about her; but Mrs. Hertzy was a more rugged plant, blatant and earthy. She pouted, eyed me with a thoughtful speculative glance that seemed for an instant to divest me of my clothes, turned helpless youth on Adams.

"It is a bore about Georges. I was certain he would be here with you, Phillip. He said his business appointment would only keep him—"

"Business?" I asked.

"I don't blame you!" she said brightly. "That's exactly the way I said it to him. Business? Nonsense. The kind of business there is on this island is monkey business!"

"He told you he had a business appointment, Gigi?" Phillip asked.

"But of course, Phillip. I thought you knew. I thought—" She caught herself up. "He had too many cocktails at Count Cassi's. I suppose some unscrupulous female ... Ah, well, I for one refuse to worry about him. He knows we will be with Elsa at the Casino."

Adams gave me a look of warning. I had an idea she caught it. The big eyes were turned in my direction again. I expressed interest in my drink.

"Is something wrong?"

"Certainly not, Gigi," Adams said quickly.

He gave her a look that was more revealing than he intended. For a moment he was an open book; a book that would have been banned in Boston.

She laughed hoarsely. "Ah! I see. You are protecting him. Really! You men! Georges is such a baby. Ah, I was afraid of the competition of this island!" She said this in a voice that did not expect to be believed. "Ah, well, he has been such a good hard-working little boy for so long, he is permitted a little flirtation, no? Still, I will make his life miserable when he shows up." She made no move toward the door. Instead she arranged herself on the sofa in a series of undulating waves.

Adams cleared his throat impatiently. "I'll get you that memo, Muldoon."

"Thanks. Then I'll be on my way."

"You're not going on to the Casino with us?"

"I'll be back. A couple of things I must do."

He looked at his watch. "We'll be leaving about eleven-twenty."

"We?"

"The Hertzys and myself, of course. If Georges isn't back, I'll take Gigi on to Elsa's party."

When Adams left the room, Mrs. Hertzy said, "Elsa will be surprised to see you walk into her party with me."

There was a flash of irony in her eyes I couldn't figure. How much had Elsa told her? For that matter, how much was there to tell? I still was not certain as to how far things had gone between me and Elsa Planquet.

From where I stood above the sofa I was getting an unobstructed view of the mountain ranges. I thought, she's working at it hard. But I retained enough objectivity to wonder why she had come to Adams' room instead of phoning. The upturned eyes revealed a cool calculation beneath the studied innocence. One thing was certain, she didn't seem too much perturbed over the whereabouts of her missing husband.

"Elsa is such a dear," she said almost mechanically. "We adore one another. It's such fun to see her and Mother after so long. It's been over a year."

"Your mother is here too?"

"But surely you have met Mother? Everyone has! She is staying with Elsa and Pepe. Elsa insisted she have a vacation."

"From what?"

"Mother has a dress shop in New York. She's an angel. Everyone loves her!"

She bent forward for a cigarette and I saw beyond the ranges to the valleys.

She sighed. "I'm afraid Pepe is too much for poor Elsa. Too much for any woman! You know Pepe."

"I've met him," I said shortly. I knew she was fishing.

"Ah, he is so naughty, so dreadfully naughty."

"To say the least."

"He can be cruel, really thoughtless. This redhead, his new discovery ... poor Lorna Parks."

"What about Lorna Parks?"

"I thought everyone knew. She was to play the lead in the film Pepe is going to make here on Venzola. But he saw this redhead in Paris and threw poor Lorna out. How he still managed to hang on to Babs Wentworth's money is beyond me."

"Babs Wentworth?"

"She is financing the film. She really put money into it with the understanding that Lorna would play the lead. We all thought Pepe had gone too far. But apparently he knows his danger line better than we do. Fantastic!"

Adams came back into the room. I wondered what had taken him so long. He handed me a slip of folded paper and I put it into my pocket and moved toward the door. Adams had gone to the sofa and was about to sit there. I thought they looked pretty damned chummy. I wondered whether the dead man had had the same idea.

"We'll meet you at the hotel entrance at eleven-fifteen," Adams said.

"I'm sure Georges will be back by then," Gigi said.

"I wouldn't count on it," I said.

There was a sudden silence. The smile died on her lips. She looked quickly from me to Adams.

"What does he mean, Phillip?"

Phillip Adams was staring at me in a puzzled manner. "I don't know."

I put on a grin. "Just a wishful thought," I said.

"He's flirting with you," Adams said. There was a note of relief in his voice.

"Ah? So?" But I saw the cloud of fear still there behind the baby blue.

I went out into the hall and shut the door behind me. A shadow moved far down at the end of the corridor. I ran quickly down across the thick carpet. When I reached the corner and turned there was nothing to be seen. I stood there a moment listening. From behind one of the doors came the muffled sound of a woman laughing. I went back to the elevators and rang the bell. The car seemed to take a long time in coming. When I got down into the lobby I saw the redhead who had been with Planquet sitting alone at one of the tables in the garden. As I made my way toward the main entrance she stared at me with a sort of brazen contempt in her eyes. I got a carriage and directed the driver to take me to the Planquets' villa out on the mountain road. Then I settled back, lit a match, and unfolded the note. In the flickering light I saw immediately that the anonymous note that had been written to Adams was in the same handwriting as the note I had found on Hertzy's body. The same miserly crossbar on the "t's," the careful, pinched letters.

I used the second match to light a cigarette. Then I began to think.

Chapter Six

THE PLANQUET VILLA, 10:45 P.M.

I left the carriage at the gates and walked up through the gardens toward the low ultramodern house with its curved glass shimmering pools, illuminated statuary, black marble terraces. A maid asked me to wait in a small sitting room overlooking the gardens and the swimming pool. Rising out of the darkened gardens were life-sized statues, male and female, realistically executed nudes apparently all created by the same artist. The stone figures had a certain brutal power, and spotlit as they were in the soft night they seemed to fill the artificial gardens with a sense of pulsating sensuality. Dominating one end of the pool was the stone figure of a stocky, powerful male, shocking in its lusty realism.

I felt a moment's anger. It was impossible to think of Elsa, with her delicate beauty, wandering among these obscene figures. At least the Elsa who, recreated from my drunken days, had become almost a dream figure of the desirable.

Behind me in the room she said, "Well?"

I turned. She rose like some exotic flower from a pink cloud of a gown, and though she had assumed the attitude of cool hauteur there was a look in the depths of her eyes that might have meant she had been standing there in the center of this vulgar room waiting for me all of her life. All my calculated words went hurtling down into limbo.

"Elsa ..."

I started to move toward her. For a moment she still waited, then suddenly, as though stricken, she backed away and made a warning gesture.

"No!"

"Elsa ..."

"Mother will join us at any moment," she said swiftly.

I got hold of myself. "We haven't got much time. There are some things I've got to ask. But aside from that, when ... when?"

She walked to the windows overlooking the gardens. "I waited for you," she said.

"You knew what happened. Mamma Peroni told you when you phoned. I got away from Ferechini as quickly as I could. Anyway, our date was for nine-thirty."

"No," she said decisively, "it was for eight-thirty."

The maid came back into the room with drinks. Elsa stood by the window regarding the naked stone man by the pool with a sort of cold indifference. When the maid had gone I said, indicating the statue, "Doesn't it embarrass you?"

She shrugged. "Pepe posed for it. Most of the other statues were modeled by stars in his pictures. Pepe tells everyone he posed for it. It amuses him to see their shocked reactions."

"And your reactions?"

"It makes me ill," she said quietly.

Then she turned. "What has happened?"

She caught me off guard. "There's ... I can't tell you. Not yet."

"So!" She came close to me and lowered her voice. "Something terrible has happened!"

"What makes you so certain?"

"A feeling. I've had it all evening. And when you phoned ..."

"Why didn't you wait for me at the Caffè del Porto?"

She turned away. "You're in some trouble, Hart."

"Tell me, why didn't you wait?"

She hesitated. "You surely didn't expect me to go on making a spectacle of myself sitting in the Caffè del Porto alone?"

I counted ten, decided not to say it. Not yet.

"I came back here then," she went on quickly. "As it was, Pepe was terribly annoyed with me for having left the cocktail party of the Count Cassi."

"It that all he was annoyed about?"

"I see that you don't know Pepe very well," she said with sudden bitterness. "Still, as Mamma always says, he is, after all, a genius!" And then before I could reply she went on in a chiding voice, "Pepe will be disconsolate at missing you. Unfortunately he had an engagement to pick up his latest discovery at the Miramar. I'm told she is quite lovely. I'm giving this little supper party at the Casino for her."

"That's decent of you."

"Under the circumstances, very! Still ..."

We lapsed back into silence. I was uneasily aware of the statue at the end of the pool. "What the hell kind of an exhibitionist is he?"

"French," she said cryptically. She took a sip of her wine. She looked me in the eyes for a moment and I saw that she was either puzzled or nervous or maybe both. What did she expect? How far was I committed ... or was I lucky enough to be committed at all?

She seemed again to be waiting. Finally I said, "You know I meant what I said last night." That sounded safe.

She turned her wide innocent eyes on me. "Did you, Hart? Say it again."

"Well, darling ..." I stumbled on. "You remember ..."

Deadpan still, she said, "Yes. But I want you to say it again."

"Well, sweetie ... you know that ... that ..."

And then she laughed. She put back her head and laughed until the tears came to her eyes. Finally she said, "You haven't the faintest idea what you said last night and you know it."

"The words don't matter," I said, reaching for a straw. "You know that ... you and I ..."

"Have nothing further to discuss on that subject at the moment!" Her words were clipped and final.

"For God's sake, give me a break. I know I'm behaving like a first-class louse, but—"

She put her hand on my aim. "No," she said gently. "You're not that, Hart. I wouldn't have permitted you to come here if I thought that. It's just that tonight ..."

"Yes," I said, feeling suddenly deflated and tired. "Tonight. What were you doing with Georges Hertzy at the Caffè del Porto?"

She gasped and stepped away from me. "Who told you that?"

"It's a small island, baby. You know that."

"Yes, but ..."

"Then you don't deny it?"

After a moment she said coldly, "He happened to be there. After all, he is my brother-in-law. You can't make a scandal out of that."

"Depends. What were you quarreling about?"

The color rose to her face. "You have no right to question me like this. I didn't expect it from you. What difference does it make?" And then in sudden anger, "This island—these people—they spoil everything! Everything becomes soiled and ugly. The way you ask me about Georges, the nasty implication ..."

"Don't get me wrong. It's not that, Elsa. There's something else ... worse, maybe."

"Worse?"

Her word hung there in the sudden silence. I heard a movement in the hall and turned quickly. A short, plump woman of middle age, fashionably dressed, was standing in the doorway.

She didn't have time to get the expression out of her eyes, an expression that was obviously meant for me. The sheer malevolence of her gaze was disconcerting.

Elsa wheeled about. "Mother!"

The woman took one step across the threshold, then held her ground. "It's almost eleven, Elsa," she said coldly. "We promised to pick up Armando at that time."

"Yes, of course." It was disturbing to see the sophisticated woman I had felt Elsa to be changed in an instant into a docile child. "This is my mother, Hart ... Mrs. Bennol. Mother, this is Mr. Muldoon."

"I know," the woman said flatly.

"He is coming to the Casino with us," Elsa said almost defiantly.

"No," I said. "I promised to go with Mr. Adams. I'm to meet him at his hotel."

"Adams!" Mrs. Bennol said in astonishment. "Phillip Adams?"

"Yes," I said, enjoying myself. "He's an old friend."

"An old friend. How odd! I don't remember Phillip ever mentioning ..." She thawed a bit. "How nice. Well, Elsa?"

"Can we drop you anywhere, Hart?" Elsa asked nervously.

"You're picking up the Count Cassi?"

"Yes."

"Good. I have to see him about something. I'll go along with you."

"You have to see Armando? Whatever for?"

"I'm not quite certain yet."

Mrs. Bennol had been watching me with narrowed, appraising

eyes.

"A mysterious young man, to say the least. Get your wrap, Elsa."

"Yes, mother."

Elsa left the room. Mrs. Bennol still stood by the door. I noticed her eyes were small and very bright.

"You are a friend of Armando Cassi's?" she asked. There was something more than mere curiosity in her voice.

I shrugged, implying that it was a subject that I didn't choose to discuss.

"Ah," she said.

"You know him well, madame?"

"Oh, no," she said quickly. "He's someone I meet at parties ... charming ... Last year he visited with some friends of mine in New York." She shifted to a social falsetto. "I'm having the most marvelous time on Venzola. It was so sweet of Pepe to insist I stay with them."

"You are lucky to have such beautiful daughters, madame."

She gave me a sharp, questioning look. "Yes. Very. You know Gigi, then, also?"

"Yes," I said, and then very carefully, "and Georges Hertzy, of course."

"Oh." Her voice was suddenly bleak.

Elsa came back into the room with a white wrap about her shoulders. We went out to the front, where a smart limousine waited. I wondered how Pepe Planquet managed all this luxury on films that failed at the box office.

When we were about to get into the car Mrs. Bennol said suddenly, "Oh, dear ... I forgot I was expecting a call from New York. I must tell Maria to have it transferred to the Casino. I'll be only one moment."

When we were alone, standing in the drive beside the car, Elsa suddenly whispered, "I will go to see the sun come up from the Palace of Tiberius. It's a lovely sight, Hart ... and no one else goes there."

It was so unexpected that it took a full minute before my blood began to respond.

"Elsa ..."

She laughed and raised her voice to the artificial timbre of her mother's. "And, now, shall we join the children?"

Mrs. Bennol came down the path, her bracelets jangling in the stillness of the night.

Chapter Seven

COUNT CASSI'S FLAT, 11:00 P.M.

The flat was in a renovated palace just off the Via Minerva. I climbed through spacious halls to a gleaming red door on the second floor and rang the bell under the crest. After a moment the door was opened by a young man in a butler's coat. He was too young and too handsome for his job; he would have looked more at home in the prow of a fishing craft. He smiled in a manner that was not service, that was, in fact, unpleasantly conspiratorial.

"Sì, signore?"

I stepped quickly past him into a Romanesque reception hall. "Tell the Count that Muldoon is here to see him."

The boy disappeared through an archway. I could hear low voices from somewhere back in the vast apartment. Then I heard the boy speak and sudden silence, followed a moment later by a whispered consultation. After a bit the boy came back and now his eyes were wary.

"This way, if you please."

I followed him through a long hall into an enormous sitting room, heavy with brocades and ornate furniture and weighted by a vaulted ceiling seething with cupids. The Count Cassi awaited me before a marble fireplace. He was like a long string bean on which had been attached a Hapsburg nose. His dinner clothes were elegantly shabby and he wore a monocle in a manner more Prussian than Neopolitan.

"Ah, Mr. Muldoon," he said in excellent English. "I was so sorry you could not make it to my little cocktail party."

"I didn't know I was invited."

"But certainly. Madame Planquet asked especially that I send you an invitation."

"I was otherwise engaged."

Beyond him I saw the knob of a closed door turn, then fall back into place. The boy servant had disappeared. Most of the debris of the cocktail party had been cleared away. The place had the frozen look of a museum.

"I would ask you to have a drink with me, but at any moment I expect Madame Planquet and her mother to call for me to—"

"Yes," I said. "They're downstairs, waiting now. I came with them."

"So. In that case, we should not keep the ladies waiting."

"They understand that I wanted a moment with you."

The Count flicked an ash from his cigarette. He sighed and looked down into the fire. He gave me no opening, but waited, letting me charge into unknown country blindly.

"What time did you last see Georges Hertzy?"

He showed not the faintest sign of surprise. "Hertzy. Ah, you mean Madame   Planquet's   charming   brother-in-law? He was here at my party. Why do you ask?"

"What time did he leave?"

The Count smiled. "Really, Mr. Muldoon, there were many people here. I haven't the faintest idea when Mr. Hertzy left."

"You didn't see him after the party?"

"After?" The Count frowned, perplexed. "No. I haven't been out of my apartment. But why do you ask?"

"He's disappeared," I said.

The Count straightened up and for the first time allowed some emotion to flicker over his face.

"You are joking?"

"He left this party and went to the Caffè del Porto. After that he spent a short time with a French girl at the Villa Rosa."

"A French girl?" His voice was really sharp now. Sharp and, I felt, somewhat apprehensive.

"The one they call Yvonne. You know her?"

He hesitated, looked down to his cigarette, readjusted his monocle.

"There are so many people of this sort, it is hard to say. Perhaps I have met her." He shrugged.

"She said she did some work for you. What was it?"

"Work for me?" he exploded. "Fantastic! What sort of work?"

"I thought you might tell me that," I said quietly.

He laughed dryly. "Nonsense. The girl has fantasies. I am not in the habit of employing female prostitutes for ..."

"Political work?"

The words drifted off into the vast room up toward the fat cupids. He moved away from the fireplace. Somewhere in the front of the apartment a phone began to ring.

After a moment he said, "May I ask, Mr. Muldoon, why you are making this your business?"

"I've always been a snooper."

"Yes," he said coldly. "For a price. For whom do you work?"

The boy butler appeared in the arch to the hall.

"*Vostre' eccellenza*, the telephone. It is important."

"Ah." The two exchanged a meaningful glance. The Count excused himself and followed the boy out into the hall. I could hear him talking in a low voice but the words were unintelligible. Quickly I smashed out my cigarette and crossed to the door on the opposite side of the room, the one in which I had seen the knob turn. I listened. There was no sound from within. Carefully I took hold of the knob, turned it, and pushed inward.

I stood on the threshold of a room, dark, except for a stream of harsh light that fell from an open bathroom door. What I saw on the edge of this beam of light was like something in a surrealist nightmare. Standing facing the light, face in profile to me, was a woman in an elaborate evening gown, a silver gown that billowed out from her slim body. Her face was rather pretty in an oddly childish manner and I felt I had seen her somewhere before ... in a dream? Jet-black hair, straight and lacquered in a long bob, jeweled bracelets glistening at powdered wrists. She stood there, facing the lighted bathroom like a figure of wax, expressionless and waiting.

A shadow fell across the threshold of the bathroom and a man came out. He was stark naked and in his hand he held something that glittered metallically, something that might have been a knife. Neither of them was, as yet aware of me. I stood transfixed, watching the man come to the waiting woman. His back was to the light. But now, at her side, he turned in profile and raised the glittering metal. For one sickening moment I thought he would plunge the knife into her heart. Instead he brought it down to the woman's arm, high up, under the lace that fell from her shoulders. And then I realized that the instrument was not a knife, but a hypodermic needle. The woman closed docile eyes and the man muttered something in Italian.

It was only then that I recognized the guy. It was the *Comandante* of the local *carabinieri*, Ferechini.

I must have made some sound standing there just inside the door. He whirled about. I stepped back into the living room and softly closed the door. I thought, This is a nightmare, some mad dream of things that are not happening. Out there in the hall the Count was still talking in a low voice. Then I heard the click of the receiver. I went back to the center of the room and lit a cigarette, waiting. I didn't have to wait long. The door to the bedroom was flung open and Ferechini came bursting forth, clutching a blanket about himself with one hand. In the other he held an automatic.

"So!" he said breathlessly. "You! What are you doing here?"

"I came for a shot," I said.

"Pig! I have had enough of you! I warned you earlier. I warned you!"

Behind me Cassi said in a calm voice, "Get hold of yourself, Ferechini."

"He went to the bedroom. He saw—"

"Quiet!" Cassi's voice was an order. "Perhaps next time you will have sense enough to lock the bedroom door."

"I tell you, Armando, this man is dangerous. I told you that we should—"

"Stop talking!" Cassi barked out the order. Slowly Ferechini dropped the gun to his side and pulled the blanket tighter about himself as though for warmth. "There is nothing to worry about. I will take care of things."

He said it quietly and smiled as he said it and looked into my eyes with a kind of chilly friendliness. I would have preferred Ferechini's bluster.

The *Comandante* shrugged, annoyed but submissive. He turned and went back into the bedroom. Up in the front of the apartment a bell tinkled.

"So," I said. "You will take care of things."

"Ferechini is somewhat impulsive. As a gentleman I am sure you will forget whatever it is that you saw. Human nature is, at best, fallible."

"I'm not much of a gentleman," I said.

"Perhaps," he said coldly, "before the evening is over I can persuade you to become one."

I still couldn't seem to get my feet down into reality. The sinister scene I had witnessed in the bedroom, Ferechini's anger, Cassi's calm and cold threat. What were they about? Who was the strange woman who had waited like wax for the hypodermic needle?

There were voices in the outer hall and a moment later Elsa came into the room.

"Really, there is a limit to waiting, you know, even for such two desirable men."

"My dear," Cassi said contritely, "I am so sorry. Mr. Muldoon and I were discussing a little matter."

"I can't imagine what."

I looked at my watch. It was eleven-ten. "I must be going," I said.

Neither of them made a move to follow. I turned at the arch. I noticed that Elsa was very pale. She was looking at Cassi as though for instructions. Cassi didn't move.

"We will see you at the Casino," he said coldly.

I hesitated. Why were they not coming down to the car? What did

Cassi wish to speak with Elsa about? And why was she so loath to look me in the eyes?

I shrugged and stepped past her and went down the long hall. The boy butler waited, unsmiling, by the door. Behind me I heard Cassi say, "Now, Elsa ..." and then stop, waiting obviously for the sound of the outer door closing behind me. I gave it to him. I went down the vast stairs, through the marble lobby to the street. Mrs. Bennol leaned forward to stare at me from the glass box of the limousine. She didn't smile. She simply stared with small, unblinking eyes. I bowed ironically and went up toward the Via Minerva with the silence of the lower town at my back.

Chapter Eight

THE CASINO, 12:05 A.M.

The Casino, flooded blue with artificial moonlight, came floating to us down around the long sweep of a neat gravel driveway. A rococo palace constructed during the closing years of the last century, it retained the curiously raffish elegance of the period. Royalty in its more irresponsible moments and a once wealthy aristocracy had made this marble pleasure dome its headquarters during the short but fashionable season of spring.

Gigi Hertzy said, "It's the way things should be."

"It is said," Phillip Adams remarked, "that on an evening in April 1914, the King of Bulgaria lost over a million dollars at the roulette tables in the space of four hours. But then I have heard the same tale at Monte Carlo and Deauville."

"I wish to believe it!" Gigi cried. "It is so romantic!"

"So is the Chase National Bank," I said.

"Phillip!" she said with a laugh. "Your friend is an appalling cynic. An enemy of charm. I will not have it!"

For reasons neither had bothered to explain, they had kept me waiting in the lobby of the Miramar for more than twenty minutes. Now she sat between Adams and me, and though the carriage seat was deep and fairly wide, she managed to make me very much aware of her presence through a series of evenly spaced and apparently accidental pressures. It was as impossible to be objective or impersonal about Gigi Hertzy as it would have been to engage in speculation over a sleek black panther crouching at one's side. Her arm, her hand would lightly touch my leg, her childish laugh would tinkle out above the slow clop-clop of the ancient horses' hoofs, and I would forget to wonder at her airy unconcern to the whereabouts of her missing husband. Her mechanical doll-like gaiety added to the unreality of my situation. This was dream stuff. Down behind me, death, grotesque and final, was locked into a room of a tawdry pension, while I moved through icy laughter toward a marble palace bathed in blue moonlight and the music of a Strauss waltz whispering across hedges rigid as granite. A liveried footman in a costume that might have been retrieved from a Romberg operetta waited for us at the entrance. We mounted wide steps and went into a vast foyer of mahogany, red damask, gold-trimmed panels, and crystal chandeliers. Small tables were set up before banquettes around three sides of the room. At the moment they were deserted except for an aged woman who sat at a corner table playing solitaire while a waiter hovered near her shoulder. Through the thick draperies masking the arch that led into the main restaurant came the muffled sound of laughter and music and the clink of silver on china, and from a similar arch on the opposite wall came the monotonous chant of the croupiers, the click of an ivory ball on metal, the hum that ceased as the ball fell onto its number. There was something eerie about the vast elegant silence of the foyer and the lone woman playing solitaire.

Slowly her hands moved over the cards as though impeded by the many bracelets glittering on her pudgy arms. Somehow she gave the impression of being part of the decor, some daring new mechanical innovation dreamed up by a decorator, a grotesque doll whose movements were motivated by exquisitely wrought cogs and springs. Her gestures were evenly spaced, considered and patient, and she seemed not to be waiting, but to have arrived at some fixed point in her destiny. She looked up from her cards and eyed us with the frank curiosity of the socially secure, in which arrogance would have been affectation and hostility bad manners.

Gigi smiled radiantly at the old woman but said to me in an ironic undertone. "Mad as a hatter, poor dear. The Duchessa di Cabrieni."

"Cabrieni!" Adams said, startled. "Impossible!"

"It's true, Phillip. One of the great names of Italy, and now look."

"She must be the widow of the old Duc. When I was a boy he visited my father's house in Washington. He was a distinguished man and a great liberal. What in the world is she doing here?"

"My dear!" Gigi said. "Don't you know? She lives in one little room down near the mole. Poor as a church mouse. The diamonds are glass and the rubies paste. She comes here every night and imagines she is receiving at a great soiree in her former palace, the lovely palace on the top of the mountain, the one that is now owned by Babs Wentworth. She has lost all sense of time and place."

"This is pitiful!" Adams said.

"The Casino management thinks she brings the place luck. They supply her with supper and champagne nightly during the season. The clientele is amused!"

There was scorn for the weak and aged in her voice and the blindness of health to illness. And there was something else; something edgy and bitter, out of all proportion to the episode or the character involved.

Rather coldly Adams said, "Mussolini destroyed her husband. Mercifully enough, he died just before the beginning of the Second World War. I haven't heard of his wife in years. This is shocking. Come."

We approached the befuddled Duchessa, who offered her hand to Adams and bestowed on me a warm smile of greeting. "Ah! I am delighted that you could come to my modest little entertainment, *signori*. It is not like the old days, of course, but since Versailles we must accommodate ourselves to the times. Is it not so?"

Fortunately she didn't expect her time lag to be corroborated, but turned to Gigi. "Such beauty is rare these days, my dear. Of a special place, I would guess. Silesia, no?"

"No," Gigi said coldly. "I am an American, madame."

"How convenient." There was unexpected acid in the voice of the Duchessa. She turned her mild curiosity on me. "And you, young man—you are, of course, an American. Very appealing. Sometimes I feel you are all a bit too serious—inclined to turn the game into the hunt."

"I haven't been here long enough to engage in either the game or the hunt," I lied.

"Watch out for the women of Rome! They are spiders. Man-eating spiders. I myself am of Tuscany. My family was there when the Medicis were mere upstarts from the country. Ah, well ..."

"A charming party," Adams said somewhat uneasily.

"*Grazie, signore.* But I am somewhat guilty. You see, my beloved husband is away. On a mission for his government. He is now visiting with your distinguished President, Mr. Woodrow Wilson, and they have important plans to discuss." She lowered her voice. "If you should see him upon his return, will you be kind enough not to tell him of this lighthearted little entertainment. He does not approve of frivolity in these difficult times. Our friends do not understand him. Those with whom I danced as a young girl in the white and gold ballrooms ..." She stopped suddenly and frowned in a dazed manner. "An old man toppled over like a flower cut at the stem.... His hair was white and in the sunlight it looked like a halo. They told me he was dead. I do not believe them. I turned away and never looked back."

She extended a shaking hand toward the champagne. She glanced at the waiter almost fearfully. "Today I do not even recognize the faces of my staff. Perhaps the old ones, the faithful ones, have gone to Africa to fight the savages." She looked at us again with pale blind eyes. "It is odd. In the old days we did not discuss unpleasant subjects at a ball. But I could not help but be touched and shocked. They spoke of murder."

For a moment no one said anything. From the restaurant came the sound of a Strauss waltz, muted and as unreal as music from a dusty music box.

"Murder, madame?" I finally said. "They?"

The Duchessa contemplated the pale bubbles. "They sat at the next table and spoke in low voices in deference to me, I imagine, but I heard. The names fell hard as hail in a summer day. I find it disturbing."

"They were people you knew, madame?" I asked intently. Adams gave me a puzzled frown.

Impatiently Gigi said, "Don't tease the old dear, Mr. Muldoon. She has fantasies."

The pale faded eyes focused on Gigi. "The young are lacking in manners these days. I know everyone at my parties, of course ... everyone. Strangers never come through my doors. And yet ... and yet ... they had charming manners. Charming. And they spoke of this dreadful murder. Poor young man."

"When did this crime take place?"

"Tonight. Tonight, of course."

Gigi dug her fingers into my arm. "We must go in! Elsa is waiting." Her voice sounded shrill and ugly.

"That lovely waltz ..." the Duchessa said.

"People gossip a great deal. Perhaps you misunderstood, madame. Perhaps you misunderstood what they said about this crime."

"This is absurd!" Gigi said.

"I don't get it, Muldoon," Adams said.

"Oh, no," the Duchessa said. "I heard every word. Every word. But so many people ... charming people ... so many people since. Why are you so insistent, young man?"

"Yes," Gigi said, "why?"

"You heard the name of the man who was murdered?"

"Yes. But ..."

"Was it Hertzy? Georges Hertzy?"

Adams' head snapped up. Gigi's fingers literally dug into my arm. The Duchessa shook her head. "No. That was not the name. I would have known. The name was different. Odd. But I can't ... Not now. I do think we should speak of more pleasant matters."

Gigi whispered, "This is a cruel joke! You're trying to scare me."

I watched the Duchessa. She avoided my eyes now and smiled mechanically toward a party that had just come in through the main entrance. I began to wonder about her. Aloud I said, "Yes. It was cruel. It was a joke."

Adams frowned. He was waiting for some enlightenment. I grinned. Gigi snatched away her arm. "Come on!" she said harshly, and started for the entrance to the restaurant. As we followed her I filed the Duchessa away for future reference. Behind us one of the incoming party said, "Madame, what a marvelous ball!"

Still angry, Gigi said, "You're a sadist. What a terrible thing to have said." And then with an astounding shift of mood, "I refuse to worry about Georges! We all have to grow up sometime. Maybe it's Georges' time tonight!"

When we were halfway to the great arch, Ferechini came through the gold curtains. He was dressed in tight fitting dinner clothes and his manner was more like a floorwalker's than ever. A murderous floorwalker, if his glance at me meant anything. It was impossible to believe that a little more than a half hour before I had been witness to the macabre scene when he had stood beside the strange woman in Cassi's grandiose apartment, with a hypodermic needle in his hand. He raised his eyebrows when he realized I was with Gigi Hertzy and Adams.

"*Signor* Ferechini!" Gigi cried gaily. "Do you have a bureau for missing husbands?"

"Missing husbands, *signora*?"

"Mine. Mr. Muldoon here thinks he has been murdered!"

A sort of dullness clouded Ferechini's eyes. He looked at me and I was disturbed to see a kind of growing speculation growing behind that oily mask. "I have met Mr. Muldoon. He has a delightful sense of, shall we say, fantasy. I am sure he will agree with me that missing husbands on the island of Venzola usually turn up very much alive."

"Ah!" Gigi cried with that unnatural laugh. "Then you guarantee this!"

He shrugged. "Except for unsavory portions of the lower town, we have had no crimes of violence on this island for many years."

"The lower town?" For just an instant Gigi's smile faded.

"He means the lower classes," I said.

Ferechini had turned his back on me and was smiling in an oily, anxious manner at Adams. "I hope, Mr. Adams, you are enjoying your visit on our modest little island."

"Very much," Adams said shortly. But as we started past him toward the arch, Ferechini said softly, "Sometimes—not often, but sometimes—one is, out of the generosity of the heart, too kind to those who are not too desirable. Fabricators of slander. We try to warn our distinguished visitors."

Adams winked at me. "I know exactly what and who you mean, *Comandante*. Thank you for the warning."

The wink had not escaped Ferechini's notice. He scowled at me with something in his eyes I didn't like. He seemed too goddamned sure of himself about something. What had Cassi decided? I wondered if Ferechini came every night to the Casino or whether this was a special occasion.

In a low, malicious voice Gigi said, "So. You are undesirable, and Phillip knows it. How intriguing. I will think of you differently from now on."

"That was more than I hoped for so soon," I said, and interested myself in the lower extremities of the plunging neckline.

We went through the gold draperies covering the great arch and helped Gigi form a suitable picture at the top of the wide stairs as we waited for the maître d'hôtel.

For a moment I was hardly aware of the glittering scene before us. I was thinking of Hertzy, sprawled stiffly on the floor of my room; his wife, who at least appeared to be callously indifferent to his whereabouts; the odd timing of Adams' request to meet him at the Miramar; the knife that had been hurled at me in the Via Cellini; the macabre scene in the bedroom at Count Cassi's; and now the mention of murder by the mad Duchessa. Had she really overheard such a conversation? And, if so, was she as mad as she pretended? I had the sensation of being drawn into the heart of a web strung with tight golden strands.

Gigi said, "My dears! So much more chic than even Rome at the height of the season!"

Phillip nodded and muttered something polite. I knew he was still trying to figure out why I had asked the Duchessa about Hertzy. I turned from him and cased the room.

The scene had some of the aspects of a pageant dedicated to the restoration of a Europe where such words as "elegant" and "chic" and "*haut monde*" had been paramount. The props and the costumes were there; a pink illuminated glass dance floor amid rosewood paneling, gilt Louis Quinze chairs, arched windows opening on a marble balcony overlooking the synthetically moonlit garden, vintage wine in silver ice buckets, crystal chandeliers and the sparkle of rubies, diamonds, and emeralds against gowns from the best couturiers of Paris and Rome, two orchestras.

But somehow the actors in this pageant, despite the richness of decor and costume, did not seem at ease in their roles. Wealthy Americans from Texas, California, Detroit, and New York had not, as yet, got much below the surface of their parts, and in the leading roles assigned to them they lived in the shadow of the splendid performances of the original production, given, of course, by their late departed British cousins. Remnants of Edda Ciano's sinister version of Roman café society—the nasty little playboys and girls of fascism, expensively garbed and derisive—carried with them the odor of a fourth-rate road-company edition of "The Borgias at Play." Plump and aging women, denationalized by common longing—widows, ersatz or otherwise—clung to bronzed young men who had been plucked not so fresh from the swimming pools and beaches of the Riviera or the bars and hotel lobbies of Venice, Rome, and Paris. Newly rich film stars were hectically gay as they rubbed elbows with titled communists, merchants from Antwerp and Lyon, weary remnants of noble families, sloe-eyed ballet entrepreneurs, fashionable writers, steamship owners, highly paid spies, fashionable whores, bright young men whose eyes met knowingly over the shoulders of their dance partners, wealthy drug addicts, and munitions kings. But there was one common thread in this polyglot assemblage: an almost hysterical search for youth, and, in youth, reassurance. So it was the young and beautiful who secretly ruled this room.

For a moment the sound of dance music faded and I thought: This is the ancient pleasure house of the Romans and somewhere out in the night Vesuvius waits again.

"Mr. Muldoon! What *are* you dreaming about?"

Out of the corner of my eye I saw Ferechini move like a shadow behind the opening in the draperies.

"Death," I said.

Gigi's smile faded. "How cheerful! Do you intend to be the skeleton at the feast?"

I didn't reply. Adams looked at me and frowned. The maître d'hôtel dangled before us like parchment, waiting. I knew now that somewhere in or near this tawdry splendor was a murderer, and perhaps the mad Duchessa knew. I felt I should turn and go back to the lobby and talk to the woman who sat alone with her cards and champagne. I couldn't see Ferechini now. But I knew that he, too, was out there waiting for something in the vast empty room. Waiting for what?

"My God, Phillip!" Gigi said with an explosive laugh. "What is this Muldoon? A minister? Or just a general bore?"

I hesitated, still feeling strongly the impulse to turn and question the Duchessa. But Phillip touched my arm and said, "Elsa is waiting." And then I saw her across the sea of faces looking straight into my eyes, and for just an instant I remembered something that made my wrists throb, and, remembering that, I forgot the other. The heavy gold draperies hissed softly as they fell into place behind us and we walked down the steps and out across the laughter and music toward Elsa, and she waited, unsmiling, looking into my eyes as we approached, and for the first time there was no attempt at guile. The message in her eyes was for me alone.

Chapter Nine

THE CASINO, 12:20 P.M.

The direct challenge in Elsa's eyes as I approached the table had been breath-taking. Why had she reserved it for this moment? Why had she avoided it when we were alone in that house among the obscene statues? And why had she stayed on in the Count Cassi's apartment after I had left?

But even with the questions and the doubts in my mind, I knew, looking down on her incredible beauty, that this was the reason I had stayed on in Venzola, and it was as good a reason as any I had ever had in my somewhat checkered career.

Her husband wasn't at the table at the moment. I figured the extra empty chairs belonged to him and the redhead I had seen at the Miramar. Mrs. Bennol sat next to the Count Cassi and neither of them gave me more than a distant nod. I looked at Elsa for a cue, but she was once again an impenetrable mask of good manners.

"You are outrageous guests!" she cried, addressing Gigi and Philip. "Almost an hour late. My table has been like a desert! Where in the world have you been?"

"Trying to track down Georges," Gigi said with a pout.

"Darling!" Elsa darted a quick uneasy look at me. "You have not found him? I don't understand. It's so unlike Georges."

Gigi shrugged. "He's like a boy let out of school. And you know what Venzola can be at recess! If he wants to make a fool of himself ..."

She caught herself up and looked almost guiltily toward her mother. Mrs. Bennol smiled a lacquered smile. "My pet, he will turn up, more contrite, a better husband than ever. I can assure you."

Quickly Elsa said, "How nice of you to bring Mr. Muldoon, Gigi." For just an instant her eyes laughed into mine. "We can always use an extra man, you know."

I took the empty chair next to Mrs. Bennol. The Count leaned around her and peered at me in a manner that made me think of photographs I had seen of De Gaulle regarding Churchill and F.D.R. at Casablanca. There was nothing in his eyes to recall the scene that had taken place at his apartment.

"It is pleasant," he said in a bored voice, "to think that in the darkness of our times there is still some light, some gaiety, some charm in such places as the Casino of Venzola."

"The darkness of our times," Mrs. Bennol said with a grating laugh. "Count Cassi has been telling me the most fascinating things about politics." Her voice was like a husky caricature of a baby's.

"Imagine!" I said. "Politics in such surroundings. Beautiful women, gay music, vintage wine ..."

"Still," the Count said, and now there was a slight edge to his voice, "the danger is ignorance. Naïveté, misinterpretation. Yet in this room it is perhaps a foolish subject. Especially when any newcomer to the table might turn out to be a G.P.U. agent or a member, say, of your own F.B.I."

"Or," I said deliberately, "a big wheel in the resurgent Fascist party."

"Yes," Cassi said coolly, "even that."

The dream, I thought, the insane, meaningless dream.

Mrs. Bennol cleared her throat uncomfortably and said with a shrill laugh, "But the Count makes even politics interesting to such an ignorant woman as I. I am convinced that he is a genius."

"You use that word generously, madame," the Count said, not without irony. "If I am not mistaken, you used it in connection with your son-in-law, Pepe Planquet ..."

"But after all," Mrs. Bennol said, "all the world knows Pepe is a genius!"

"Maybe," I said, "because he has informed the world of that fact."

I scanned the dance floor and finally found Planquet dancing with the luscious redhead who had come forth with him from the elevator at the Miramar. He clung to her as though she were about to be snatched from his arms. The orchestra was playing a rumba but they were engaged in their own variation of that dance; practically every part of their bodies moving except their feet.

The Count laughed wearily. "Sometimes it's a wonder to me that Pepe ever has anything left over for the bedroom."

"Such a naughty boy." Mrs. Bennol smiled indulgently. "He adores women, and they, poor dears, adore him." I noticed her small bright eyes turn anxiously toward Elsa, who was elaborately ignoring the spectacle her husband was making on the floor.

"And the redhead?" I asked.

Mrs. Bennol shrugged. "Pepe's latest discovery. A little American. She arrived from Paris this afternoon. I believe he found her in some Paris music hall. I'm told she did an act where she hung by her toes from a trapeze or something equally absurd."

"Her toes?" said the Count. "Such a lovely creature to do such an unnecessarily dangerous thing." And then almost as an afterthought, "That is, if you care for that sort of thing."

Mrs. Bennol laughed sharply. "Perhaps I should have mentioned that she performed this dangerous feat in the nude."

"Ah! How amusing!"

The Count turned with a concealed yawn to Elsa.

"You are Hungarian, madame?" I asked Mrs. Bennol.

"Certainly not! I am Rumanian. My husband was General Bennol, a very great friend of the late Queen Marie. He died of a broken heart over the destruction of his country."

"But your heart, fortunately, remained intact."

"I had my two precious girls to think of."

"And how did your thinking go?"

"To the United States, of course. I was then—how do you say—broke?"

"That's how I say it, yes."

"The Americans ... How such kindness! Friends help. I now have for myself a dress shop just off Madison Avenue. Small but chic. And, if I do say it myself, do very well. I was able to send my two treasures to good schools. They met the right people. This is always important, yes. And, well ... *voilà* ... you see!"

"Not quite."

"I beg your pardon?"

"You knew Georges Hertzy in Rumania?"

She lost a little of her aplomb. "Georges? But no. I never laid eyes on Georges until the day my dear Gigi announces she intended to marry him. Ah, that girl. She could have had anything, anyone—the richest man in the world."

"And she married a nobody named Hertzy. Why?"

"Why? You ask me why?" Her voice was suddenly serious. "Ask her. And then tell me." And then, as though she couldn't prevent the reflex action, she looked toward Phillip Adams.

I laughed. "All is not lost yet!"

"You speak in riddles, Mr. Muldoon."

She turned her back on me and I heard her say to Count Cassi. "But now I see what you mean exactly, Count Cassi. If Il Duce had only listened to Ciano—or yourself—surely you would never have permitted such stupid blunders."

I managed not to gag on the champagne, got up, and asked Elsa to dance. She hesitated a moment, frowned, changed her mind, came to meet me on the edge of the floor.

We drifted out over illuminated glass. For a moment we said nothing. And it was as though for just that moment she submitted to me without question. After a bit I whispered, "I can't wait until sunrise."

"Hart, please be more discreet."

"Your husband isn't quite so fastidious."

Like a fool I had broken the spell. She stiffened in my arms. In a stilted voice she said, "He loves dancing."

When I laughed she whispered, "You know the truth. You knew it last night. I hate him!"

"Pepe? Why do you stick, then?"

"Mother."

"What's she got to do with it?"

"She's sacrificed so much for us, Gigi and I."

"Is marriage to Pepe the only career that Mamma sees fit for you?"

"I'm not much good for anything else!"

"For God's sake!"

"No. It's true. I wanted to be an actress. A good one, I mean. Through some of Mother's friends I got small parts on Broadway. I was—well, I was pretty damned terrible." She paused, then went on: "There were other men, but Pepe seemed—well, it was as though he couldn't touch me very much ... I can't explain it. And Mother ..."

"The old bitch!"

"Hart!" She turned to draw away from me but I held her fast. After a while I felt her resistance weaken. She seemed to cling to me. And then suddenly she gasped. I swung her around to see what had brought on the reaction. We were at the edge of the dance floor opposite the orchestra. At a ringside table almost beside us were Mrs. Wentworth and her party. Mrs. Wentworth was keeping up her reputation as one of the best-dressed women in the world. She was cool and chic and yet in some manner seemed to be playing a parody of the role of hostess. Lorna Parks was at the table, transformed into a boudoir kewpie doll of bows and ribbons and tulle. Freddie had been lost in transit from the Villa Rosa to the Casino, but there were three other Freddies, blond and vivacious, chirping away at Babs like excited sparrows. The third woman in the party was Yvonne, the French girl from the Villa Rosa. She sat demurely in the midst of the chattering party, looking like a schoolgirl down for the holidays. And right away I knew the sight of her had been the reason for Elsa's gasp of surprise.

"You know that girl, Elsa?"

"What girl?" Her voice was strained and unnatural.

It seemed incredible that the sight of Yvonne could have had this effect on Elsa; in fact, it seemed hardly likely that she would have known who she was. What was the French girl doing at the table of the reputedly smart Mrs. Wentworth. Was it some kind of cruel joke on the part of the American woman, or was it more sinister. And then another idea crossed my mind like a dark shadow.

"Look, sweetie," I whispered. "Can't you skip this party of Babs Wentworth's?"

"No," she said. "We are all going on there."

"Isn't it a funny hour for a party to begin?"

"Babs always does things in an original manner."

"So I've heard!"

"There is some young actress she wants Pepe to meet. It's important to him. She is financing his film, you know."

"Listen, baby. Is Babs Wentworth making a play for you?"

"Hart, really!"

"If not, you're the only woman under thirty on this island she hasn't tried to get her hands on. You know as well as I do what her tastes are."

"People tell such dreadful lies! Just because she is rich and rather eccentric ..." There was something uneasy in her voice now that I would rather not have heard.

When I said nothing she pressed against me. "You must come to Babs' party, Hart. We can get away from them. I want you to see the sunrise from the Palace of Tiberius."

My blood began to move faster. But I got down beyond my reflexes. "What's Cassi got on you, Elsa?"

"What *are* you talking about now?"

"Who is he? What's his racket? Where does he fit in?"

"Everyone knows Armando," she said coolly. "He's as much a fixture on this island as the Hotel Miramar."

"In what way? Fascist totem? Drug peddler?"

"Don't be absurd, Hart. Armando comes of a very ancient family."

"I'm not so much interested in where he comes from as where he has arrived. What if I were to tell you that while you were talking to him in his impressive living room—"

I caught myself up. She didn't seem interested. She was looking beyond me once more to the Wentworth table.

"Elsa ..."

I felt a sudden hopelessness. It was as though a film of ice had descended between us. For a moment everything else was driven from my mind. We circled the floor in silence. Once we almost collided with her husband and the redhead. Planquet seemed riveted to the girl and stared over his shoulder at us with glassy eyes in which there was no recognition of anything save his momentary preoccupation.

"The bastard! Is he crazy? Any guy who has you tied up legally and even looks at another woman must be losing his marbles."

"Pepe is nervous," she said. And then we laughed. "Oh, Hart, sometimes I think ... I wake up and I think, no, not another day. I could tell you ..." But she didn't.

I saw the Duchessa come through the gold curtains. She stood smiling, as though pleased that her guests seemed to be having such a good time. Near us someone on the dance floor laughed and said, "Crazy as a loon!" I wondered. As she began to descend the stairs toward the restaurant, Ferechini came through the curtains and stood there surveying the room like a warden in the prison yard. I noticed that he watched the Duchessa closely as she made her way between the tables, stopping now and again for a gracious word with one of her "guests." After a bit Ferechini turned and went back into the foyer.

As we revolved slowly to the waltz, the room became a kaleidoscope where faces and names danced a slow, stately dance of death in the gilt mirrors. Babs Wentworth, Yvonne, Ferechini, Mrs. Bennol, the insane Duchessa, Adams and Gigi, Count Cassi, Planquet and his uninhibited redhead, and Elsa and myself seemed part of some nightmarish ballet that had for its center the dead body of a man called Georges Hertzy. And as we danced I had the odd feeling that I was moving into a vortex where I would be smothered, obliterated by the perfumed dancers.

Into the midst of this odd fancy Elsa whispered, "I'm afraid, Hart. Desperately afraid."

I drew her close.

"Tell me, Elsa."

"I can't now. I must think. Later."

"Is it about Georges Hertzy?"

She said nothing. I went on, "Your sister doesn't seem very much concerned over the fact that he hasn't shown up."

"Gigi is like me. She's learned not to show what she really feels."

"Elsa, tell me. I might be able to help you."

"I want to, Hart, really I do, but not now. Not now."

Relentlessly I went on, "It might be convenient to your sister if Georges never showed up at all."

"What do you mean by that?"

"Maybe then her friendship with Adams could be more legal."

She broke away from me. "Take me back to our table!" she said frigidly.

"Elsa ..."

"You're an oaf!"

She turned and marched across the floor while I cursed myself for being a fool. Over near the arched windows leading out to the terrace I saw the Duchessa. She was looking anxiously about the room. Suddenly our eyes met. She smiled slightly. For a moment I thought she was trying to communicate some message over the heads of the dancers. Then she turned and went out into the electric moonlight on the terrace.

Chapter Ten

THE CASINO, 12:45 A.M.

Planquet and the redhead came up for air. I found myself seated between her and Mrs. Bennol. The redhead gave an impression of being breathless and disheveled, an impression that I surmised was, perhaps, consciously professional. Where Gigi's sexuality was almost childishly blatant and Elsa's supremely subtle, this one was one of those beautiful babies who might do anything for a buck and probably had. Her first look was a challenge and an appraisal. Apparently she was in the right company with Planquet. She gave Elsa a hard, indifferent smile, almost openly derisive, while Planquet leaned around her to case me with one of his genius-at-work looks. Then he sat back and stopped all conversation with a baritone monologue.

"You know," he said, "I do not know why I waste my time in such places. This scene—regard it—it has no interest for me whatever. As an artist, I mean. These beautiful people, these dolls, this exquisite room—a setting for mannequins. I would have to undress them, strip them down, begin all over again—get to the primitive sources of their beings."

He leaned around the redhead and glowered at me. I noticed that he seemed to need her leg for support. "You, Muldoon. You have seen in your experience what I mean—the drama, the ancient drama behind the polite charade. You understand what I say?"

"About stripping people?" I looked significantly at his hand. The redhead giggled.

"Well, getting to what makes them really tick. Surely you must realize what I mean, in your delicate work."

He caught me unawares. "In my delicate work?"

He laughed. "Your secret, monsieur, is safe with me. For the moment."

"Goodness!" Elsa said with forced gaiety. "You make it sound rather sinister, Pepe."

"Do I? Perhaps it is."

The redhead snickered again. Adams gave me a worried look. Elsa was obviously puzzled. Planquet seemed to lose interest. He went back to his pronouncements, this time to Gigi and Adams. He had almost caught me off guard. I wondered if he really had dug up my dossier or was just making wild stabs in the dark.

In a low voice the redhead said, "My name is Loretta Kelly. Not that it matters."

"It might to Mrs. Planquet," I said.

She shrugged and looked me in the eyes with that odd fixed and sultry expression.

"You're kind of cute," she said.

"I've got other plans," I said shortly.

"I've heard that before." She smiled.

I changed the subject. "So Planquet is featuring you in his new film?"

"Yes. If all goes well."

"In what way?"

"Something vulgar about financing," she said derisively. "Some woman who has to pass on me. From what I hear about her, I'll make the grade."

"Babs Wentworth?"

"I think that's it. Some dyke."

"You're pretty sure of yourself."

"I've had to be. Men, women, and children. Nothing surprises me anymore." Then, with cool detachment, "Now that we've got that straight ..."

She seemed entirely sure of Planquet's wandering hand. Mrs. Bennol turned from the Count and gave her a murderous look.

"Well, my dear Miss Kelly, how does it feel to be a movie star?"

"I'll wait and find out."

"How wise of you," Mrs. Bennol purred venomously. She got an overly sweet note in her voice. "I'm sure you will be much more effective in the part than poor Lorna Parks would have been. It was a great shock to her to discover that she wouldn't be in Pepe's film."

"I don't know about that," Miss Kelly said coldly. "I had nothing to do with her being dropped from the film."

"But, my dear child, it never occurred to me that you had. However, you know, it is odd, but somehow or other Pepe's 'discoveries' always seem to have such bad luck after the first film. Maybe after all, poor Lorna is the lucky one. Then, too, you know that Babs Wentworth is producing some young Swedish actress for Pepe to pass on before she makes her decision."

"I'm not worried," the redhead said. For the first time I realized the girl was quite drunk.

Pepe, overhearing the last part of Mrs. Bennol's conversation, exploded to the table at large, "Who is this Swede that Babs insists I meet tonight? I do not see anyone such as this at her table. Does anyone know her?"

For a moment no one spoke. Then to my surprise Count Cassi spoke. "As a matter of fact, I have met her. A Miss Bernson. Quite striking, really. Mrs. Wentworth seems to think she can act."

Before the whole table the redhead patted Pepe's hand and said, "Don't you worry about a thing, honey. I'll handle her."

Pepe laughed and shouted across the table to Elsa, "Elsa! Isn't she magnificent, my new discovery?"

Quietly Elsa said, "Miss Kelly is very beautiful."

"Beautiful? Yes, yes, of course. But it is more than that meaningless word. It is the pure uninhibited animal appeal. You see ..." And to everyone's shocked surprise he lifted his hands and cupped them over Miss Kelly's prominent breasts, allowing them to remain there for a long moment. "With these I expect to make a fortune in America!"

There was complete silence. For once even Mrs. Bennol was speechless. I controlled a desire to smash my glass in Planquet's face. Elsa looked down into her wine.

To my surprise Gigi was the first to recover. Her face was white and tense. "I think," she began hoarsely, "I think ..." But Adams touched her arm and she choked off her words. Adams cleared his throat, gave Pepe a contemptuous glance, and asked Gigi to dance. As they left the table, Elsa looked up for the first time and I saw the two sisters exchange an intense glance. For just a moment they seemed to be locked together by some deep emotion.

The redhead said, "Whoops! Someone get me my Emily Post!"

Mrs. Bennol found healing words, "Really, Pepe darling, you are a naughty boy."

Pepe grinned. "You understand me, Mamma, if no one else does."

Count Cassi rose like a statue, bowed formally to Elsa, and asked her to dance. She looked neither at me nor at her husband, but joined the unbending Count at the edge of the dance floor. I watched her move, stiff as a mannequin, into the crowd, revolving slowly in a stately waltz.

Planquet laughed. "Hypocrites! I adore to shock people! Loretta will be a big star. And for the reasons I have said. Her acting I will take care of. The critics will compare her to Duse and think of how she would be in bed." His hand on her leg was more urgent.

"And they'd be right," the redhead said thickly.

"As for Babs Wentworth ..." Planquet waved his free hand in the direction of her table. "As for—" And suddenly stopped, hand frozen in the air. Across the dancers I saw the French girl watching us with a kind of detached dreaminess.

"What is it, Pepe, honey?"

For a moment he didn't answer. Then he turned back to the table and I saw a small V of worry on his forehead. He reached for his wineglass and took a big gulp.

Miss Kelly swayed to her feet. "I'm going to the can," she said elegantly.

Planquet gave Mrs. Bennol a meaningful look. The older woman sighed, shrugged, and rose to accompany the redhead. Planquet moved quickly over to the chair the redhead had vacated.

"You're a bastard, Planquet," I said quietly.

"Perhaps you're right." The little line of worry was still there but he managed a mechanical grin. "I daresay you have worked for bastards before."

"Worked for—"

"Quite baldly, and without wasting more words, I am offering you employment. Something that I believe you can accomplish well."

"I'm not available," I said.

He smiled. "That is not clever of you. I know enough about you, Mr. Muldoon. You are far too worldly to go on working at a job that might get you quietly—" He stopped and, shrugged significantly.

"I'm the beachcomber type. No bosses."

"Nonsense. I know you're working for Phillip Adams."

"Ah?"

"After all, it is more or less a family affair."

"Assuming you were right, Planquet—which is a hell of an assumption—why would Adams want my services?"

He smiled. "Come now, Muldoon. Let's not be naïve. He wants you to get something on Georges."

I smiled back as though he had found me out. "Well ..." Palms upward I surrendered to his superior intelligence. The flattery worked.

"After all, it's pretty common gossip, you know. Gigi has been Adams' mistress of three years. Adams' wife began making trouble. He couldn't afford a scandal, so friend Georges was called to the rescue. A marriage of convenience, if you understand."

"Quite."

"Unfortunately, that idiot Georges fell in love with Gigi after the marriage. He's a sanctimonious troublemaker. We all—for various reasons, of course—would like to shut him up."

"I see."

For various reasons. For various reasons many people would be damned glad to see Hertzy out of the way. Including, it seemed, Phillip Adams.

"What difference does it make to you?"

"Well," he said, "I understand Phillips' concern over the matter. But there are other aspects of the case—things that perhaps Phillip doesn't realize. It might be dangerous to go too far."

"Political things?"

He shrugged. "Perhaps." And then quickly, "You understand that I myself am not involved in this. But a scandal at this moment ... I depend a great deal for my financing on the good will of Mrs. Wentworth. She might ... You see I am being very frank."

"Yes," I said. "And I wonder why."

Planquet looked across the room toward the Wentworth table. I waited a moment and then said, "What sort of work did you have in mind?"

"Ah!" He snapped his head around to me again. "You are good-looking, discreet, clever. I wish you to help me persuade Mrs. Wentworth tonight that Miss Kelly is right for the leading role in my film. I believe she has some Swedish creature she wishes me to meet. But after all, although I need Mrs. Wentworth's backing for this film, I am an artist."

"I don't see how I could help."

"For tonight you could be an American film distributor. Your word would then count in such matters."

"It's an odd sort of job."

"I tell you," he said in an almost childishly confidential manner, "it will pay well. That is, if you give up your—ah, other work."

"I see. A bribe, eh?"

He shrugged. "We are both men of the world."

"Why the hell are you so anxious to call me off?"

He hesitated, then said, "I can't afford a scandal now."

"Like murder?"

He snapped his head around and for the first time he looked me directly in the eyes. He lowered his voice.

"You're not serious. Georges? I mean ... My God!"

"Just an idea," I said.

"No. He couldn't. He wouldn't."

"He?"

"Phillip Adams."

The dancers moved slowly to a tango. Elsa and Cassi were on the far side of the floor. They seemed engaged in some sort of altercation.

"Tell me why I shouldn't go on with my job," I said.

He looked at me again with a mask of candor. "I'll tell you, Muldoon. You are hired for one purpose, or one seeming purpose, and maybe just by accident you are in a position to meddle with things that do not concern you. You become, therefore, dangerous. I am offering you a way out. Besides," and his smile was now downright lascivious, "Elsa is amused by you. Why not enjoy yourself?"

For a moment I saw red. The room vanished. I pushed back my chair and half rose to my feet with the intention of shoving his face down into the crockery. But a hand on my shoulder brought me back to my senses. It was the redhead.

"Oh, the man looks so angry. What has Pepe said?"

Planquet was on his feet by this time. Quickly he said, "Come on, Loretta. I promised to show you how to play baccarat."

They moved off across the room, leaving me with Mrs. Bennol.

"The girl is terribly intoxicated," Mrs. Bennol said distastefully. I noticed that her eyes and her manner seemed a little brighter. She sat, gave me a brassy, amused glance. "Pepe is such a little boy, but so charming!"

"All the charm of a bull let loose."

"Even a bull can be charming, you know."

Her eyes had the sparkle of an iceberg in the sun.

"Your daughter Elsa shows great patience," I said.

"I hope so. It is not easy to be married to a genius. But then, it is not easy to be married to any man. However, Elsa is quite capable of managing without outside help."

"You, too, like to keep it in the family, eh?"

"I beg your pardon?"

"Skip it." I changed course quickly, hoping to catch her off guard. "Is Count Cassi connected with the Balkan Eagles?"

The shot reached home before she could rearrange her expression. She sucked in her breath, recovered, and said as casually as possible. "I haven't the faintest notion of what you speak about."

"Oh, come now, Mrs. Bennol. You told me your husband was a general in the Rumanian army. Certainly you must have heard of the organization called the Balkan Eagles."

"I am an American now, monsieur. Rumania is in the past. I do not speak of such things."

"You speak only of money now, eh?"

"Comment?"

That did it. The charge that had been forming inside me since

Planquet's vulgar scene in front of Elsa exploded. "*Comment* yourself, sweetheart! Don't give me that *grande dame* act! Why, you'd serve your two daughters on a plastic tray for dinner to the highest bidder. How much does Cassi pay you? How much did he pay Hertzy? Or did Hertzy get too cute to handle?"

"You're drunk!" she sputtered, and looked around as though for help. At the moment Elsa came back to the table with Cassi. Mrs. Bennol cried, "Elsa! This young man, he is mad! He raves about something called—what is it?—the Eagles of the Balkans."

The Count stood by his chair as though suddenly frozen. Elsa was jerked out of her lethargy. The color seemed to drain from her face. In a low voice she said, "Hart! You've been teasing poor Mother. Stop it immediately!"

"Who is he? Who is he, Elsa?" Mrs. Bennol continued shrilly. "What do you know about him?"

And Elsa said, "Know about him? Nothing. Nothing at all. He's just a man I met on a beach."

"Well, really!" Mrs. Bennol gasped. "Armando! You heard. He has insulted me. What are you going to do?" And she repeated it, this time with a garish fear behind her words. "What are you going to do?"

"I know what I'm going to do?" I said. "I need air!"

I left the table and made my way across the room toward the terrace. At Mrs. Wentworth's table I saw the French girl watching me with a sort of schoolgirl gravity. The air seemed choked with heavy perfume.

I stepped through the French windows onto a wide terrace that was raised high over formal gardens. A few couples wandered between stiff hedges along the gravel paths that branched off from the foot of a long flight of marble stairs leading down from the terrace. But on the long sweep of marble there was only one other person. It was the Duchessa, who stood near the top of the stairs as though waiting. I lit a cigarette and approached her.

"Ah!" she said gently. "The young American. I thought you would never come."

"You have been waiting here for me, madame?"

"*Sì.*"

"But why?"

"Why?" She turned her haggard face toward the moon. There was something like despair in the old eyes. "Because in all this great assemblage there is only one who cares."

"Cares? About what?"

"About human life," she said sadly. "About the young man who was murdered."

Beyond her, out beyond the reach of the marble steps, in the depths of the garden, I saw a shadow move slowly along the hedges. I watched it until it disappeared into the farther darkness. Down behind me, far down the terrace, I heard the scrape of a foot on stone.

"I have remembered," she said.

"Remembered?"

"The name they mentioned. The name of the young man who was murdered."

I thought, she's crazy after all. She never heard anything. But I smiled encouragingly.

"And the name?"

"It was Muldoon," she said, "Hart Muldoon."

The shadow was moving again. For an instant it came out of the deeper darkness into the faint light of the moon and I saw clearly the face upturned toward the terrace. It was Pietro, the concertina player from the Villa Rosa. Far down behind me on the terrace someone coughed.

The Duchessa was looking into my eyes with that strange, terribly sad expression. Obviously she was not aware that she had spoken my name. I felt a coldness on my spine.

"And this Muldoon," I finally said. "The one you heard them talking about. Where was he murdered?"

She passed her hand across her eyes and frowned.

"They were afraid he would find out about the ship." she said.

"Ship?"

"I believe so. Yes. Or perhaps I only imagined that. But I know where he was murdered. Oh, yes. That's what you asked, isn't it?"

"Yes."

She looked beyond me and lowered her voice. "They murdered him in the ruins of the Palace of Tiberius."

Chapter Eleven

THE CASINO, 1:15 A.M.

"It is a dream," she said. "We are dreaming. But there is more in the dream ... more I must tell you."

The shadow that had been Pietro had vanished off into the outer darkness. Someone was walking slowly down the length of the marble terrace. I felt tired and angry. I didn't want to believe the Duchessa. I suspected someone had put her up to this, someone who knew, in what manner it was difficult to figure, that I had a rendezvous in the Palace of Tiberius with Elsa at sunrise. Planquet had tried to buy me off, now the Duchessa was trying to scare me off. Her old hand touched my sleeve.

"We are being watched," she said in a low voice.

I wheeled about. Adams was standing two feet away in the act of lighting a cigarette. He looked amused. "Sorry," he said. "I didn't mean to interrupt you in your work."

"What do you want?" My own voice sounded melodramatic and harsh.

He raised his eyebrows. "Information," he reminded me dryly. And then, "But to be more specific, I have been sent as a delegate to find you and to inform you that you will accompany Mrs. Planquet in her car to Mrs. Wentworth's party. Elsa wants you to meet her in the lobby in five minutes."

"There is something strange in this night," the Duchessa said. "It's as though ... as though I had been cheated. Perhaps the party isn't fun after all. Perhaps there is no fun left in the world."

"I need a drink," I said rudely, and brushed past Adams and started down the terrace. But he caught up with me and took my arm.

"You wouldn't be going off the deep end, Muldoon? I thought you were the calm, cool type."

I stopped dead and turned and looked at him. "Did you hire me as a cover-up, Adams?"

The smile disappeared. "Who told you that?"

"I figured it out myself."

"Your figuring is 'way out of bounds, old man."

"Maybe," I said shortly. "But this I will tell you. Once I get on a deal it takes several kinds of devils to call me off."

"Good!" He sounded genuine enough. I began to simmer down.

Down the terrace the Duchessa called, "Young man, come back. Come back. There is more I have to say."

"Tell it to him," I said, pointing to Adams. I turned on my heel and went through the French windows into the Casino, out of the blue artificial moonlight, between the glittering tables, out beyond the gold draperies and the main lobby to a small bar just off the entrance to the baccarat rooms.

A gaunt ghost of a woman, painted like a corpse, waved cornstalk arms covered with emeralds and diamond bracelets under the chin of a square-faced young blonde as they prepared to leave the bar. "I warn you," she said intensely. "I warn you for the last time. I won't, I simply won't put up with it!"

"Yes, yes, I heard you," the girl said sulkily.

"If I catch you around that Wentworth bitch once more, just once more ..."

They went out into the lobby. Except for the barman I was alone in the room. It was curiously insulated against sound in here; dance music barely trickled through the walls. My own voice sounded muffled and the barman's dead. I ordered a cognac and tried to think.

Was Adams a phony? Was his elaborate story of spy-work merely a cover? Had he engaged me as insurance against possible future investigation? Was it possible that he not only knew Hertzy was dead but had actually killed him?

It was possible, but improbable. From the little I had been able to learn about the industrialist, his methods would not have been so blatant.

Planquet? He seemed too damned sure of himself. He knew something, perhaps the key that would solve the riddle. His offered bribe was proof of that. And he was scared. Of what? Of whom?

Count Cassi? Ever since the scene in the Count's apartment I had been certain that Ferechini and Cassi were connected in some manner with the death of Hertzy. Was this connection political? Somehow I doubted it. The unpleasant vision of Ferechini clutching that hypodermic needle put a new light on things. It didn't take a mastermind to figure that somewhere in the background was the grim shadow of drug traffic. Had Hertzy been one of their American connections?

And Elsa?

I took a swig of the cognac. Here reason stopped. I couldn't—I wouldn't—believe that Elsa was party to some plan to lure me to my death in the ruins of the Palace of Tiberius. Either the Duchessa had been coached or she had misinterpreted what she had overheard.

Maybe.

The barman looked at me with dead marble eyes. I thought, Someone in this place is planning to kill me. I took another swig of brandy.

What was Pietro doing out there in the Casino gardens? And above all, who was the strange woman in the silver dress who had stood waiting like a wax figure in the light of the bathroom at the Count's apartment?

And yet above all the confusing crosscurrents I was certain of one thing: Unless I got the answer to this one quickly, probably before the night was out, I would be, in one way or another, a dead duck. As long as they—whoever they were—knew that Hertzy lay dead in my room, I was still comparatively safe; obviously they planned to get me out of the way by pinning murder on me. But not if I got too close to home base before morning.

Behind me a woman's voice said quietly, "Hello."

I turned to find Yvonne, the French girl from Room 26 of the Villa Rosa.

"Cognac?"

"A vermouth would be nice."

"Must keep a clear head, eh?"

"*Oui*," she said calmly.

I ordered the vermouth and moved with her to one of the small tables, out of earshot of the deadpan bartender.

"You wanted to speak with me?"

"Not particularly," she said. "I wanted to get away from the others a moment. My stomach is not as strong as it should be."

"How do you happen to be in the Wentworth party?"

She shrugged. "Maybe she is a philanthropist. But I doubt it. It suits her purpose. Whatever that may be."

"You've met her before?"

"Once," she said curtly. "In Paris. With someone I knew there."

"And she looked you up at the Villa Rosa?"

She shrugged. "She saw me earlier at the Caffè del Porto."

"Is it business?" I said cruelly.

She turned and looked at me with that queer, placid expression. "It might be. What of it?"

"Everyone to his own taste."

"Yes," she said.

And after a moment I said, "Good Lord!"

She laughed. "For a man of the world you are easily shocked."

"Not shocked. Disgusted."

"Oh, come."

"Stop acting!" I said roughly. "You yourself said you had to get away from them, that you didn't have a strong stomach."

She said nothing. She twisted her glass around. I noticed she kept one hand on the shabby little beaded bag. "Aren't you afraid Ferechini will boot you out of here?"

"Not while I'm with the Wentworth woman. Besides ..."

"Besides, you've got something on him!"

She smiled remotely. "Perhaps."

"Drugs?"

She showed no surprise. Her silence told me a lot.

"Cassi wanted me to work for him and Ferechini," I said. "They're in this together."

She looked quickly around and lowered her voice. "You talk too much."

"Is Pietro working for them too?"

The effect of this question was startling. She snapped up her head and I saw the pupils of her eyes dilate. "Pietro? What are you talking about?"

"I saw him not five minutes ago lurking around the Casino gardens."

She half rose, her mouth pressed tight, and then sank back again.

"The fool! The young fool!"

"So," I said. "You and Pietro, eh?"

"Nonsense!" she said harshly. "He is only a boy. A silly romantic boy! I've told him—" She broke off. The hard mask slipped a little and she allowed the despair to shine through her eyes.

"Was Pietro jealous of Hertzy?"

"Oh, no, no, not at all. You must not think—"

"You're not very convincing."

"Mr. Muldoon." She put her hand on my aim. "Listen to me. You are wrong. Pietro had nothing to do with Hertzy's death."

She stopped, horrified. Her hand slid away from my arm. The room seemed smothered in cotton.

Quietly I said, "So you knew all along."

In a dead voice she said, "Yes."

"How?"

She stared down into the drink. "When he was in my room he asked me a question. I didn't want to answer. Not then. But after he left and went to your room I got to thinking about it. I decided to tell him what he wanted to know. I went to your room and pushed open the door, and I saw. Then I went back to my own room."

"Why didn't you call the police?"

"Ferechini?" She laughed ironically.

"Why didn't you tell me?"

"It was none of my business," she said coldly. Then she looked into my eyes. "You see, I have business of my own. Tonight. After tonight it will not matter too much. But—perhaps I am foolish—I think you're decent. Or at least nearer to being decent than—than the others. I will tell you this much. Get off this island as quickly as you can. They will kill you!"

"They?"

"Cassi, Ferechini ... and associates."

"Who are the associates?"

"I don't know," she said. "But this I can tell you. Hertzy started to leave my room when he saw someone in the hall and closed the door quickly. Someone he didn't wish to be seen by. He waited until she had gone."

"She?"

"Yes. I know it was a woman because he said, 'What in God's name is she doing here?' He seemed horribly shocked."

"Thanks," I said. I began to feel terribly tired. If the girl wasn't lying, there were things behind her words I didn't want to face.

After a moment she said quietly, "Mr. Muldoon, one man can do nothing. Evil is highly organized and powerful here. You are wise enough to understand this. Nothing can win out against it."

"Not even love?" I said softly. "Not even Pietro?"

The shot hit home. She pushed her glass from her and stood. In that moment she took her hand off the beaded bag and before she could prevent it I snatched it up and snapped open the catch. Nestling among the cheap cosmetics was a small automatic.

She stood by the table very still, looking down into my eyes. Slowly I closed the bag and stood. Without a word I handed it to her.

After a moment I said, "It's your funeral, baby. Who is it for?"

"A monster," she said quietly.

"I know several of that species. Which one?"

She hesitated and for a moment I thought she was going to tell me. But suddenly the expression in her eyes changed. She was looking beyond me. I turned. Elsa was standing in the doorway to the bar. When she saw the French girl she turned quickly as though to retreat.

"It's all right," I said, "You're not interrupting."

Yvonne stood there watching Elsa. Her face was once more a mask. Elsa came reluctantly across the threshold. She looked very pale. Her hands were clasped tight.

In a low voice the French girl said vehemently, "Not even love. It is a trap."

And without another word she walked past Elsa and out of the bar.

"What did she mean?" Elsa asked tensely. "What was she talking about?"

"A little joke," I said lightly. Then, "What's wrong, Elsa? You look as though you've seen a ghost."

She shivered. "I don't know, Hart. I'm frightened. I'm desperately frightened."

The bartender was looking at us curiously. I lowered my voice. "You've got to tell me, Elsa. You're concealing something. It's dangerous."

She looked up at me and her hand found mine and held it tight as though for reassurance. "Hart, you will go with me to the Wentworth party. We will be alone. We can talk. Pepe is taking the Kelly girl in another car. Mother and the Count are going with Gigi and Mr. Adams. We can talk. I must—"

She broke off as a stout little man in a shiny black suit came into the bar. "*Signor* Muldoon?"

"Yes."

"The *Comandante* Ferechini wishes to see you immediately on the terrace."

Elsa's fingers tightened about my hand.

"Of course," I said, managing to conceal any uneasiness.

"I'm coming too," Elsa said.

"Baby, maybe you'd better wait here."

"No," she said tensely. "I'm coming."

We followed the man in the shiny suit out to the terrace. We went to the head of the marble steps and a little beyond them. Ferechini and two men, obviously of the *carabinieri*, were standing down in the shrubbery. I felt a sudden coldness.

Ferechini looked up at me, his face blue in the synthetic moonlight.

"Ah, Mr. Muldoon. You were out here a short time ago, talking with the Duchessa?"

"Yes."

Out of the corner of my eye, like a figure in a dream, I saw a woman far down at the end of the terrace. She stood by the balustrade looking out into the gardens. Her gown glittered silver in the moonlight. There was something sinister and frighteningly unreal about her; the quality of wax I had felt when I had first seen her in the bedroom at the Count Cassi's. And in the other dream I heard Ferechini's words:

"There has been an accident. Most unfortunate. Apparently the poor lady had too much champagne. She must have leaned too far over the balustrade, and unluckily for her, the little stone satyr was right below. Her head must have hit it as she fell."

"It wasn't an accident," I said wearily.

"There is no question about that, Mr. Muldoon. It was an accident. We have ascertained this fact."

Elsa pressed close to me and began to sob. Ferechini stepped aside. Down in the shrubbery, beside the hideous little stone satyr, a face was turned up, looking, it seemed, beyond the synthetic moonlight to the dim distant reflection of the real moon rising now high above the bay of Naples. And in death the face of the old Duchessa di Cabrieni had taken on an eerie aspect of a long forgotten, innocent youth, full of the sound of tinkling music.

Chapter Twelve

THE CASINO, 1:45 A.M.

The office of the director of the Casino was vast and gloomy, an oppressive room of thick red carpets, dark paneling, a portrait of a vanished monarch, and a permanent odor of cigars and port and lemon furniture oil. It was windowless and soundproof. Ferechini had commandeered the director's imposing desk and sat facing us like a latter-day Mussolini. The silence was stale and heavy.

"I simply don't understand," Elsa said. She was still pale and shaken by what we had seen outside on the terrace, but was coming away from the boundaries of shock now like a sleepwalker from sleep.

Quite pleasantly, as though he were discussing some comparatively minor business matter, Ferechini said, "I assure you, Madame Planquet, that this is but a formality. There are some matters I must discuss with Mr. Muldoon."

Some matters, I thought bitterly, remembering my last glimpse of the Duchessa, an inert little rag doll all tinsel and paint, being bundled into the green cloth and discreetly whisked away across the gardens among the rigid hedges by the Casino attendants and

Ferechini's policemen before any of the clientele could become aware that there had been a tragedy.

"But it doesn't make sense," Elsa persisted. "Why must you question Mr. Muldoon? He was with me in the bar at the time it happened."

Ferechini stopped smiling for a moment. Then he recovered. "But of course. Still there are certain aspects of this incident ..."

It was as though he were talking in a dream. I heard the words but they didn't make much sense. Yet somehow they seemed to be making sense to Ferechini and even to Elsa. They felt at home in this dream, knew the symbols, the hidden meaning behind the words, some unspeakable silent knowledge. What am I doing here? I thought. What am I doing in this sealed room? Had it been only a few hours ago that I had discovered the body of Georges Hertzy in my bedroom at the Villa Rosa? Had I ever really seen, through the doorway of another bedroom, this oily little monster, naked, poised with a hypodermic needle beside that strange woman in the silver dress? As I watched him now, cocky and self-assured, it was difficult to believe. And the woman in the silver dress; the nameless woman, oddly unreal and sinister despite a certain peculiar beauty—what had she been doing only a few minutes before on the far reaches of the terrace? Who was she? Had I dreamed her too?

I heard their polite words, and as I listened I became more and more convinced that there was a bond between these two. The Duchessa had prophesied my death in the ruins of the Palace of Tiberius, the very place that Elsa had suggested for our rendezvous at sunrise. Surely it was more than a fantastic coincidence. And yet, even with a growing conviction in me, I looked at her and thought, She's like a Lorelei whom I might go to meet anyway, even knowing that it meant my death. Was Ferechini counting on that?

The gods of evil have come to life, Mamma Peroni had said. But something else was coming to life within me; a slow burning anger and disgust. A harmless, half-mad old woman had been struck down for words she had apparently accidentally overheard. And I knew that the man sitting so smugly before us at the desk was somehow involved in that death. And out of the welter of words and motives and people I had encountered since finding the body of Georges Hertzy in my room, I was beginning to sense a pattern, a central theme that held fast all the painted dolls that danced around its edges. And the pattern was greed and money and drugs.

"But, *Comandante*," Elsa was saying, "surely you don't think it was murder?"

Ferechini's eyes contracted. He seemed to be warning her. "Madame," he said shortly, "the Casino does not have a scandal of that nature. We must all—all—be most discreet."

The word hung there for a moment as his gaze slid almost imperceptibly toward me. "As Madame knows quite well, life is seldom simple. There are many sides to the diamond. Is this not so? Sides to consider."

What was he trying to say? Was it a threat? If so, I might yet be able to reserve final judgment on Elsa.

Elsa looked at me quickly, then away. Her chair was near the desk and she reached forward to smash out a newly lit cigarette.

"It is hardly the time, *Signor* Ferechini," she said in a low voice, "for philosophy."

"Ah, but Madame is wiser than that. There are so many things to consider."

"Like what?" I said.

Without looking at Elsa he said, "Loyalty, for instance."

Elsa sucked in her breath sharply. I laughed. "That's a dirty word, coming from you, *Comandante*!"

Unruffled, he said, "For me there are other words. I do not speak of my—how do you say?—my own point of reference. But for others ..."

"What the hell are you talking about? So you're threatening Madame Planquet?"

"Threatening? What a melodramatic idea! Madame doesn't think so, does she?"

"What does he mean, Elsa?"

Elsa avoided my eyes. Suddenly the effort of making words seemed too much for her.

"Elsa!" I said recklessly. "This little bastard has you scared to death. What has he got on you? Are you protecting someone? That louse of a husband?"

She looked me in the eyes for an instant and I thought she was about to blurt out something but Ferechini cleared his throat and she turned quickly away. "What an idea, Hart," she said in a calm voice. "What a fantastic idea."

"O.K.," I said harshly. "I can take care of myself. Go on to the Wentworth party and enjoy yourself."

"Hart, you'll come." She turned to Ferechini. "You're not going to—to hold him?"

"Certainly not, Madame. In a very short time he will join you."

"Sure," I said. "Have a drink and forget the untidy little scene on the terrace."

She stood and looked down at me as though waiting for some kind of signal. When she got none she suddenly cried, "Hart! I ... You must ..."

But almost instantly Ferechini was on his feet. "Madame!" he interrupted quickly. "There is something you must know."

She caught herself up, turned to him almost fearfully. "Well?"

"I have a message for you. The friend you were expecting from Cairo is arriving by ship this morning. The ship is the S.S. Lyon, due to arrive about dawn."

Now there was no doubt of it. The bastard had something on her and this was a final warning. And suddenly I remembered that the Duchessa had spoken of a ship.

In a dead voice Elsa said, "Oh. Yes. Thank you."

"Since when are you acting as a telegraph office, Ferechini?" I asked.

He looked at me and smiled. The smile had a chilling effect on me. The guy didn't care what I thought. He thought he had me too. Otherwise he never would have revealed his hand so openly. He thought he had me where he wanted me. But about what? He couldn't very well pin the death of the Duchessa on me. As witness number one I had no less a personage than Phillip Adams, who had seen me leave the terrace to go to the bar. Logic and reason were on my side.

Ferechini led Elsa to the door. "I would suggest, madame, that you do not upset the guests of Mrs. Wentworth with the story of what you saw here at the Casino. This is a night, after all, for festivities. And, I might add, jokes."

"Jokes?"

"One of these jokes Madame will perhaps appreciate more than anyone!"

"What *are* you talking about?" Elsa asked uneasily.

He shrugged and smirked. Elsa looked beyond him to me. "Hart," she said swiftly, "I don't know what you are thinking, but—"

She stopped again and I could almost feel the pressure of Ferechini's hand on her arm. "Madame Planquet!" he said warningly. There was a silence during which Ferechini looked at her with a kind of intense speculation. I had a feeling that he was hesitating about letting her leave the room. But some further thought made him change his mind. With a flourish, he opened the door. Dance music came drifting down the long corridor. Across the threshold one of Ferechini's smartly uniformed young policemen jumped aside to let

Elsa pass. Ferechini went out into the hall with her and closed the door behind him. I got up quickly and started across the room with some vague idea of trying to hear what was being said out there, but before I could reach the door Ferechini came back, closed the door behind him, and went to the desk.

He took a long moment to light a cigarette.

Without looking at me he said, "Sit down!"

I drew up a chair and waited. He took his time, tilting back his head and blowing a thin stream of smoke toward the ceiling. There was a hell of a lot of ham in Ferechini; he would have looked entirely at home on an opera stage between Tosca's candlesticks.

I said, "I've lost my cues in this hassle. I'm waiting."

"Cues? Ah, yes. The theatre. I myself am a great theatre fan. Intrigue and murder, deceit and betrayal—these are the fantasies of the stage. Not like real life, Mr. Muldoon. Not like real life at all."

He grinned in a manner that might have been misread as naïve by anyone who didn't know.

"You Americans! How you amuse me! Little boys with tough talk and hearts like jellyfish."

"You mean we get mawkish over the murder of helpless old women?"

"Precisely," he said with cold directness. "As a European I have seen much of violence and much of death. Many old women quite dead. Many young men. I have seen young girls torn out of the convent to lie in the mud among the ruins for the pleasure of the little boys with the tough talk who came to save Europe for democracy. I have seen many destroyed. I survive." He repeated it slowly and carefully. "I ... survive."

"You're like a corrupt little spider, Ferechini."

He laughed. "The moralist. The dishonest moralist! I have learned that the only incorruptibles are the corrupt. I have learned—because, *signore*, I am not stupid—that I am surrounded by a sea of corruption, and it is only necessary to attend to the somewhat simple needs of the corrupt in order to survive."

"You are being honest for a change."

"That's because I have nothing to lose."

"What about Mamma Peroni? Have you been able to corrupt her?"

For a moment the smile left his face and I saw something like perplexity in his eyes. "She is a peasant. Or rather, one of the fisherman class. These people are clods. They are not to be taken too seriously. No, not at all. One treats them as clods." He leaned forward. "It's amusing. I'll tell you. This Peroni woman and some of

her fishermen cronies, they got ideas about me. It was really very
funny. They went to the mainland and spoke to a high official of their
suspicions. The results? I could have told them before they went to
the trouble. Absolutely nothing. Talk without proof! I am still
Comandante and they are still clods who are somewhat troublesome,
but no more than that." His eyes narrowed. "Why do you mention
her?"

I shrugged. "I was just thinking. I don't suppose you could go so far
as to have a mass massacre of the clods. They are always there,
underfoot."

"Like insects," he said. Then he leaned back and blew more smoke
to the ceiling. "However, they do make a quaint background for the
tourists."

"Who killed the Duchessa, Ferechini?"

He shook his head in mock regret. "A sad incident. Who killed her?
Who knows? Perhaps the same thing that killed the cat."

"What the hell do you want with me?"

"A little reasonableness," he said quietly.

"To be specific?"

"I have means of securing information, *signore*, that led me earlier
tonight to request you to leave this island. I believe now I made a
mistake."

"In what way?"

"Information is my obsession, Muldoon. It is also my livelihood.
Facts. Facts about weakness and behavior. These are the weapons.
With facts of this nature I am enabled, for example, to nullify the
power of the local mayor. I know the women and the beds, if you
understand."

"Blackmail!"

He shrugged. "On the contrary. Merely the statement of certain
facts. Now there are some—I believe you to be one of these—to whom
the statement of such facts would mean no embarrassment. You do
not live in society, but skirt its edges. Therefore, my only other
weapon is ... money."

"You're being damned candid, anyway."

"What have I to lose? Your word against mine."

I decided this was the waiting time; the wrong word might spoil
it. When I said nothing he went on. "For what purpose did Mr. Phillip
Adams hire you?"

"You're having fantasies, Ferechini!"

"Not at all," he said calmly. "This is one of these facts I make it my
business to know." He bent slightly forward now, stiffly leaning on

his elbows, eyes narrowed. Softly he said, "Did he hire you to kill Georges Hertzy?"

And he smiled.

"Georges Hertzy? I don't think I ever met him," I managed to say.

He kept smiling. "I understand Mr. Phillip Adams has been somewhat annoyed by an unexpected element in the pattern of his life."

"Unexpected element?"

"These facts were not difficult to procure. It is in the realm of fashionable gossip. Gigi Hertzy became Phillip Adams' mistress two years ago, when she was, of course, Gigi Bennol. Adams had an unreasonable wife. He persuaded his confidant and friend Georges Hertzy to go through a wedding ceremony with Miss Bennol on the theory that Mrs. Adams would then have no valid weapon. Unfortunately he forgot what the sentimentalists call human nature."

"In what way?"

"The young man—the foolish young man—Georges Hertzy fell madly in love with his wife. He has been making difficulties. He didn't understand the rules of the game. Mr. Adams has, correctly enough, found him to be embarrassing and even dangerous. Emotion is so unpredictable. But all this, of course, you know. How much did he offer you to do away with Mr. Georges Hertzy?"

I began to feel slightly sick to my stomach. Ferechini was closing the trap about me. He stopped smiling and said directly, "How much do you want to work with me, Muldoon?"

"As a policeman?"

"Don't be facetious. I could use a man like you. How much?"

"More than you could pay."

"Name a price and we'll go on from there."

His cynical audacity was more extreme than even I had expected. But its cocksure theatricality gave me an opportunity to try for a rift in his armor.

"Look, Ferechini, I've had offers from the same sources, in different cities, in different countries. You can tell the big boss that I'm still not working for him."

"The big boss?"

"Luciano."

Right away I knew I had hit home. For a moment his face sagged in astonishment and fear flickered his eyes.

"You're mad!"

The silence of the room pressed down on us. The bottled anger

within me began to seethe and boil. Ever since I had seen that
hypodermic needle, I'd suspected, but now that his moment of lost
control had confirmed my suspicions the anger almost defeated
me.

"You stupid little son-of-a-bitch!"

He stared at me, a masochist waiting for more of the whip. My
sense of preservation put anger where it belonged for the moment
and I changed tack.

"It's none of my goddamned business," I said. "You and your pal
Cassi can have it out one of these days with the narcotic squads of
two or three nations. And there's no reason to be so astonished that
I guessed."

"Guessing is one thing," he said with trembling softness. "There
have been many guessers. The proof?" He shrugged expressively.
Then with feline swiftness he added, "Mrs. Planquet told you this
crazy story?"

I grinned affably, wordlessly. He stumped out his cigarette. "You're
bluffing," he said.

"Oh, sure."

He stood up. "You are a very foolish young man. You might have
walked off this island in a few days considerably richer. As it is ..."

And I ran for home now, reckless beyond reason. "Tell me,
Ferechini, did Hertzy play it too cute? As your American contact did
he hold you up for too much?"

Immediately I knew I had made a bad mistake. The tightness
about Ferechini's eyes relaxed. I knew I had been a damned fool to
overplay my hand. Up until the time I had mentioned Hertzy's name
I had been doing fine. But in my career as a wrong guesser, this was
the wrongest guess of all. Whatever Hertzy had been, it was obvious
now that he had not been one of them.

Now the oily little bastard was on top again. He stood and sighed.
"Too bad," he said. "Really too bad. You will wait here."

He went out into the hall and closed the door, and I heard the key
turning in the lock. This time I didn't move from my chair. Only
termites could have escaped from this room. I stumped out my
cigarette and tried to think. Although I was certain that Ferechini
and Cassi were mixed up in a big-time drug operation, there were
many puzzling aspects of the situation. If the island had become the
center of a European base for drug traffic, how had Ferechini
managed to involve a woman like Elsa Planquet in the deal? Was it
her husband, the exhibitionist French film director, who was really
their man, and was she only trying to protect him? Was it possible

that she had made the rendezvous with me in the Palace of Tiberius without knowing that someone planned to bump me off there? Or was she being blackmailed? And the woman in the silver dress? Who the hell was she and where did she fit into this cobweb atmosphere of a bad dream?

The key turned in the lock and Ferechini came back into the room. He was brusque and businesslike now. "If you please, Mr. Muldoon, you will come with me."

"Where?"

"I have just had a message from my headquarters," he said glibly. "There has been an anonymous telephone call. Utterly fantastic and improbable. Still, it is my duty to investigate even such a wild tale."

"Wild tale?"

He smiled coldly. "It seems, Mr. Muldoon, according to the caller, that in your room at the Villa Rosa is the body of a dead man."

Chapter Thirteen

THE CASINO, 2:10 A.M.

He waited by the door. Perhaps if I had not mentioned Hertzy's name he would never have played this trump. It was doubtful. It was too easy for him. I'd been expecting it, of course, but not so soon. Not in this way. Now that it had come, my stomach muscles refused to accept the inevitable; they contracted with a sort of chill. Also something seemed to be happening to my mind. I couldn't think straight. But somehow I managed a laugh.

"That's something for the comics on the borscht circuit," I, said, and stood. "Now that we've had our little chuckle, I think I'll be going to Mrs. Wentworth's."

He kept smiling. His manner now was elaborately polite and distant. "I'm afraid not. At least for the moment. I realize, of course, that this call is probably sheer nonsense. Still, the lady who called me was quite—"

"Lady?"

He sighed with mock sympathy. "The ladies are so unreliable, Mr. Muldoon."

Maybe he was right there. "What the hell are you trying to do, Ferechini? Am I under arrest or something?"

"Certainly not! And what I am trying to do is nothing more than any conscientious police officer would do. It will take but a few minutes out of your time. We will go to the Villa Rosa, disprove this idiotic tale and then you will be as free as a bird."

"Only a minute ago you were trying to buy me off!"

"Buy you off? But, *signore*, you must have been drinking."

I took a step toward him with some vague idea of leaving my fingers in his face. With the agility of a ballet dancer, and still smiling, he backed into the hall, into the protective circle of three of his stalwart and elegantly uniformed young policemen. Deeply ironic in his courtesy now, he stepped aside as I went out into the hall. There wasn't any point in throwing fists around, not with eight to my two. I didn't feel any too good. Ferechini had me where it was going to hurt bad.

We went out to the main entrance. Ferechini's limousine came creeping up the drive like a tiger at night. One of the crisply uniformed coppers opened the door and in a minute I was between Ferechini and a gleaming young goon in the perfumed, glassed-in silence of the rear. Ferechini lit a cigarette. Obviously he was enjoying himself.

"You seem somewhat nervous, Mr. Muldoon."

"I twitch easy."

In my mind I was rehearsing the shocked surprise I would have to display at the sight of Hertzy's body. The young goon giggled about something, choked off the sound at a glance from Ferechini. I wondered where the hell the reek of perfume was coming from.

The car swung into the wide Via Minerva. There wasn't much good trying to figure how a police *commandante* rated a custom job like this; it was all too obvious. Ferechini had the island and its people by the short hairs. You could almost hear them calling "Uncle" as they spat out the lire.

The handsome new boulevard was almost deserted at this hour. But after a moment a low-slung Bugatti sports racer whistled past us, her bonnet headed out for the mountain road. A woman in an evening cape beside the driver turned back to stare into our headlights. Her face was a pale mask, too white, too unreal, a painted doll hurtling off into the darkness.

After a bit I said, "How long do you figure your show can last, Ferechini?"

"My show?"

"It's only a matter of time," I said. "You and your pals can't expect to have it good through eternity."

"Time," he said reflectively. "Pals?" he laughed. "This is one of these sentimental American words. My dear Mr. Muldoon, in my time I have had many of these 'pals.' Some of them have been indiscreet and hysterical and in one or two cases leveled absurd charges against me to higher authorities. But, poor dears, they have not been very lucky. You see I have survived time."

The limousine turned off the Via Minerva, tilted downward, began to descend toward the port. Below the moon fell among the quiet yachts and the fishing craft. The only sign of movement in the harbor was a fat launch, far out now, chugging painfully toward the lights that marked the breakwater, heading for the open waters of the Bay of Naples. Ferechini stumped out his cigarette and turned sharply to the goon.

"What is the meaning of that?"

"Of what, *Comandante?*"

"Where are your eyes, you fool? That boat out there."

The boy followed the direction of Ferechini's pointed finger. He gasped. "I—I do not understand."

"What is this? You know I gave orders that no craft was to leave the harbor this night!"

"But certainly, *Comandante!* I do not understand."

"I deal with idiots!" He tapped on the window for the chauffeur to put on more speed and we began to slide downhill at an uncomfortable rate. "Now then," Ferechini snapped. "When you leave Mr. Muldoon and me at the Villa Rosa you will go as quickly as possible to the municipal pier. Order the municipal launch to intercept that boat immediately and bring it back. Find out who is in it and report to me!"

"*Sì, Comandante!*" If it had been possible the young man would have risen and bowed.

The limousine jerked to a stop at the entrance to the narrow Via Cellini. The narrow alley through which no vehicle could pass appeared to be even darker than usual. It seemed to me that there had once been a street lamp near the entrance to the pension, but if so it was now out of commission. Ferechini gave a command and the limousine with the young policeman whisked off across the square in the direction of the municipal pier. Out of the shadows another goon appeared; apparently Ferechini was afraid of being alone in this world. Or more likely he wasn't taking any chances of my slipping out of this one. I lit a cigarette and tried to appear nonchalant. Followed by the policemen, we walked up the alley toward the entrance to the Villa Rosa.

I tried the court of last appeals. "I suppose you realize you might be involving important people in this little joke of yours."

"Important people?"

"Phillip Adams wouldn't be overjoyed by any scandal."

He laughed, but I thought I detected a note of uneasiness in his voice. "Mr. Adams is a very distinguished gentleman. If he made the mistake of employing someone who—" He shrugged expressively. "I believe his name can be kept out of the public press, if that's what you mean."

"But suppose he makes trouble for you?"

"But I don't know what you are worrying about. So far, there has been no scandal in which you are directly involved. So far."

He had me there, of course. He stepped aside and I went past him into the dimly lit entrance hall of the Villa Rosa. The bar was dark and silent. Ferechini stopped, suddenly tense, and held out his hand for silence. Quietly, but with a certain disturbing relish, the young goon at my side took out a revolver. Somewhere up in the house there was the sound of a door being quietly closed, then a quick scurry of feet and another door closing. Ferechini stood there frozen, his hand still raised, as though he were Toscanini reaching for a downbeat. After a moment there was another sound; a chain lock being unbolted and then a door creaking open. After a moment the familiar voice of Mamma Peroni called angrily from the top of the stairs, "Who is it?"

Quickly Ferechini whirled about and put his finger to his lips. But I beat him to the draw. I cleared my throat and called, "Hello, Mamma!"

Ferechini whispered, "You will outsmart yourself yet!"

Mamma Peroni came clumping down the stairs, stopping a few feet from the bottom. "Well?" she called fearlessly. "Come into the light where I can see you."

Ferechini sighed, stepped forward under the spattered bulb.

"So! The Americans bring only trouble, as usual!"

Her gaze went, beyond Ferechini to the young policeman. Her lip curled. "Tony Aderni! You're poor old father would turn over in his grave if he could see you now. Dressed up like a toy soldier, licking the boots of this little tin Duce! Mother of God, may she forgive you!"

"Quiet, old woman!" the boy said petulantly. "You can't use your lip on me!"

"Ha! I know all about you! In the Count Cassi's bed before you were sixteen for a few lire and now look at you!"

"*Signora!*" Ferechini said sharply. "I am engaged on official business."

"Official business for monkeys! I know your business and so do many of us. I have no business with your kind. There are no young men in my house to engage in your kind of business. Has he put the needle to your arm yet, Tony? I'm told that is his pleasure!"

The boy's face darkened angrily. Ferechini took a step toward her.

"Easy, Mamma," I said warningly. I don't want Ferechini goaded too far—not with what was up on my bedroom carpet.

"Easy!" she cried. "*Sì!* Easy. Keep quiet and don't talk. Keep your eyes shut and don't hear. You, too?"

Ferechini regarded her as though she were some unpleasant insect. "I have not time for gossip on the tavern stairs." He gestured for me to follow him. I didn't have much choice. Tony was prodding me in the ribs with something metallic. But Mamma Peroni held her ground, barring the narrow stairs.

"You have not the right to break into an honest woman's house. You have no papers. No real authority. Get out!"

Ferechini, for his own reasons, was trying hard to keep his temper. "You are insolent, *signora*. I warn you, we have had too much trouble with you as it is. In the past I have been too tolerant."

"Tolerant!" She cackled mirthlessly. "You lap dog! You would not dare put your hand on me—officially, that is. Otherwise you would have got rid of me long ago. There are people on this island who would tear you limb from limb! Ask Tony. He knows. And we know who you are, *Comandante* of nothing! A thief and a corrupter of young men. We have a name for you, *Signor* Bootlicker! Our sons and brothers know who you are and they spit when your name is mentioned! Like this!" And she illustrated.

"Ugly bitch!"

Beside himself with rage, Ferechini leaped forward and brought the back of his hand across her face. Some reflex drove me forward almost at the same moment, but before I could get my hands on him Tony had a half nelson on me from the rear and the revolver was biting into my back.

Mamma didn't budge. Ferechini backed away, breathing hard. For some reason he seemed scared. "And now," he said in a hoarse whisper, "we shall see what you conceal in your bedrooms, *signora*. We shall see if you protect American murderers!"

She hesitated a moment, then stepped aside and said in cold contempt, "Excrement of a pig! You have the hospitality of my house."

Did I detect a note of weary surrender in her voice? She avoided my gaze.

"I am not responsible for what the American brings into my house," Mamma said. "That is his business alone."

Tony urged me on and I mounted the stairs behind Ferechini. We went down the hall to the door of my room.

"No doubt you have the key, *signore*?"

I thought, This it is. I dug into my pocket, trying to find the key. One corner of my mind was aware of a slight movement in Room 26. I wondered if the French girl had finished whatever business she was up to. While I was still fishing, the young policeman who had been with us in the limousine came bounding up the stairs.

"*Comandante!*"

"Well? What is it?" Ferechini's nerves were stretched tight. They showed through the whiteness of his voice.

"I have been to the pier, *Comandante*. There is trouble!"

"What trouble?"

"The municipal launch! Someone has tampered with the engine. It refuses to turn over, even. They are working on it now, but—"

"Mother of God!" Ferechini shouted. "What fools do I have to contend with? The municipal launch must meet the Lyon at six A.M. It is imperative!" And then quickly, "What of the craft we saw in the harbor?"

"It is through the breakwater already, *Comandante*. It seems to be heading toward Naples. It belongs to one of the fishermen."

At the end of the hall Mamma Peroni laughed. Ferechini whirled about to face her. "What do you know about this, woman?"

She stood there, arms across her great bosom, a slight smile touching the corners of her mouth.

"Maybe this time on the mainland they will listen, eh?"

"You're bluffing."

Ferechini whipped around to the young policeman. "Go back to the pier. If the engine of the launch is not repaired, commandeer a fast boat in the harbor. Never mind about the legalities. I will fix that later. I want that boat of the fisherman brought back into the harbor!"

"*Sì, Signor Comandante.*"

As he brushed past Mamma on the way down to the street, she said softly, "So ... it is the Lyon."

"You fool!" Ferechini said in an icy voice. "Haven't you learned yet? There's nothing you can do."

He got hold of himself and turned back to me. "And now, if you please, Mr. Muldoon, it is your turn."

His eyes glittered with a kind of cold triumph. I realized that his dislike for me had developed into white hatred. I got the key and approached the door. Only then did I notice that it was slightly ajar. I knew I had locked it when I went out. My heart began to thump in an unpleasant manner. I kicked the door inward and stepped across the threshold. I didn't reach for the light switch. Ferechini did that. A sickly pink light flooded the sleazy cupid under the threadbare shade. The bureau drawers were open and my suitcase spilled forth its contents on the rug.

The rug, I thought dully. Not the familiar rug with its faded rose pattern, but a different rug, equally threadbare but new to this room.

And the body of Georges Hertzy was gone.

Chapter Fourteen

THE VILLA ROSA, 2:40 A.M.

Behind me there was a sound like air escaping from a punctured balloon. It was Ferechini expelling his breath. I turned and managed an ironic look. Over his shoulder I saw Mamma Peroni, arms akimbo, and the young man she had called Tony with a puzzled look on his stupid face.

I did even better than the ironic look. I summoned up a shaky laugh. "You see, *Comandante*, you were right in the first place. Whoever called you was a crackpot."

Ferechini moved quickly past me to the closet and threw open the door. When he found it empty, he stood there a moment, his back to us, staring into its moldy interior. In the hall Mamma Peroni chuckled. I tried to get her eye but she looked beyond me, dark and impassive. I fished out a cigarette and lit it. It felt damp between my fingers. I had trouble getting rid of the match, like the character in the old vaudeville flypaper act.

"Now," Mamma Peroni said calmly, "you will apologize, *Signor* Ferechini!"

I expected an explosion. Instead there was a rigid silence for a moment, then slowly Ferechini turned and said with remarkable control, "There seems to have been a mistake. It is a night for bad jokes. It is also a night that will be bad for jokesters. Still, you realize I was engaged only in my duty." His eyes seemed to have gone out of focus, looking through and beyond me. "I sincerely hope, Mr. Muldoon, that you will forgive me."

The switch in his manner made me uneasy. I was sure that he had known Hertzy's body was in my room and that part of his plan was to pin the murder on me. Mamma Peroni voiced my own reactions. "When you are polite, Ferechini, my blood runs cold!"

Ferechini made a sound that might have been a laugh; a sound as brittle as a fingernail snapping against glass. "Perhaps more will be implicated in the jokes of the night than I had planned on. One stone, many birds. Now then. You will be going on to the party of Mrs. Wentworth, Mr. Muldoon. I myself will be there later. Perhaps you will join me there in a glass of wine."

The thin, calm veneer couldn't quite hide his inner panic. He still played the part that had made him successful in his constant war for "survival," but I sensed that something foreign to his way of thinking, something outside his Machiavellian consciousness, had occurred, and for the moment it was the shock of this discovery, rather than its results, that had unnerved him. But even allowing for this unscheduled assault upon his ego, it didn't quite explain his sudden changed manner or the fact that he did not immediately demand a search of the Villa Rosa.

"Is that all you want of me?" I asked.

"But certainly. For the moment."

Tony, his young disciple, was watching his master for some sign. Ferechini made an impatient gesture and Tony put away the revolver. Ferechini stood there a moment on the threshold as though engaged in a balancing act. Then almost like a ballet dancer he twirled and faced Mamma Peroni and for just an instant his face was animated by naked hatred. But the moment was brief. He bowed and, like an opera tenor at his next to last exit, not waiting for applause, hoarding it for his big number, moved swiftly toward the stairs with his minion behind him.

We stood there listening until the street door slammed. Mamma put her finger to her lips in time to stop my words, snapped out the bedroom light, crossed to the window, and gestured to me. I joined her and looked down into the alley. Tony was marching off toward the limousine that stood at the mouth of the alley in the square. But several yards from the entrance I could barely make out Ferechini in low-voiced conversation with two rather tough-looking characters who were not in uniform.

"Ferechini's imports," she whispered, "from Sicily."

In a moment Ferechini went marching off toward the car and the characters melted into the shadows.

"Come," Mamma said.

I followed her from my room down the long hall to her own. As we passed the door of Room 26 I thought I heard some movement inside. Mamma was too busy with her thoughts to have noticed. I realized for the first time that despite the late hour she was fully dressed.

Her room was small and chaste; a surprising contrast to the flamboyant earthiness of her public personality. Whitewashed walls, one small window overlooking the Via Cellini, a simple cot, a crucifix, a chest of drawers, and one photograph—that of a handsome giant of a man with flashing black eyes and a ferocious mustache who stood proudly in the stern of a moored fishing vessel. For a moment she seemed overcome by an unaccustomed shyness and I had a sudden disinclination to mention what had just occurred until she broached the subject first. Just as though I were paying a social visit, I lit a cigarette, regarded the photograph, and said, "Your husband?"

She nodded.

"I see no photographs of children."

"There were none," she said harshly. And then almost as though the question were being answered in another manner, she said anxiously, "*Signor* Muldoon, you have been at the Casino. Did you see Pietro there?"

"Pietro? What in the world would he be doing at the Casino?"

"Playing the fool!" she said darkly. "What else does a man do? And tonight of all nights, when we need his help so badly."

"We?"

She sank to the edge of the bed and leaned forward wearily.

"There are a few decent people left on this island."

"Look, Mamma. You and your friends—you're not trying to buck Ferechini alone?"

"Who else!"

"Have you any proof?"

"Proof?" She looked at me sharply. "You sound like the high and mighty officials on the mainland. Bring us proof, they have said. Well ..." She caught herself up. "This is not your affair. Tell me, did you see Pietro?"

"Yes."

She straightened up on the bed, her eyes wide. "Ah! Then he was at the Casino. With whom?"

"First, does this have anything to do with the Ferechini business?"

"No, it is an affair of the heart. The young ass is madly in love with the poor little French girl in Room Twenty-six. She has told him some story—the usual thing, you know—a man who ruined her or some such business. I have heard only an hour ago that Pietro intends to kill this man! I am out of my mind!"

"Who is the man?"

"I wish I knew."

I took a deep breath and said, "There was a murder at the Casino."

"Holy Jesus. No!"

"The old Duchessa di Cabrieni was murdered."

Horror changed to astonishment and disbelief. "But why ... Who ... Not even a monster like Cassi or Ferechini would.... I don't understand."

"She overheard something said at a neighboring table. She overheard a plan to murder me, as a matter of fact."

"Ah! So! This comes of meddling." She stood decisively. "You will not listen to me. Already you have given me enough trouble."

"Where is Georges Hertzy, Mamma—or what's left of him?"

Calmly she said, "You speak in riddles. I don't know what you're talking about. All I know is I must get you out of here safely. Ferechini's gunmen will be waiting for you outside. This much I know. Now then. They will be expecting you to leave by the Via Cellini. I will show you another way out. I will tell you where to hide and before morning you will be taken to the mainland and safety."

"You expect me to run out?"

"This isn't your affair.

"I have a certain stake in it."

Suddenly she crossed the room and grasped the lapels of my dinner jacket. "I have things to do. You waste my time. I will show you the way out, over the roofs to the Via Marina. Then you will go through the arcades, beyond the fish market to the big warehouse the other side of the mole. The warehouse is half on a pier. You will hide under the pier until someone comes to fetch you."

I opened my mouth to protest but decided not to argue. She pushed me out into the hall toward the stairs. I didn't give the door of Room 26 a glance. We went up two flights to a small attic. There she carefully opened a dormer in the slanting roof and beckoned me to her side. "Now," she whispered, "let yourself down to the gutter. Work your way over behind the big chimney. There you will find the roof of the next house. Cross it and lower yourself to the roof of the Caffè del Porto. After that it is simple. There is an iron ladder down into the alley beside the restaurant. You know where the warehouse is."

"Yes." Close to her I said, "Why do you bother about me, Mamma?"

"That's what Pietro says, God help him. Sometimes I cannot think why!"

"But you are in danger yourself."

"Not from Ferechini. I have too many friends among the fishermen. Go quickly."

"Where did you put the body of Georges Hertzy?" I whispered.

"I don't know what you are saying," she said coldly.

I crawled over the ledge to the slanting roof. The slates were worn and broken in many places and even with the help of the drainpipe I had a precarious moment when my feet seemed to be sliding on ice.

Above me Mamma hissed, "Clumsy fool! You will have me in trouble yet!"

"You seem to thrive on trouble," I whispered back.

"Go back to America," she said in a low voice. And then with a breathy suggestion of a laugh, "And be certain you send me the rent you owe or I will hold your luggage through eternity."

I worked my way down the drainpipe to the rusted gutter. Then, lying flat against the slant of the roof, I began to edge my way toward the chimney. This was for Mamma's benefit. I had other plans, but I didn't intend to waste the night arguing with her about them. When I had the chimney between me and the dormer I took time out. Down below the Via Cellini was a dark slash in the moonlit night. I thought I saw a shadow move from the protection of a moldering arch but couldn't be sure. After three or four minutes I edged my way back to the drain, and like a mountain climber pulled myself back up to the dormer. As I had hoped, Mamma was gone. I climbed back into the musty attic room and removed my shoes. Then, holding them in one hand, I descended the stairs to the second floor. I could hear Mamma down in the lobby talking in a low urgent voice into the phone. I heard her say, "Don't come here. Ferechini's men ..." And then the words sank back into a meaningless drone.

Quietly I went down the hall to the door of Room 26. I pushed it open, found the light switch, and snapped it on. The room seemed to be empty. But there was another door half open on a darkened interior. I remembered seeing a lavatory here, perhaps the only private lavatory in the Villa Rosa. I closed the hall door behind me and crossed to the lavatory door and threw it open. The light from the bedroom fell on a woman crouching against the basin. In her hand was a very businesslike German Luger.

I looked from the Luger up into the face of the frightened woman. It was the widow of the man who had been murdered in my room, Gigi Hertzy.

Chapter Fifteen

THE VILLA ROSA, 3:00 A.M.

Carefully I backed into the bedroom. I didn't like the way her hand was white on the revolver. She came out after me like a tigress stalking prey. She stood near the bed and said in a low voice: "Where is he?"

"You've been waiting here a long while," I said. "Ever since you searched my room."

"Where is he?" she repeated tensely.

"There are so many 'he's.' Even you must get them confused. The Luger spoils the effect of the gown. Dior wouldn't approve."

"I've had my fill of funny bastards for tonight," she said. "I'm fed up with jokesters."

But I noticed that the hand that held the Luger so tightly was trembling. I took a step forward, purely exploratory, to test the true nature of the climate. The Luger came up sharply. I held my ground then; the weather was still too uncertain for unnecessary risks.

"Tell me where Georges is," she said tensely.

Was she on the level? It was hard to tell. I decided to settle for the literal truth. "I wish I knew."

Downstairs I heard the distant drone of Mamma Peroni suddenly cut off.

"It's like this," she said. "When you start making an idiot of yourself, the way I'm doing now, you can't go halfway. I'm all the way in now with a gun in my hand. Phillip hired you to get rid of Georges, didn't he?"

"Hell, no!"

"You don't have to pretend to me. Nothing shocks or surprises me much anymore. Nothing!"

"Obviously."

"I knew when I walked into Phillip's suite tonight that he was up to something like that."

"For God's sake, you don't really think that Adams would hire me to bump your husband off. Why?"

"Don't be naïve. Poor Georges, he's a sweet boy. He's been kind to me. That's why I'm here."

"You're in love with your husband?"

"Love?" She laughed. "What books have you been reading?"

"I'm just a country boy."

"The hell you are!" she said. "And the only thing I know about the country is hay."

She was relaxing a little, back on the footing of hard banter where she felt at home. I heard Mamma clumping up the stairs and held my hand up for silence. Gigi, resplendent in her white and gold gown, kept a bead on me while we listened to Mamma enter her room and put the chain lock in place.

"How did you get here?" I asked.

"Simple enough. I called a taxi. I was at Babs Wentworth's party, you know—or what passes for a party. Phillip was down in the garden talking to some people and in that mob I knew he wouldn't miss me. For a while, anyway. Some dyke began pawing me on a Louis Quinze sofa and suddenly I thought I'd go in search of Georges ... and things."

"Ah? And why my room?"

"Because I knew Georges came here to see you earlier in the evening."

I didn't show what that did to me. Almost casually I said, "Why would he want to see me?"

"At Count Cassi's cocktail party he told me. He was terribly upset about something. He wouldn't tell me what. Somehow he had got hold of your name. He told me you were some sort of agent or private eye or whatever they call a person like you. But why do you ask? He must have told you."

"I never saw him," I said. And then I amended it to the truth: "I never spoke to him."

Something in my rearranged words communicated a new uneasiness to her. "You know something. You're not telling me."

"How did you know my room?"

"I—I believe Georges ... I don't know. What does it matter? What is it you are hiding from me?"

"I'll tell you," I said glibly. "Georges may have gone to Naples." And then quickly, "It may interest you to know that this joint is surrounded by thugs. They're lying in wait out there for me now."

"You? But why?"

I took advantage of the moment of surprise to reach over and turn off the light.

"I'll use this gun," she whispered breathlessly. And then when I said nothing, "Stay where you are."

I knew by her tone that she couldn't see me. Carefully I bent down and placed my shoes on the rug. Then, with only the darkness between us, I began to edge across the room to her.

"Turn on that light!" she whispered urgently.

The moon fell in a long slant to the hem of the white and gold dress. She must have been aware of this because suddenly she moved from the moon's path, but too late. I fell on her, pulling her close in a bear hug. There was a nasty moment with the Luger between us when I wondered whether the finger would tighten on the trigger. But her hand on the gun was in an awkward position, with the wrist twisted about by the weight of my body, and in a moment I felt the fingers opening and the Luger slipping down between my legs, and then I heard the soft plopping sound as it hit the carpet.

Quickly now I got hold of her and twisted her around to the side of the bed. While she was still off balance I smacked her hard across the face and she went sprawling across the bed. I threw myself on her and she struggled, trying to work free, sobbing and breathing hard. And suddenly in the midst of the struggle I was very much aware of her body.

"Don't kill me," she gasped.

"Kill you!" I whispered huskily.

My voice told her, if nothing else had. She said, "Oh ..." and then in a flash her arms went up about me, drawing me close to her. "It's all right," she said. "Nothing else matters. Nothing ..."

And in the sudden urgency of the moment nothing else did matter.

The nightmarish pattern moved on through unreality. It seemed a lifetime later, but, of course, the dawn was only a few minutes closer. We were held together now by the sad aftertime, the moment when we were left for a short period of respite without urgency. Our cigarettes made orange pinpricks in the darkness of Room 26.

"It always happens like this," she said after a bit, "without meaning."

"I still can't quite believe it happened," I said.

"All my life it has been like this—like a dream."

I, too, was caught in her dream. All the events of this strange night belonged in some haunted realm of sleep. And now, strangest of all, this woman whom I barely knew had clung to me in the center of a strangeness as though this brief and violent unpremeditated contact was the only reality and we knew it in the midst of fear and apprehension. It seemed natural that I should lie beside her despite the danger of the hour and fleeting time and the threat of death that waited in the shadows of arches and moldering doorways all about the Villa Rosa. Time was suspended and seemed to hang rigid, like our cigarette smoke in the stale air of the tiny bedroom,

"It was like a dream, my coming here," she said. "Georges had been kind to me. I felt sorry for him. I wanted to find out what you were up to. I went to Phillip's room at the Miramar. I knew where that Luger was. I don't know what I planned to do with it. And now ... look."

She gave a little mirthless laugh.

I thought of Elsa and felt a moment's guilt. Not for the act that had just taken place, but because, despite it, it was still Elsa who was the object of my final desire. And yet, despite her brazen hardness, there was something somewhat touching about Gigi Heretzy, something that disturbed me.

Almost as though she had heard my thought, she said, "Elsa would be annoyed with me if she knew. You are, after all, her young man."

"That has an unpleasant ring."

"I don't mean it that way. It's just that Elsa has always been able to get what she wanted. With me it's been different."

"You have Phillip Adams."

"Oh, yes," she said with sudden bitterness. "I settled down finally and promised to be a good girl."

"Settled down from what?"

"I liked the wrong people. People without money. People who lived in little apartments in Greenwich Village and ... Oh, well, that's in the past. Elsa ..." She stopped.

"You were saying?"

"Nothing. Not much of anything. I guess I've always been the girl who never held out. What the hell." She turned restlessly on her side. "It's strange, Hart, it's mad, but I can talk to you. You know what that means. You know how few people there are in the world to whom one can talk? It's as though I'd known you all my life."

"All your life can't be too long."

"I suppose not. It seems so. The dream again, you see.... Like a long senseless dream. My childhood in Bucharest ... it's like an illustration from someone else's picture book. The snow on the boulevard in December, the palace on the hill, and the dark little flat where we lived. Mother sewing far into the night on some society lady's gown, perhaps for one of the ladies of Michael's court."

"She was a *couturière* even then?"

"She was a seamstress."

"What? The wife of a general?"

She laughed dryly. "It's naughty of me to expose Mother's little white lies, but actually the only uniform my father ever wore was the uniform of his trade. He was a conductor on the Bucharest street railways."

"Ah ..."

"He died when I was six." She hesitated a moment. "I don't know why I tell you this. I've never told anyone, even Phillip—especially Phillip. But it was then, after my father died, that I began to learn about—well, discipline and men. Mamma had a gentleman friend, you see. A manufacturer of children's toys, I believe. He took Mamma and Elsa and me to Paris. He didn't last long. There were several other gentlemen friends, and even as a girl I could see the cold smile of contempt on Mamma's face when the door closed behind them. Then there a friend richer than the others and we went to New York. But he didn't last long either. There were some bad years, but somehow Mother saw to it that we went to the right schools and met the right people. And then suddenly there were no more gentlemen friends for Mamma."

"I see. The daughters became old enough for the market, eh?"

"You make it sound sordid. Well, maybe it was. But so is poverty. Mamma had scrimped and sacrificed and God knows we had gone a long way from that dreary little flat in Bucharest. We were popular, Elsa and I—Elsa more than I, but ..."

"It paid off in spades for Mamma, eh?"

"Mother believes that love is a weakness—something for the rich and sentimental. A luxury. I wouldn't know. I've never been in love. Not the way I hear about, anyway. It's always as if I were getting into bed with some man to forget something. What, I wouldn't know. With Phillip it's different. He was kind to Mother, put money in her dress shop."

"Did her shop do well?"

For a moment she didn't answer. Then she said, "Not really. In fact, until last year it lost money. But now ..."

"Gigi," I said carefully, "did the shop begin to pick up after Count Cassi visited New York last year?"

The effect was immediate. She crushed out her cigarette. She got out of the bed, and, trailing her gown behind her, went to the bathroom and closed the door behind her. I lay there thinking a moment, then dressed and turned on the light. She came out of the bathroom looking as fresh as ever, a schoolgirl waiting for her diploma.

"All right, Sweetie," I said. "Come clean. Did Georges come to see me about the Eagles of the Balkans?"

"I haven't the faintest idea." She was cool and in command once again.

"Now you listen to me!" I started for her but stopped halfway across the room, stopped by a sudden clatter in the quiet night. Someone was pounding on the street door downstairs.

"Hart!" she said fearfully. "What is it? I must get out of here."

"Quiet."

I heard the chain of Mamma Peroni's lock and a moment later her footsteps clumping down the hall and the stairs to the entrance foyer. Quickly I opened the bedroom door. Gigi stood close behind me, breathing hard.

We heard the street door being unbolted and Mamma's deep challenge. "Well?"

A man's voice said in English, "Is Mrs. Hertzy here?"

Gigi's hand dug into my arm. "My God!" she whispered. "It's Phillip!"

"Take it easy. Now, no matter how screwy it may sound, do exactly as I say."

"Hart! He must not find me here. Mamma would never forgive—"

"To hell with Mamma. Do as I say! This may be a lucky break. Ferechini's men are all about this joint. You might never get out of here healthy without the proper escort. And what could be more proper than Mr. Phillip Adams of the well-known American dollar?"

Downstairs Mamma was saying, "You will have to look elsewhere for your woman, *signore*. This is a respectable house!"

"One moment, please. I know Mrs. Hertzy came here. Unless you wish me to call the police ..."

"The police!" Mamma's laugh rose derisively. "Just raise your voice, *signore*. They will come running."

I broke from Gigi's grasp and went to the head of the stairs, making sure as I went that my clothes were, as they say in the theatre, decent. From the top I called out, "Is that you, Adams? Mrs. Hertzy is up here."

"Muldoon!" In a moment Adams came bounding up the stairs. His face was red and he was puffing angrily. "What the devil is this? Where is Gigi?"

"She came in the hope that I would be able to tell her about her missing husband."

Gigi came down the hall. To my relief she looked as though she had just stepped out of a beauty parlor. Practice, I thought cynically. She gave Adams a ravishing smile. "Isn't it naughty of me, darling?"

Adams gave me a murderous look. "Well? Who is going to explain?"

Below Adams, Mamma Peroni's face appeared in the stairwell. She gave me an expressive look as though to say, Nothing surprises me anymore.

Gigi was as calm as a May day. Her mother's rigid training came in handy now. "Don't look like such a bear, Phillip darling. Anyone would think I had an assignation here with Mr. Muldoon, or something equally absurd. Don't embarrass me, darling, please."

"Speak up, Muldoon!"

"You've got an evil mind," I said insolently.

"Now, listen here. If it hadn't been for Miss Parks, who overheard Gigi call for a taxi to bring her to the Miramar, I wouldn't have known what to think. I traced you there, Gigi, and found the driver. He told me he brought you here."

"But, darling, I didn't want to worry you. Someone told me Georges had come here to the Villa Rosa. I thought I'd better fetch him. There is a French girl here, you know, he was interested in. People at the party were beginning to talk. It was you I was thinking of."

"Well!" Adams said. "Did you find him?"

If it was an act, it was a damned good one. He almost convinced me. Almost.

"No, darling. Isn't it a bore? Where in the world do you suppose the boy has gone to?"

Instead of replying, he said, "Where did Muldoon come into the picture?"

Mamma Peroni came to the rescue. "My halls are not for social conversation at this hour of the morning. You will be good enough, *signore*, to take your woman and leave!"

It was good strategy. Adams turned his anger on Mamma Peroni, forgetting me for the moment. "Now look here, my good woman—"

"I'm not your woman, good or otherwise. Now, all of you, clear out. I am fed up with crazy Americans."

Gigi gave me a wide innocent look and smiled at Mamma Peroni and, like a well-behaved child, walked down the stairs to the foyer. I realized Mamma Peroni had seen a way to get me safely away from the vicinity of the Villa Rosa and off her hands. She suspected, as did I, that Ferechini's men would not dare pull any rough stuff as long as I was with the influential American.

"Come on, Adams," I said. "I'll explain in the taxi."

Trying to retain some semblance of dignity, Adams followed me down to the foyer. I looked back at Mamma Peroni and winked. She shrugged in a gesture of hopeless outrage. I went out into the street between Gigi and Adams.

A shadow moved quickly out from an arch farther up the alley, hesitated, and retreated. Unmolested, we walked to the taxi that waited in the lighted square. None of us said a word until the taxi was climbing the cobblestones up toward the Via Minerva. I lit a cigarette and waited.

When Adams could stand it no longer he said, "All right, you bastard, talk!"

Gigi said, "Phillip, I assure you that—"

"Stay out of this a moment, Gigi!"

I leaned back and half closed my eyes. "Look, Adams. You hired me for a job. Oddly enough, I'm going to finish it tonight. But first, would you kindly tell me why the hell you pulled all that phony political stuff about the Balkan Eagles? You know goddamned well that isn't what you want to find out about Georges Hertzy."

That took the wind out of him. I could feel him stiffen at my side. "What are you driving at, Muldoon?"

"Who are you protecting, Adams? What is it that Hertzy discovered? Why was it imperative that you find out what he was up to and with whom?"

"Now look here, Muldoon. It seems to me—"

"No!" I said in sudden fury. "You look here! You're as bad as all the rest of them, despite your high and mighty moral tone. There's something you wanted Hertzy to shut up about. You hired me as insurance. If anything happened to Hertzy as a result of his misguided curiosity, you could always prove that you were worried about his political connections and had actually hired me to investigate. In other words, if Georges Hertzy should be bumped off, you would be perfectly willing to throw up a smoke screen, hide the real murderers, make it look like a political assassination!"

"Phillip!" Gigi cried. "What is he talking about?"

For a moment Adams said nothing. Then very quietly he said, "You're cleverer than I thought, Muldoon. And reckless."

"You don't deny it?"

"I don't have to affirm or deny anything, Muldoon."

"I'm going up to this Wentworth house and dig up some skeletons. What are you planning to do?"

He hesitated a moment, and then said in a weary voice. "I think perhaps we will go back to Babs' party also. If this brash young man insists on upsetting apple-carts, we might as well be there to see the apples roll out. Or perhaps his head."

Chapter Sixteen

THE WENTWORTH VILLA, 4:00 A.M.

I stopped in the shadow of a loggia that was heavy with the odor of grapes. Behind me, the great house—once the property of the Dukes of Cabrieni—was, except for a few drunks in the reception room, almost deserted. Gigi and Adams, whose relationship at the moment was in a state of cool suspension, had gone on ahead through the hanging gardens. The scene below me was fantastically unreal. Here the cliff was bitten into by the sea, and at the base of the terraced gardens, on the edge of a small half-moon of a beach, was a gaily lighted pavilion where some of Babs Wentworth's late lingering guests were sipping champagne while a man whom I recognized as Pietro sang to them over his concertina. Light spilled out along the beach, barely touching a row of cabanas where couples were stretched out on chaise lounges and rubber mats, while several yards offshore a floating bar had been set up at the foot of a floodlit high dive. Many of the guests had changed into bathing costumes. The handsome and the beautiful still played tag with the rich and anxious; only now, as dawn drew near, the game, at least for this night, was less elusive. The laughter and the mutter of voices drifting up from the beach had taken on a darker, more urgent tone than that heard in the Casino.

In the very center of the pavilion, as though holding court, was the woman in the silver dress, the one I had seen in the bedroom at Count Cassi's apartment and later on the Casino terrace. And among those who formed a semicircle at her feet was Planquet. The woman, from this distance, looked like a doll from the court of Marie Antoinette. Near the edge of the pavilion, talking to Cassi, was Elsa, looking as fresh and beautiful as she had earlier in the evening. And despite my recent experience with her sister at the Villa Rosa, I felt a hot stab of desire.

In my sight were some of the other actors in the strange melodrama of this night. Yvonne, the French girl from Room 26, who sat alone and remote from the others, touching with both hands a glass of champagne as she watched Pietro, who was singing, oblivious of the noisy guests, apparently only for her. Lorna Parks, looking haggard in the overhead light, was chatting in what appeared to be a frenzied manner with a bored young man. Mrs.

Bennol, still very much the *grande dame* despite the fast disintegrating semblance of decent society all around her, the tailor shop in Bucharest forgotten, seemed to be making pronouncements to a fat little man in green slacks and an orange shirt. Like a spectator in a gallery of a theatre I watched Gigi and Adams enter the pavilion and drift apart, Gigi toward the cabanas and Adams to Elsa's side. Through the crowd wandered sturdy women in sturdy slacks accompanied by graceful nymphs, while along the sands the arrangement of the sexes in couples or trios would have offered interesting material to a Kinsey investigator.

For a moment I was unable to spot Loretta Kelly. Then suddenly she came into the light of the pavilion in the company of two young men who were more or less clad in bikinis. She herself wore the daring gown, which, with the hours, had become more revealing, and she swayed dangerously on her feet as she waved an empty glass in mid-air. She said something to one of the young men, who laughed, then turned in a curious half crouch in the direction of the pavilion. Her face, turned up into the light, was a picture of malevolence.

Behind me a pebble was dislodged. I wheeled about to find Mrs. Wentworth standing not a foot away. She had changed from evening gown to velvet slacks and a glittering silver blouse. One hand holding a cigarette holder rigidly in my direction, she was smiling ironically.

"I abhor gate-crashers!" she said.

"I can see, from the scene below, how exclusive your guest list is."

She kept smiling. "In a way it is. No bores. Some of them are my friends. Others amuse me. You don't fit into either category."

"So?"

"So," she said calmly, "since you are neither friend nor clown, it's possible I have other, more practical, interests in you."

Taken by surprise, I said, "That's what I like—practicality at four A.M."

"One of the servants told me I would find you here. I'm glad. I've been expecting you. You see, since I first saw you in the hall of that disgusting little pension, I've made it my business to find out something about you. As a result I would have words with you. Come into my parlor, Mr. Muldoon."

Curious now and puzzled, I followed her back through the loggia into a large reception hall. From an open doorway to one of the sitting rooms came a querulous voice, female and middle-aged. "It's unforgivable of you, Blanche, unforgivable. Getting drunk like this. Like a common slut. After coming all the way from Rome and knowing Babs might be good for at least four hundred if you behaved. And then you have to go and get stinking! She never gave you a second look!"

We went quietly past the door, unobserved. Mrs. Wentworth gave me a quizzical, amused glance. "Some of my dearest friends," she whispered, and laughed. She led me into a small study, closed the door behind us, and, much in the manner of a business executive, indicated that she desired me to sit on the sofa. And again like the executive, she stood, legs apart, in front of a fireplace, facing me from the advantage of a higher level. I half expected her to offer me a cigar.

"So?" I said.

"The Duchessa di Cambieni was murdered tonight at the Casino. I was fond of the poor dear. Things have gone much too far."

"I'm glad someone around here seems to think so."

"I gather from a dear little friend of mine that certain people find you annoying—inconvenient."

"A dear little friend?"

"A boy called Freddie."

"The one who was with Miss Lorna Parks at the bar of the Villa Rosa when you walked in earlier this evening?"

"Yes. That Freddie. The Freddie that Count Cassi keeps."

"So ... it's that way with the Count."

"It appears to be 'that way' with many of my dearest friends. However, though I adore Freddie, I can't abide Cassi."

"What does Freddie know about the murder of the Duchessa?"

"Poor thing," she said calmly enough, "Freddie and I have planned this little party for several weeks. We have a little private joke that I can't reveal at the moment. But he has been barely able to go through with it. Because, you see, poor Freddie happened to see the Duchessa murdered."

"What!"

Through the open window the sound of Pietro's voice rose from the beach like singing on another planet. I was confused. Although I was pretty good at remembering faces—after all, it was part of my job— I had no recollection of seeing the young man named Freddie at the Casino.

"Who did it?" I asked.

Instead of answering, she went to a bell rope and pulled it. When a servant appeared at the door, she instructed him to go to the beach and tell Miss Lorna Parks to come to the study immediately.

Then she turned back to me. "I have a reputation for many things, most of them completely justified. I amuse myself, and until tonight the sleigh ride has been fun."

"And tonight?"

She frowned, tore the cigarette from the jade holder, flung it into the fireplace. "I don't know. There is something about tonight, something odd.... Maybe for the first time I'm afraid of death. Oh, God, what drivel am I talking?"

She strode to the window, stood there with her back to me staring out over the gardens.

"Why are you telling me this?" I asked.

"Because, damn it all, I need help. For once I'm up a tree."

"You're in trouble?"

"Not me. But someone of whom I am—well, very fond."

"Lorna Parks?"

"Yes," she said quietly. After a moment she laughed again. "It's really the damnedest thing, you know. I've plowed through things and people all my life, and now look at me—having heart palpitations over a rather silly, fading movie star. It's ridiculous. Still ..."

"And Mr. Wentworth?"

"Henry? Oh, my God, Henry and I have gone our own ways for many years now. Everyone knows that. He has some tart he keeps in doubtful taste but what is referred to as luxury in a Park Avenue apartment. He—" Again she stopped and stood there with her back to me, staring out into the night. "You know," she said finally, "people say dreadful things about me—men, women and dogs ... that sort of thing. And they are partly right. I don't mind what they say. I'm rich enough to be unconventional and throw it in their faces. But ... but ..." And suddenly a sort of harsh emotion crept into her voice. "I won't let them destroy Lorna!"

I leaned back on the sofa, thinking that of all the odd scenes of this odd night, this was most certainly the strangest. A rich and notorious woman with whom I had exchanged only a few words in the lobby of the Villa Rosa was now divulging her innermost secrets to me as though we had known one another all our lives.

"You still haven't told me who killed the Duchessa."

"I want Lorna to be here. I want her shocked into reality. You see, there are things about Lorna that she doesn't know I have discovered. I've tried to be discreet, hoping it would end, but I've failed."

"But where do I fit into this picture?"

She turned and looked at me directly. "Georges Hertzy knew what I had discovered. I told him this afternoon at the cocktail party at Cassi's. He had suspected the truth but couldn't bring himself to believe it. Someone gave him your name. He was going to see you in the hope that you would undertake a private investigation. Did he reach you?'"

I hesitated.

"Ah!" she said sharply. "I might have known! What filthy monsters!"

"Cassi? Ferechini?"

"Oh, yes, of course. And—well, the others."

"The others being?"

She looked toward the door almost furtively. "What the hell is keeping Lorna? She can be such a little fool after a few glasses of champagne." She paced back and forth a moment, then settled once more in the position of business before the fireplace.

"I've seen enough in my time, young man, to be pretty damned cynical about accepted morality. I believe people should do whatever they feel like doing, if they can afford it. But this thing has me stopped. Freddie is a bright little darling and his not so innocent ears hear everything. He has heard things, and repeated them to me, that neither he nor I can prove. At first I shrugged it off as none of my business. But when I realized Lorna was mixed up in it, the picture was changed. I don't want any part of the authorities. I don't want any unpleasant publicity. So I'm going to hand on to you what I know, and then you can go to the proper authorities with it. And I'm going to pay you five thousand dollars to handle it in such a manner that Lorna will not be involved."

"You flatter me."

"Nonsense. I've checked on you. You can do it. But before I tell you, I must be certain, absolutely certain, that you will keep Lorna out of this mess."

"You'll have to tell me first."

"No. I want your promise."

I tried diversive tactics. "Let me tell you, then. Cassi and Ferechini are part of a big drug ring. Ferechini used this island as headquarters for distribution. Cassi is the contact man. Cassi has used a crackpot outfit called the Balkan Eagles as a front. He and his agents have found it convenient to camouflage, especially as some quite respectable Americans have vouched for them in the States for lectures and so on."

"You're right. And smart as you have been represented."

"Furthermore," I said, "this morning, just after dawn, a ship called the Lyon will put into the lower port. On it is a shipment of drugs marked for Ferechini."

"Then you *do* know!" she said in astonishment.

"This much I have guessed. I almost know that in some manner Ferechini has involved Elsa Planquet in this rotten deal. It is she who is supposed to pick up the shipment, as she ostensibly visits a friend who is supposedly ill aboard the Lyon."

"Elsa!" she said, startled. "Oh, no! Not Elsa."

A feeling of relief surged through me. Mrs. Wentworth's shock was genuine.

"But I don't understand," she said. "Unless ... unless..."

"Unless what?"

The door opened and Lorna Parks came into the room. She looked questioningly from Babs Wentworth to me. Then I saw the sudden flicker of fear in her eyes.

"Close the door, Lorna," Mrs. Wentworth snapped.

Without a word she obeyed. Then she came back into the room, smiled shyly at me, and began to speak almost hysterically. "It's about the joke. Oh, I know it's about the joke. And I'm so frightened. Pepe has no sense of humor. I don't know ..."

"I didn't send for you for that reason, Lorna. Sit down."

She darted a frightened glance at Babs and like a docile child sat, very prim and straight, on the chair facing me.

"Now, Lorna," Mrs. Wentworth said, "I find this very painful, but the time for lying is past."

"Lying? Lying? I don't know what—"

"Now, darling, you must not waste our time. You can speak freely before Mr. Muldoon. He is going to help us."

"Help? About what?"

Mrs. Wentworth frowned, looked away, and began to speak in a quick monotone. "Freddie told me, my dear. About the drugs."

"Drugs? Oh, Babs, what are you talking about?" The ex-movie star's voice rose shrilly. She gave me a wild, imploring look.

"Oh, I don't blame you," Mrs. Wentworth went on. "Perhaps it's my fault for not realizing. I know now how desperately discouraged you were about your career. You never were able to face up to things. And after that bastard Planquet—Well, he'll pay tonight, all right. After he threw you out of the film—I should have known. I knew it wasn't like you to run up those enormous bills at the dress shop, but ..."

"What dress shop?" I broke in.

"Mrs. Bennol's shop in New York."

There was a complete silence. After a moment I said, "Of course. I might have known. She works for Cassi. Ferechini got Elsa into this through blackmail. She has to do it to protect her mother."

"Possibly. But my interest is seeing that Bennol bitch put behind bars, where she belongs. She started poor Lorna on the habit, and by God, she's going to pay."

Lorna Parks put her hands to her face. "Oh, I can't bear it. I can't."

"Now, then, Lorna," Mrs. Wentworth said sharply, "no histrionics, if you please. It won't help any of us."

"But to think you have known ... I was so ashamed. But I couldn't help myself. And it was so easy ... put on the bills from the shop. Clothes I never even saw, of course. Only here on Venzola they have been making it difficult for me—demanding money and—I think I shall kill myself."

"I think, my dear," Mrs. Wentworth said coldly, "that good medical attention, for a while, is more to the point."

"But you must hate me now."

"No," Mrs. Wentworth said harshly, "I don't."

For a moment the two women looked in each other's eyes. I turned away, feeling uncomfortable.

"Look," I said. "Time is going by. That ship is due at six."

"You're quite right. Now you have the facts—"

"You haven't told me who killed the Duchessa."

"It was Ferechini," she said quietly. "He smashed the poor thing up against the balustrade, and then he pushed her over the rail."

"Oh, no!" Lorna Parks cried. "Oh, no! It's a nightmare. I can't bear any more. I must go away from here, far away somewhere. And you've got to stop that farce. It's not funny, Babs. Pepe will be wild."

"I'll take care of Pepe!" Mrs. Wentworth said coldly. "And now I would suggest that you go to your bedroom. Mr. Muldoon has some fast work to do."

Already I was at the phone. After a great deal of sputtering I finally managed to raise an operator. "I want to get through to Naples," I said.

"I am sorry, *signore*. It is impossible."

"Impossible?"

"*Sì, signore*. I regret that the line has been out for two hours now ... an accident to the cable."

"An accident named Ferechini!" I shouted, and hung up.

Mrs. Wentworth was startled. "My God," she said. "You know what that means."

"I have a hunch. What's yours?"

"It's obvious," she said. "Ferechini suspected someone would try to get through before the arrival of the Lyon. And it's equally obvious that he cannot afford to let that person live to tell his tale."

"In that case, my dear Mrs. Wentworth, we're both in trouble."

She laughed harshly. "Not me, Ferechini knows I wouldn't intervene because of Lorna."

I walked toward the door. "One little Indian," I said.

"You can still get away. There's time. I could hide you until late in the day."

"Thanks," I said. "I think I'd rather celebrate in champagne."

Chapter Seventeen

THE WENTWORTH BEACH, 4:30 A.M.

The woman in the silver dress still dominated the pavilion. She sat in the center, gracefully manipulating in one hand a glass of champagne and in the other an ivory cigarette holder and speaking in low husky accents of art, the theatre, and the cinema. She seemed to have almost a hypnotic appeal to the group around her, and among the most attentive was Pepe Planquet.

"Who in God's name is she?" I asked Babs Wentworth.

"Sigrid Bergson is as good a name as any, don't you think? She is a protégée of mine. Very talented."

She was amused by something behind her words. Considering the conversation we had just held in the study, her calm was either admirable or foolish.

"It might interest you to know," I said, "that your talented protégée is also a hophead."

She stopped smiling.

"What are you talking about?"

"Look," I said. "What goes with this Bergson dame? If she's such a close friend of yours, why wasn't she in your party at the Casino?"

"She came too late. She was—she was visiting friends."

A young man in the briefest of bathing trunks came sauntering up. "Babs, darling, introduce me to the new number. So attractive!"

"This isn't in your league, Jerry."

"Well, sweet, no harm in *asking*."

They chattered on while I cased the crowd. Elsa, talking with a group on the far side of the pavilion, was watching me across the heads of the guests. I thought she looked pale and tense. Ferechini had just come in and had joined a group that included Cassi and Mrs. Bennol. Ferechini caught my eye, smiled coldly, and came across the room, having acquired a glass of champagne from a servant.

"Ah, Mrs. Wentworth. A delightful party. I'm sorry I could not be here earlier. Some boring duties ..."

"I'm certain of that!" Mrs. Wentworth said coldly. She gave me a worried, questioning look and wandered off with Jerry.

"And now, *Signor* Muldoon," Ferechini said, "we might have that glass of champagne we talked about."

"You'd better drink while you can," I said. "Despite certain reforms, I doubt that you'll be able to get it in an Italian jail."

He laughed. "So among your many other accomplishments you are, too, a penologist. It would be a tragedy to see such a brilliant career cut short!" He squinted reflectively at the retreating back of his hostess. "A charming woman, yes. And rich. A lovely combination. And intelligent, also, as sort of an unexpected bonus. It is her intelligence that keeps her out of the business of others." He looked around. "And where is the delightful Miss Parks?"

"She swam to Naples to have a chat with the police."

He smiled benignly. The man's gall was supreme. "No, she will never do that. She has neither the courage nor the fortitude."

"Mr. Phillip Adams has both."

He shrugged. "He has also his private life. He wishes to keep it quiet. I am willing to co-operate for mutual quiet. Do you understand?"

"You don't think you can blackmail a man like Adams?"

"But, my dear Mr. Muldoon, a man like Adams, as you put it—this is the most vulnerable subject for the ugly word you use. A virtuous reputation is difficult to part with."

"What have you got on Elsa Planquet?"

For a moment he stopped smiling and his eyes narrowed, boring into me with a question. But he didn't give voice to it. He said nothing.

"In other words," I said, "there is no one here who knows what you are up to who would give your show away?"

He inclined his head. "Everyone to his own garden, *signore*."

"And devil take the hindmost! Well, goddamn it, you haven't got anything on me!"

He sighed. "Nothing of any value. That makes it difficult. Most unfortunate ... for you."

Despite the chill at my spine, I said, "You've forgotten someone, Ferechini."

"Who?"

"Mamma Peroni and her friends."

His face darkened. "Bah! Clods. You think I fear such scum?"

"And ... there's me."

He lifted his glass of champagne. "Yes," he said with an explosive laugh, "there is, for the moment, you."

Quickly I added before he could get the glass to his lips, "And there is Georges Hertzy—wherever he may show up."

Slowly he lowered the glass. "You know, *signore*, it is odd about the disappearance of *Signor* Hertzy. I am inclined to the belief that Mamma Peroni thought she was performing an act of kindness in covering up for you. Perhaps if Mr. Hertzy has completely disappeared—say to the fish—she has been kind also to me!"

Elsa had managed to get away from her group and came up to us. "Hart! I've been so worried about you! I couldn't imagine why you didn't show up. What happened?"

"Ferechini wanted to ask me some questions about blackmail and a passenger coming in on the Lyon."

She gasped and turned quickly to Ferechini, who merely looked amused. "Mr. Muldoon hears a great deal of gossip—harmless talk that harms no one."

"But—" She broke off as Mrs. Bennol came gushing up to us.

"What an amusing party! Only Babs could gather together such an odd assortment. Not at all the sort of thing for Palm Beach or Newport, but here ..."

I watched Elsa closely. There was no doubt that her nerves were near the breaking point. Her hands were clenched tightly together as her mother spoke. Mrs. Bennol suddenly stopped gushing and frowned. "My dear, what is all this business about that Bergson woman? Pepe is making a perfect ass of himself over her. And I just heard the strangest rumor."

"What's that?"

"It can't be true, of course—even Pepe can't be that much of an idiot—but Lady Nevell just told me Pepe had just offered the leading role in the film he's going to make here to Miss Bergson."

"Impossible. Loretta Kelly is set to play that part. There must be a contract."

"If I know Pepe, the only contract was verbal—and over the pillow, at that. He's wildly enthusiastic about the Swedish woman."

Elsa frowned. "I don't understand. Who is she?"

"A guest of Babs. Lady Nevell said that Babs has offered to put money into the film if Pepe stars Miss Bergson."

"But it doesn't make sense. Why should Babs ... I mean after ..."

"Exactly. I don't like it. It's quite odd, really. And you know how difficult Pepe has been recently. There's no telling what—" She broke off and gave me a glassy smile. "Come, *Signor* Ferechini, tell me all about crime on Venzola."

She took Ferechini's arm and led him away. Elsa gave me a quick nervous glance. For a moment neither of us said anything. After a moment I said, "Well?"

To my surprise she jerked her head toward me angrily. "For God's sake, who do you think you are, standing there like a paragon of virtue?"

"Listen, Elsa. You can't be such a fool as to go to that boat."

"Who told you about that?"

"I heard Ferechini pull that phony about a 'sick friend' in the office of the Casino."

"How do you know it isn't true?" she asked defiantly.

"Elsa," I said urgently, "Ferechini and his whole crowd are riding for a big fall. He's drunk with power. But there is more of the world to contend with than just the island of Venzola. He hasn't got something on everyone in the world, you know."

"I don't know what you're talking about!"

Someone had begun to play the blues at a piano in the far corner of the pavilion, where Pietro had been singing until a few minutes before. I thought, Maybe I'm mad; none of this can be real.

"Elsa, I want to help you. You don't belong in all this."

"It's too late for moralizing," she said bitterly. "Far too late. I know what I'm doing ... what I have to do. Stay out of it!"

"You're protecting your mother!"

Startled, she looked for a moment into my eyes, then turned on her heel and marched off across the pavilion. I saw her take a glass of champagne from a waiter and drain it in one gulp. She looked across the pavilion to me with an expression that was half defiant, half despairing, then turned to some chattering people and said something that made them laugh.

I managed to find a Scotch and went down to the beach. On the opposite end of the beach from the cabanas and their whispering occupants, I found Yvonne and Pietro. They were sitting silently on the sand in the shadow of a rock and I saw their hands were locked tightly together. I came up behind them without making a sound. Yvonne drew her hand from Pietro's and said softly, "You will forget me."

Pietro said hoarsely, "Never!"

"But, Pietro, you are young ... but not that young. You know what I am."

"I know you have been driven to what you have done ... by that devil Planquet. I have vowed to kill him and I will!"

Quietly I said, "It wouldn't be worth it, Pietro."

He jerked about, on the defensive. "You have been spying!"

I disregarded him. "So," I said to Yvonne, "it was Planquet who brought you to Venzola."

In a tired voice she said, "He picked me out of a Paris department store, promised to make me a star. He brought me here. I thought I was in love with him, God help me. He got tired in a week. He threw me out."

"And you were going to kill him."

"Earlier tonight I planned to kill him, yes. Now, when I hear Pietro talking like this, I realize how stupid I was. Make him understand."

I squatted down in the sand beside them. Here we were in a little oasis of darkness away from the shrill laughter and the grotesque exhibitionists.

"Pietro," I said, "you have deserted Mamma Peroni on the very night she needs you most."

"A man has his own problems!" he said sulkily.

"There has been enough murder on this island tonight. What kind of future would Yvonne have—what good would a murderer be to her?"

"She won't have me anyway!"

Yvonne scrambled to her feet. "Make him go home. There is no good in this talk. I've tried to make him understand. I want another glass of champagne."

Pietro jumped up and grabbed her, holding her fiercely to him.

"You will not go back to that rotten garbage! They are no good—filth!"

She tried to shake herself free. "Please, Pietro."

"No! You will stay with me! Here!"

I lifted my glass. Yvonne smiled ruefully. "What can I do with him?"

"You might marry him," I said, and walked away.

Halfway back to the pavilion I came upon Loretta Kelly, who was lying on the sand with a young man in bathing trunks. When she saw me she pushed the young man away and staggered to her feet. Somewhere she seemed to have lost her shoes. With drunken primness she yanked her neckline up to a more respectable position.

"Hey, you," she said. "I wanna talk to you."

"She's a talkative wench," the young man said.

"Scram!" she said.

"I can take a hint," he said. He rolled over, scrambled nimbly to his feet, and walked toward the pavilion and, obviously, any available female.

"Well?" I said.

"Who's the dame in the silver dress?"

"A Swede."

"I'll Swede her and Pepe, too, if she doesn't lay off. I've got an option on the guy—at least for a few weeks."

"You know how mercurial Pepe is."

"Give me a little sip."

I handed her my glass and she finished off the Scotch. She was roaring drunk and beyond caring.

"I've been around," she said thickly. "All around. In, out, and under, if you know what I mean. But this crowd beats anything I've come up with yet. Some of the propositions I've had tonight would turn your hair. What is this, anyway—a cat house?"

"What you need is a little sleep. Why don't you go back to your hotel?"

She paid no attention. "All right, so Pepe is making for a Swede. Let him! Who the hell wants to be a star, anyway? And the thing that gets me ... the politeness, asking you the goddamnedest things in an Oxford accent. I'd like to blow the lid off this little shindig. I'd like to—"

She staggered up against me. "All right," she muttered. "All right. So I hang from a trapeze with my bosom showing for the yokels. At least it's work. I'd rather—" She hiccuped. "Tell you what. You and me ... let's get stinking and tell the whole lousy crowd off!"

"Sure," I said. "Later."

I managed to get free of her and went back to the pavilion. A tall gaunt woman in slacks was talking shrilly at a pale young man on the platform's edge. "Such ego! The man is incredible! Announcing to the world at large that he is the world's greatest expert on women in Europe. How Elsa puts up with him—"

"Don't I know," the young man said. "Pepe is the world's worst bore. Have you ever seen that statue he has of himself at his swimming pool?"

"Isn't it loathesome?"

"But so terribly virile. Sometimes I suspect—'The lady doth protest too much,' if you understand...."

I went past them to find Adams and Gigi in a low-voiced altercation. Gigi had changed to a scanty swimming suit.

"I won't have you making an exhibition of yourself."

"I'll do what I damned please," Gigi said heatedly. "Until you tell me where Georges is—"

"Gigi, I haven't the faintest idea." He stopped as he saw me approaching. Without a word Gigi turned, ran to the water's edge, and dived in. She began to swim furiously toward the float.

"Women!" I said.

"You're damned right. I'm glad you're here, Muldoon. I've been thinking about our little deal."

"Well?"

"It's off."

I took a long moment thinking of the ten thousand, then I said, "I'm afraid it's too late, Mr. Adams. Once I've been hired for a job, I don't leave it until the payoff."

"Now look here, Muldoon ..."

"No," I said quietly, "*you* look here. And look well! You lied to me tonight. You know as well as I do that Georges Hertzy was not mixed up in anything political. He had merely heard some ugly rumors about his wife's mother and wanted to track them down. You were just as anxious to stop him."

"Nothing of the sort," he sputtered.

"Maybe your motives were good," I said. "I don't know. Maybe you merely wanted to protect your lady love from the sordid truth. But whether you like it or not, I'm finishing up this job, if I live through it. And you will pay off."

He didn't answer. He was very pale now and his lips were drawn into a tight line. After a moment he lowered his voice and said, "All right. It's true. I wanted to throw you off the track, discredit Georges—because I knew he was going to you with that ugly bit of gossip about Mrs. Bennol."

"The gossip being ..."

"Oh, that she was engaged in some sort of smuggling racket."

"Some sort being drugs!"

He groaned. "You're too good for me, Muldoon. But now that you know, I'm actually relieved. I don't want Gigi hurt. I thought perhaps I could arrange this business without a scandal. Persuade Mrs. Bennol ... It was wrong, I know that now. And then, too, frankly, I suppose I was a little jealous of Georges."

"Listen to me, Mr. Adams. This is more than merely a little bit of scandal. There have been two murders tonight, and unless I'm very careful, there may be three."

His mouth fell open. "What!"

"And," I said quietly, "I'm not at all certain yet that you had nothing to do with the first murder!"

He started to speak but broke off as the sound of a gong boomed out over our heads. We turned toward the center of the pavilion. A servant was striking the gong with a felt hammer. Someone helped Babs Wentworth up to a gilt chair, where she stood smiling and waving her arms for silence. Gradually, except for the low laughter out in the shadows of the cabanas, the noise died down. Something tense behind Babs Wentworth's smile caught my attention. I had a sudden premonition of disaster, sharp and utterly inexplicable.

When the pavilion was comparatively quiet Babs Wentworth started to speak. "My dear friends, I know it is selfish of me, but I want you to share my excitement over something that has just occurred—something rather extraordinary."

Faces were turned to her now in puzzled attention. I saw Loretta Kelly stagger across the beach and grab one of the pavilion pillars for support and lean forward, mouth half open, trying to take in what was being said. On the other side of the crowd Elsa stood almost as though she were a prisoner, surrounded by her mother, Count Cassi, and Ferechini. Her gaze held mine for a moment, then slid away.

"As you all know," Babs Wentworth continued, "one of my guests is the famous motion-picture director Pepe Planquet. Now Monsieur Planquet is not only a genius, but a great connoisseur of beautiful women."

There was a ripple of polite, uneasy laughter.

"Well, my friends, tonight he met for the first time the lovely Swedish actress Sigrid Bergson, and believe it or not, on the strength of that one meeting, Mr. Planquet has just engaged Miss Bergson as the star in his new film!"

There was scattered applause. A woman in front of me whispered to her companion, "Since when has Babs gone in for commercial announcements?"

"And now ... I give you that formidable male among males, the great Pepe Planquet!"

If there had been any irony in her words, Pepe Planquet, for one, seemed happily oblivious of it. As Babs got down from the chair he took her place and began to boom out in his deep baritone:

"Ladies and gentlemen! As Mrs. Wentworth has just told you, perhaps with some kind flattery, I have some reputation in my particular field. But it is very rare indeed that I have had the privilege of knowing practically on sight that I am face to face with a very great talent. I pride myself on my instinct in these matters. And tonight I have taken what some may consider a gamble, but what I know to be a sure thing. There are some women who are beautiful. Others are witty or intelligent. But there are very few who combine those mysterious qualities that I can only describe as being 'pure female.' I have met such a woman tonight, and I am willing to stake my professional career on the fact that she will soon be the idol of millions of screen fans throughout the civilized world. Ladies and gentlemen, it is with great pleasure that I present to you the star of my new film, Miss Sigrid Bergson."

Flushed and excited, Planquet stepped down from the chair and helped the woman in the silver dress climb to the place where he had stood. As she rose up over the heads of the crowd, I remembered her as I had first seen her, standing in the semidarkness in the bedroom at Count Cassi's with the hypodermic needle raised over her arm. I noticed that the gown she wore cleverly concealed the upper portions of her arms. Although the night was warm, I shivered.

The woman ahead of me said, "What *is* this all about?"

Loretta Kelly was clutching the pillar, leaning forward, staring almost idiotically at the woman in the silver dress. I had the feeling that as yet she did not comprehend the situation.

The woman in the silver dress was striking in an odd, spectacular manner, but there was still something about her that made me think of wax. Her strange beauty had a peculiar effect on the crowd. During Planquet's speech it was quite obvious that most of them had become bored with what they considered a trivial and tasteless exhibition. But now, as the woman stood there, silent and smiling, there was a sudden, complete silence.

The woman in the silver dress said not a word. Instead, slowly she raised her hand toward her black hair. And then with a sudden swift movement she removed the wig. There was a gasp of amazement from the crowd. For a moment I was too stunned to register what I was seeing. And then, as though coming up from underwater, I realized that I was staring at the face of the young man who had been with Lorna Parks in the bar of the Villa Rosa; the young man named Freddie.

For a moment there was no sound. Then suddenly harsh laughter broke into our midst. I turned to find Loretta Kelly shouting with laughter, still hanging on to the pillar. "Hallelujah! The world's greatest expert on women!"

The laughter spread across the crowd like wildfire. I saw Babs Wentworth, head thrown back, laughing almost hysterically into Planquet's face. It was then that I realized this was the "little joke" she had planned with Freddie, a way of getting even with Planquet for having thrown Lorna Parks out of his film.

At my side someone said, "My God. He'll never forgive her for this!"

It was Yvonne tugging at my sleeve. I looked toward Planquet. He stood like a stone statue staring up at the boy in the silver dress. And then he lunged forward. Freddie was too quick for him, leaping to one side like a dancer, out into the crowd. Planquet started after him, but two men grabbed him from behind and held fast. Freddie laughed gaily and bounded out across the pavilion toward the cabanas. "My dears," he cried, "no one even *guessed!*"

Cassi, red-faced and angry, intercepted Freddie on the platform's edge. They were only a few feet from us and I heard Cassi hiss, "You little fool! He'll never forget this!"

"Don't be such a killjoy!" Freddie said petulantly. He broke away from Cassi and ran down the beach. Elsa was standing where I had last seen her. She looked as though she were transfixed. The laughter of the crowd had risen to hysterical proportions.

And then suddenly Planquet broke away from the men who held him and leaped to the chair. He crouched there like some sort of trapped animal. The laughter was choked off. "How dare!" Planquet shouted incoherently. "How dare!"

"Come, come," someone said. "Can't you take a joke, old man?"

"Joke? Joke!" Planquet shouted. "A joke to make me, Planquet, the laughingstock of Europe. No! I know who is behind this. I know—"

He pointed a shaking arm toward Elsa.

"That bitch! She planned it. But she'll pay. I've kept quiet long enough. I will tell everything—the whole damned crowd ... I'll spill the story all over every front page!"

"For God's sake, shut him up!" someone said. Hands reached up and dragged Planquet down from the chair. He shook himself free and pushed his way through the crowd toward the stairs leading up to the villa, and a moment later I saw him scrambling blindly up the incline toward the outer darkness.

Someone tapped me on the shoulder. It was a servant. He handed me a folded note.

Adams said in disgust, "I've had about enough."

"Not quite," I said, and pointed toward the beach. A shout of hectic laughter went up from the guests. I saw Elsa and Mrs. Bennol hurrying up the steps toward the villa, and a moment later Cassi and Ferechini. But no one else would have noticed. The scene on the beach was an unexpected diversion.

At the water's edge was Loretta Kelly. Already she had removed her gown and was now in the process of discarding a pair of lace pants. In a moment she stood stark naked except for her stockings, bold and defiant and breath-taking despite her drunken state.

"All right, you bastards!" she shouted. "The first one to reach the raft gets the booby prize!"

With that she turned, ran into the water, dived gracefully, and headed for the raft with an Australian crawl that would have made an Olympic champion envious. Out on the raft I saw Gigi Hertzy laughing with the crowd as Loretta approached the raft. Several men had followed her into the water and were swimming manfully after her. From the crowd I heard Babs Wentworth shout angrily, "This is too much! Someone go quickly to the house and have one of the servants put out the lights on the raft!"

It was all a mad dream. Almost calmly I opened the note. It was from Elsa. "Forgive me. I'm so frightened. Perhaps you can help. Meet me in twenty minutes at the foot of the path leading to the Palace of Tiberius."

I stared at the note feeling suddenly dead. So, I thought. So ...

Dimly I was aware of the sound of cloth tearing somewhere near me and Loretta Kelly rising from the water like a sleek seal, and Gigi laughing wildly, hanging on to the diving board for support. A sickening odor of heavy perfume passed very close to me and someone laughed softly. Loretta stood facing us, brilliantly white on the floodlit platform, shouting obscenities at the arms churning the water toward her.

From the crowd around me a shrill voice, vaguely male, said, "Really, do people still go in for such nonsense?"

And then I saw the shadow out beyond the diving board, a shadow floating slowly in from the sea.

Mrs. Wentworth was screaming, "Turn off that goddamned light!"

But the light remained merciless and the shadow floated closer.

At that moment Loretta Kelly froze, with her arms above her head, staring with her mouth open in shock at the water, and Gigi Hertzy began to scream.

A shudder of horror went through the crowd, even before they saw. I watched the shadow with a kind of awful fascination. It bumped up against the raft, then came swinging around into the light. It was a man in water-soaked dinner clothes, stiff and open-eyed between two oars that had been strapped to his side. He stared unseeing at the naked woman and her screaming companion and there seemed to be a waxen smile on his face. The figure bumped stiffly against the boards of the raft. Georges Hertzy had come back to his wife.

Chapter Eighteen

THE WENTWORTH BEACH, 5:00 A.M.

The raft and the pavilion, the figures on the beach and under the scarlet canopy were plunged into sudden darkness. Apparently a nervous servant had pulled all the switches. Gigi had stopped screaming and now there was a slow-gathering sigh of fear sweeping over the guests of the party. Out on the eastern horizon an ominous pink dawn was edging the sea. Was the man who had been murdered in my room at the Villa Rosa floating quietly away from the raft now to some outer loneliness, or in death did he still nudge the feet of the woman he had been foolish enough to love? For the moment the inferno-like scene had vanished from its cruelly lighted stage but the madness of the night was still on me, focused now like the merciless beam of a searchlight on a battlefield on one object, one person. My fingers closed tight and tense about the note in my pocket.

Someone grasped my arm. "Is that you, Muldoon?" Adams' voice rasped with anger.

"Yes."

"I was a fool to think I could handle it. You can't compromise with evil."

"If it's time for platitudes, I might add you can't rationalize with madness."

"Madness?"

"What else? Ferechini and Cassi and ... and the others. Mad enough to believe that the power they had gained could not be challenged. Mad to the point of reckless exhibitionism and murder."

"I suppose you're right. But this— My God! Poor Georges ..."

"Poor Georges," I repeated dully. "Poor Georges. No one would listen to him. Even you ..."

"I couldn't believe it was as serious as he suspected. He told some wild tale of having heard that Mrs. Bennol's New York shop was a front for the drug syndicate. At the very worst, I felt that if there were any truth in it she had been blackmailed into it. I wanted time. I wanted to go slow. At any rate, I wanted to protect Gigi."

"And Elsa?"

After a moment he said, "I ... I don't know."

"I know."

"I can't believe ... Surely Planquet isn't ..."

"Not an active collaborator. He probably only stumbled on the truth recently. My guess is that he kept quiet—for a price. Cassi was a fool to permit his boy friend to goad Planquet in the place it would hurt most. Planquet will sing now. That is, if—"

"If what?"

"If he lives to sing."

"God, Muldoon, you don't think they really would! Not after two murders tonight."

"They have to go on killing now. It's their only hope. And the insane part of it is they probably still imagine all will work out right for them. As it has in the past. Step on the canaries and turn your heel, if you can't blackmail or buy them off. They feel fairly safe about you, for instance. They think you will stay clear of the mess to protect Gigi."

He groaned. "If anyone had ever told me I would try to hush up a thing like this, I would have punched him in the nose. But Gigi— Nothing like Gigi ever happened to me. I thought I could reason with Mrs. Bennol. I thought Georges was going to scream what he thought to the world. I thought— Oh, Lord. What difference does it make? Why excuse myself?"

"It's possible that you might have succeeded in reasoning with Mrs. Bennol. In time. But there is one person you could never have reasoned with—"

"Who?"

"I have a date," I said wearily. "I've got to keep it."

His hand closed on my arm. "You'd better watch out, Muldoon. They're out for you now."

"Maybe I'm a masochist."

People were milling about in the dark, most of them pushing toward the stairs leading up to the villa.

"Can you swim?" I asked.

"Of course. Why?"

"You'd better go out and get Gigi," I said, and left him abruptly.

Someone had found candles by the buffet. In their fluttering light I found Babs Wentworth. She was trying without much success to quiet some hysterical women. I managed to draw her aside.

"Look. I want you to do something for me."

"Good God, what a time to ask for favors!"

"Pietro, the boy you hired to sing—he's somewhere on the beach." I got out my address book, scribbled a note, tore off the page, and thrust it at her. "Find him and give him this."

She took it automatically. "Muldoon, you're not welching on our agreement...."

"I may not be around to keep agreements with anyone. It's a personal matter."

She hesitated, looking me in the eyes. "I'll find the boy. Good luck!"

I blessed her for asking no more questions and headed for the stairs. I was rough on some of Mrs. Wentworth's guests in my hasty ascent to the main house.

In the loggia I turned and looked back for a second. The pale streak of dawn in the east was playing tricks with the scene below. White faces turned up to me in fear, and they seemed to be floating up from a crumbling city. Sodom and Gomorrah? Babel? Far out on the motionless dark gray sea a shadow was moving in toward Venzola. The Lyon?

I turned, strangely calm now, and pushed my way through the throng at the main entrance, where they were huddled waiting in strained tension for their limousines to become disentangled from the snarl in the drive. A shrill-voiced woman waved bony arms laden with diamonds as she cried, "This time Babs has gone too far!" And near me someone said, "My dear, we *must* get away before the police arrive. We simply can't afford a scandal!"

Too late, brother, I thought with some relish.

I went down around the half-moon swing of the drive, out between the imposing entrance gates to the highway. There I turned my back on the town and began to hurry along the narrow ancient ribbon of twisting road that skirted the cliffs and mounted ever higher and higher up the mountain. The traffic of elegant refugees from Babs Wentworth's most sensational party were, for the most part, behind me, headed back to the town and the luxury hotels. But occasionally a car would whiz past me and I would step off the road into the protective cover of the shrubbery. I didn't want Ferechini to snafu this last date.

Once I stopped to make certain that the Luger I had taken from Gigi Hertzy was loaded. It was. With my hand on the cold steel, standing still for a moment beside the deserted highway, I had the sensation once again of drifting back through time to some pre-Roman dawn.

After a bit I came to a shattered marble arch and turned off the highway into a sort of courtyard cut into the mountainside. I went carefully now, alert as a cat in the dark, my hand ready on the revolver.

At the foot of ruined stone steps she waited. For a moment she didn't see me. She stood there leaning against an ancient pillar, a light wrap over her shoulders, her arm rising gracefully as she puffed at a cigarette. The gown fluttered in the slight breeze. From somewhere far away came an odd sound, as though someone had plucked the string of a harp and then quickly placed the flat of a hand against the string to choke off the sound.

A pebble rattled beneath my shoe. She turned quickly. She laughed. "I thought I was being stood up!" The laughter kept bubbling through her words.

"Not a chance."

I stopped a few feet from her, not touching her, waiting. One part of me listened to the shadows in the foliage and among the fallen marble.

"Hart! Is something wrong?"

"Not for me," I said.

Nothing moved out there. My senses were so acute now I think I would have heard the slightest intake of breath. My hunch was right, then. It wouldn't be here, not down by that road. The Duchessa had said "the ruins of the palace," and that was up above, looming against the dawn.

"You sound—well, odd."

"Do I? I wonder if the sirens bothered to say anything so prosaic to Ulysses?"

The silence. The faint rustle of the morning breeze among the branches of the olive trees. My hand touched something cold. I looked down into the shattered face of a mutilated Venus.

"Have you been drinking, Hart?" Elsa said. "Have you had too much champagne?"

"What's too much?" I asked harshly. And then with deliberate coarseness, "Don't worry. I'll function all right!"

She took a step backward, the act of a lady properly shocked. "Hart! Really ..."

"You can change your mind!" I said coldly. "You can run home to Mamma and the destroyed cuckold!"

She darted a nervous look toward the road, then at the narrow steps arched by the branches of lemon trees. She had to disregard the insult in my voice now. Under the circumstances, she had no choice. She tried to laugh it off. "You have such a crude sense of humor, darling. You almost destroy the romantic aspects of this place. It will be a lovely dawn."

"Can you guarantee that?"

And then the sweet voice of the harpy, the dulcet tones of the executioner: "We must hurry, darling. I insist you see the first of the sun from the terrace at the top. The very top!"

"After you, my sweet," I said.

I waited, still not touching her. She hesitated, drew the wrap tighter as though a sudden chill had struck her, then came close and found my hand. Whether by accident or intention, she drew it across her breasts, turning my fingers inward as the wrap fell open. A wave of unreasoning, sadistic desire swept over me. For the moment I managed to keep it in control. But she was quick to sense the trembling in my fingers and it gave her confidence once again.

"Come," she whispered.

For a moment I couldn't move. She pressed up against me. "Hart, darling, you act as though you were performing some unpleasant duty!"

I drew her to me then. "I saw you," I whispered incoherently. "I saw you once and stayed on here in Venzola. You could have ... I never wanted anything more. No other women ever. You were everything I ever wanted in a woman."

"Were?" She gave me a husky laugh. "Don't put me in the past tense so definitely, my dear."

Despite the throbbing of her closeness, I fumbled, with apparent clumsiness, the hand that held the little gold handbag. I squeezed the sequined cloth tight for the feel of a gun. She didn't have one. At least not there. My guessing was right so far. I was still safely balanced on the tightrope. This wasn't a solo job. She was the decoy on this one. They were probably up there among the ruins, waiting tensely among the toppled pillars. For the first time since compulsion had driven me to this dangerous tryst I felt a twinge of uneasiness. Could I really handle this one? They were desperate now and ready for any reckless act. Suppose Babs Wentworth had not been able to find Pietro or, having found him, faced a refusal to take the message to Mamma Peroni? And even if Mamma Peroni got the message, would she understand?

Under the pretext of amorous play, I frisked her carefully. I don't think she realized it. There was something as cool as stone, as professional as a medico in her response.

"There is no other man I would have met here, darling!" she whispered. "I can't bear Pepe. Life has been so dull!"

I stepped back from her. "Get going!" I said.

"Where?" she whispered.

"To the top. To meet your pals."

She turned a stricken face up to me, "I don't know what you're talking about. Oh, Hart, you of all people!"

"You're breaking my heart. Get going!"

She jerked her head away from me with a dry sob.

"Some things ..." she whispered. "Some things are so dreadful that you can't believe ...."

"Is that what you told your mother when you first persuaded her to act as a front for the gang you're working for?"

"Gang? Oh, God, what is this? Have you gone mad?"

Somewhere up above a pebble was dislodged on the path. I caught her roughly by the shoulder and hissed, "You do exactly as I say or you'll get this right through the back of the head!" I took the Luger from my pocket.

And no guilt, I thought, no guilt at all. She had it coming to her. But there was something in her eyes as she turned once more that went to my heart like a knife. Suppose ... suppose I was wrong?

"Never mind the histrionics," I said harshly. "Go on!"

Without a word she began to walk slowly up the steps. There was something listless now in her movements that scared me. The uneasiness increased. I had been so certain when I had read that note. And yet ...

I stifled my misgivings and caught hold of her again in the shadow of the last arbor. Ahead of us was the long stretch of ruined marbled terrace, destroyed pillars, some of them jagged against the half-light, a scene of eerie desolation like something in a surrealist painting.

I put my mouth close to her ear. "Go out there on the terrace," I said. "I know they are hiding up here. Go out alone and draw them out. Remember I am an excellent shot and I'll have a bead on you."

She leaned back against me for a moment in an attitude of utter weariness. Then without turning she straightened up and walked resolutely out onto the carpet of marble and weeds. She looked like a child lost in a vast stony space. She did exactly what I had told her to do. She stood there finally in the center of the terrace with the crumbling façade of the palace and the sea beyond her. She shivered again and drew the torn wrap close.

Nothing happened. The only sound in the gray morning was that of a car far below on the mountain road. I held the Luger, trying to fight off the flood of guilty doubt. She stood very still with the breeze rippling the hem of her gown.

My misgivings increased now to panic. If I had made a mistake, the thing I had done to her was unforgivable. Suppose she was, after all, merely an innocent victim? Suppose I had, in the melodramatic atmosphere of Babs Wentworth's macabre party, been wrong about that handwriting?

But no. It was impossible. The same cramped letters, and the tiny crossbars on the "t's." And yet ...

She turned back to me, not moving from the spot. She was weeping now and she lifted an arm toward me imploringly.

And I completely lost my head. I moved forward, out of the remnants of night in the arbor, out across the ancient flagstones.

She stood waiting, arms outstretched as though for mercy. I was halfway to her when I saw the smile. She threw her head back smiling. And she was looking beyond me. I got it too late. A hand came down from behind and struck my arm and the Luger went clattering out across the terrace. I wheeled about to look into a shiny revolver and behind it Ferechini.

"Good work, Elsa," he said in a businesslike voice. "But my God, I thought you would never come. We must work fast now!"

Elsa had snatched the Luger from the flagstones and was already at my side. Her face was pale and twisted with hatred and malevolence.

"You didn't imagine I would let you ruin things?" she said almost calmly. "Not after all the hard work, the chances, the planning ... You are a soft, idiotic fool. And I am sorry to inform you that there is no place in the world for people like you. It's like drowning in jelly to hear you talk! My God, how I ever put up with it I don't know. I was very much tempted to give the show away at the Casino. In the office, I mean, after *Signor* Ferechini had finished off that stupid old woman, the crazy Duchessa. Maybe we would have saved ourselves a lot of trouble if we had done it then. But Ferechini needed someone to arrest for the unfortunate death of Georges Hertzy."

"You murdered Georges in cold blood!" I said.

"What a lovely phrase. 'Cold blood.' I had to kill Georges, yes. He thought Mother was the queen of the narcotics racket! He thought I didn't know anything about it. He came to me for advice. I knew you were at that very moment being questioned by Ferechini, so I wrote your name on a note for Georges when he became difficult. He thought you might be able to carry on a discreet investigation of the 'rumor.' He told me he had talked to Adams. I sent off a note to Adams implicating Georges in the Balkan Eagles, just in case. You should have stuck to your whisky, Mr. Muldoon!"

"Elsa!" Ferechini said urgently. "This is no time to—"

"I wanted him to know!" she said in cold fury. "I wanted him to know what an ass he has been. I wanted him to see how I have wrapped him around my finger."

"Elsa! I have never seen you like this. Calm down. We have no time to waste. Unless we use our heads—"

She whipped around on him. "What about Pepe?"

"He didn't go back to the villa."

"What!"

"Don't worry." There was a scratching nervousness in Ferechini's voice. "He can't get off the island. We'll pick him up before—"

"But suppose the authorities—"

"We can handle them as we have handled them before. They can question all they want. But with Mr. Muldoon out of the way, who will talk?"

"Adams," I said quickly. "He'll talk. He probably is talking now!"

Ferechini laughed harshly. "That lovesick old goat! He'll never talk. I could ruin him in five minutes!" He turned to Elsa. "The Wentworth woman may make trouble. But she can't prove anything. You will have to handle your mother."

"That bitch!" Elsa said with cold vehemence. "As long as she keeps getting her cut, she won't talk. She never loved anything but money."

"Good! My men are down at the Wentworth villa, 'investigating' the unfortunate death of Mr. Hertzy. Already I have arranged for a witness who will swear he last saw Georges Hertzy alive in the company of Mr. Muldoon, as they went to Mr. Muldoon's room at the Villa Rosa."

"How did the body get into the water?"

"The work of that Peroni woman! She had some of the fishermen tie oars to the body and dump it near the Wentworth beach. However, it will help. It will only implicate her. A stupid clod of a woman."

Elsa was looking at me. A little cloud of uncertainty passed across her eyes, but only for a moment. Had she, in that brief moment, awakened from her mad dream of power and wealth? Had she caught a glimpse of the inevitable end? Surely she must have caught the grim truth behind Ferechini's fantasies. They couldn't murder everyone in the world.

Ferechini stuck the gun in my guts and prodded me forward. For a moment I saw myself through their eyes, an inconvenient sort of dummy robbed of heart, feeling, or meaning. But beneath their bravado I had detected the theme of growing panic in their voices. But it was beginning to look as though this nightmare would end for me in blackness with no waking-up time.

I stumbled over an obscene satyr smirking up at me from among the weeds and then suddenly we were around the corner of the main façade. Before us a narrow terrace stretched out on a promontory to end in the delicate columns of what had obviously once been a charming little circular temple. Far down to the right sprawled the town of Venzola, a toy town stuck onto a papier-mâché cliff. And out beyond it, just inside the breakwater, a small steamer had come to anchor. I knew it must be the Lyon. From the mole the municipal launch, Ferechini's pride, was cutting through the harbor toward the newly arrived ship.

"Your sick friend will be disappointed," I said to Elsa.

"Count Cassi is taking care of my sick friend," she said with a cold smile. "He's very much concerned about her health."

"Maybe he should be!" I cried. I raised my arm and pointed out beyond the breakwater to the open sea.

The first shaft of the morning sun glistened on metal and brass and the unmistakable silhouette of a government cruiser skimming in across the Bay of Naples like a bird to the prey.

Elsa gasped. I could feel Ferechini freezing behind me.

"What does that mean?" she whispered.

"Apparently," I said with far more calm than I felt, "the clods got someone into Naples last night to report murder, among other crimes against the state."

"My God!" Elsa said furiously. "You said no one would leave the harbor!"

"Keep your head, Elsa!" Ferechini said shrilly. "Just a few crazy fishermen. Nothing they can prove—nothing ..." His voice died out into uncertainty.

"But look. Cassi is at the ship. He's going up the ladder."

"Cassi is no fool. He'll get the stuff overboard before they reach him."

"But—but—oh, my God, suppose your men don't pick up Pepe before they land. The government men. Suppose—"

"We can't think of that now!" Ferechini snapped. "All the more reason to get this over with quickly."

"Yes. Yes!" Elsa cried.

"And now, *Signor* Muldoon," Ferechini said in a trembling voice, "I will act as your last guide. I will perform my duties for the American tourist. All the points of historic interest. Look. Before you is the great morning terrace of the Emperor Tiberius. At the very end— see the white columns—there is the sweet little temple overhanging the sea. It is from this temple that the Emperor, after a night of strange pleasures, was in the habit of driving the objects of that night's pleasure into the dawn—and, incidentally, to their deaths on the jagged rocks a hundred and five feet below. No one ever lived to tell of the sweet horrors of the night before."

"Charming," I said.

I'd give him another minute before I made the break. Better a shot in the back than that last fumbling step off into space, the futile grasping at empty air, the lost scream.

"Hurry!" Elsa cried. "The government boat is already beside the Lyon."

Even in that last hopeless moment I saw her with a kind of cold objectivity, as someone conditioned as a child to believe the world was populated by fools who must be fleeced. The hard chromium ruthlessness was showing now behind the gift of beauty. Now there was something as inhuman as metal about this woman for whom I had stayed on the dreamlike island.

Ferechini shoved me forward toward the temple.

And then it happened, just as it might happen in a dream where the censor refuses to permit the final self-annihilation. Like ghosts and apparitions from another world, rising as though by magic from among the fallen pillars and toppled stones, came the fishermen of Venzola brandishing their boat hooks. There must have been fifteen of them, at least. At their head, like a symbol of earthy vengeance, waving a vicious-looking hook, was Mamma Peroni.

I took a quick side step as Ferechini wheeled about, waving his revolver. Taken completely by surprise, Elsa was hardly aware of my hand smashing down on her wrist, or the Luger clattering to the stones.

"Get back!" Ferechini screamed. "Get back or I'll fire!"

It was obvious that he was confronted now by the darkest fears of his worst nightmares. The fishermen hesitated for a moment, drawn up in a semicircle about Mamma Peroni. Mamma threw back her head, eyes glittering, teeth flashing. "You can't kill twenty men with that little popgun, *signore*. Pig!"

"The clods!" I cried. "The blessed clods!"

"Obey me!" Ferechini screamed. "Get back! I am the law!"

Mamma laughed scornfully. "The law! You don't have a chance now, *signore*. We have, at last, witnesses and proof. Some of your pretty boys are waiting to talk with the authorities. There is the waiter from the Casino who saw you kill the Duchessa with your own hands. At this very minute some of my friends are sitting in the elegant apartment of the Count Cassi, where they are guarding your cache of drugs! Also with them is that film director Pepe Planquet, come for our protection and waiting to talk! No, *signore*, your evil night is finished!"

"You're bluffing! They're only bluffing, Elsa!"

I looked at Elsa. Her face was a mask. She looked at Ferechini as though he were some stranger on another planet.

The fishermen began to close in. Ferechini started to back away. His face was white with fear. I made a sound with my foot on the flagstones. He twirled about like a nervous cat and in that moment two young men pinned him down. Above the hubbub I heard Mamma suddenly scream, "Watch out! The girl!"

Something in her voice sent a chill through me. I turned toward the spot where Elsa had been standing. She was gone. Then I saw her, far out across the flagstones, and she seemed to be floating through the morning light toward the ruins of the little temple. With a cry I started out after her. But already I was too late. She leaped up into the heart of the little temple. There she turned, smiled coldly, and spoke, the words distinct, prim, like those of a little girl leaving a party: "It's been a most interesting evening."

And then she took a step backward, off into space.

Chapter Nineteen

THE HOTEL MIRAMAR, 9:30 A.M.

Gigi was sobbing in the next room. Adams turned from the great picture window in his suite and said quietly, "Here's your check."

Without a word I took it and put it into my wallet.

"It's incredible to me," Adams said. "A woman with her beauty. She could have had anything. But to get mixed up with Ferechini and that crowd—and murder! It's incredible!"

I sighed. "Something went wrong a long time ago. Probably when she was a child. Better ask the mother. But then, I suppose you will have to visit a penitentiary to do that."

"Terrible. Terrible. Poor Gigi—poor little kid. It's such a shock. After all, her own mother and sister ..."

I said nothing. After a minute he stopped looking me in the eyes. The boy-scout expression wasn't coming easily for him anymore. "We're leaving for Paris on the evening plane," he said.

"We?"

"Gigi and I."

"How will that look to the gossip columns? What about your political career?"

"Oh, that," he said quietly. "That, of course, is finished."

"Just like that, eh?"

"Just like that." He turned and went back to the window. Over his shoulder he said, "I've just talked to my wife in Rome. She's going ahead with the divorce. She's naming Gigi as co-respondent. Gigi knows. It will be a filthy mess and my wife will get about everything she has been holding out for, but ..."

"It's worth it to you?"

He hesitated and then said in an oddly remote voice, "It's strange, but all the things I believed, the things I thought were so important—honor, public responsibility, all the standards that have ruled my life—they don't seem important to me anymore. Nothing matters now but Gigi."

A sea gull went floating past the window, as stiff and unreal as a stuffed bird.

"I see," I said.

He turned about impatiently. "What the hell do you see?"

"I see that the island has done its well-advertised job on you."

"It has nothing to do with that!" he sputtered.

At the door I had one final word. "There are more ways of dying than jumping from cliffs."

I shut the door between us and went down to the lobby. Babs Wentworth was waiting there for me. We went to a deserted writing room.

"Well?" she asked tensely.

"I've been down at Ferechini's old headquarters with the big brass from Naples for the past two hours. They're finished with me."

"Yes, but—"

"It's all right. They've agreed to keep Miss Parks out of it. In fact, they're not much interested. It seems that everyone is hopping on the bandwagon now. Witnesses are turning up by the score, from beneath every rock."

"Thank God!"

Brusquely, in a businesslike manner, she sat at one of the desks and opened a checkbook.

"Make it two checks," I said. "One for a thousand, the other for the balance."

When she had turned them over to me she said, "Is it true what they are saying, that Elsa Planquet was one of the top people in this hideous business? That she murdered Georges Hertzy?"

"Yes. Georges had stumbled onto the facts about Mrs. Bennol's dress shop. He wanted to protect Gigi from a scandal. He didn't suspect Elsa. He thought when he told her what he knew she would co-operate. She did. She sent him to see me at the Villa Rosa knowing I would not be in my room, followed him there, and stuck a knife in his back. She and Ferechini thought they would plant the job on me, if and when it was necessary, but first they wanted to see if I couldn't be useful to them. In the meantime Mamma Peroni and her pals got the body out of my room and out to sea."

"The Italians!" Babs Wentworth said wryly. "They must have their dramatics at all costs!"

"I guess we've all had enough dramatics in the past night for a lifetime."

"Yes. I understand that my party is being splashed all over the New York papers and I'm being compared to Lucrezia Borgia. What the hell! Talk can't hurt me now. I've decided to buy a place out in Kenya. I'm taking Lorna out there as soon as the doctors think it wise. Maybe we will make one of those films with Lorna defying a pack of lions with her trusty rifle. It's possible that with the help of a cork helmet and a thin film of mosquito netting over her face she might make a comeback!" She laughed.

"Don't get caught in any revolutions!"

I went out to the front of the hotel and got a cab. In a few minutes I was at the Villa Rosa. My bags were packed and waiting for me in the hall. I found Mamma in the bar. You'd never have known that she had not slept. She was as dark and imperturbable as ever.

"You have little time," she said. "The morning boat leaves in twenty minutes."

"Did the authorities give you a bad time, Mamma?"

"No one ever gives Mamma Peroni a bad time!"

I looked around the deserted bar, suddenly reluctant to leave.

"I'll be seeing you again one of these days, Mamma."

"No. Not if you are wise. I was born on this island. Here I will always stay. But you—if you are sensible, you will never return."

"How is Pietro?"

She shrugged. "Tomorrow morning he joins the fishing fleet. Like his father before him. No more playing the concertina and flirting with the rich garbage!"

"And Yvonne?"

Mamma became interested in wiping a speck of imaginary dust from the bar. She sighed. "She stays."

"With Pietro?"

"Who else? It is mad. It is insane. No money—it will be years before he can afford to have his own fishing boat. I cannot help them. I am a poor woman. Still, she chooses to stay."

"They will be married?"

"On Saturday." She scowled. "Young fools!"

I took up the pen that Mamma kept by the account book and endorsed the check for a thousand over to her.

I handed it to her, saying, "Use what you think wise of this for their wedding present. Maybe it will buy Pietro his own boat."

Before she could recover I started for the door.

Behind me she gasped. "Mother of God! There is not this much money in the world. And I thought you were an honest man!"

Without turning back, I quickly picked up my bags and went out into the Via Cellini. But in a moment she was at the door, behind me, calling, "*Signore!* May the Gods bless your grandchildren! I will light a candle for you every day of my life!"

"I'll need them, Mamma!"

At the corner I turned. She was still standing in the doorway, arm upraised in farewell. She looked very beautiful standing there in the ancient doorway; beautiful and indestructible.

"*Arrivederci!*"

I managed to make the dock just in time to hop aboard before the gangplank was pulled up. The little steamer groaned away from the mole out toward the breakwater. I stood in the stern looking back.

Through the morning haze Venzola spilled down its hills in riotous color. There was nothing in the scene to suggest the evil of the night before. For the moment, at least, Mamma's gods of evil slept among the gay villas, smart hotel, and an ancient ruin.

The fat old boat went through the breakwater into the open sea. The island began to float away from me in the filtered light. Was it real? Or had the happenings of the past few hours been a part of dreaming? Far out to the right, the ruins of the Palace of Tiberius was a mere heap of rubble on the high cliff. I shuddered when I thought of the inert little rag doll they had found on the rocks below.

Someone touched my shoulder. I looked down into the face of Loretta Kelly. She didn't look too good.

"God, was I drunk," she said. "And do I need a drink now!"

"I'll buy you one when we hit Naples."

"And then I'll buy you one. Where are you headed, lover boy?"

"Maine. U.S.A. The first plane out."

"I was there once," she said. "When I was a kid. My folks were playing the old Orpheum Circuit. They got a place there called Portland."

"I've heard tell. What about you? Where are you headed?"

"Back to the trapeze, unless I can hook a weak-minded Frenchman. Back to an honest day's work. Now that my former great film director is going to be star witness or something at a criminal trial ..."

For a moment we said nothing. Then she laughed harshly. "The gay international set!" she said scathingly. "Gay like a reformatory. Hopheads and dykes and nymphs and anything else you never saw outside a zoo. And a woman like that Planquet dame, snooty and looking like something on a cover of Vogue, and all the time working with the toughest bunch of goons this side of the Iron Curtain. Nothing can surprise me anymore. Nothing."

"Ever seen the aquarium at Naples?"

"Why?"

"They've got an octopus there. We can watch him between drinks."

"That's all I need. An octopus."

"And there is a charming little hotel up at the top of the town."

She looked up at me, then away. "Why not?" she said. "This damned tub is rocking. I'm going down where I can't see the bay come up at me."

Suddenly I was alone in the stern. The island was fading into the morning mists. The light was playing tricks with my eyes. For just a moment I thought I saw, rising high above the ruins of the Palace of Tiberius, the fluttering pages of a calendar, and among them the figure of a beautiful harpy waving farewell with a dreadful smile.

THE END

John Flagg Bibliography
(1911-1993)

The Persian Cat (1950)
Death and the Naked Lady (1951)
The Lady and the Cheetah (1951)

Hart Muldoon series
Woman of Cairo (1953)
Dear, Deadly Beloved (1954)
Murder in Monaco (1957)
Death's Lovely Mask (1958)
The Paradise Gun (1961)

As John Gearon

The Velvet Well (1946; reprinted in Australia as
  The Deadly Web, 1956; and in France as
  Le Puits de velours, 1949)
"Faces Turned Against Him" (1951, *Suspense*)

Plays

Without Guile (1934; with Edward Crandall)
De Luxe (1935; with Louis Bromfield)
A Bright Young Thing (1936; with Edward Crandall)
Two Hearts in Candid Camera Time: A Revue (1937;
  with Wilson McCarty and Edward Crandall)

And for more twisted tales of obsession, we offer...

Douglas Sanderson

"There is more going on than you can believe, with backstabbing and double crosses galore."—Bruce Grossman, *Bookgasm*

**Pure Sweet Hell /
Cath a Fallen Starlet
978-0-9749438-2-4 $19.95**
"The plots read like a shotgun marriage between Jim Thompson and Mickey Spillane—on speed." Kevin Burton Smith, from his Introduction.

**The Deadly Dames /
A Dum-Dum for the President
978-1-933586-06-9 $19.95**
"One of those fast and furious novels with so much going on, so many dead bodies, and so many plot complications that you can't believe the author can pull it all together...but [Sanderson] manages just fine."
—Bill Crider, *Mystery File.*

**Night of the Horns /
Cry Wolfram
978-1-933586-72-4 $19.95**
"Exceptionally well written, action-packed, fast paced, and thoroughly entertaining...very highly recommended... the action is non-stop"—*Midwest Book Review*

**Prey by Night / Rain of Terror
978-1-951473-00-6 $19.95**
"This is 50s pulp noir at its cynical, nihilistic best. The characters in both these novels are mendacious and duplicitous... But beware, the non-stop action and double dealing belie subtle and complex plotting... savage, breath-taking fun." —Paul Burke, *Crime Time*

"Retro-crime fans will be clamoring for more." —Wes Lukowsky, *Booklist*

STARK HOUSE

Stark House Press, 1315 H Street, Eureka, CA 95501
griffinskye3@sbcglobal.net / www.StarkHousePress.com
Available from your local bookstore, or order direct or via our website.

CPSIA information can be obtained
at www.ICGtesting.com
Printed in the USA
LVHW021650031220
673319LV00018B/1650